MW00880830

THE MAN
FROM SWEET LOAF

A NOVEL BY

G. FRANKLIN PRUE

ISBN: 1481025937
ISBN 13: 9781481025935

DEDICATED TO

Jill and Julian

1

Sunday, 22 August 1985. There's a kiss and a noble ending not meant for them as they awake in each other's arms. Mabel Friday, with brown, rainbow, sun hair is just a child of jazz from the sixties. She's a cool, chocolate, sassy woman, with a high heel walk that will make you melt in five minutes. She rides out the sticky, hot summer season with her boyfriend Sam, who drives a dented-up red truck. He carries carpets to new office buildings from a dusty, quiet city on the Eastern Maryland shores, Sweet Loaf. He makes his runs through the I-95 Beltway: D.C., Maryland and Virginia. They met like other children in the past, on the streets. It was ten years after a war and the death of his soul in a Viet Cong raid. Sam came out in broken pieces of a no-nonsense, selfish man. He even had the sailor nerve to paint on the side of his truck: *EL, ZORRO.*

Sam Murphy is a womanizer. He's a gambler, common sense, drinking man. She would do almost anything for this man of many puzzling qualities. He's tough on his life. Sam isn't around most of the time, which makes their screwing just a Sunday handshake. Now his other women don't make her mad and damn sure don't make her sad. Mabel knows she's a good woman for any man. But with Sam, she's been on this road a long time, a long time. They're cuddling, bouncing in the back woods to the Sweet Loaf Carnival. They're both drinking up a lot of gin with the radio turned up to James Brown begging for love on WKSL-AM Soul station, as they move behind the purple valley city and white corner moon.

Folks forgive Sweet Sam Murphy. He's one of the living dead, chain-smoking, with the face of a dark storm wind coming to the shore's edge. Most of the time he wears a greasy, pale blue golf cap on his head, over wide, brown, soft eyes that take in the yellow and green day, and sometimes another man's wife.

Mabel gives him that lullaby stare: drugs, money or love over on the side of the road? Naw! She wants something else as she rolls her moon-shaped butt on the black vinyl seats of the truck.

"Baby, what you want?" Sam pleads. "Tell me! But don't just sit there like a fly on a elephant's ass."

Mabel scoots over closer to his ear, "I need another cigarette, Daddy."

"Mabel, I just bought you some. Darlin', you got's to be supportin' your own habits!" Sam takes the pack from his pocket, hands it to her. Then he gets real cruel. "Dey be cutting your tits off one of these days."

"Sam, you don't have to talk like that to me!" Mabel lights up, gives him back the pack. "You a thirty-two-year-old asshole!" She sucks in the smoke, and scoots away from him. "Shit, man! As much as I give you." She gazes out to the sights of yellow, brown, burned summer, alabaster leaves, and sees butchers in her dreams. "Maybe I'll just die before they cut dem off! Butcher bastards! Sons-of-bitches cut my momma up too! I ain't never going to let them put the knife to my pretty tits!" She grabs and cuddles them. "Sam, feel these! Feel these!" She rolls her eyes, drags hard on the cigarette. "Goddamn butcher men... that's all the fuck they are anyways!"

Sam knows it's the gin talking. She's sad, kissable, a chocolate milk woman from Sweet Loaf County. He's sorry he put fear in her face. But people he cares about are sacred to him, their lives a part of his life, secure in his web. He made her think about the knife her mother died under, tender memories of a wife, a sister, a lover, mother. He notices her tucking pieces of her brownish-black hair behind her right ear. Gold earrings flash, the ones he bought her for her birthday. He rubs a thumb across her cheek to take the pain from her lips. He searches for that blueberry, apple smile. He surrenders his love and forgiveness in the silence of a dusty road, a wand over her heart, summer madness concocted under a hell and fire sun. A bead of sweat drips from her neck. He peeks down her v-neck red dress. When the truck shakes, her breasts jump, jiggle, pow, boom, wow in the dress. He slows down over a dead squirrel. Dry, red leaves crackle under the wheels that take up the space between their lives and the red clay, chain gang road.

He squeezes up behind a red and white Chevy station wagon. He scares the hell out of a family man with his long-neck wife, two kids and a hound dog. Mabel laughs as the man's horn curses Sam out.

Sweet Sam becomes childish, drinking gin with his Mabel, mixed up with the dog shit on a county road: Route 87, to Bailey's Cross. He sips his brown bag gin from a bottle. All he cares about is the fire from a pretty woman in the middle of a lost country road. It starves away the dream nightmares of a war. He lost a Vietnamese wife, a son. He found Mabel after, after a country lost another son in Vietnam. He's alive, alive to taste, smell the sun, moon, and sweet smells of a woman's panties. He has time to hear the silence in his heart, play the sax in the night, kiss up an angel's tears that fall with the rain.

"We almost there, baby."

"I know." She puts his right hand on her left breast. "And they going to stay there too." She draws closer to him. "I love you."

"I'm sorry I scared you. You know that."

"Yeah I know." She teases him, "Watch that pole."

"I just love you… that's all." He sticks his golf cap on his right knee. "I can't stand somebody else dying in my life, 'specially you."

"You made that clear."

Earth winds blow from east to west.

Gas fumes drift in their noses. Sam looks over her eyes of blossoms and lips of red watermelon lipstick? Yes! Yes! He wouldn't give a fuck if he did die

4

with her. It's better than leaving in some war with dog tags around your neck at nineteen. He puts more gas on the pedal, shifts some gears before she gets sick in the cab of the truck. Hell! He knows she has to be tired. He doesn't look at her as she uses his sweaty yellow towel and wipes it up. She throws the towel of vomit out the window. He counts to ten over and over, before the sleeveless, tight, red dress almost makes him smash right into a three hundred-year-old oak. Pleasant surroundings of her French perfume mix in with the sun and gin. He gets up the nerve to see if she's calmed down. Is she still looking for a fight? He throws an arm over her bare shoulders. He leaves one eye on the road to keep from hitting the cows. Sam sneaks a kiss on her cheek. He takes his arm from around her to concentrate on the road, Voodoo jazz music, and her rich creamy thighs.

She sneaks a peek at Sam behind the wheel. He has control of the clutch, and her too. He plays in the traffic, and he plays in soft tissue, proud black, white, Asian, Spanish women. They are his fountains to drink: Kool-aid, white wine, rum, bourbon, Coke, Pepsi, ginger ale and ice tea to get rid of the fires in his belly.

"Don't worry, Mabel… " he says. "Old Sam here going to take good care of you."

She gazes out the window at the horses eating grass on the farm. She lifts her leg up some to touch his knee, rub it, next to the stick, just letting him know, she's still there with him. Dust winds have her not caring what people say about him. He doesn't beat her and he doesn't steal her money for drugs. He just steals her heart. Her Gypsy man is just restless, a good looking man she doesn't mind sharing. She just makes him keep his women straight and her name in place, like a thousand year dinosaur footprint in the city of Sweet Loaf.

The radio plays some Miles; Boplicity. Horns rage in the stage of the cab.

She doesn't have much except a secretary's job with the State Department. She sleeps in a one-bedroom apartment with some nice linens her mother gave her just before she died in a psychotic fit. She has that American CocaCola bottle shape, a sweet gal with a big butt and firm, melon-shaped tits that all the white boys try to touch on her job. The gin has her feeling Miles' fingers going down her stomach. She rolls up a joint. When she hears "Sketches of Spain," the Black Prince makes her want to open up her legs. She pulls on the weed. "Damn, that's nice."

"Colombian Red." He smokes. "Uhhhhh!" Pushes it down his lungs.

The trumpet makes her want to give it up, right over on the side of the road. "Sketches" makes her just that crazy. This is her liberation, just like Sam's. She doesn't care about Miles shitting on everybody. All black people got Mississippi lynching, white man's blues problems. The music is sad to her as the sun breaks out, until she falls into the waves of sounds from this man's fingers. Death surrounds all of them. No black folks live long. Death is our freedom, our theme song to get away from this past and present of jive day. And the music is the strutting death march they play down in Storyville. Ask Satchmo.

And they finally arrive, around about two.

Carnival games are played between the suckers and the hipsters, dice, balls, bottles, shooting ducks, dropping the clown in the water or the basketball in the hoop. People stop by booths for beer, kosher mustard hot dogs and Milk Duds. Sam buys food, couple of rib sandwiches with potato salad on the side and two cokes.

Beer and laughter, hustling crooked teeth rednecks, toothpicks in their mouths, just love beating you out of your money. All just for fun! Old friends shake hands, wave bye and bye. Sam is cool when Mabel rolls her eyes at Josie Saunders, one of his young things from Calvary, Maryland. He's so cool that he takes her up in a Ferris wheel, just to keep her calm in the skies.

"I stole me a kiss! I stole me a kiss!" He hugs her up in his arms. "Now!"

She pushes her nose up against his. "Sam, you look like you about five years old at this carnival!" Her eyes get wider as they get higher.

"I am, baby! I am!" He swings his feet. "Boy! This takes me back when my mother and father use to bring me to these places!" He rocks the seat. "You look kind of scared, baby!" He tickles her in the rib.

"Sammmmm!" She looks down. Closes her eyes. "Sam, stop it!"

"Stop! It! Stop! It!" He recites her sweet voice over in the breeze.

A tear comes down her face.

"Okay, I'll stop it." He kisses the teasing away. "I just got lost for a second there... remembering and all." He looks down at the people. "Those were just some happy times in my life... when my parents were together, not on that dope." He rests back, searches the blue horizon of trees under their feet. "You know, when I was just a kid growing up on the block... this carnival would be my only escape from the stuff going on in my house with my mom and dad." He pulls out a couple of sticks of Juicy Fruit from his pants pocket. "Here." Hands her one.

She unwraps the gum. "It's so blue up here." Sticks it in her mouth.

"Yeah, baby. Blue as blue can get." He kisses her forehead. "The Ferris wheel makes you closer to the man upstairs." He points up at the clouds. "Gravity and God is working with us today."

"That's right. I don't need a brick building to talk to him." He looks down at her in his arm. "But you betta watch the devil in me."

"Give me a kiss," she says.

He sticks his tongue in her Juicy Fruit mouth. "Mabel, you so silly."

"You too!" She looks down at the ant people. "My mother use to bring me and my brother Jeff to the circus in the summer."

"What acts did you like watching?"

"Them big cats. Honey! I always wanted to see one of them tigers eat up the man with the whip."

"Don't be cruel!" He gives her his Elvis Presley voice.

"Elvis, they probably had them cats drugged on something," she plays with him.

"Are you having a nice time?" He digs a ticklish breeze out his right ear.

"Yes," she says, pecking at his leaf vein neck. "A bunch of old people, but it's cool."

He picks his cap off, places it on his left knee, and throws an arm around her. "You know, it's the last days of summer... so I thought getting away from Sweet Loaf for a while would be nice." He pulls on his ear. "We played chess all summer long, and I needed a break from you taking my king."

"With my queen," she laughs in his face.

"Yes, it's true... your queen did do all the damage." His gentle voice sounds like a husky southern sonnet.

They circle in the sky one more time and do a comical rock and roll over the festivities of a band playing under their feet. Her eyes search over this man with the long-distance view of trying to get away from a cursed life. She slips three fingers under his shirt. Mabel looks up in his buffalo black eyes; licks his heavy lips as their tongues start a nice dance.

Sam backs away from the music and her warm face of gin. "Thanks for winning me a teddy bear." He sits the prize between her legs as his right hand roams over her harmonious territorial landscape.

2

Monday, 7:30 a.m. Sam's dying for a second cup of black coffee on the doorsteps of recovery... such a hangover. Mabel is his missing link of love that he doesn't want in his shirt pocket. His wandering soul will not give in to her buttery, warm heart. Small talk drowns out his lust for her. Eyes that shine place him in a sand box, press him into a pinecone frozen to a vine. He follows his dreams and nightmares away from love, his dreams of the past, a place in his nightmares of a mother's screams. Mickey Mouse speaks in false tongues to him. He takes a cigarette, coughs into a Twilight Zone. He's pissed at his boss man, Posie; stiffed him on some carpets. Pentagon brass had money waiting for him, but some nice shag didn't come through. Shit, everybody gots to piss, eat, spill up their guts to pay a mortgage or rent. Live again, and die in the streets of a dead country. God bless all assholes on the I-95. Maybe one day he'll stop smoking? Drinking? Kissing rainbow women, just before they close the casket on his humpback ass.

He checks his watch; 7:43a.m.. He needs a drink. Time is the wrecked revenge of his past and future. He gets lost in Clint Eastwood movies, passes time at the Zoo Bar. He watches some drunk getting John Wayne whipped upside the head, over a woman. He wants to drive over the civil servants, just the kind that drive around in VW vans with cheap blue suits on. He jams a few cab drivers. He listens to the drivers holler profanities of shame and lust, one finger up, long-lasting music to his ears. Stop up the traffic in and around the bow ribbon expressway, just get the hell out of his way. Sam got a delivery to make.

He searches in his cotton blue shirt, the one with the alligator on his chest, very bad taste from an old dead flame, Alice Jackson. She bought this for him. He left her after that on a rainy street corner, pagan eyes of goddess, whore. He didn't feel the rain, he didn't feel her pain. He just felt like a bullfighter, running from her bull. He never wanted to hear her lies again. He sucks down the orange sun in his chest, tries to catch it over the exit ramp. It blinds him. He wants to take some more cocaine and Novocain, crash test Norgesic Forte, Robaxisal, a little bottle of Xanax and Valiums, some weed to cap off this morning drive. He lights up another Camel's over the Teddy Roosevelt bridge. Don't look down because he wants to jump off.

He brakes, rattles and twists his red truck up Fourteenth and Pennsylvania Avenue, beeps his horn at a long-legged, pale, horse woman. Fine, white girl, she's an injured angel in a fashionable gray suit.

11

Lawyer? Paralegal? Or just a GS-3 sucking the pipes off her GS-17 boss for a raise? Sam hollers out the truck, "Morning, darling!"

He slows down with the steps of the woman, sticks his face out the truck and whistles. "Have a nice day, hon!" plucks his cap off his head. Then he speeds by the untouchable, winged angel, who is afraid out in the morning sky.

He's going to Barkley & Brothers Construction Company, as mud splashes up on the giant wheels of the truck. He drives by the Donkey Girl Club. New office buildings are going up. A guy with a fire orange flag waves him through the yellow light, sleepy wink of morning.

He greets them. "Big John! McGee! Al! Joe Pops!" Wooden sawhorse lines trapped mad men on a hot, muggy morning in D.C.. Voila! He's happy to be working. Daddy had him on the streets early, taking drugs around different businesses; no kind of life for a young pup. Sam is unconfused in these jungles of steel beams, green frog men with shining teeth, raisin eyes. He's a part of the big twelve-story building going up on New York Avenue. Foreign Japanese auction of apple pie; Tokyo branches stretch out to feed them cream and honey from a Pacific Rim breeze.

Sam slows down when he sees the chain link fence, a hundred-foot drop hole of mud. Black, white, yellow faces lift, constantly moving with the floating day. Gouging, dragging, pulling, nailing, drilling, banging, tugging; cussing up steel girders in the nuclear sky. Silver hard hats reflect from the sun. Bare backs crack, break. Ankles twist. Foul air of blind sweat creeps from scaffold tops. A flatbed of bricks comes in from North Carolina. Around the corner, he comes upon a line of men begging for a job, day laborers. Twist! Shout! Sam has one slipped disk. Other men with sad blue, brown eyes, showing nothing but hunger of men- dogs, eating at the flesh of another for money to feed yourself and feed your family. In the early morning dead sun, muscles flex, reach, grab, chase down the cement into the hole. Die with American corporations, die in the cement hole to feed your family; so far, three died in the pits of Barium Construction. So far, black wreaths lay up on wooden planks of Union men, Mafia dues just enough off the top, kind sir.

Sam pulls his truck over to the side and hops down from the cab. He yells over at his friends: Big Lou hammering down some planks, Dickie Jefferson setting up the electrical wiring, Howie standing around waiting for his cement truck to finish mixing, Tony the Terrible washing down some water from his thermos. Amen! Nobody died last week. Harry Smith is catching hell for leaving his tools. Bo-Dick is chomping on an Egg McMuffin before going up the scaffolding. Beanie Thompson is picking up bets for the first football game between the Washington Redskins and Dallas Cowboys. All say a prayer for Mike Pickett, who died last year in the hole.

Nino Julio walks over to Sam. He's a third generation foreman from Nowheresville, his body beet-swine red, nose broken in three places. He's the latest version of a schoolboy rat. He's a man you'd like to whip up on in front of a cop, worth going to jail for. He would report on his mother for a two dollar raise.

"Murphy," he asks, "how many rolls of carpet you got this morning for us?"

Sam rubs his chin, reads his clipboard. "Compliments of Sweet Loaf Carpets, five rolls of blue shag and ten rolls of Oriental." He gives him the invoice.

Nino counts off his carpets. "Looks good!" He gestures with a gloved paw. "Hey, Jimmy! You and Tommy get over here!" He snatches off a copy. "Here!"

"Thank ya', boss!" Sam walks away from Nino. He goes over to talk to Richie Valentine, an old bear-hug friend. They grew up chasing the same girls under the second grade moon. Richie's lifting up some two by fours. He stops everything, slips his gloves off and shakes Sam's hand. "Heyyyy! My mannnn!"

"Working hard today, I see." He looks down at the planks of nails. "Boss man got you humping?" He pulls out his handkerchief, blows his nose, slaps the snot from his face. "What you been up to?"

They lean on a brick wall near the soda pop machine.

"A little dis... a little dat... You?" Richie offers him a cigarette. "Want one?"

Sam takes it. "Tryin' to make some money, like always." He leans into the match. Drags. "Ummm!" He waves to Charlie, Frank, Rudy Johnson moving through the yard pushing wheelbarrows. "So, you heard anything?"Richie spits. "I heard about this rich white woman over on Capitol Hill might need a few feet of Persian for her dining room."

"Good... I check back with you tomorrow morning for her address," Sam says. "So what you got going this weekend?"

Richie rolls his eyes up. "Something you not about, Sam." He plops fifty cents in the soda machine.

Sam challenges him. "Well! That must be gambling, then... Shit! I've seen too many Brothers get killed over the roll of the dice." He sees the men pull off the last roll of carpet from the truck. "Where the game going to be at this weekend?"

"Jimmy Lee's." He kicks the machine. A can of Coke plops in his hand. He pops the top, drinks. "Ahhhh! Right down the street from your place."

"Well, I hope you win... Then you can pay me back my twenty I loaned you in boot camp," Sam says. "I don't like the crowd at his place... You ain't going to win."

"Shit! That was back in seventy-two," Richie says. He reaches in his back pocket, opens up his wallet. "Here, man! Here's your money! Now go on, move El, Zorro out of here!" Richie grins up in his face like he has a can of worms in his hands.

Sam takes his money. "Thanks, Richie... See you later." Tips his dirty cap at him. "See you tomorrow." Sam starts to leave. "And don't be talking about my truck! That's my baby over there." Sam warns him, "Be cool at Jimmy's."

"Yeah! Okay," He watches Sam hop back up in his truck and slowly pull the truck back in the middle of the booming chaos of jack-hammers screaming up to the mountains of Jericho.

Back in traffic, sunspots shimmer in his rearview mirror. He slaps his sun visor down to shade his eyes. He yawns off last night's lovemaking with his Mabel Girl, thinks of her warm night snoozes as she cried before, during and after his kisses. He had cried with her. He didn't want to, but the release of tears over her breasts just had him back in his mother's womb. She made him blind to the fear of a war, a past, but all the time making him feel guilty when he made love to another. She talked to him like he was a baby, nestling him... before, during and after his kisses.

3

It's close to lunch time. Sam is driving off his load of carpets to different building sites in the diamond shape highway of the I-95 nightmare. Within an hour he's in Sweet Loaf heading back to his company's warehouse on Albermarle Place. He had to swing the truck through a narrow street they called Otis Road and an alley just wide enough to get his tailgates through to the loading docks of Sweet Loaf Carpets. It's owned and run by three southern gentlemen of World War II: Mr. Albert, Mr. Pinchon, and Mr. Finney, big white men belonging to country clubs in the backwoods of Middlesex Virginia. They didn't mind having the help over their estates, just to wash their car or cut their immaculate lawns for a bit extra on your paycheck every Friday. You could even peek at their milky, white daughters diving in the pool with their boyfriends, while you was working like them old Negro slaves of Maryland. But when he turns into the alley, three green and white police cars are at the entrance, checking people coming in, people coming out. He hits his brakes hard to stop inches from the rear end of car Two-One-Two. His boss, Posie, is coming out the back door in handcuffs, a thick necked cop on both sides.

Sam gets out of his truck. "What the fuck is this?"

Two other drivers come to him, Duck and Kenny.

Duck warns him with his hands up. "All right, Sam. Just calm down." He grabs him up in the arm. "Calm down!" his voice lowers, "don't say nothin'."

Kenny hollers at Posie, "Don't worry, boss! We'll get you out of this!"

Posie yells, just before his head is pushed in the car, "Sam! Call Rose!" He sits back; two other cops get in the car.

Sam cuffs his hands over his mouth. "All right, Posie! I'll call her."

The cars pull out, screeching out the alley with sirens and lights, breaking up the lunchtime calm of a normal working day. Dogs run right behind the tires of the law.

Life and skimming carpet off the top to feed your family... Ain't no Black man going to work a job if he can't make no extra, but Sam and the others know they can't fire all of them. So, the deal is to get the head brother, and that's Posie.

Men stand around by their trucks, scratching their heads, acting like they don't know what day it is. Twelve black men, all with barrel-hard arms and chests, speak with gin and garlic potato chip breath, shattered rumors of hidden truths, searching in their wallets for bail money.

Robby King flashes, "I got two hundred, Sam."

Mack pulls out a wad. "One-fifty right here... Damn! There goes my rent."

Duck picks his nose. "I got to get to the First National."

"Well, you better get your ass on then," Kenny says, slapping down some money in Sam's hands. " 'Cause Posie been good to you, boy."

"Don't nobody panic. We going to get him out," Junior reassures them. "Wasn't for Posie helping me with my drinking problem... I'd be a dead man today." He kicks a hundred in Sam's smelly golf cap.

"Shit! He helped all of us." Joe Buck opens up his wallet. "Yaw remember when he let me take off a week to take care of my mama." He sticks some bills in.

"His wife babysit my kids all the time... Posie and Rose are some good people." Nods at the men. "Shit! I can spare a couple of hundred," Jesse Jenkins says. He sticks fifty in the hat.

"Sam, you just make sure you get him out," Darnell Turner tells him. "If you need any more... just come this way."

"Thanks. This should be enough to get him a lawyer," Sam says to the mortified, scared faces of his fellow drivers. He folds it all up, sticks the wad down in his pocket.

Mr. Pinchon comes out the back door to them. "Men, come on in here. We got a meeting to start."

They stroll behind him into the dark cool caverns of the cobwebbed warehouse to the back offices. All three of the bosses standing in a line. All wearing dress gray wool suits, wrinkled in Christian dignity. All white, clean-shaven men with the country manners of pseudo, hide-your-words Klansmen to get along with the blue, brown, black, yellow Brothers.

Mr. Albert is drinking a cup of coffee. Mr. Finney is smoking on a long cigar. Mr. Pinchon sniffs the rose in his lapel, clipboard in hand. They huddle for a few minutes. Then they come back around to the drivers.

It's quiet; the drivers just mingling around. Some of them are scared of going next, some of them just pull out their hook-bill knives to play with the edges. Some just stand and wait to hear the payback of firings, new hirings. The questions hang in the air: Am I next? Will I see jail bars like Posie?

Mr. Finney pulls his cigar from his teeth, spits. "What we got here?" He looks around at the bowl of fruit faces. "Thieves!" Grits his teeth. "You know, we want to fire the whole lot of you!" He plucks cigar ash on the concrete floor. "But we got a job to do around here... We decided to lynch just one of you!" He smiles with a wink like he was Santa Claus for fifty cents on the dollar. "Posie was hired to watch the chickens. But when we turn our backs... he's stealing them right from under us!"

The drivers look at each other like a UFO has sprayed hydrogen piss on them.

A side door opens. Out comes a husky, short, red-bearded man, with a stare that's straight from Bella Lugosi. He's a crazy white boy from a teen horror movie.

"Gentlemen," Mr. Albert says, "this is my son-in-law... Michael Milano. He's going to watch the chickens... starting today."

The three men huddle up again.

Mr. Finney comes out of the cocoon to look over the faces wanting to cut his throat with their hook-bill knives. Even some too scared and bugged-out, that they are ready to beg like wounded dogs for their jobs. "Ummm! Uhhh! We decided to drop the charges against Posie... but his ass will never set foot in this warehouse again!" Straightens his tie. "This is all we got to say for now." He points his finger at them. "But if we catch this stealing around here again, we gonna chop some hands off!" Searches the sea of eyes to make sure they understood this edict. "Now get back to work!"

•　•　•

Sam drives over to Posie's apartment with his second load. Rose opens up. Her face is wet, scared. As soon as she sees him, she grabs him by the arm.

Sam says, "I just want to give you this money, Rose." He closes the door. "How you holding up?" He touches her face, kneels lower to pat their little boy, Reggie, on his curly head of hair. He's just seventeen months.

"I'm okay. Posie just got in from the jail." She calls, "Posie! Sam is here."

Posie comes out the back bedroom, his face relieved. His eyes smile up, and he shakes Sam's hand.

Sam slaps him on the shoulder. "I can't stay long... I got a load to take to Aberdeen... but, I just want to check on you and Rose." He reaches in his pocket.

Posie picks up his son. "Whewww! I'm just glad they dropped the charges." He looks at Rose in her blouse and jeans. He's more worried about her than himself. He kisses his baby on the cheek.

"I had to tell them you were on drugs, man... to get that sympathy vote for you."

Posie scratches his head about the lie. "Ah, shit! That all right!" Hugs his boy. "As long as I don't have to stay in that jail, you could tell them I was a Communist. I don't care!"

The little boy's face lights up. "Dadddd! Daaaadddy!" Punches his small fingers in his father's face.

Sam grabs Rose's hand, sticks the money in. "Here's a little something from the gang."

Posie looks at Sam, tearing up. "Thanks, Sam... You tell the rest of them, I said that too."

He tickles the baby boy in his ribs. "No problem! Let me go make this trip... I see you later." He goes to the door.

Posie opens it up. "All right! See you later, man. Thanks!"

Sam turns back to him, Rose and the baby. "Okay!" He leaves, runs down the steps right back to his truck to make his last runs.

• • •

At the end of this day, by five, Sarah Vaughan is singing her guts out on WQSL radio station.

In the back and front seats of Sam's seventy-two Impala, Duck, Kenny and Joe Buck are having a little taste in the back alley of the warehouse. Drivers are pulling off, going home to wives, girlfriends, children, most of them in a hurry for that hot, soapy bubble bath and cool drink. Just get your mind off the hard work and being in a hot coffin truck.

Duck holds his paper cup of gin in his hand. "Sam, did you get the money to Rose?"

Sam searches in the plastic bag for ice cubes. "Ah, ha!" Plops the ice in his drink. He takes a long pull. "Ahhhhhh!" Licks his bottom lip. "Posie was there."

Kenny asks, "How was he holdin' up?" He unscrews the top off the orange juice chaser for his vodka. Pours it in his cup, drinks up.

Sam takes his golf cap off his head. "He was all right. I told him what I said at the meeting about his drug problem." He sticks it on the dashboard right under the giant dice dangling from his rearview mirror. He taps the horn. "Beeeep!" at Jesse and Darnell getting in their cars.

"How did he take that?" Joe asks. "Because I was shocked to hear you say that to Finney."

"He didn't care." Sam shrugs. "He was just glad somebody said something to get his ass out of jail."

Kenny slaps Sam five. "I hear dat!"

Duck was getting worried. "So! We got a new man to deal with?"

"Shit! Don't worry about him," Sam tells them. "He looks like a thief to me." He thumbs his steering wheel upholstery. He cools off with Sarah's sweet voice and Duke Ellington's piano.

Joe Buck laughs. "Sam, you always could spot a crook two hundred paces."

Sam plays with his mustache. "By the time he gets to talking to them foremen on the construction sites... it'll be business as usual." He makes himself another drink. "Believe this!"

23

"And he gots to go through us to make the deliveries," Kenny says.

"That's right. He gots to go through somebody," Duck says.

"Was you scared, Sam?" Kenny asks him, huddling towards him.

Sam drinks up. "Shit, yeah!"

Kenny gets serious about this. "I already been to jail... and I wasn't going to do any more time... If they called my name... I was going to hop in my car and get the hell out of Sweet Loaf."

"We all were scared," Joe says to him. "Ain't no shame in that."

Duck bounces his head to the sassy lady. "They got one of us."

Kenny says, "Well, Posie took a chance like the rest of us." He scratches his three-day beard. "He knew what time it was."

Sam isn't worried. "He'll land back on his feet." He shakes the ice around in his drink. "He was a damn good driver before taking the supervisor job here." Pulls on his ear. "Somebody will pick 'im up." He knocks a fly from his arm. "I'm gonna miss him."

"He got a nice wife too." Kenny asks, "Sam, you ever fuck her?"

"Naw," Sam says to them. "I'm a dog, but he ain't never do nothin' to me."

"Ah, you lying, Sam!" Duck doesn't believe this.

"But don't think... I didn't think about it."

"We all have," Duck says. "She's a fine yella woman."

Kenny messes with him. "Mr. Sam Romeo man... I betta watch you around my old lady."

"Yaw drank up my liquor. Now yaw gonna talk about me." Sam smiles over the high faces of his coworkers. "I betta watch ya' around my lady."

"Let's get on home to our wives before Sam gets them." Duck drinks up.

"See ya' in the morning," Sam says. He starts the car, listens for the voice of a cat coming from the engine.

The men leave the banana-yellow car, feeling like feathers. Kenny waves Sam through the alley. Two hound dogs bark right behind the car.

Sam decides to drive towards Main Street, take the long way home.

Sweet Loaf is full of traffic. Most of it comes from the Sandstone Defense Factory letting out. A traffic cop whistles him by. He gets stuck in his first traffic jam. Sam muscles his car into the right lane. He then makes a right turn on Dakota and Main. That will put him near Luigi's Italian Deli, Sweet Loaf Bakery, Samurai Used Cars. Around the corner on Baker and Monroe is Saint Peter and Paul Catholic School. The Bijou Theater on the corner shows: *From Russia With Love*. He lights up a cigarette, and calms his mad nerves out in the nicotine, knowing Posie is no different than him or any other man. He's just a refugee from the big leaf tobacco fields of South Carolina. He's a hardworking man, cool to everybody. He's the kind of man that doesn't want to see anybody starve, but he's a Robin Hood thief. Not saying that wasn't wrong, but he'd steal for you and his family too. And it's never enough from the boss to put shoes on your kids' feet, food on the table and pay your rent or mortgage too. Never enough to see the next day clear, and take care of two-three families at the same time. Never enough in just trying to make it to work in one piece and pray they don't lay me off today.

Sam knows the game about more dope coming to Sweet Loaf instead of jobs. He was born and raised in white powder dreams. Cold nightmares roam a city in drag. It got worse after Vietnam. Everybody had their hands out. At the stop light, the car purrs like Eartha Kitt. He just gave it a tune-up. Green light, he drives past Bobbi's Liquor Store. A couple of wine-heads dwindle in the front door. They vanish in radio waves next to Little Mo's Barber Shop, where lime green, popsicle whores stand three paces to the right from the door. The day sun falls like pieces of thread from a half-done dress. A night calls forth the Transsexual Vampires of Broadway and Main. He finishes his cigarette, flicks it out the window in the sun orange dust. Herbie and Wayne Shorter play some "Indigo Blue" from his radio. Sam's going to get drunk tonight, call up his Mabel and cry in her cup of lemon grass tea.

4

"Elthel, we glad you came over here," Mabel says to Richie's wife. "Come on in here and sit down." She closes the door. "Take your jacket off."

Elthel slips off her jacket, peeks around the apartment of books, African statues, stereo playing Al Green, "Let's Stay Together." She sits at the dining room table. "Where Sam at? I know he's not at Jimmy Lee's."

Mabel hangs up the jacket in the hall closet. "Oh, noooo! I sent him out to get some beer." She sits across from her at the table. "He'll be right back."

Elthel pulls her pink blouse sleeves down. "Ummmmm!" She sniffs. "Look like I came a good time." She looks over in the kitchen. "What you cooking, Mabel?"

Mabel opens up a wooden box with carved flower designs on the top. "Sam's favorite." She starts to unwrap a plastic bag. "Beef bar-b-que ribs, potato salad, collards." She pulls out some weed, rolls up a joint, lights up, sucks down the smoke. She holds it in. "Ahhhhh!"

Elthel takes the joint, puffs. "Ummmmmm!"

"So Richie gambling tonight, huh?" Mabel asks, while sucking down the herb real slow into her lungs.

"Yep. But I made sure he left some home… so he don't lose all of it." She plucks some of the ash in a large ashtray. She looks out the picture window overlooking the front part of Longmeadow Street, not quite dark. Some children still jump rope, kick a ball to each other. She feels the room getting lighter. "This some good herb," hands it back. "Where you buy this, Mabel?"

Mabel takes another puff, hands it back. "Oh, Jimmy Lee's." She gets up from the table and goes to check on the food. She opens up the oven, sticks a fork in the ribs, and bastes them with some sweet, Georgia, homemade hot sauce.

Elthel walks in the kitchen with the weed still in her fingers, "Jimmie Lee rolling, huh?"

Mabel squints up from the heat of the small oven. "For now… Girl, you know how it is…"

Elthel gives her the joint back. "He probably been in and out of jail fifty times."

Mabel's feeling good talking with a girlfriend. Al's music and the weed make her relax. She finishes off the joint, plucks it out in the trash basket, picks up a large spoon, lifts up the top on the collards, and stirs.

They hear the door bang closed.

Sam comes in with the bag of beer. "Baby!"

Mabel winks up. "Right here, Sam!"

"Ohhhh! We got some company!" He pecks Elthel on the cheek.

"Hey, Sam."

He puts the bag down on the counter. "Got some beers here!" He gets out three cans of Schlitz, opens up the refrigerator, and slips the rest in. "I see yaw started without me… That's all right!" hugs Mabel around the hips. "Enjoy! Enjoy!" nibbles on her neck.

She pushes him. "Stop! Sam, let me cook!"

He winks at Elthel. "Baby, you are cooking!"

"And you said Sam didn't love you, Mabel!" Elthel shakes her head, takes her beer back in the living room by the stereo.

Mabel kisses him hard on the lips. "Now, that should hold you for a while."

He sniffs around. "Is dinner almost ready?" He starts to check on the collards.

She smacks his hand with the spoon. "Get out of there!"

He opens his beer. "Just let me know… I'll keep Elthel company." He leaves out the kitchen.

"Okay!" Mabel checks on the ribs. She should have made some cornbread; that's what she was getting a taste for. Never mind, she has some wheat bread left. She listens to Al Green, "Loving you forever! Times the good! the bad! the happy, the saaadddd! Let's stay together!" She taps her foot to the beats, and dabs the sweat rolling down the side of her face. "Ohhhhhhh! Sing it, Al!" as she shakes her aproned hips. Her Saturday is going on okay so far. Sam isn't complaining about the Redskins, Black people, White people, Indian people, Chinese people, and he's cooled off some about Posie losing his job. She's gotten her period back on track. Her days of tampons, Kotex, blotting, were all wrapped up in a heavy life of bleeding rivers.

Motherhood isn't near, after three abortions, ten doctors correcting the tubes, and six months of dealing with attorneys about her life's will. She has a niece from a nasty-ass brother who never remembers her birthday. Maybe she'll leave her money to her Calico cat, another man feline who never stays home. She pulls out the potato salad. Mavis Staples is singing in the other room, she licks her thumb. She doesn't want Sam to touch her until Sunday, when her blood rivers slow down for him to taste the salt from her body again. Over and over she plays with this thought. Blood rivers flow, so does her body go. Blood rivers flow, so does her body go. She turns off the greens, and picks out the smoke neck bones for her man.

Elthel comes back. "You need any help?"

Mabel opens the oven, grabs the mitten and the potholder from the counter. "Oh, thanks! You can help me take the plates in." She pulls out the pan of ribs. The pan pops juice from the heat. She turns the oven off. "Ummmmm! Yeah, they ready." She slaps off the mitten. "Elthel, get me that bottle of wine from the refrigerator."

"Okay." She squeezes behind her, takes out the bottle, and pulls down three wine glasses from the cabinet.

Mabel is fixing the plates. "Let me know how much you want."

Elthel licks her lips. "Oh, that's enough!" Pats her hip. "Gots to watch my weight."

"Yeah, right! What Black man you know want a skinny ass woman?..." She starts to fix Sam's plate. "And I know Richie don't want one." She licks the rib sauce off her fingers.

"Haaaa! Haaaa! I couldn't get rid of this big butt if I tried."

"You been watching too many Slim Fast commercials. Haaaa! Haaaa! Girl, you full of shit!" She works on her plate. "I wanted to cook some cornbread, but I said, 'Let me watch my weight!' Haaaa! Haaaa! But we got some wheat bread here." She takes the loaf of Roman Meal down from the top of the refrigerator. "Come on, Elthel, time to get down!"

They march in the room with the plates, shaking their hips to Momma Staples: "Shum! On! Now! Play on it! Play on it!"

•   •   •

"DeeDee, get your ass up them stairs!" Jimmy Lee pushes her in the back. He has a pocket full of hundreds, with a house packed with people. Greywhite smoke of dope smokers drifts in the air on the first floor, crap shooters in the third bedroom. Dark, chocolate women selling their tails in the other two bedrooms. His redbone from Southeast D.C. is his best prize for tonight. He doesn't want to take his belt off, but he will. "Come on, baby, now just give Stan some of your sweet stuff and you can go for tonight." He pulls her closer to him, rubs his hands down her waist and butt.

She doesn't want her face touched by him, but she knows he can get real crazy in front of the people he tries to impress the most. When he's coked up, he could kill his own mother for a buck. She roams her long fingernails over his smooth face, matching his bald head. "Okay, baby! But I don't want no rough

31

shit going down in that bedroom… or I'm gonna cut him." She licks the side of his face. "And that be three hundred for tonight, and after this, I'm going home."

"Okay! Okay, DeeDee." He watches her go upstairs, lights a cigarette and gets back to his poker game. He watches the place get to jumping with some men and women dancing around, humping on each other to some of that James Brown "Get On the Good Foot." His woman, Sandra Brown, is sitting beside him watching the money pot. Her hair's all over her face, nose dripping over a white trail of coke. He grins around at the players. "Baby, did you watch my hand?"

She wipes hair from her eyes, cleans off her nose. "Yeah, Jimmy, I watched your hand."

He glances at her soaked, wet-baby, China doll face, hauls his hand back and slaps her. "Bitch! You a goddamn lie! Now get your ass up from this table, and go clean your face!" He snatches her up from the chair. "Shhhhh!"

She scampers out of the dining room crying, with blood coming through her hands.

Richie looks away, doesn't want to get involved between a crazy man and his woman. It's almost nine. He has to get over to Sam's place to pick up Elthel. He's lost two hundred. That's all his home life can stand for tonight. The cards he has aren't going to send him to Hawaii, throws his hand down. "Shiiiittttt! That's enough for me tonight." He pushes back from the table.

Jimmy leans back in his chair, covers his fingers over his cards. "Ah, all right! So how'd you do for tonight?" He drinks some of his scotch, plays with his suspenders.

"Not too good… but I never do." Richie smiles as the other men laugh with him around the table, understanding this plight. He stands up. "Just something to do, you know."

Jimmy looks up. "You think you could do me a favor?… It'll be a couple of bucks in it for you." He gets up. "You can go home and be a winner tonight."

"Awright! I'm with that." Richie rubs his chin. "What is it?"

"I need you to go upstairs, and watch the door that DeeDee and Fat Stan in… If you hear any problems," slips a hundred in his hand, "you come and get me."

"Um, huh!" Richie sticks a toothpick in his mouth, and pushes his way through the crowd. The stairs have some of the girls waiting to go in the two occupied rooms with their customers.

One tall one with a red wig on, black lipstick, tits almost hanging out, rubs against him. "How about you, Richie? You want a spin around the world, baby?"

He's polite, but moves his face away from hers. "Naw, Sweet Charlotte, I'm all right tonight." He gets to the door, next to the bathroom, crosses his arms, and leans back. He doesn't hear anything getting out of hand. But minutes later, voices can be heard:

"Motherfucker! I said no!"

"Bitch! What you mean, no? I just gave you three hundred dollars!"

Richie backs up, but the door swings open. He sees DeeDee running in her silk red bra and panties. "The motherfucker's got a gun!" ducking. "Awwwwwwww!"

Stan shouts, "Bitch!" Aims and starts firing at her.

The crowd scrambles as the bullets have no particular name who they going to hit. Men, and women fall. Eyes search out for God. A couple of the men from the dice game not hit yet, fire their guns.

They stop him with some rounds to the chest.

Women's screams call out like the sounds of Saint Agnes Church bells on a Sunday morning, for all sinners to come and pray.

Jimmy Lee, with his gun drawn, goes over the bodies on the steps. "Move out my way!" But one of the people he stumbles over is Richie Valentine.

Richie's eyes stare up to heaven.

Jimmy Lee reaches into the dead man's pockets, takes his hundred dollars back. He turns around, to the mess of hiding dice, cards, and dope before the police arrive.

5

In a song for the dead…

Mabel Friday sits in the Lotus position at the feet of Sam, who's playing Richie's favorite tune, "Round Midnight." Other guests sit around quietly listening to the notes of a friend saying goodbye. Mabel drinks some white wine as her tears trail down her face. In silence, and only that, she washes away the loss. She holds on tight to a small couch pillow, her grip wanting to tear the pieces apart, treat it as if it was Death, surrendering its claim on a people. Nothing but the notes ease her down this path of the night. Her man plays slow, deliberate, as if to give his friend every piece of the song that others have played, many, many times before him. Yes, yesterday's laughter will be remembered in all their dreams… of Richie's smile, his bad attitude, his clamp on Elthel. How he watched out for her safety, taking her to work, picking her up in the evenings. She knows Sam is taking it hard, in silence, the way a man works the pain of his past. He wants friends around this day after the funeral: Doris and Tony Gathers, Mike Malone, the cats from work, Rob and Jill Lee, Minnie, Sarah, Ralph Jenkins, Diane and Joseph Singleton, Kathy, Ralph and Bobbi, Denise and Jeff Lewis, even his brother Ray.

She looks at Sam's face, his closed eyes, puffed cheeks... in a trance with nothing but the music to comfort him. But she wants him to know that she's there for him, not to nag him. Let him be with his own God. The games, his car, his truck, other women, his family. His work that's not for a normal man. Every day after the next... she would be there for him... when he is able to hold her and say, "Baby, I love you." She looks at the solemn faces of the people from the neighborhoods of Sweet Loaf. Old, new friends, some his, some hers, all came to be with them, came to hold them, for the music. Some of them knew Richie Valentine, some didn't. But they came to be with Sam and her, that's all they had to do. Drink wine, eat some French bread, talk about life... Yeah, talk about life. She sways with her man's feet tapping with the beats. She sways to the notes of her man's heart pumping, twisting, hitting, kicking with his whole body, just playing for the love of another man.

Mabel feels the last days of summer breezes come through the windows of the apartment. Liquor, cigarette, marijuana smoke float through their heads. Wine tasting with the melancholy refrain of Sam's sax, carrying them all through the maze of realizing that we are here for just a short minute at a time. She feels the sounds tickle her in the ribs. She shakes her head to the riffs of a man who cared so much, who loved so deeply, but didn't show it... only in his obtuse actions of playing for another. Final passages of death she knows so well. Final passages of sweet surrender she watched her mother go through... screams in the night of a morphine-subdued life. Suffer sweet angel of seeing someone you love die in the alcoholic aroma of a hospital room, skinny, bald-headed woman who brought her in this world. Her mother was always there for her, even as her words slipped away in the early morning light dew of room five-o-six. Her mother grasped her hand and whispered, "Marry a man who will make love to you." Mabel sees from these words the man standing above her, playing to the angels.

Whispered prayers:

Kathy comes and hugs her around the shoulders on the floor. She reflects, wipes the tears from her cheeks, and faces her friend with just a long, frozen smile. She rests her head down on her to feel the last notes tremble through her body. Her soft female friend of many years teases her, "Now, Mabel, don't you go on make yourself sick with all these tears. You don't want your face all dried up, looking like Mr. Raisin."

Sniffles, "Nooooo! I'm so glad you came."

"Girllll! To hear that man of yours play that sax! Ummmm! Ummmmm!" Rubs her back. "I'm just sorry it's over this mess." She gives her a Kleenex. "How's Elthel holdin' up?"

"She's okay, staying with her mother for a while," plays with the Kleenex, blows her nose.

Sam comes to her and bends down. "I feel better."

"Good." She looks at him. "I know Richie appreciates it."

"You want some more wine?" He touches her knee, caresses the hair from her cold cotton cheeks. He's drained from the playing, especially this tune.

"I'm fine... Go on and talk to your brother."

"Okay." He goes to his brother, grabs him around the neck. "Hey, Ray! Glad you came."

"I was going to be here with my little brother." Ray slaps him on the back. "I see Mabel taking this pretty hard."

"We all are... Richie come from where we come from..."

Ray agrees. "That's right! The same neighborhood here in Sweet Loaf." He drinks his glass of wine, nods over to Minnie. "Three blocks of us! All squeezed in."

"Ha! That's right, bro'." Sam rubs his sax. "That piece was for him."

"I know." Pulls on his ear. "He was a Dexter Gordon fan."

They go over to the table, pour some more glasses of wine.

Joe Buck comes over, gives him a hug. Kenny, Duck, Posie and Rose all surround their friend of many years. They just give him their hearts... drink his wine, eat his bread. All talk of the life of a man.

Richie and him were close, same age, same school, same gals—the Jackson twins, played a lot of ball together over at the Sweet Loaf Rec Center. The same fucking war: Vietnam: 1972-1974, the Mekong Delta. On a clear fucked-up day, you could kill forever and ever. Amen! They were friends who fought for and against any and everything that mattered: jail, drugs, women, children, jazz, Rhythm and Blues, Malcolm X, Martin Luther King, Jr., peace, war, mothers, fathers, brothers, archaic free thinkers, unrepaired articles of clothing borrowed for a dance, unrepaired articles of figures singing in the rain. Two boys drifting under a tree from the ball game, waiting for the lightning to strike one of them, taking bets on who gets hit first. Getting drunk on some Colt 45 in the attic, listening out for your mama. Jerking off on some *Playboy* magazines, on naked paper pieces of flesh that made you drown into a cesspool of love. At the age of thirteen, calling up little girls on the phone and groaning over their voices when they pick up. Hang ups. Old whores just giving it up for old times' sake. Beating the shit out of a punk from another neighborhood. Coming home. Running from bullies trying to get your lunch money. Sam crying to his mama because Richie cheated at marbles. He crying to his mama, because you got a new bike for Christmas. With both of you ending up crying in each other's arms, because the day was gone.

Ray looks kind of sad at his brother slipping the sax from around his neck. He knows Sam is a hard man to soften up when things from the past come up to haunt him. Maybe this is the right time to take him on. "Sam, I talked to Daddy a couple of days ago."

"Um, how is he doing?" He lays his sax in the corner by a floor plant.

Ray follows him out of the circle of friends. "Okay. He just want to know how you doing." Sticks a hand in his pocket. "That's a lie. He's not really doing too good."

Sam stands by the window, turns his back. "It's not good to lie, Ray," turns and pats him on the shoulder.

He takes a drink of wine, winks over to Mabel eating some cheese and crackers. Kathy is making her get rid of those Round Midnight tears.

Ray remembers with the scratching of his chin. "Um, I know… Mama would always tell us that." He looks him over. "He wants to see you."

Some of his friends laugh around in the living room.

"Man, fuck him."

Ray hunches, backs up some. "Okay, Sam."

"And fuck you too!"

Ray coughs up a stupid grin. "I remember when you was a little boy I use to bust you upside your head when you said stuff like that to me." Nods closer to him. "You ain't little no more."

"That's right, I ain't little no more."

"Memories hurt. I know, I know they hurt." Ray lights up a cigarette, blows smoke.

Sam taps the side of his head. "That's right, they hurt… so I just try to remember the good and leave the rest alone." He peeps at him, then back to his shoes to just keep the pain down in his throat. "You could learn that lesson, Ray."

"I'm sorry. I thought this was a good time."

"It ain't never a good time, Ray." He looks at his brother standing two inches taller than him. "It ain't never a good time." Looks at his glass. "Our mother was a whore and a saint. She was always there for us."

"He just wants to talk to you, that's all…"

A weird feeling comes over Sam, he gets kind of cold. "The bastard killed her… I found her calling out his name! Butt naked on the bed! Wet with sweat, piss, vomit and tears for him." He sets his drink down. "Where was he at, Ray? Where was he at?" He shakes his head, walks from the face of his brother.

No more voices, no more laughter.

Mabel rushes to him, lets him drop on her shoulder, pulls him back in the bedroom and waves them out of the apartment. She nudges his body back on the pillow, pulls off his socks and shoes, "Just close your eyes, Sam," lifts him towards her, unbuttons his shirt. She feels him helping her in the darkness of the bedroom. She drops down, unbuckles, pulls off his pants. Over him, she pulls her sweater over her head, unzips the back of her denim skirt, kicks off her moccasins. She mounts. On top of his chest she listens to his breaths put her to sleep.

6

Sunday before Thanksgiving:

In her magical dressing mirror, Mabel's face lights up as if the fireflies of St. Croix had taken her hostage. A colored red, black, green afro pick lays between a jar of Noxema cold cream and twisted Bobbie pins Sam has picked out of her hair. Seven forty-watt oyster shell lights frost over her honey hourglass body and various silk chokers in colorful blues, yellows, browns. When Sam sees her, he turns into a man with heat in his drawers. His lips kiss away his favorite things. Cheap perfume from the houses of East Flatbush, West Los Angeles, Southside Chicago, and Paris, Texas. A brooch from her mother, Ruthie, pearl necklace from her Grandma Ivey, nothing from her daddy, ivory and imitation painted gold brush set from her brother Leroy. She got that when she graduated from high school: last heard, last got anything from him since then. She picks her hair up, out, all about, bare-assed. She lotions her face, arms, legs, feet. She'll go

without a bra today, slips on some French-cut panties. Then she gets real comfortable in a long-sleeve,
white sheer blouse and a matching black and gold
necklace of an Island- African woman… going to see
another, Island-African woman. She has to see her,
this woman saved her. Her grandma is an old roots
woman, by way of Tortola, by way of the Motherland.
Mabel sticks in big loop earrings, and lifts from her
red lip love seat a hand-made red, black, and green
shawl over her shoulders. She slips into a pair of
Lee's, points her feet into some penny loafers, and
looks around the room, checks over the mess Mabel
in Wonderland vibe. She grabs thirty-three dollars,
car keys, cigarette butts, and leather change purse
from the dresser, lifts up her Rosary beads. There's an
Oxford dictionary under the *Vogue* magazine, white
girl winter fashions issue. She slips her small phone
book in her purse. Memorabilia of tainted pieces
of junk mail lay about, coffee stains over the winning entry prize number of the Johnson Afro-Sheen
Sweepstakes. She's mad now. Other curled up pieces
of phone numbers lying around. display past, present
girlfriends, family enemies that choose to be quiet.
They know who they are! They know who they are!
Her checkbook captures a treasure chest of three-
hundred dollars. Her rent is just five hundred. Damn!
Short again. Inside is a torn Greyhound bus ticket
from Detroit, just to visit ghosts of the past. Mabel
listens to the Temptations sing one last song, she has
that thing for David Ruffin. You know, girls! When
your man ain't around! Another will do. A treaty
exists between her and Sam. He hustles. She shuffles between family and a vanishing-act man.

She's just about ready to visit her Grandma Ivey down at Crocker's Boat Landing. Some old people coddle up to death, her grandmother coddles up to life. She keeps traveling, rows her own boat, plays softball, goes to dances with men in their fifties, bird-watches tight asses at Sparrows Beach. She even drinks sherry on a cold day, sips lemon rum ice tea on a hot one. Grandma Ivey took care of her when she was just nine. Nobody else, after her mother died in a place folks called Saint Mary's Corners, and behind your back they called it the Crazy House. But she was told by her grandma and others that her mother died of breast cancer. She doesn't need to know nothing else, except life for a woman is a hard love affair. "There!" She mugs in the magical mirror of her bedroom, loosens the top button on the blouse. "Damn! Girl, you sure look good!" A smile of stars comes in her eye. She dabs at her afro hairstyle, and grabs her car keys out of her purse.

She's out the door, leaving behind her porcelain dolls of *Gone with the Wind*, peach colored walls, high school banners of an ex-cheerleader in the path of a man with the storm in his eyes.

It's cool beneath the apple blossoms.

Up a hill, in a yard, leaves spray sweet fragrances. Arms of a huge oak reach out to a long porch swing. Grandma Ivey and her special girl sit under the golden yellow leaves, in it all. With different ways, the women take in the greyish blue Indian Summer day. Thunderous sounds of boats can be heard from this hill. Just behind them is a red brick, two-story house, white shutters.

Ducks peck in the yard. This used to be Mabel's home, a place that once kept fairy tale wolves from her door. Grandma Ivey had seen it all, damn near just about, sitting there in her green sweater. She holds a cutting knife, switches it over in her left hand to skin the orange. A cloak of knowledge lives behind the pointy, white shell eyeglasses. She would peek over the glasses to make sure you got her meaning, or you got pinched, made sure you listened. She just flipped the orange skin over to her granddaughter's lap. It always used to be this way every Sunday afternoon round about two. The both of them would sit and wait. Grandma would call that old oak, Gran'pa, eating, gazing down at the canoes and sailboats. Buoys kept the line between deep and shallow waters. Two pondering women rest their feet with the swishing of waves and the peeling of an orange.

Peeking from the clouds, the heart and soul of the sun's hands lay down upon Ivey's grey and white hair. It's pulled back in a bun, forming a halo with the sprinkling shade from the fingers of the leaves. Folks would say, when the sun was cool and the breeze tickled your ears, as the tree shade come just above your head, she could talk for hours upon a moon owl's laughter. Turkey, gobble-neck woman just about shows her age of eighty. White pearls take care to cover up these fading star years. But her brown eyes still reign proud over her few acres above the landing. Granpa Earl bought her this property in the thirties.

He kept his wife in the back woods, near the shore. Always with a boat ready to get away from the

Klan, if they ever decided to visit one night, and they came a couple of times.

Ivey reflects and pauses with her two thumbs splitting the orange in half. "Here, child," she puts a piece in her mouth, "you still going with that crazy Sam Murphy?"

"Yes, Grandma," Mabel looks up from the napkin. She bites on the sweet orange, wipes some of the juice from the side of her mouth. "Ummmm!" She asks, "Mr. Fox sold you these?"

"Um, hum! He got some good ones in this week." peers over her eyeglasses with a glint. "He just needed a little dab... for me to get a good price."

They laugh.

"Grandma Ivey, still fresh, ain't you?"

"Child! I just needs a little dab every now and then. Heee! Heeee! Heee!" She bites into another piece. "Um, gonna be fresh till I die." Sun shines over the trees and lake on Crocker's Landing, a good day. She taps her feet, rocks the swing some.

Mabel scans the lake. "Men, they seem to be such fragile creatures." She licks her fingers and lips, rubs her hands with a napkin.

Ivey closes her eyes, wandering and swinging, looks at her all-grown-up Mabel. "Dey like to stray from home every now and again... but sometimes you gots to bring 'em back." She pats her bun some, points the knife up towards the sky, trying to remember long ago. "Let's me tell you bouts when I was a little girl back in Tortola, what happened to this man dey calls Jala Jala." She sits back with the orange and knife in her hands, and tells her this story...

Massive arms of a whore come up from the sea.

St. James Bay waves splash up on muddy wet sands. Just below his balcony he can see the combative soft rains towards the west, gasping for its last breath. Sunlight morning creeps over his back as he has one last cup of coffee. Speculation grows as palm trees flap mosquitoes from his face. To the east a cruise ship moves over the light blue horizon. On this Sunday he has given birth to a hangover.

He stays at the Villa Allegro, on the isle of shame.

A tornado of Carnivals, root people from Africa's hands, rich white shoppers, everybody from around the world, all coming through the gates of dreams and for that elusive gypsy woman of love. Little cars roam over our island, with some buses too. We hurt each other, buy and barter the White man's paper money. Heat, swat huge flies, drink up good rum, and run from the devil's hands; all want to go to America, not live here anymore longer under this greedy savage.

But this man is from everywhere.

He's messing with his landlady, Madame Susie, his drunken rum lover, coconut haunting pretty girl with a flower in her hair. She is from St. Maarten, I thinks! Owner and a wolf, runs her place like a plantation master. But she gives her body only to White men, to the gold. Doesn't have an ounce of love in her bones. She would beat a maid with belt, if she found dem stealing.

He roams over the island on his third day there.

Tucks his shirt down in his pants, soaks up the beach and the sun people. Watching the children have a life without hatred; because of the colors of their rainbow skin. He rests under the papaya palms, and remembers all the women he hurt during his life. A selfish man, who has been hurt by many himself: a father who left, his mother who gave him birth, then tried to make him marry the local girl. He sleeps well no more at thirty-five. He listens to the steel bands call out heart to these women, the beach, the sea.

Jala! Jala! Mon! Jala! Mon! Jala Jala Mon!

He waves to some folks from the States as smoke floats in the air. He sucks on a cigarette and keeps the pain to himself, like so many others. It's killing him, this unrest, this unease.

Beyond the beach edge, red flowers bloom.

Imprints of the palms' hands rest over his sleepy eyes in the shade. Not a family man, not no particular hand to hold to his heart. He relaxes under the small wonders of the sun, listens to the band play some farewell notes in the breeze. He got married once or twice. One girl, Marta Abraham from Domenica, such a sweet flower child. He took her from her parents, carried her around the world. Hurt her with other women in his bed… he didn't give a drunken stare about her. He just believed in love and pain.

She cusses him in Creole. "*Cochon! Maron! Malandrin!*"

He turned back, to keep from slapping her. He lifted up his baggage, left her in London Daily Square. He traveled away to other islands: Puerto

Rico with the street women, Martinique with long legged girls from the bushes, Cuban whores with big lips, breasts, small waists, British Guinea to Indian women praying to their night Gods. Chased the girls of Haiti to island shacks for a three-finger shot of rum, love and an American dollar.

Stupid band plays something about making love to a woman and eating salt fish at the same time, stayed in his head. Trumpets shit out a wobble. Women and men soak in the waters, bathe in aloe and cassis, plug in their sun-black bodies to some Hemp God. He waits for a grey cloud to pass over. It turns back into chalk white skies. He dips in the waves, watches lovers roam, kiss thick soft lips. Heads go down into wet golden breasts. He rests his eyes over the blue, green bay. But, in all this splendor he would never be able to rest.

Someone calls out his name: "Jala Mon! Ohhhh! Jala Mon!" It's a snake-eyed devil, that rescues him from the edge.

He fights back the thirst for Betancourt rum.

He comes up, shakes his head. "Good to see you, mon!"

He looks into the sun reddish face… hazel eyes. He's a bearded man with pants rolled up above his ankles, toasted, brown burned chest with long blonde hair of being a mulatto.

"No, I'm okay, Captain Billy."

"You need some hemp, Jala Jala Mon?" He rolls his eyes up. "I got some good hemp."

"Maybe later." He walks down the beach. "You been here long?"

He smiles, plays with this for a minute. Winks at the girl washing her legs off at the edges of the beach, her skirt up over her thighs, not paying attention to any man.

"Captain Billy's been here quite awhile." He points at the islands across the waters. "Dese! Here is my home!" He gets proud. "The White mon drops me people off here... to do some plantin'."

He gets a little dizzy from the sun. "Ha, I forgot... Some people do stay home." Dabs his brow with a handkerchief, sweating hard.

"Mon, you don'ts looks too good."

"Maybe it's a fever, Captain Billy. I'll get a cold beer to wash down this heat some." He feels his stomach getting uneasy.

"Don't sits around, mon! You gots to keeps bizzay."

He points to the dark chocolate women bathing their naked bodies. "With them?" He gets moist over the jiggling breasts and butts running in the waters, laughing girls dripping over the scorched earth.

Captain Billy corrects him. "No! No, mon, not dem!" Frustration comes up in him. "They don't keeps you bizzay! They keeps you sweatin'!"

"Ha! Haaaarr! You right, Captain Billy." Slaps him on the back.

His head and mouth rise up. "Dey never keeps a mon peaceful." He rubs his hairy stomach. "Kids now! Dey make you wise... Makes you looks back at your mistakes." He flings a shell back into the waters. He comes back to the White man with tired eyes, with hairy bow legs. He points to him with some information. "What you needs, mon, is Ti Cousine! Now, she keeps your head on straight… Go drinks some of her tea. And it will brings your life back to you."

Ti Cousine lives in the Hamilton Fancy mountain area, clouds, fog, thick brush surrounding the rock dirt path to her home.

She's the local medicine woman with the bad teeth, long hair down her back. She takes care of the ills in the blue water world, makes sure the goats give milk, the women bleed on time during the month. She has the plantation men drink some of her fine brews to keep their strength up, to cut the tall weeds up the mountain side. Well now, he takes a mule ride up the hard rock path of narrow curves in a dark purple night. Billy goat laughter makes him out of sorts, uneasy in his fever under the quarter moon.

White Caribbean stars flicker over his head.

Up about a mile, from a window clear a candle leads him to her front door, a wooden, black shack covered in moss. He gets off the mule, walks over a white rock gravel path to the front door. Two small knocks.

She opens up. "Yes, may I helps you, mister?"

He looks down at the little woman with bad teeth and hair down her back. "I come to see Ti Cousine."

"Come."

He follows behind her into a house of shadows with just candles burning all over. They say she's as old as the history of the St. Jan slaves, older than the blood drip mountains on Cay Bay.

But her soft brown eyes give off a youthful wonder of the stars, moon, seas.

A large red, yellow, blue parrot is perched in the corner. Wax falls to the floor, a black, yellow, white cat crawls from the drippings.

She takes him to a parlor. "Seat, mon."

He sits in a comfortable chair, then hears drum music, but doesn't know where it comes. She's in a black shawl, sandals, long mauve dress of satin. A thick fat neck is over a pair of thin shoulders. Her voice is gentle, but as strong as the hurricane winds.

She puts her hand out. "Your gun, mon."

He's startled. "What?"

"Your gun."

He gets powerless from the soft rabbit eyes. Lifts up his shirt, pulls it from his belt. He gives it to her. "How did you know?"

Sadly, but with comfort in her words, "I just knew, mon." She puts the gun on the table across from them. "Now, let me gets ya some tea, and tin we can talk, mon."

"Okay."

She leaves out the room, the cat following behind her.

He rests. Maybe at one time she had a bunch of babies sucking at her breasts. Hump back, soft steps of a woman, an old gal who just does her daily chores and talks to God by the seas. Maybe? Just maybe, he talks back?

A few minutes pass, when she comes back with two cups. He takes the cup from her tree root fingers. "Thank you." A honey smell comes up in his nose. It's very dark and hot. "Ohhh!" He drinks, rests back in the chair. It's bitter and sweet all at once.

She sits, the cat curls up on her sandaled feet. "Now, let's talk... Ti Cousine can see." She pauses, takes a sip as her long nail finger points at him. "You were selected, Jala Jala Mon."

"Selected?" He starts thinking this ol' woman is putting on a show to get more money. He's going to question her every stuttered phrase. He's going to have some fun with this old gal.

"Dese hole is a place to rest ollllddd souls." A smile comes over her, as if she just met a friend. "Old souls that were once bahnnnnn here." Places her teacup on the floor. The cat licks up from the cup. "Dese is your home, Jala Jala Mon."

He challenges her. "Ti Cousine! I don't want to be disrespectful to an old woman who just given me a cup of funny tasting tea." He puts his cup on the floor by his shoes. "But I think you been smelling too much mountain air." Shakes his head. "Ha! Old souls, shhh!"

Her face becomes a dark storm. "You are a disbeliever, mon."

"Disbelieve! I want to hear the truth."

"What truth is dat? Your truth or mine?... You don't get it, mon! Dese is your place ... your home... your waystayshun!" Her chin goes up at him. "Your place to come kleeennnn!"

The cat scrambles from the rising voices, its tail knocking over a teacup on the floor. The tea stain starts to soak the rug. "Mon! You must come kleeennnnn!"

He's heard enough, opening his wallet. "Ti Cousine, here's something for your time." He gets up to hand her a twenty. She pushes his hand back. "Eets not abouts money, mon!"

"Then what? What, old woman?" He sticks the money back in his wallet, moves towards the parlor door. But his legs start to get tired, heavy, his fingers start to itch. He falls back in his chair. Looks at her face, it's spinning, shakes to clear his vision. Peers down at his hands, they start getting hairy, changing into goat hoofs. He strains to get back up, but his feet turn into goat hoofs. He feels a prickling in his neck and back. He sees her smiling, going about her business to clean the stain. A spasm hits as the floor comes up. "Damn!"

She stops cleaning when the transformation is complete. "It's about blood, mon, olllddd blood." At the table she pulls the knife out of a slice of sweet potato bread. "Sometimes, we have to make you stay home, mon... We have to make you stay home."

She lifts up the goat, pushes it up between her thighs. Squeezes, and takes the knife right between its back legs. "You beens running scared mon... you beens running scared."

Mabel slaps her hand. "Oh! Grandma Ivey!" shakes her head, "you and your tales!"

"Sometimes you gots to do that, baby... heeee! heeee! heeee!" She slips the last piece in her mouth. "Um! hum!" Chews. "You just listen to your grandma now, if you want to keep that Sam all to yourself." Swallows, wipes her lips with a napkin.

"Can I fix us a Thanksgiving turkey this year, Grandma?"

She gives her a schoolgirl grin. "That's very nice of ya' but I'll be on a date."

"Where," Mabel worries for her. "you going, Grandma?"

"In Cambridge. I'll be eating my turkeys with Mr. Fox this year."

"That's nice, Grandma."

Ivey cross her legs, rests back, swings some. Tree shade hides her pretty face of reddish brown summer leaves. Grandma Ivey gazes down the grassy walkway. "I'll be fine! You just go on and fix your turkey for you and that Sam fella." She never knew when this could be her last time watching these johnboats coming into the Landing.

"Do you love him Mabel?"

"God only knows."

7

"Sam! Get ready for the Christmas party! We going to be late!" Mabel watches him cleaning his shoes for the fifth time. His head hangs low at the edge of the bed. Her watch says it's after eleven p.m. He is out of it, with splotches of black shoe polish on his left cheek. His hand is gripping the brush and his elbow is just speeding over the shine. She can't stand this invisible knife digging in his guts any further. She straightens her red knit cotton mini in Sam's bedroom mirror, checks her hair. She can't stand this nervous buffing of his wing tips. Damn! Sure didn't want to miss Kathy Isaac's pot of Christmas chitterlings. She goes to him, kneels down. Stops the brushing. He looks in her eyes, gives a faint smile. "I'm coming, Mabel."

She kisses him on his neck. "You just settle down, baby."

He looks down at the brush and the shoe. "I said I'm coming!"

"Sam, don't try to fool me, okay? I sleep with you."

He puffs out with a weight on his chest. "What are you talking about, Mabel?"

She lifts his chin up. "Look at me... It's your father, isn't it?"

He tries to throw her off as if she missed the "Jeopardy" question. "Wrong!"

She challenges him. "Liar!"

He stands up. "It's about work, that's all!" He shrugs. "Bills, my car, Richie, you know, shit in general." He lays the shoes and brush on the floor. Checks himself out in the mirror.

She looks at her man's face in the mirror. "Ever since you had that talk with Ray you been out of it." She clutches his arm, stops him from uncorking his bottle of Old Spice cologne. "Why don't you just go see him... before..."

"Before what, Mabel?" He turns around to her. "Before what?"

She gets bold. "Before he dies."

He backs up to the mirror. He can see his face, his father's face, his face. A life flickers, slowly out. His mother's face. His brother's face. He can see his father crawling in the night over another woman's place. His mother crying out to him. His face, his father's face. He can see his father picking up a woman on the street corner. It isn't his mother. His face, his father's face. He can see his father slapping another woman in a gambling joint. It isn't his mother. His face, his father's face, his face, his father's face. He sees his father dancing, dancing, dancing with others at the Hot House Grille on Route Seven. He sees his father kissing another woman in the dark. His father jumping out the back window of Sarah Brown's, before her husband Reverend Brown got home from preaching his sermon. His face, his father's face. His mother always crying out to him. Alone, so alone. In her bedroom by the window, waiting. His face, his father's face. He turns back to Mabel and hugs her. "Come on, let's go to a party."

"Wait, Sam. I'm not ready yet!"

"But, but you was rushing me up!" He fixes his blue silk tie in the mirror. "What are you playing, Mabel? Some kind of a game?"

"I know you, Sam. I have to rush you up because you usually take longer than me." She turns her back to him. "Zip me up, darlin'."

He holds her waist, growling. "Grrrrrrr!" He bites at her ear. "Grrrruffff! Ruffffff!"

She turns, pushes him from her neck. "Sanmmmm! Stopppp it! We going to be late for the party!" She pokes out her tongue, wiggles her hips, entices him with a finger. "Gruffffff! Gruffffff!"

Kathy greeted the guests as an elf. Mistletoe in her hair had her kissing all the men at the door. Some of the wives pull their husbands away. Table spread out with food: chicken, ribs, sliced beef, greens, potato salad, macaroni salad, crackers, tuna salad, candy yams, sweet potato pies, seven-up cakes, pineapple upside-down on the side. Red, yellow, blue balloons tied up in corners of the room. Mabel put a lamp-shade on Sam's head. He dances with Mabel with a glass of champagne in her hand. James Brown sings. Pass the peas! Ha! Good God! Ha! One time Maceo! Sister Aretha has to get her Respect!

He spins Mabel around on the good foot.

She jerks her arms to the beat of nineteen seventy rhythm-blues horns and stomps her feet to the beat. Ain't nothin' but the Bugaloo. Feels all good inside to see Sam dance and shout, clap with the crowd; call and response in the Christmas eve night. Black folks need this. Ain't nothin' but the Bugaloo! Sweat, get loose. Unbutton your collar. Shout and holler. Dance with your gal. Eat some more chicken, don't worry about lickin'. Sweat off the problems. Ain't nothin' but the Bugaloo! Sing with the music. Circle the party. Get on the train. Blow the whistle in the Conga line. Mabel watches Sam do a split and almost break his back. Joe Buck flips his wife over his shoulder, then catches her in time before she hollers. Ain't nothin' but the Bugaloo! Elthel gets there with her new man. All her friends greet her at the door. Under the balloons they take her fake fox wrap.

She introduces him. "Sam and Mabel… I likes to introduce yaw to… Terrence."

Sam shakes his hand. "Hey, Terrence."

Mabel looks him over. He's shorter than Richie. "How you doing, Terrence?"

"Good! Glad to be here." He puts his arm around Elthel.

Elthel grabs his hand. "Come on, baby, let's get on that floor with the rest of them."

"Okay!" He leads her into the screaming crowd.

Mabel gives Kathy a wink as she puts Elthel's wrap in the kitchen closet. She takes Sam's hand. "You all right?"

They move back some from the crowd.

"Yeah, I'm okay."

"Life gots to go on, right?" Mabel isn't going to baby him. "We all gots to get up in the morning to deal with it."

"I know, baby. It's just a little strange seeing her with another man."

Duck came over finger popping to "The Midnight Train to Georgia." "Sam, can I borrow your woman for this dance?"

"Sure!" Sam leaves them and goes out in the Christmas eve night.

Black skies on Christmas night. Stars roam here and there. Other couples stand on the dark porch, kissing, holding hands in the cool winter chill. Marijuana smoke lingers in the air.

Sam pulls up his sports coat collar. He squints through the night shadows, rests his foot on the porch rail. Freezes a gentle smile at the partygoers hanging around the front door.

A woman hands him a joint. He sucks, holds, releases, drifts up in the stars, passes it back. Muffled sounds of Marvin Gaye singing with Tammy come from inside. Giggles erupt in the soft cold air. He leans, watches people talk, give Christmas greetings. Pass a wine bottle around. Wipe off the sweat from the hot dance floor. Pass champagne around. More drunks are born this night. Cars honk. Junkies walk with their heads down, lost children this night, seek out some cheer, some family. Sweet Loaf streets are adorned in Christmas lights. Stumbling men, women fall out the door. One woman pukes over the railing. Her girlfriends rescue her from the deep intoxication of the holiday. People laugh at the poor, loose gal trying to hail a taxi. Across the street, just under the lamppost a car of people explodes. One woman pulls another out from the seat. "Bitch! I told you leave my man alone!"

The guy runs from the steering wheel to break them up.

But the mad woman of Christmas takes her pocketbook to his head, swinging. "Jerry! I told you to leave that snaggle tooth whore alone!" She whacks him. "No good son-of-a-bitch!" She hits him with the purse again.

He dives at her. "Goddamnit! Bitch! Diane! Diane, stop actin' like a fool out here in the streets! Baby!" He wrestles her up against the car, takes the purse from her.

The other woman runs. She slaps him. "Mutherfucker! I'll fix your ass!"

He pins her arms back. "Diane! Stop it! Stop it!"

She quits struggling. Cries out, "Who is she? Who is she, Jerry?" Snatches her red wig off. "You ain't shit! No good bastard!" Pushes the wig in his face. "Let me go, Mutherfucker!"

"Baby! Come on, get in the car... Get in the car." He backs up and touches her arm.

She tears away. "Get off of me!"

"Get in the car," he says, stepping to the side of the door.

She sticks her wig on. "I'm getting in, Mutherfucker! But you going to hear from me!" She stumbles, lifts her skirt up. Ducks in, still cussing him out.

He gets in, takes off down the street before the police come.

The crowd on the porch applaud. Whistle. Cheer as the car speeds away. "Jerry! Jerry! Jerry! Jerry! Jerry! Jerry!"

Sam claps. "Haaaaa! Awwwww!" Shakes his head when snowflakes start to come down. A tap on his shoulder. "Mabel"

She hugs him. "I missed you, I came out here to check on you." She rubs his butt under his coat. "Um, it's cold out here."

He looks at the snowflakes coming down. "Naw! It's Christmas."

She kisses him. Nods up, "Yeah, baby, it's Christmas."

"And, I think I'm going to see my dad." He hugs her up closer in his arms.

She looks at his wet face. "Good!" Lays her head on his chest. "That'll be a nice Christmas for him."

He kisses her brow. "For the both of us."

8

It's the eyes.

His are purple, brown, closed, in a land of shadows. Moist, cold surroundings. Voices, smells, tastes that soak the tongue with sweet, sour, fresh foods. Air of frost, face of chills. It's the sounds that keeps Jim Murphy alive. Sirens, guns popping off, babies crying, women fussing, cussing out their husbands. Dogs barking, scratching at the door. Cats sneaking around, under, through the window. An oven door opens, closes. A woman cries for her children to come home. A father cries for his wife to leave him alone. Death creeps from closet doors. The shadows touch his shoulder. She isn't there. Nobody is there to love him anymore, just use his Social Security check to pay for his life, love, happiness, the Statue of Liberty, his medicine. A walk by his little boy guide, Pookie. His girlfriend Earlene Johnson keeps him fed. Up and down, up and down, their bedpost creaks. Remembering her soft cotton mouth, up and down. Her bosom heaves, up and down. He cries out for peace, sanctity. God! Let me see! Let me see! But God does not. He listens to some opera, not knowing what the hell they saying. But the music soothes him, puts him into some Italian fantasy: pale pink women, bosoms pushing, begging some man for forgiveness. The violins resting his heart, keeping the devil of sorrows away. Hold back the hurt feelings of a man. He's in a forest, sneaking behind a tree. Sword in his hand, he's ready to play or cut off the heads of tree elves, rescue the pale white woman on his pale white horse. He smiles. Was that Donizetti? He hears the door open. It's her, not saying anything, just smelling up the room with that five and dime Christmas perfume. He fingers the eagle head cane. Music, more music, violins, trumpets, cellos, cymbals blast up a calming storm in his chest. Rest his soul, please rest his soul. He scratches his balls, rocks in his chair, imagines figures of his boys and wife. Sarah, sweet, sweet Sarah, forgive me. Forgive me. The opera ends, Christmas carols begin. He rocks, rocks, rocks, leans down, pats the cat under his chair. He rocks, rocks, smells the snow in the one-room air. He rocks, rocks, licks his tongue at the slow day. He listens to chestnuts on the roasted fire with Brother Nat, for the hundredth time in his life. He rocks, rocks, listens to her feet shuffle back and forth. She's humming, whipping up something in a bowl. His head cocks back, the cat tickles his slippered ankle. He rocks, rocks, moves his feet away, slips a hand under the cat. He lays him in his lap, brushes his ears back. Rocks, rocks, he waits for her to call his name, tell him how much snow came. He waits for her to rub his belly, tell him he's getting like jelly. He waits for her to cuss him out, tell him he's getting old as a fart. He smiles, listens to her slamming doors, waits for her to love him some more. He plays with his girlfriend, the one he left Sarah for. He wants his women to find peace, either dead or alive. He damn sure can't help them. But he gives what he can, and that never is much. Old blind man sitting on a train track waiting for that son of a bitch to hit, he gives up, stops. Drops the cat to the floor.

It's the eyes.

Christmas morning fills with flavors of cakes, pies, pine cones, wet snow, new outfits, new hair, new lives made over for a new year. Jingles erupt over the radio. He's getting nauseous, twists the knob. Damn! Turns it off. Earlene clicks the TV on. The parade. And hear Nat King Cole Chestnut song...

He wants to close his ears, rest. He lets his heart find peace in the room. He lifts his spirits up by imagining himself hurting the giant floating balloons or strangling Mickey Mouse or kicking Donald Duck in his tail feathers and taking care to slap Goofy a couple of times, knocking that laugh out his throat. He cocks his head, rocks. This is a children's holiday. But he played along on the swings with them. He once bought his little boys cowboy and Indian outfits. Funny, how things end up now, Sam is a Redskin fan, and Ray is a Dallas Cowboys man. Huh! The announcer: "Little children! Santa Claus has arrived! He's passing out gifts! Lots of toys and prizes!" He picks up a little girl in his arms. Santa Claus waves to the crowd "Ahhhh!"

Listening to this makes him glad be can't see worth a Santa Claus Tinker's damn! He hums along with the songs, beside him on the table, a cup of coffee. He drinks from his mug. Hums, rocks, hums. Puts the cup on the table. Coughs, buttons his sweater up to his neck. Ah! Braves the cold hands of death. He had one stroke already that laid him up for three months, left side of his body frozen. Seventy percent better now, but he'll never be good enough to knock another man out like he used to in them old Joe Louis days. He was once the 1947 Junior Welterweight Champ of Sweet Loaf. He trained right out of Bobby Frye's Gym. He was a great left jab too, ain't take shit off no man. But one thing got to him, took his strength away; that was Sarah Robbins. A lovely black bird came down out of the sky, and she built a nest right in his heart. Then a hundred piece marching band gives him a trombone blow to the ear drums.

Jim Murphy likes this little ditty, makes him want a glass of Manischewitz Concord Grape Wine, has his head swinging back and forth to this high stepping band. It's too early in the morning. He keeps clapping to the tune, grinning as if he was marching right along with them.

Her voice awakes him from the stomping feet. "Honey, here's a pillow for your back."

He leans forward, lets her puff it up. "Thanks, baby."

"See, Christmas not that bad." She pats his shoulder, gazes down at his thick, wavy, white head of hair. His neck chokes up tight. She kisses his ear.

He moves his ear away. "Earlene, you just got the fever, that's all." He takes her hand off his shoulder.

"It's nothing wrong with that, is it?" She looks at the TV, not paying attention really to his grumpiness.

"Not unless you're Santa Claus now."

She ties up her apron. "Oh, hush, Jim. You got the fever too!"

He's going to come back at her on this. "Is that the door?" His head rises up, listens to hear the soft knocks, grips his rocker. "Must be Ray."

She walks to the door. "Let me get it." When she opens it, her dentures almost drop. "Why, if it ain't…"

Jim commands. "Earlene! Who in the hell is it?"

"Come on in, honey." She takes him by the arm and leads him to his father. "It's Sam, Jim."

Jim's head searches the footsteps. "Well, I'll be…" His shoulders slump back at the surprise.

Sam sees his father perched up in his chair. The cane has him looking proud, smart. He's a cold stone that whirls and turns into a Gargoyle.

•　　•　　•

Dialogue with a Gargoyle:

"You like to see an old man suffer, don't you, son?" He rocks back. "Well! Merry Christmas to you!" He scratches behind his ear. "Um, this is a surprise you know…"

"I know Dad, just wanted to see you for Christmas." He sits on the couch in front of him. Watches the wings flap out. The skinny claw-arms rest loosely on the chair. "And I don't want to see you suffer."

"No. well," his wings flapping, "I'm glad you could come by to see the living dead. Ha! Ha! Ha!"

"No, I come by to see a living cold bastard."

"Say what you got to say and get the hell off my roof."

67

Sam kicks his legs out, takes off his Army fatigue jacket. "Was my momma a whore?"

"Boy, she was the queen of the whores, and I was her pimp." He leans forward. "And I went to jail for her." He plays with his dark eyeglasses. "But boy, this was all before you was born." He spits yellow flames, "so how'd you hear bout dis?"

"You forget. Your son… my brother, is a cop."

He wishes he could see his face, the face of a man now. "Well, we all got our demons, son…"

"And you one of them." Sam felt his heart. It was beating fast. "Did you kill her?"

He flaps his wings. "No. I loved her."

"Why did you mess over her?" Sam asks. He follows the closed grey face of the sightless man. Sees the claws spread wider, the web feet grip out for a ledge. He could kill the monster without thinking of the future.

"It wasn't our time, son." His ears guide him to the man's hollow soft voice. "I messed over a lot of women, boy." He scratches his hairy chest. "To me, she had stopped taking care of business."

Sam felt the heat go up in his chest. "So you threw her away like she was a piece of trash." His arms go out with the wing span of the Gargoyle. "Goddamn you! She was my mother!"

The Gargoyle plays with his beard. "She was my wife, boy." His head jerks. "She died the way she wanted to…"

"Suffering over you…"

"If that's what she wanted to do," he said. "I ain't got no control over how a woman wants to kill herself." His fire-red tongue flicks out. "Like I said, I loved her."

Sam stares at him. "You don't think you should pay for this?"

He smiles up at the invisible angels. "I paid for it a thousand times over. You gots to remember, Sam, I come from another time. A place where men would beat the shit out of a woman if they sassed back, a time when women knew their so-called place in this world." His tongue licks out. "There was no liberation thing! We were all fighting to be free. It was her place to walk soft, love me good, and do what I say." His claw points up. "That was the law… Wasn't no police going to get in between a man and his woman." He blinks though the dark glasses. "We were to make babies… good strong babies. That's you and your brother." His long ears wiggle. "Anything after that could have just been jail for my ass." His head searches towards the voice. "Now, I know you don't want to know this… Hell! You might even kill me on Baby Jesus' birthday, but since you here, you might as well hear this. Your mother ran a whorehouse! And I didn't want her to!"

Sam got smug. "Oh! Like you wanted her out of the business?"

"You damn right I did!" He pulls on his long, devil-looking ears. "I wanted her ass home taking care of you and your brother Ray. But she couldn't hear none of this." His long tongue drips spit. "She was gone… too caught up in the action."

Sam doesn't believe this. "Man! You full of shit!"

"Let me ask you one thing, boy." His wings flap down. "Do you remember who took care of you?"

Sam thinks, bites the side of his lip. "I don't know. But I do know one night... the night of the storm. Her crying out for you, butt naked on the bed. And I was crying beside her body when I was just a little boy." Tears froze, drop hard to the floor. "You was not there."

"Boy! You momma was sick. She was sick in her body, and she was sick in her head." He lifts his face from the tears coming through the eyeglasses. "I damn sure couldn't save her!"

Sam jumps in his face. "You couldn't save her?" Grabs the Gargoyle's skinny arms, watches out for the long claw-fingers.

He twists. "That's right! I tried, but I couldn't."

"You couldn't!"

His snake tongue flicks out. "Boy, get out of my face."

Sam sits back down, staring at the Gargoyle. His father's face amasses into some hideous grey stone., the nose dripping with snot, the claws long, ready to scratch the life out of a man. But he isn't afraid. No, he just wants answers about her life.

"Now, I ask you before. Who took care of you?"

"What are you getting at, old man?"

"Was it just her and your brother in that house all alone the night she died?"

Sam's anger comes up in his throat. "I don't know! I was just five or six!"

"Well, son. You needs to sit your ass down and listen." His mouth droops as if he's on a high that's about to take him over a cliff. "I wasn't going to go down for her again." His claw points. "There some bad women out there. Now, they can either take you up or take you down. And I wasn't going to go down for her again." He pulls back the wings in the chair. "But, I had to look out for you two boys. That's why I had my mother come stay with you boys at the house... Your momma wasn't taking care of business and my ass was hustlin' on the road."

Sam gazes away. He can't look up at his father.

"Boy! Look at me. Look at my face... my claws... my wings." He points. "I don't want you to be no parts of me!" His arms move up, and his wings expand out. "I'm a monster... I don't want you to be no parts of me."

"But I am a part of you."

The Gargoyle shifts slowly in his chair. "I know. I know... but you got time to learn from your daddy's mistakes." He wipes the sweat from his brow. "I was mean to your momma... but I loved her." He flaps his wings. "I wanted to be there for her... but that bad dope had my ass. You hear me boy! I said that bad juggie had my ass... I wasn't good to nobody at that time, especially your ma."

Sam sits quietly, his head hurting, his foot shaking nervously. He's tired, mad, drunk with relief over this conversation. He's spent, emotions lost in the winter frost. There's nothing to celebrate, just cherish. Her time spent, her voice arising from his heart for him to let it go. Let it all go...

Tears fall from Sam's eyes.

The Gargoyle's head cocks back. "Boy! You listen!" He listens. His son says nothing. They just sit across from each other. taking in the silence of the words... the truth... the lies. "Listen to what?" Falling out the sky into the snow-covered streets, just Christmas music comes between the father and son, under the noise of the band. A family story is told with two men trying to reach out for a mother, a wife, in a cold grave, but to come finally together in this silence and wish each other, Merry Christmas. The gargoyle spits yellow and blue flames, "Listen to the angels."

9

Ten thousand streets, white stripe highways wrap through his thoughts. Sam lets the March winds blow El, Zorro towards Embassy Row. He has a new partner with him, Pete Jessup, Petey-Pete for short, a dude from D.C… Sam always catches him reading romance novels, chewing on a toothpick. He's nervous, always ready to jump from three gals trying to hit him up for child-support. Tall and skinny, in his late thirties, with a beer gut that isn't fit to fuck a four-legged gal from the Fourteenth Street Grille. He's kind of funny, strange, writes poetry, and even reads some of the weird shit out loud when they're making their rounds.

"Petey, do you drink?" Sam asks him and slaps a hand underneath his seat. Bounces. And stops at the light.

Petey closes the paperback. "Yeah, Sam." He scratches his chin, looks down to the woman in the next car over, with her dress hiked up. He winks and hits the side of the truck.

"I got Seagrams." Hands him the paper bag. "Take a swig."

He sits up, unscrews the cap.

Sam reminds him. "Keep your head low. Cops!" The light changes, and he starts back up.

Ducks. "Ahhhh!" Winces. "Whewww." Petey-Pete wipes his lips, and hands the bag back. "Thanks."

Sam takes a drink. "Um huh!" Hands it back to him. "Go on, take another one... Get your head right."

"Okay." Sips, bounces. He watches the stores, buildings, concrete speed on. Drift, knock, shake. Feels the heat of the gin down his stomach. Sips. "You want some more?"

"Naw, I'm all right!" Sam hits his horn. "Asshole! Get that mutherfucker out the way!" He grabs his steering wheel, zips around a concrete truck backing up. Petey puts the cap back on. Jerks, knocks, rattles against the door. Hands it to him. "Here you go." Twists his cap around to the back of his head, and opens his book back up.

Sam takes it and sticks it back under his seat. "So, uh, Petey, why you always reading them books on them mixed-up White girls?" Hits his brakes. "Uh, you want one or something?" Sam looks at him and the book in his hand.

Hunches. "It's an escape Sam... that's all it is, just an escape."

"Escape, huh!" Sam smiles. He watches the cop pass him through the road work. "Shit, man, I can take you to an escape." He spins the wheel to the

74

right. "Have you ever heard this place called The Devils Fork?"

"No, I haven't."

Sam grins, and looks at him. "Now, that's an escape."

Petey gets interested. "Oh, yeah? What they got there?"

Sam starts to look for the embassy. "Everything you imagine Hell to be, plenty of women, plenty of chitterlings, potato salad, bar-b-que, and plenty to drink." He picks up the receipt. "Twelve hundred Massachusetts Avenue. Okay! One more block."

Petey frowns. He didn't like to be left out of nothing. "How come I never heard of this place?" He watches the face of Sam focusing on the street numbers.

Sam gets sly on him. "It's a secret, Petey-Pete!" Taps the pencil behind his ear. "What you call a speakeasy… You need a special card to get in."

"And I suppose you got one?"

"That's right!" He reaches in his top shirt pocket and flips him the card.

Petey takes the card. It's red with a black figure of a devil grinning and a pitchfork in his hand. "Where you get this at, Sam?" Hands it back to him.

He sticks it back down in his shirt pocket. "Friends. You got to get out and about… You can't be reading them romance novels all the time." Sam grins at him with a wink. "Uh! here we go." He slows down.

"What embassy is this, Sam?" He sticks the paperback in his back pocket.

Sam reads the receipt. "Haitian… They just want a couple of rolls of moth-blue shag." Shakes his head. "Ain't gonna take long." He parks the truck right in the front. "Oh, and they need a can of Flexarall floor glue." He hops out.

Petey gets out on his side and zips up his jacket from the winds. He follows Sam to the front door, rubs his hands and blows in them. "Shit! I can't wait for the spring."

Sam hits the doorbell "You ain't kiddin'. I can't stand the cold myself."

"So, when can I go with you, Sam?"

"Oh, you don't want to read no more romance novels?"

"Come on, man, stop playing…"

"Friday night be okay with you?"

Petey nods his head. "Fine with me."

A few seconds pass. A bearded, bald man opens up. "Yes?"

Sam gives him the order. "Delivery. Rugs."

He peeks around the two men, spots the truck, and reads the order. Nods. "Wait right here." He leaves, closing the door in their faces. A German shepherd follows right behind him.

Petey doesn't like this. "Ain't this a bitch!"

Sam says, "Calm down. We on Embassy Row… People got a lot of secrets."

Petey messes with him. "Like you, huh, Sam?"

"Haa! Haa! Haa! Man, don't mess with me." He takes the pencil from behind his ear. "Shut up and go get the flat-dolly… so we can get rid of these rugs."

Petey sticks a toothpick in his month. "Okay. You the man." He walks back to the truck.

Sam answers him back. "That's right! I'm the man."

• • •

Directions from the man with the dog guide them through a large vestibule of wood, glass flowing designs. The rooms have ivory covered alabaster walls, and cupid water figurines sitting on a fountain in the middle of a pale atrium. White and black marble floors take them to a long conference room. In this room, Sam sees a woman standing by a window, her arms folded, face transfixed out the window. Wavy black cascades past her ears and lays on her shoulders. She turns to hear the wheels of the dolly roll in. She stands for a few seconds, then leaves out a door at the other end of the room. Sam and Petey unload the carpets. Then they stand for a minute gazing out the long windows. All they see are the street corners, lights on this early in the winter day. Nasty winds push people around. Jaywalkers dodge death. Petey asks, "Did you see her?"

"See what?"

Petey pulls out the toothpick in his mouth. "That woman when we came in."

"Uh! Her. Yeah, I saw her."

"She looked all right, didn't she?"

Sam sticks his hand in the pocket of his Army fatigue jacket. "I guess so." Shrugs. "It's a lot of that around here." He lights up a cigarette. "She reminded me of somebody too." He starts to leave the ocean quiet room.

"Oh yeah? Who?"

He blows out smoke from his nose. "Old girlfriend when I was in Vietnam." Pulls the cigarette out his mouth, cuffs it under his hand. He doesn't want the man and his dog to cause no fuss about the smoke.

Petey walks by him. "Well, maybe we be back."

Sam keeps moving. "Maybe we will, Petey-Pete. Maybe we will."

• • •

Friday, 12:45 p.m.

Sam meets Pete at the front door of The Devil's Fork. It's a back alley spot, up three flights of stairs, then a dark hall. One way in, one way out joint. The room has one pool table, bar on the side, kitchen behind that, leather couches and a large movie screen. Men mingle around, bikini-clad women on their arms. Jazz fills the room from a speaker.

A movie starts up. It's a black and white flick. A naked woman is doing it to herself in a room on a bed. In a corner, the door opens. A German shepherd comes in. She coaxes it to jump on the bed, then grabs it around the collar, kissing it in the mouth, petting its nose. She pushes its claws back, cuddles it, turns her butt away, then slips underneath him.

A couple of women come up to them. A blonde in panties and a halter top hugs him. "Sam!" Licks his ear.

"Hey, baby." Sam isn't ticklish. "Brenda." He kisses her on a pair of cherry red lips. "Pete! I want you to meet a friend of mine."

She surprises Pete with a kiss.

"Uh, hi, Brenda. Who's your friend?" Pete shines over to the woman with a neat short afro haircut, face of candy, body decked in a red bikini. High heels made her taller than him.

"This is Zoey… She doesn't talk much… but boy, the things she can do with her mouth."

"Haaaa! Haaa!" Sam shakes his head. "I'll bet."

Brenda isn't hedging around. "Sam!" Hands on her hips. "Which one of us you want for tonight?"

Sam grabs Petey around the shoulder. "Brenda, I'm going to have to take Zoey, because my buddy here got a thing for romance novels. I think he likes to have you." He pulls his ear. "You know. Show him a fantasy or two or three." Hunches up. "Is that okay with you Petey-Pete?"

Pete reaches out for her hand. "Fine with me, Sam. Fine with me."

Brenda gets closer to him, strokes his chin. "Fine with me too, Pete. Come on, let me show you where we going to have this fantasy of yours." She leads him off to the back. Waves. "Bye, Sam."

He nods. "Whewww! Zoey, that was fast." He unlooses his collar. "I haven't even ordered a drink yet."

She hugs him. "What you having from the bar? I'll get it for you."

He messes with her. "Ah! She does talk." He gives her a smooth peck on her lips. "Ummm, soft." Closes his eyes. "Yeah, baby." He pulls out his wallet. "Scotch on the rocks with lemon," he rubs her on her ass, "get yourself something too." He sticks a ten in her hand and watches her walk over to the bar. She's definitely the one for him tonight. He watches her poise, her lean, the circle-shape of her hips, thighs, legs. She's a runway model who looks good in red. He will be the matador to play with her in the ring tonight. But he isn't ready. No. He's going to take it slow with her, listen to her whispers, in his ear. A woman's truth, her truth in pleasing a man. No, she doesn't talk much, but he's going to feel her fingers waltz. Her body charms, moves, surrenders, dances to the music.

The red moonlight woman brings back the drinks. They take a seat on the couch right in front of the blue movie. Between peaks and valleys they drink each other up. Others roam in the red moonlight. Lovers look for love, all strangers in blue land. Sam peeks down her front. Sweet Jesus. Sweet Jesus. He puts his drink down, takes her for a slow dance, holds her gently, gently, gently to the sounds of the Chi-Lites.

He looks at Zoey's caramel face, a warmth of love, woman of pleasure. Where is his Mabel? Home alone? Waiting for him or another? He doesn't want to think about the pieces of the puzzle. He just falls deeper, with his eyes closed in the hair, neck, face of Zoey. Sweet Jesus. Sweet Jesus.

• • •

An EEOC notice is pinned on a display board outside the cafeteria door. Government workers stand in lines with trays, knives, forks. Secretaries speak of their bosses, husbands, little girls' recitals, little boys' football games, and their boyfriends either tipping out or around on them before, during and after they tell them the news of a baby coming. Special for today: Chicken Fried Steak, Buffalo Wings, or Fish Fillet patties. String beans on the side, mashed potatoes, or corn on the cob will go nice with a slice of apple pie á la mode. Mabel dabs at her mashed potatoes. "Kathy, I told you, I didn't do anything this weekend."

Kathy Isaacs is disgusted. "Girl, this ain't the fifties… You staying home waiting for some man." She bites into her Buffalo wings. "Shit! If he was my man… I'll tell him either shit or get off the pot!" Licks three greasy fingers.

She plays with her black pearls around her neck. "Well, he ain't your man… Like I told you before, we don't have a relationship like that!"

"I just don't want to see you hurt." Kathy frowns with her mouth down, wipes her hands with a napkin, and waves to some other friends. "Hey, Charlie, I thought your wife put you on a low-fat diet!"

Mabel laughs. "Why don't you stop embarrassing people around here?" She cuts up her chicken fried steak. "Um, um."

Kathy rolls her eyes at this. "Child, they embarrass me…" She drinks on a can of Coke. "Mabel, you getting too old for this shit! That man could bring you back something awfully bad."

"Kathy," she stirs her cup of coffee, "we use protection."

"Sam," Kathy didn't believe this, "Yeah! Right!" She gets to squirming in her seat like she has a hot poker between her legs. "When it's getting good, girl, you don't want protection all the time."

Mabel is shocked at this display. "What is wrong with you?" Her voice lowers. "Stop it."

"You stop it!" Kathy says back to her. "I'll tell you what… let's double date this weekend."

She gets cute, sticks a fork of potatoes in her mouth. "Ummm! I don't know. I might have to do my hair this weekend." Chews. "And my fingernails, toenails, nose hair…" She swallows.

Kathy cuts her off. "Ha! You might have to wait around for Sam."

"Don't get smart now," Mabel says. "And don't set me up with a frog!" She knows Kathy's into playing jokes. "Or I'll kill you!"

Kathy grins up at this warning. "*Moi?*"

Mabel gets sort of excited. "So who the frogs going to be?"

"Shiiit! You ever seen me date a frog?" Shakes hot sauce on her wings.

"Haaaa! Haaa! I don't want to make you mad… but what was his name?" She thinks for a split second, pops her fingers. "Fred! We called him Black Fred!" She takes her hand across the table "Oh, now that was a ugly man!"

Kathy agrees. "Haaaa! Ahhhhh! Yeah, girl!" Breaks some bread. "But he had some goood stuff." She hides her face, trying to keep her giggles down in her stomach. "Ouch! That hurts."

They both bust out laughing. Hands reach out for napkins to wipe away the tears. Some of the crowd look their way. But friends all know when these two get together, they have that crazy love-sister-hate effect on each other. They speak of men, old girl-friends and who's doing it to who, in a silly laugh of green-slimy Jell-O with tired lunchtime greetings. Damn! They don't want to go back to work, but some-body has to make that money. You can't depend on any Prince Charmings to rescue you nowadays.

82

"So where you going to have this surprise frog take me? Mabel blows off the hot cup of tea. She watches Kathy make a face. "And don't think so hard."

She taps her chin as if she's Sherlock Holmes. "McDonald's and a movie."

Mabel closes her eyes. "Oh. God! This is going to be a nightmare."

"With this frog you going to have a nice time," Kathy says, trying to reassure her that you can have fun on a cheap date and popcorn. "Besides, you don't want to make him think you a gold digger, do you?"

"Yeah!" She pushes her plate. "Let me get back to my desk." Finishes her tea. "What time to be ready for you and this frog?" She stands up.

Kathy pays more attention to her wings than this question. "Saturday at eight o'clock… We'll catch a late movie." Shakes hot sauce on her bread. "See ya', darlin'."

Mabel walks out of the cafeteria. In the hall at the elevator, she wonders what she has done with Kathy this time. But as many years as she known her, she was the type that always kept things stirred up. She hits the button, taps her black pumps, waits, lights up. Maybe she needs her coffee stirred up? Sam isn't doing it. She gets in and braces for the ride up to the seventh floor.

•　　•　　•

An early spring shower closes windows. Bunions soaking in warm water in a washing tub, her butt and back ache as Mabel sits on the toilet stool at the end of the day, feels the pain subside in her feet. She closes her eyes, robe undone, just bra and panties. It sure would be nice to have Sam here right now, massaging these feet. Yes, a man would be good for just that. She rubs her feet, especially the left big toe. Them damn high heels have men whistling, but have her in pain all at the same time. A fifty dollar pair of alligator hide shoes; the 'gator must still be alive, the way her feet feel. Ummmm! Rest. Closing her eyes, she feels a headache coming on. She reaches for the calendar over the sink, thinks. Yep! It's about that time for her period. Rest, relax, think the headache away. Ummm! She lets the hot steam soak down those corns. Sinks, massaging her temples. She lets her right hand roam, over, over, lower, lower.

"Mabel! Mabel! Open the door!"

She stops. "Who the hell is that calling me?" She runs to a window that overlooks the back parking lot, and sticks her head out. "Sam!"

Sam's arms spread out. "Open up, baby!"

She hollers, "Okay! Coming…," ties her robe up. "The back door must be locked." She puts her pink slippers on, takes her key from the mantel, rushes out her door from her second floor apartment. All the way down in the cold basement, she lets him in.

He looks at her. "You even beautiful in the cold… butt naked too!" He tries to touch her robe.

She slaps his hand. "Don't touch me!" Turns to go back upstairs, running.

"I'm glad you was home. We haven't seen each other since Christmas." He takes three giant steps at a time, "I know you mad at me," hunches and loses his breath at the same time. "Whew!"

84

She unlocks her door. "I should let your ass stay out there." Folds her arms over her robe.

He leans back on the wall. "You calling the shots."

Mabel remembers what he's good at. "Come on in here and massage my feet."

10

"Joe, come on, man!" Sam hollers at him, leaning on the truck. "What did Mike say?"

Joe Buck rushes out the door with the orders, winded. "Whew! Uhh!" Hands him the papers. "Hey! We back in the saddle, Sam… He wants you to take an extra order off… that red Monsanto around the back of the Navy yard, Building C for a Lou… Lou Stringfellow."

Sam grins at him and Petey, rolls the orders up. "I knew Mr. Milano would come around… took long enough." He twists the edge of his golf cap. "Let's go, Petey."

Pete walks around to the side of the truck and gets in. He listens to the money talk. Just in time… he needs some extra for his Captain Hook wives and his party life.

"Sam, I forgot… He wants you to take two more cans of that Flexarall floor glue over to the Haitian embassy."

"Uh, Petey, get two cans out the warehouse." Sam jumps in the truck.

"Okay!" Petey gets back down and goes in the warehouse.

Joe Buck slaps the side of the truck. "Sam, just like old times again?"

He taps his thumb on the stirring wheel "Mannn! I tell you what... Since this is the boss's future son-in-law, we ain't going to have to look over our shoulders no more."

"I swear!" Joe sticks a shoe up on the running board. "He told me back in the warehouse that the cut for all of us will be bigger, too." He fiddles with his watchband. "I got to talking to him and found out he was over in 'Nam too."

"Oh yeah? What company?"

"A medic with the First Cav in Long Bin." He spits. Slap his mustache. "But he was in a couple of peace marches first before he left for 'Nam."

"Ain't this something... One of them good ol' hippie boys!"

"Aaaaahaaaahaa!" Joe Buck sees Pete coming out the door. "Okay, I'm going to let you go now."

"See you quitting time, maybe we have a little taste for you."

He moves from the truck. "I hear you a hard drinking gin man."

"You buying today?" Sam's dented helmet face asks.

"Not me... Jesse hit the number."

"Come on, Petey-Pete, let's go."

Pete hops up. "Let's go!"

They take off out of the parking lot, into the traffic of cars, fools, drunks and a spring afternoon. Back in the saddle again, getting a piece of that Sweet Loaf American apple pie for your pockets. El, Zorro rattles, shakes the men in low gear right out the alley.

He makes a left on Massachusetts. "Um, Pete you a hard man to please."

"Not really, Sam." He takes a folded piece of paper from his top shirt pocket. "By the way, Sam... I wrote a poem about you over the weekend."

"Petey-Pete, don't play with me, man... I ain't got time for jokes," Sam says.

"Here we go." Pete unfolds it.

Sam points a thick finger at him. "It better be good, or there's going to be a traffic accident." He keeps driving, making sure he doesn't pass the Embassy. Pete starts to read...

> Winds blow over black flower streets
> A sun rises, a day begins
> From a sad night moon
> There is a man
> That raises cane
> Just him and his truck
> That's all in the rain
> Women reach out
> Touch his thorns
> But one thing they
> Didn't touch
> Was his soul
> That nodded
> At the heavens
> And a crying moon.

Sam doesn't say anything when he finishes. He bites his bottom lip, taps his thumb on the large donut steering wheel. He becomes mellow, relaxed, because Pete has him down like a fly on a piece of dog shit.

"Sam, you like it?" Pete asks him. He needs to know does this poem need more work, a little salt or a little pepper.

"I didn't have an accident… Go on and read your book." He reaches for his pack of cigarettes, one left hand on the wheel, slowing down with the bumps in the road behind a bunch of cars. He takes a drag, plucks ash out the window. Sam drifts, meditates on the lines: 'Heaven and a crying moon.' Huh! He ain't dead yet, so that means he better party some more. He reaches under his seat, uncaps his bottle of Seagram's, drinks from the top, no cup. He hands the bottle to his partner. Pete can write. If he stopped smoking so much dope, his shit could be better. But Sam starts getting a little closer to this funny little man who smokes dope, drinks, and loves plenty of women, just like him. Yeah, they're fit for each other most of the time.

Sam finds the street, parks a few cars down from the embassy. "Petey, go on and take the cans in. Have them sign for it." He passes him the white and yellow receipts.

Pete looks at him. "You don't want to come with me? Maybe you can see that brown songbird at the window again."

He flicks his cigarette out the window. "Yeah! Maybe I will." He gets out of the truck and goes with Pete.

They get closer and see her snipping roses out on the side of the building, in a black and white toggle coat and hood. Oversized, it hides her back from whatever is bothering her. Off-white knit pants, her face is a warm peach spring day. Teary black eyes will open the windows to any man's soul. She smells the roses, moves to the next as if she's a bee about to taste their sweet nectar.

Petey takes his shot. "Hi, baby."

She doesn't look his way.

Sam nudges him. "You okay, Petey?" He knows that isn't the way to approach the Caribbean songbird. "Come on, let's give them their glue." He slaps his back.

"She's a cold bitch!"

Sam straightens him out. "Man, don't disregard her beauty for coldness... Think of her like your mama." He rings the bell.

Door opens. "Yes sir?" The guard and his dog are ready to bite.

"Delivery. Two cans of glue." Sam pops the papers in his face.

Pete turns back. "They must be smelling the stuff." He's still mad. He watches her clip a rose off, lay it down in her basket. "Mannnn! I like to pop that."

The guard takes the orders, not the cans. "I'll be right back."

Sam tells him, "Pete, you don't approach them with 'Hi, baby'." He takes his cap off, slicks a hand over his hair. "Always be a gentleman."

The door opens. "I'll sign for it." The dog growls for blood.

Pete hands him the cans. The guard keeps the yellow copy. "Thank you, monsieur." He closes the door.

Sam leaves the steps. "Watch this, Pete." He walks to the woman by the flowers. Sun hits her face. "Um, ummm! Good day."

She turns. "Yes?"

"I saw you by the rose bush… and I thought it was such a beautiful picture," he spots a strand of hair undone on the side of her left cheek, "that I wanted to bring you some roses."

She smiles, lowers her eyes at the man in jeans, thick mud boots, but a face that shows sincerity for a woman, for just her. "Yes, *monsieur*, you can bring me some roses."

His heart leaps. "When can I bring them to you?"

She clips another rose. "Wednesday be nice… but come around the back. There is another garden there." She clips the thorns. "Uhhhh, any time after two." She smiles up at this man with a big heart and lonely brown eyes that tell more of the world than he wants to say.

"My name's Sam Murphy." He asks, "Yours?"

"Myrthe Presumé" She goes back to her roses. He walks back to his truck.

• • •

Under the cloak of a spring storm, Sam comes back to her with the flowers. Seven-foot gates open up a rock concrete garden to this woman. He stands to see a small blue bird next to her as she sits on the edge of a large water fountain, three steps leading up to her red high heel shoes. It's as if the bird is talking to her, but that can't be. Intimate soft white sheer dress, hair of black waterfalls comes down like the waters of the fountain, and servants with garden tools, a few feet separating them from the outside streets. All traffic noise disappears when he gets closer to her and the bird.

It flies away.

Myrthe looks at him. "Sam, you here." She stands up from the fountain. "Such lovely roses, *monsieur*."

He gives them to her.

"Thank you."

He takes his cap off. "You welcome." He sees her face sparkle from the waterfalls, and a round sunshine face that is his eclipse this day. "I see your little friend left us."

She questions this. "Friend?"

"The little blue bird."

"Haa haaa! That's Pierre. He's very shy." She pats the stone. "Sit."

He looks into eyes of black stars. He almost gets lost, but he blinks away in time to notice the gardeners carrying wheelbarrows around them, trimming the twenty-foot circle lawn. Her voice of French trumpets swings between African drums, pushes him between two worlds. Children of three have playmates, but she still has these qualities of being able to have fun in an insane world. It's a place with trees, birds, working men in gloves. She comes upon this day, connecting with all things. Clear, silly… romantic, even in calling a bird Pierre. But what gets to him is that of this small bird, she has made a friend.

She asks, "Sam, do you have friends?"

He plays with the waters in the fountain. "I have some… A good friend of mines just died awhile back." He seeks his reflection in the pool. It's unclear, a face waving, and a man creeping over in a liquid blue mirror, just him wanting to drown.

"I'm sorry to hear that." She touches his hand… rough fingers, thick flesh of a man with a few things of goodness left in him. He has time to see a rose of beauty. He has time to talk to her in her insular world of men with dogs, guns.

He looks down at his mud boots. "Uhhhh, it takes a lot out of you when good friends leave." He straightens up. "They never return your calls."

She smiles and sweeps her hair back. "But we find peace with them… yes?"

"Yes, in the long run, we do… we do recover." He asks, "How long will you be in Washington?"

"I don't know… The colonel will tell me when we will leave." She says this and it makes her feel out of place in this beauty again, this peace with this man and the flowers. It's as if the thunder has clapped over her chest, ashamed of ever mentioning this man to him.

"Is this man supposed to be a secret?"

"Colonel Labossier is my lover," she tells the face of a dark hurricane wind.

"Love is hard on us with the wrong person," Sam answers, knowing of this by being with Mabel Friday.

"I come from a hard and beautiful land, Sam… A country that has a saying in Creole, '*Le mise' bare' ou se le ya oua konin sak brav ak sak kapon.*' Myrthe can see the question in his eyes. "It is: 'Easily men shall tell who are the brave and who are the cowards at this time of misery.' "

"You are part of the brave," he says, leaning back on the fountain's edge. "I have killed many of the brave."

"You were a soldier?" She touches his knee, thinks of his soul burning in the flames of an endless dream, finger people dying under his gun.

"I was a soldier... in Vietnam." He stares at his dirty fingernails that strangled the life out of old men, women, children, and burned down homes for the price of wheat-rice puffs for daddy Rockefeller.

"Then you know what I must do?" She searches his eyes of cold brown stones.

"There is no shame in what you must do." When he says this, he spots the guard with the dog coming their way. "I better go."

"Yes, it's time to go." She holds the roses in her hands of brown, in the soft, twisting light.

"Will I see you again?" He walks slowly from her, asking.

The guard is getting closer.

"It's not possible..."

"Yes it is," he says. "Have faith."

The dog growls ten feet away from them.

He drives back in the narrow yellow strip concrete streets. He leaves behind a woman who doesn't need to be left with dogs and guns. He taps his horn at the driver switching lanes at the wrong time. Unspoken words between them pass in rush hour madness. He catches a red light, amazed that his heart is beating like he's drunk bug juice instead of gin... especially for her. He feels the left hand of death, but he also

94

feels the right hand of love tugging at him, all at the same time, twice around the strawberry avenue. He wipes his hot cheeks as sweat of the visit pours from his neck and back, in view of unfinished clouds coming ahead. He wants to reach out to her, even if it ends up cutting his heart out. He flicks on his windshield wipers as it starts to rain.

11

"Mabel, you look fine. Come on," Kathy says. "We all got jeans on." She winks at her girlfriend. "I'm telling you, you going to have a nice time."

Mabel opens the door. "Yeah, but with who?" Closes it shut.

"Don't you worry about that. Come on, child!" She pulls her out the door to her apartment.and lets her lock up. It's hard holding this secret. Mabel had been in her face all day at work about this man. Whew! It's finally over.

From her hall to downstairs seems like a thousand years. Is her hair done right? Do the curls from the side of her face bounce enough? No mascara on, just lipstick. Do the jeans show her butt too much? Is the third button open, just enough to show him what he's not getting. But the future can be bright if he is a handsome frog? A mask disguise of politeness, but don't mess with her, because she's the Proud Mary type. She won't eat much. She will just order salad, no burger, no fries. She doesn't want him to think she's a pig. Grandma Ivey always told her not to talk much on the first date. Keep quiet, let him do all the gabbing. She opens her big purse of cowhide: keys, cigarettes, if she wants to be nasty, twenty bucks to catch a ride back home, a switch-blade Sam gave her to protect herself against the monsters at night, matches, a bottle of perfume. She sprays her neck again. That's enough. If the frog looks like Kathy's last boyfriend, she will just say at the car door, "Sorry! I got a stomach ache. Maybe some other time... 'but not in this life'." Then she'll run and lock her apartment door shut, all the way to the bathroom to puke.

She finally gets to the lobby. Kathy grabs hold of her arm. "I ain't letting you run back in that apart-ment, Mabel" She means this. "Or we going to fight out here on the streets tonight."

Mabel said, "If he's a frog... if he's an ugly frog, I'm going to kick your ass."

Kathy reassures her. "You my best friend. You know I'm going to do you right." She pushes the door for her. "You first."

In the night she can't see much. "Where's the car?"

Kathy helps her out. "That blue Mustang right there." Points.

She gets closer. "I'll be goddamned! Ray!" The look on his face tells her that he knew all about this. She peeks in the back seat behind him. He's with his other friend Felix Jefferson, both cops. She turns to Kathy. "Girl! I can't do this."

"Girl, come on, stop acting like a damn fool."

She goes after Kathy. "Why you set me up with Sam's brother?"

Ray gets out of the car to get between the women with the bulky purses. "Mabel, Mabel, it's not her fault." His voice is lumpy-nervous. "I didn't know how to ask you... because I been wanting to go out with you for a long time."

Kathy gets in the back seat.

Mabel is frozen. "A long time?"

"Yeah," he says, "a long time."

She looks at him in his blue sport coat, white button-down collar shirt, Lee jeans, penny loafers. His face resembles Sam, but is fatter, clean-shaven, a man with some grey at the sides. But a position in life that makes him straight, he doesn't have time to joke with people. He's shy around women, but speaks his mind when the time is right. And this must be the right time. "I'm going to kill Kathy." She peeps down, points with a smile.

"No. Kill me first," he says, leaning back on the sharp Mustang.

She can't kill him. "Okay, I'll go."

"Great!" He opens the car door for her. They drive off for McDonald's.

•　•　•

It's almost two weeks later. People sit around on a grey, warm, cartoonish morning, in Little Mo's Barbershop at Third and Taylor Avenue in Sweet Loaf. It's packed in by talking, jiving, walk-tall men with not much to do a Saturday morning. Haircuts for five bucks, a trim for two, oil, grease, lilac lotion is slapped in and through scalps. Smoke filters about. Good reading material lays around, toilet stool confessionals of sports and girlie magazine fun. *Playboy* soil centerfold, Miss January 1972, is from round about. Hormone spicy-chili Black women pout from the rack behind the front door. *Players* magazine cover, Miss March 1975, is going to be a fighter pilot once the secret is out. Nobody wants to read *Life*, *Esquire*, *Washington Post*, or a *Sweet Loaf Mirror*, but fingers fight for the pages of Ebony and Jet, all twenty-eight back issues.

Dance back high chairs swivel, wiggle with sleeping men snouts. Wing tips, sneakers, desert boots punch up in the air to the fifteen years of service to the Black folks of this town. The checker board squared, red and white, brick-box storefront is the local hangout for the preachers, teachers, and just lame walkabouts.

Clipping, snipping, shaving. lifeless face-up men; goateed, bald, mustache is too long today, sir? We clean you up, slick you down, give you that just-came-into-fantasy money look. There's some afros still around, a hint of that liberation voices of "I ain't going to give up my daishiki today." They came by way of ships, boats, chains, incoming sixteen hundred arrivals off the docks of Virginia. Men mess around under pictures of John, Malcolm, Martin and Bobby, all looking down from heaven.

A ceiling fan swings around as a possible candidate waits next for Little Mo, Leroy, Ernie or Ty. But talk goes on, as some smoke neck bones cook in the back on a hot plate stove. Don't nobody ask for none, just sit and wait your turn to get your head clipped.

Ray sits back. Hearing the razor strop pop reminds him of his daddy whipping his ass. Hot shaving cream eases him down under the careful, fast fingers of Little Mo, who happens to stand six feet four, World War II and Korea veteran. Ray is tired after pulling a night shift in the Third Precinct. He busted sneak thieves, a rapist, an arsonist and a drunk for pissing on the side of the Second Street Baptist Church. He tries to make it to Little Mo's at least once a month for his trim. The cats know he's a cop, but they don't want to talk much about that. In the chair, he has to pay Little Mo extra for any other information he may have heard about the dog shit out here on the streets.

Ray listens to the baseball game, Baltimore getting hurt by the Twins again and again. He closes his eyes, swivels, swings, clip, snip, clip, snip… comfortable, baby-like in the chair, in the arms of a man who could kill him. If anything or anybody wants to get bad, he still has his piece strapped under his arm. He doesn't know what fool wants to take a risk on taking out a cop for fun today, after they finish eating their Wheaties. He seen too much stuff flying out here in the streets. But it's getting meaner: dope, shootings, muggings, the population growing. Hopeless feelings come after all the heroes are slain in the streets. Nothing, not a care in the world of taking out another man, woman or child. War is always around the corner: here, overseas, the Middle East, on the streets or in your local synagogue. This isn't New York, but he's seeing some funny things going on after Vietnam. Kids are running wild. Hollering: "Fuck you! Fuck your momma! Fuck your sister!" She got two, three kids by the time she's eighteen. Clip, snip, clip, snip. A Jesus-freak president… Shit! People don't want to pray. They want blood. No Bible for me, Martha, get my gun! Riots have died down, isn't no fist pumping for freedom no more. It's, "Let's get high. Chill out. Cool down. Mao! I'm tired as shit! I betta get a job." He hugs the handles and lets the cologne, talcum powder soften up his view on the world. Let the lions sleep in his belly, but keep one eye open. Damn! The Twins hit another homer; his poor, poor Orioles.

Mabel filters through his thoughts like a warm cup of coffee. Black, no cream. The hamburger, movie and surprise turned out all right. They giggled a lot. He feels Little Mo's breath on his neck. That tickled. He wants to have breakfast with her next, but they decided to take it slow, slow like the Mississippi. If something put them on this earth together, then he damn sure isn't going to let his brother take it away. She's a nice girl. All nice girls deserve a chance on being met and kept happy. She's a woman with her head up high and keeps her mouth clean and free of bad-mouthing old lovers, friends and neighbors. But she'll kick you like a dog if you do her wrong. He knows of the pact between Sam and her, no puppets on a string. But, he thinks, she's just a little tired of this dangerous tryst… with a man who doesn't really give a damn about anybody, except his drinking buddies, a fast woman and the road.

He sneaks a peek up at the pictures of Malcolm, Martin and Bobby, probably laughing at all of them. Closes his eyes and soaks up the bullshit from the four barbers:

Little Mo: Hey, Leroy! Where your black ass going tonight, man?

Leroy: I'm gonna see your momma!

Ernie: Little Mo ain't got no momma… If he does, she's a wolf. Cheap bastard!

Ty: That'll be five dollars, sir.

Leroy: I'm going to Atlantic City.

Ty: Leroy! Pay me my twenty before you leave.

Leroy: Man! Fuck you!

Ernie: Don't come back here broke… Get in that crap game and have to sale your car to get back to Sweet Loaf.

Leroy: Don't yaw worry about me… Come Monday morning all ya hands be out!

Little Mo: You just make sure you back her Monday morning… Don't have me come looking for you with my ugly stick!

Ernie: You taking Geraldine with you to Atlantic City?

Leroy: Naw! She gots to work this weekend at the hospital.

Ty: You a lucky man.

Little Mo: He ain't no lucky man… He's a fool! I damn sure wouldn't leave my ol' lady behind. Shit! As fine as she is…

Leroy: Well, you ain't got to worry about it! I got things under control.

Ty: You ain't got shit under control! She's probably putting your ass on a bus to Atlantic City to get the fuck out her hair!

Leroy: Man! Fuck you.

Ty: Fuck you! You just pay me my twenty dollars before you leave.

Little Mo: Don't worry Ty… His ass be back here Monday broker than a mutherfucker!

Ernie: Begging as usual!

Ty: Yaw all go to hell!

Little Mo: You want me to box or feather it out?

Ray: Go on and feather it out, Mo.

Little Mo: Okay.

Ernie: Thank you, sir. Have a nice day.

Leroy: I pay my debts.

Ty: Yeah? When? You been owing me that twenty dollars for two years now.

Little Mo: Hey! Ray… I think that's your brother pulling up in that truck of his?

Ray: Hold it, Mo.

Sam comes in. Ray sticks his hand out from under the sheet to shake.

Ray: What's happening?

Sam: Get the fuck up out of that chair!

Ray: Man, what the fuck is wrong with you?

He gets up from the chair, sticks a hand up in Sam's face, snaps his gun loose. Customers start scattering like cockroaches.

Little Mo: You two brothers get the hell out of here!

He walks quick to the door, holds the door open. Ray pulls his gun right at Sam's head. The other three barbers run out.

Sam: You know why I'm here?

Ray: Come on… let's take it outside!

Sam: Shoot me!

He opens up his arms.

Sam: Shoot me Ray!

Ray: Go on out the door, Sam, before I do shoot you!

Ray lets Sam go out the door first and straps his gun down in his holster. People from the shop gather

103

around the brothers. He screams at the faces. "Yaw go on and get away from here!"

The crowd doesn't move.

Sam stops, throws a right hook.

Ray steps to his left. The fist misses his chin by inches. He ducks, tackles him to the ground. "Sam! Cooool it!" He uses his knee and right leg to keep his brother's body prone, but Sam continues by pushing him under his chin. Ray brings his fist down on Sam's jaw, yelling at him, "Asshole! Stop it, mannn!"

Sirens respond, cry out to hurt your ear drums.

Sam spits up in his face. "Shoot me, Ray! Shoot me!" Pounds his chest. "Right here! Right here!"

Two squad cars pull up. The crowd spreads open for the cops as they run to get the men apart. They recognize Officer Murphy. "Lock 'im up. He's my brother," Ray hollers up. "He's my brother."

They turn Sam over, handcuffs, sling him up in the air, push him in the squad car. He was still hollering at Ray, "Shoot me Ray! Shoot me!"

Ray speaks to one of cops. "Just cool him off for awhile... I'll be there in a few."

"Okay." He walks off with the other cops as they push the people back from the man in the car. "Go on home now. The party's over." He directs them, "Get away from here before we lock yaw all up!"

"Damn." Ray walks from the people, rubs his face.

Little Mo came to him. "You awright?"

He knocks dirt off his shirt. "Yeah, I'm all right." He pulls out his wallet. "Fifty set me right for the mess?"

"Yeah," Little Mo says, taking the money. "You just go and talk to your brother."

He pushes through the crowd. Children imitate the scuffle. Mothers hold their babies up in their arms. He feels some people slap him on the back. He doesn't flinch, but keeps trying to hold back the mess of a lifetime between him and his little brother. Ray pats his pants for keys. He stalls, tries to figure out what to say... to a brother he helped raise through Saturday James Bond, Godzilla and Mickey Mouse movies. Nursed him through baseball and football practice. He gets on his knees. A square head little boy helps him out. The boy finds the keys, between Sam's truck and his black '82 Camaro. He's in no hurry. He just wants Sam to sleep it off. He pays the boy a fiver. "You stay out the streets, son."

"Okay, mister, I will!" The boy's eyes pop. He runs off down the street.

Ray is shaken. He hopes Mabel is all right. He has to see her. He tries to start his car, but his hands shake. He peers in his rearview mirror. "Calm down, Ray... you'll be okay." He waits a few seconds for the keys to stop shaking, then he starts the car up. He spins the car into a U-turn to the precinct.

•   •   •

Foggy, toilet stool noise flushes down a slip of darkness. Sit, wait... months or years, with men that can't seem to swim towards land. It makes sense to sleep behind jail bars. Dreams of demons hollering in your face, his father's face, this brings Sam light to your tomb. A mother's womb, piss smells in corners. Mop it up with your tongue. Scream, scream for your mother, your lawyer, your wife. A piece of bread, bowl of chicken soup... you eat. To dream, dream, dream again. Spit up your name down the sink drain, blood-covered lips. A fag pokes fun at your fear as he bends over. Fish head smells in an Ovaltine jar-size cell... try to lick your way out of this mess. It has no ending... no commercial value. It has no name. The shadows of fog have fun with your name. Sam! Sam! The pretty man. Hot tongues sweat out confessions of love. I killed her! I wiped out the whole goddamn family! Yes, I killed her! Cigarette smoke as the cockroaches light up... attack cracker crumbs from a half empty can of something. Is it dog food? A memory comes back, how it all ended with his ass in here. Is it cat food?

He saw himself in trouble when she told him. When she said, "It's your brother. It's your brother, fool!" Jesus pray over your ass today. Heads duck in holes: murder, rape, arson, assault with a baseball bat, robbery, larceny, mayhem. Pretty boys punch their Black tickets. Riders of a far farewell storm to the outside. These mug shots are fabulous! 347685-R, 629825-A, 147862-T. I want my lawyer! I want my lawyer! I want my lawyer man! Main Street hookers flash tits for bribes, lick tongues, guns. Pimps parade in town under big clown hats. Don't forget the feather on top. Had you laughing when the clowns got five to ten for accidentally murdering their own street ho'.

Raisin-head men rain down into peaceful shepherd snores. Latest update, six o'clock junkies rat on their mothers for another hit. The cops, the robbers wrestle with their critics. Ivy League word spinners write about stopping crime on the streets. Answer:

more guns, more men with guns, more children with guns, more asses six feet under with guns. Lock your door! The Beasts of Bellaire are out! Spread your feet. Don't say nothing! I don't want to hear one peep about your rights. Kick him! Kick him! Whip him up the head, New York style! Reach for the sky. Jesus hands. Reach for a belt to hang from. Twist! Shout! What the fuck is it all about?

Sam feels the hammer of gin leave his head. He blinks, catches panther shadows in the cage. Radio waves of Sinatra sing in a jail, under the stars. Inside this meat pit he feels his Saturday night slipping off… heartburn over a woman he didn't even want. He remembers now. She said, "He treats me nice." Fuck! A dog could treat her nice. And he damn sure is that. He gets up off the cot. Bars stop him in the placid darkness of night. A brother stops him by giant steps of love.

Keys sing in the hall. A guard comes to the cell unleashing his name. "Sam Murphy!" He rattles the keys from his belt. "Let's go!"

Sam slides between the backs of men, making sure not to touch, not to bump or fuss. "Coming!" He comes from the jar, praying to a God he doesn't know anymore. He follows the cop towards another room with a grey steel door sign, Interrogation Room.

He walks in.

Ray waits in the blue blood-stained room. "Pull up a chair."

Sam sits down at the table. "You pull up one too."

Ray sits across from him. "You all right?"

Sam doesn't want to say much. "Yeah, I'm all right." He looks at the fist dents in the table. "Just don't mention her name." Sam crosses his arms. "But tell me, brother, why you have to fuck my woman?"

Ray answers with the hunch of his shoulders. "Sam, she's nobody's woman... " He lights up a cigarette.

"Basically, that's where I went wrong." He takes the offered cigarette from Ray's fingers. "I want to say I'm sorry... for acting like a goddamn fool"

Ray gets up and steps around the table. Sam stands, opens up his arms. They hug each other. In the silence they listen to each other's hearts beat. Pumping hard, steel black blood... a mother's, a father's blood. In the silence they let the pain die.

Sam gets excited. "Man, get me out this place."

"You sound like you don't like my house?" Ray gazes at the blood-stained walls of men lost and found in a jail cell. Chewing on their own tails to freedom and asking, "Why am I here?"

He puffs, gives him the cigarette back. "I don't!"

12

"Grandma Ivey, Ray Murphy's a kind man." Mabel has to tell her. "Takes his time with me. Not like his brother, who always seem to be in a hurry. Sam even walks fast." She rests her eyes on her grandma's big hips bending over in the gas oven.

"Baby, this Sam of yours seems to me to be a man in a hurry to die fast."

"You got a good point... He was over there in Vietnam."

Ivey keeps spooning juices over the chicken in the oven. She closes the door, wipes her hands down her apron front. "Baby, seems like your heart ready for some slow hands." She sits at the table with her and puts Mabel's hands in hers. "Soft and smooth like a baby's feet." Pats them.

"Thank you, Grandma."

"Your mother's hands were like that." She lets them go. "How much you like this brother Ray?"

Picks up her dish towel, wipes some wet spots off the kitchen table.

Mabel has to smile to herself about this man. "I always did like 'im, him being Sam's brother. But this is kind of strange." She shakes her head. "Funny, really funny."

Ivey knew her, raised her up. "You just settle down, eat that pumpkin pie in front of you and remember ain't nobody... and I mean nobody, got a hold on nobody in dis world." Winks. "Takes your time about this, if you unsure." Sits back. "Clean water don't need a dirty man or woman."

Not sure, she cuts a slice off the pie, in this kitchen where she grew up, watched her cook, clean pots, dishes for Sunday and holiday parties. Scatted her out sometimes after sticking her big nose in the stew pots. Decisions of the world were made right in this high-back wood chair. She covers up herself in cake, pie, roast, collard greens smells... But Ray is a warehouse for her love to stay in. He wants her all to himself, just himself. Around him she's comfortable like a sixty-eight degree day... no clouds in the sky, just the sun in his eyes. People talk. They have nothing else to do in Sweet Loaf. She isn't going to hide her man from them. But the pain is there for all three of them. It will work itself out of the mouths of church folks... because they all can kiss her pretty, wide ass.

"How you likes the pie?"

"It's good, Grandma." She picks some crust off. "It's melting in my mouth."

"I put some orange zest in it this time."

Sticks some in her mouth. "Ummm! I got to get the recipe from you."

Ivey kids her. "Mabel, you ain't going to make no pie."

"Yes I am!" She drinks some milk with it. "But I never be able to cook as good as you."

With her rag she dabs some crumbs up. "Yaw too busy now of days to live in your kitchen." She scratches at her hair tied up in two plaits. "Yaw free now... Ain't got to cook for a man."

"It just takes time, Grandma." She hunches. "Some men out here can cook better than me."

Ivey scolds her. "Something yaw ain't got now of days." Folds her arms on the table. "Child, if it wasn't for McDonald's, you probably wouldn't eat." Raises her voice. "Hell, Mabel, how many pounds you done lost?" Points at her. "If you too tired to cook, you just get your butt over here... Grandma Ivey will feed you! Girl, you got the bakers' genes... I don't want you looking like some magazine model, with no tits or ass."

Mabel didn't mean to get her upset. "Grandma, look at it like this... We out the kitchen now, and we cookin' in the office."

"Ha! That's full of shit!" She gets mad with her about the past.

"No it's not, Grandma. No it's not."

Ivey unfolds her arms. "Progress, uh! Can't cook worth a damn!" She goes to the sink.

Mabel smacks her lips with the last piece of pie. "You to blame!" Points the fork.

Ivey wants to laugh at this. "You blaming me... I had your ass in the kitchen, but you was too busy smacking them big lips of yours." She washes her hands under the faucet.

111

Mabel defends her skills. "Sam tells me I can cook a mean slab of ribs, homemade sauce and all." Her nose gets big with pride. She licks her fingers. "Now, tell me that recipe."

Ivey plays with her left plait whenever a question is at her. "Baby, who you going to fix this pie for? Sam or Ray?" Dries her hands off with some paper towels.

Mabel oozes down in her chair, full of the pumpkin pie. "Ohhhh! Hell! Both of them."

• • •

Sweet Loaf has two McDonald's—one east end and the other on the west side. On the borders between Washington and Maryland, Sam enters near a beltway ramp on I-95, all paths have tentacles of cars, trucks, cabs, motorcycles crossing over yellow strips. A way-station of Texaco, Exxon, Gulf, and Domino gas stations make you want to fill up on gas and hamburgers either before or after work. A few state troopers keep watch on the road mess... car accidents involved over the Roosevelt Bridge, a five-car pileup, a car or three stalled on the highway, women, men with broken taillights have to be babified or given a ticket for not having your ass fixed. On the fringes in the parking lot of the westbound McDonald's, exhaust fumes fill up a Wednesday. Close summer heat of the day has Sam turning into a piece of suffocating plastic, burning up in the cab of El, Zorro. Leftover gin and sweat pour from his skin. He's a smoking coffee filter that is running over with hot water. A blue and white bandana tied around his head, he rests back, taps his horn at the women going in the glass door. Lunch time... two cheeseburgers, large fries, and chase it down with some gin mixed in a cup of orange soda pop.

Sam had offered to buy Petey-Pete a burger, but he was into staying away from the red meat this month. He wasn't giving up on the booze yet. Not yet... maybe next month when he get back on the red meat again? In fact he's drinking more and writing more of that weird poetry shit of his.

One-third drunk, half drunk, a hundred percent drunk in the D.C. heat of flies and elephant gnats, the radio blasts WQSZ-FM. Trumpets, drums, flutes tick off the seconds of his break. Pause... pass the paper cups. Pause... listen to your car horn thoughts on Myrthe Presumé. He wants to school-boy pull her long black hair, let his fingers slide and glide through her coconut oil riches. Large waves of her smile, he hopes to taste her soft, fine body on a beach, while she teases him with her eyes. He freezes... melts when she talks of home. Pause... Tenor man, tenor man swings into "My Favorite Things." He snaps his fingers.

Petey turns the pages of a Jasmine Truelove novel. "So what's going on with you and that French chick?"

Sam winces from the orange gin. "She's not French, Pete. She's Creole, man."

He pulls on his ear. "French, Creole, damn near all the same to me."

Sam understands, he's still mad from her cold shoulder. "Never mind... It's going to take a crazy man to get with her." He peeks up to his rearview, no cops, just other truckers getting hamburgers.

Pete has to laugh on this. "Haaaa! Haaaaa! You the right man." He shakes his head, keeps a thumb in his page. "You one of them gorillas, ain't you, Sam?"

"Oh, I am, huh?" He scratches his chin and belches. "S'cuse me." Taps his fingers to some more trumpet. Freddie Hubbard on that Red Clay cut has him cracking his teeth on some ice. "Um!" Bobs his head.

"So what you going to do about her?"

He spits his ice back in his cup. "About what?"

"The French chick... since the road is clear now."

"Man, the road always been clear." He gets the hint about Mabel. "Except this time, I think I'm going to stir up some dust."

"Can I get in on this?" He gets curious and puts his book in his back pocket.

Sam shakes his McDonald's cup. "That's up to you." He watches him thinking. "You know you owe me for them fries."

Petey sits up and winks at a sweet redhead going in. "I betta pay up."

Sam rubs the sweat from his neck. "That's right! I'll be calling on you." He checks the parking lot again for cops. It's clear. He's cool, not that drunk.

Petey lights up a cigarette. "Damn! It's hot as shit!" Sucks down the smoke. "Wheww!"

"Mannn, it's not even summer yet and you already complaining... Just don't forget to drink plenty of water or you'll be hit by a sunstroke."

"I'll remember that."

"Good! Now let's get the hell on back to the ware-house." He swallows the rest of his ice, and turns the key in the ignition. Listen to El, Zorro, power under him. He reverses and drives out under the golden arches.

Bitch dogs bark behind the wheels of El, Zorro coming through the alley. They charge and yelp under the tires, growling, jumping. Pete throws an empty pop bottle, smashing the yellow one in the nose, a warning for the other two to retreat.

Sam backs up to the loading dock. When he gets out, he hears other men cussing, popping fingers. Four of them kneel down behind a giant garbage dumpster, throwing dice on the ground. Duck is praying to the good king lord. Kenny has his fist up, shooting. "Haaaa!" Slaps Joe Buck five.

Joe has his head over the dice. "Pick 'em up! Shit! Throw 'em again!"

Darnell is counting, licking his fingers over some tens and twenties.

"Come on, we get into that later." Sam sticks his hands in his pockets. He doesn't have much to lose anyway. "Let's see what Mike got for us… Make some of that easy money."

Pete looks at the men hunched over, praying. "All right, Sam."

•   •   •

Dark shadow men pass through the cavernous cold warehouse. Spider webs creep under such heavy rolls of rich fleece beige, Rocky Mountain brown, Caribbean blue carpets. Tall Indian beaded rugs rise from the concrete floors from the southwest and New Mexico ancient Indian drawings are bought and stolen for a jacked-up price for the pleasures of Eastern rites suburban luxury. One of these hand-sewn rugs went up in the thousands. Tribal women bleed, bite, stitching threads from the bird, the buffalo, the rabbit, the fox. For just a few dollars to eat beans, rice, some bread, mixed in with rabbit stew. Under their mud homes, under their mud men on a cold prairie reservation night.

Sam walks through these rolls, touching the soft, pale pink riches of a people. Mr. Milano walks out his office waving the order sheets. "Sam! I got your next run!"

Sam says, "I told you, Petey. Easy money!"

Pete rubs his hands. "On time too!" He follows him up to the office.

Mike says, "All right, here's your run." He shoves the papers in his hand. "They want you back over to the Haitian embassy, but before you go there… " points at some carpets, "… take two hundred yards of that alabaster green over in Greenbriar to this mansion…" sticks his fingers down to the address, "… to a Mrs. Woolcott. Get two thousand from the old babe." He pulls his ear. "Uhhhh! Split five between you and Petey, and bring me back the rest." He follows his eyes with a smile. "If there's a problem, get on the phone and call me."

"Okay, Mike." Sam rolls up the receipts. "What's the order for the embassy?"

He hunches his shoulder. "This woman called here and asked for you to bring over two more cans of that Flexarall glue." He lets out a mulish laugh. "Hee! Haaa!"

"What's so funny, boss?"

He plays with the pencil behind his ear. "Either she's sniffing that… or she's sniffing you!"

Sam doesn't look at him. "Naw, boss you got it all wrong… Let me get this carpet. See ya!"

"Okay, see you two later with the cash." He goes back in the office.

Pete tells him, "Haaaaa haaaa! I think yaw both sniffing that glue."

Sam pushes him. "Man, fuck you!"

"Fuck you!"

Sam slaps him with the receipts. "Mannn! Fuck you!"

"Fuck you!"

•   •   •

"You boys bring the carpet through the dining room." Mrs. Woolcott directed them to a giant size room of pushed-back wood stained tables, French doors that need to be painted, some ferns that drip from the ceiling over the head of a furry white cat curled up in the middle of the room.

Sam and Pete are two men who don't take nicely to a blue-wig hag calling them "boy." They let it go and give her their best Uncle Ben smiles for good service and the payoff at the end of the job.

"Watch my Ming vase from China… that's it… that's it." She fingers the pearls around her neck. She doesn't like their filthy shoes messing up her floors, but she puts up with it for now.

In unison, Sam and Pete say. "Yes, ma'am!"

She gets to it, lifts it off the table. "It's a parting gift from my third husband." Takes it to the dining room.

117

"That's nice, ma'am," Sam says. Sweat pops from his nose as he carries his end through the door. He winks at Pete. "Isn't it, Petey?"

"Yeah," Pete grunts, shuffles his feet. The weight is getting heavier. "Uh!"

She gets back in time. "Watch the cat!"

Sam stops. "Oops!" His foot is inches from its tail.

Pete asks him, "Sam, you like cats?" His arms are straining.

She grabs the cat up. "My babbbbbyyyy!" Scratches its head. "Fritter, come to Mommie... Bad kitty." Rubs her nose in its fur. "Those men almost squashed you."

They lay the rug down, and drop to their knees, rolling it.

"There you go, Petey-Pete... Keep the edges straight."

Pushing it and keeping it tight.

"I got it, Sam."

Sam shoves his knees into the corner. "There!"

They get off the floor, checking the display of the rug in the room. Mrs. Woolcott is still soothing the cat with kisses to the nose. "My precious... my precious."

Sam walks over to her. "Mrs. Woolcott, the money?"

"Oh, of course." She walks to a small cherry wood table in the corner, pulls out her pearl handle purse, and turns her back. She puts Fritter on the rug and takes him the money. "Here you boys go."

"Thank you, ma'am!" With a wet thumb, Sam counts. "Mrs. Woolcott, you a thousand dollars short." He looks at her shrunken, made-up cheeks that had at least three face lifts already. At the corner of his eye he sees Pete smiling at Fritter the cat.

"Boy, it's what I was told… Now you go on and get out of my house."

"Sam, let me handle this."

Sam sees the cat in Pete's arms. Mrs. Woolcott is about to shit on the new rug. "Put my cat down!"

Pete pats its head. "I will after you pay us the rest of our money… or we'll be eating cat stew for dinner today."

Mrs. Woolcott gets to her purse and pulls the rest of the money out. "Here! Here!" Slaps the money in Sam's hand. "Now my cat!" She's shaking, turning white as her pearls around her neck.

Sam counts. "It's all there."

Pete gives her the cat. "Have a nice day."

They walk out the door, leaving behind an old woman and a cat that almost was fed to the dogs of Sweet Loaf for dinner that day.

• • •

Colonel Labossier's nights are spent in unloosening Myrthe's bra strap, tasting her flower petal lips, taking bites here and there at the delicacies of her thighs. He opens her up to his world, peeling off slices of her silk white gown. Making love to her is as if he's amongst the trees, wind, rains and mountains of Kenskoff. Last night he felt her hands cold, lips dry, parched, her face an ice box of flesh.

Up on his balcony high over the living room walls, he watches her play with the servants' children, a game of Lagot.

He's her master, the maestro that conducts most of her moves. A figurehead over the bed, he commanded her to love within the blink of twelve midnight. He ordered her like he directed his troops to kill. She is trained to not seek, search or find any other voice but his. On the winds, on the rains, from the mountains of Kenskoff, his echo is heard.

He choked her, bit her nipples. She would not cry, scream or beg in the violence of the night. He plunged into her soft, brown, round hips with rapid thrusts. She would not cry, scream or beg from the mountains of the moon. His teeth sank into her ass as he told her over and over again he loved her. He fingered up in his love-enemy-slave to respond back to him these three words: I love you! I love you! I love you! She would not cry, scream or beg. He slapped her, pulled this brown, long-haired beauty from the sheets. He stood her up against the wall, kissing her, tonguing her, licking her, riding her long-legged flesh up and down. Up and down. Up and down. But she would not cry, scream or beg in the two o'clock night. Her head dropped. Unspoken words didn't appear, didn't come forth. She just let him touch, feel, taste, mountain woman flesh, perfumed. Wet, soft liquids dripped from her. He kept licking. Up and down. Up and down. Until her gown melted away in the three o'clock moon.

He spied on her, watched his love-enemy-slave cook his favorite dishes, but yet the taste was the same, no poison. Was it this man, his truck driver, this foolish, dirty fellow in the funny hat? He would watch further of this. If the Mambo was right, a rescuer one day would come to steal his songbird away. He claps his hand. "Sergeant Moreaux!"

The man comes, bows. "Sir."

"Get the car... I'm ready to go." He straightens his tie in the hall mirror. "Yes, I must watch this dirty, dirty man."

13

Sam can barely catch his breath as he looks at Myrthe in the garden by the bush of baby's breath. Her hair shimmers under the sun flecks of black, brownish strands as she pushes the hair from her eyes. In her long, white lace dress, her shape shows off a woman with hips, and legs laced in sandals. A straw hat sits on her head to keep the sun from her honeybee face. He wants to sweep her up, take her away in his truck. But the guards and dogs bark him back to their reality. In back of the mansion, they stand in the circle green garden, not saying much, just feeling each other's eyes roam, sink, swim into each other. He follows her with the two cans of carpet glue as she sits on the stone edge of the fountain, looking up at him. Her hand is up, shading the sun from her soft brown and hazel eyes.

To his astonishment, she says, "Come get me the first of September, when the moon is white and full."

He sets the two cans by her feet. "Here's your receipt." Pulls the papers from his back pocket. His heart pounding in the heat, he bites his tongue to keep from hollering with joy.

She quietly asks, as she bends downs to the cans, "Did you understand, Sam?"

He kneels down, and points at the label. "Yes, ma'am. This glue will keep your carpets in place for a hundred years."

She closes her eyes in relief. "Yes, good."

He plays with the front of his cap. He sees Pete standing by the gate, calmly watching the guards roam a few feet in the distance.

She swipes the strands of hair from her left eye. "Thank you, sir." She gets up. "The carpets in the living room seem to pull up whenever there is a bad rain."

"Ma'am." He straightens up. "Those are very expensive carpets you got. Treat them real gentle... maybe even clean them with a special rabbit hair brush you can get from the hardware store."

She wants to hold him, kiss this tall man who stands beside her. His voice makes her feel again, makes her relax in his husky decibels of calm church bells.

The children run over from some of the trimmed bushes. A little girl about six, with a thumb in her mouth, pleads, "Myrthe, come play with us!"

She gently takes the thumb away. "I will Gigi... Keep the thumb out of your mouth."

A little boy wearing eyeglasses pulls her arm. "Myrthe! Myrthe!"

123

She hugs him. "Okay, Antoine… okay!" Sadly she waves Sam away. "Thank you gentlemen very much." She picks up the girl, swings her in the air. "Haaa haaa haa! Don't be afraid. I'm not going to drop you."

Sam walks out the gate.

Sam can't say too much to Pete. He just wants to think of the night he will have her in his arms… when the moon is white and full.

He lights up and puffs down the nicotine. Sam keeps his foot on the brake mostly in the traffic coming out of Washington, D.C.. Drivers melt behind their steering wheels listening to WMZD, WHUR, WOL, WXYS radio waves. Each colored face has a taste in music, sounds, their children, wives' voices, nagging the shit out of them for money, a ride to wherever the road leads. His road, his long, long road will lead to a Creole woman and a full white moon.

Pete nods off, his Redskin baseball cap dipping down and up whenever the truck hits a bump. He can't rest much. "Sam! where we at?" he yawns, "AAAWWW!" stretches out.

"On," Sam pulls over in the right lane, "the road back to Sweet Loaf."

Pete says, "She must be a precious jewel."

He moves up on a pickup with a Rebel flag pasted on its bumper. "I guess you can say that." He flicks some ash out his window.

"Must," Pete sticks a toothpick in his mouth, "be pretty hard, with all them guards around, to be in love with somebody and never able to touch."

"You been reading too many romance novels."

"And you been living them," he smiles, "Sam, a life like yours would drive me crazy. I don't want life to be that hard for me," he pulls out the toothpick, "you got too many women."

"No. I got one woman." Sam comes off the brake a little more. "Pete, I'm going to have to take her out of there." He smokes on the cigarette, stays with the traffic engines as I-95 takes him east.

"Shit!" Pete spits out his toothpick, "you see all them guns?"

"I see," Sam turns to him, then back to the highway. "a frightened bird."

"Man! you crazy as shit!" lifts his cap up, scratches the sweat from his head. "Now you messing with a government. Sam! They hunt you down like a dog," He looks at the smoke black, sweaty face. "You serious about this?"

"You goddamn right!" Nods, flicks the butt out. "I found a woman who can stop me from acting like a fool out here in the streets, and I'm not about to give that up."

Pete shakes his head. "So what's the difference between this woman and Mabel?"

He gave a small smile to a man who didn't want to see him killed. "She's nothing like me."

"Nothing like you... You talking in riddles, man."

He slows down. "Uh, what attracts me... is that we come from two different places." Looks over to him. "And those two different places have come together."

"Yaw! Both Black... Sons and daughters of kings and slaves."

He balls his fist. "She's from a land where people are afraid to look up, and I'm from a country where we fight to look up." He speeds up, passes a Greyhound bus. "She's beautiful in here." He points at his chest. "She gives me that wholeness... something precious called life. I want to live again... and she makes me feel this."

Pete scans the highway. Slaps some sweat off his cheek. "Sam, to me, women are a great big adventure. And I got plenty of them... same as you. But when you get the one you think you really want... you'll find out they all are headaches."

"Petey! Man, you make me laugh... I agree with you." Taps the horn at another trucker. "But Pete, all you really need is just one headache... Everything else will fit in place." He watches the cows graze in the meadows. "And I truly believe there's just one woman for every man out here... You just gots to find her."

He plays with the front of his cap. "Yeah! You mean even get shot and ate up by guard dogs to get to her."

Sam says, "That's right."

"Well!" Picks his back teeth. "You going to need some firepower... I know a couple of dudes who can help you out... that is, of course, if you need them." Pete stretches out. "Ahhhhh!" Flips his cap back down over his eyes, not wanting to look at the signs to Sweet Loaf, but to just rest up before he goes out again to visit some of his headaches.

• • •

Saturday night, Sam is at the Drunken Owl Bar and Lounge.

126

Long picture mirrors roll around in the background of three dancing girls shaking bare ass in your face for a dollar. Titties jiggling like chocolate milk from a cow's belly. Hey, baby! Come, come over here! Let me get a closer peek at you, girl! Blue lights overhead. Red walls from a cops' hangout. Prostitutes come over to Ray Murphy, give him some street tips. A lick, and a feel on his ass. He pays off the night vultures in blonde wigs and bad teeth with some cash. Sam just sucks the cold ice, spits the cubes back in an empty glass of what was scotch.

Ray asks, "I haven't seen you in awhile." Nods at the dancer twirling on a pole. "What you been up to?"

Sam rubs his hand through some hair that needs to be cut off. "Nothing much. Just got a lot on my mind."

Ray tries to pep him up. "Shit! Let me buy you another drink… It will be clear in the morning why you on this planet in the first place." Raises a finger at the bartender.

"Okay. You can do that." He looks at the long brown legs waltzing in front of him, a ring in her stomach navel. The third drink comes, and he toasts to her.

She bends over him from the stage. "Here's something for you, Sam." Dips the tits in his face. Turns, shakes, bends over, squats. Does the nasty on the floor, licking the air.

He stands, plucks a five from his pocket. "All right, Coco." Places the money in her garter, blows her a kiss. "Shake it, baby!" Claps her down the stage to the next customer. He sits back down.

Ray drinks a glass of Schlitz. "What you been up to?" Shakes some salt in the beer.

He rubs his bumpy forehead. "A woman." Sips the cool, sweet, hot taste down.

"It's always a woman." He asks, "Who is she?"

"She's from the Haitian embassy." He looks at his brother's face. "I surprise you?"

"You ain't surprised me since the day you jumped out that ten foot tree…,thinking you was Superman." Drinks some. "Moving up in the world, huh?"

Sam rubs his eyes to get a closer peek at the reddish brown girl strutting in front of him. He winks, with a smile at Candy. "Could be moving six feet under."

When Ray hears this, he's worried. "This ain't no easy pussy?" He sees the crazy stare in his brother's eyes, glassy, show a hint of life. But a rugged, hard face, dented with fighter cuts over his eyebrows from school and a war that damn near killed him when he was nineteen. "Who's fucking with you, Sam?"

He peers around to the Schlitz lights flashing above the bar. Quarters going in the juke box, thumping to a beat, and a nasty black-blonde woman humping on the stage to Jimmy's "Purple Haze."

"It will be all right, Ray." Pats his arm. "Don't worry about me… Drink up, man. Enjoy the show."

Ray turns to the stage, then back to him. "I'm your big brother… Don't you ever forget that." He gets angry, points at him. "If somebody's after you… they after me too! Now we might fight over bullshit… but our blood is still the same." He points around to the other cops in the bar. "All of us in here… watch each other's back." Nods at him. "We watch your back too." Grabs Sam's arm. "You hear that? You hear that?"

Sam says, "I hear that."

Ray pats his cheek. "Good!" Sips, stands up and sticks a dollar in Ola's blue garter. "Man, what you got yourself into? You going to be running illegals in that beat-up truck of yours?"

"I'm not going to be running illegals, Ray. This is about one woman."

"One woman and a whole fucking country!"

He leans forward, plucks a cigarette from a pack on the bar. "Myrthe's her name." He lights up as some more legs come at him. A pretty brown ass romps over his drink. He puffs hard on the smoke. "I just might need some help, that's all." Finishes his scotch.

Ray shakes his head. "You after another man's woman?"

"She don't belong to nobody." Blows smoke through his nose.

"Yeah, you after another man's woman." Rubs his fingers over his lips. "I'm not judging you." His finger goes up for another round. "If he ain't treating her right," winks at him, "and this the one you would get your dick cut off to have… well, she's all yours."

The drinks come over. Sam bumps his glass up to Ray's. "To family."

Ray repeats, "To family."

• • •

Coming out of the club, Ray and Sam lean on each other. Both their cars are parked in the alley. Wet pavement, cats scratch to fuck each other, rats

129

eat out of garbage cans. The two brothers sing, "Let's stay together! Loving you wherever! Any kind of weather! Let's stay together! Ahhhh, baby!"

Ray gets to his Mustang and pats his pockets. "Shit! I forgot my keys."

"You left them on the bar."

Ray turns away. "I be right back!"

Sam walks across the alley to his car, pulling out his keys.

"Hey! American!"

Sam wavers up off the side of his car. "Huh?"

Two shadow men come from under the stage door light of the club door. One has a switchblade, the other a club.

He pulls his out, pops the button. Ducks from the fists and blade. Round house kicks one of them in the stomach. Stumbles. Runs down the alley.

They tackle him.

One head butts him.

The other uses his weight to pins his arms. "Craze *djol*!"

Sam spits back. "Fuck you!"

Blows come up in his stomach and face. Club door lights. He twists. Gunshots ring. Lights swing out. His journey, his spirit becomes a veil of darkness.

• • •

Lemon flavored gas wakes him.

Is he in the rice paddies? Fingers, bandages on his right arm. Headache circling his eyeballs. In a warehouse? Smoke, flames, babies crying. Water up to his knees. Licks his lips, reaches down. Presses a button.

VOICES:

    Doctor Kelly to O.R!

Five minutes go by.

    Doctor Kelly to O.R!

Two minutes go by.

    Chief Davis call the operator!

    Chief Davis call the operator!

Three minutes go by.

    Maintenance to Emergency!

    Maintenance to Emergency!

Sam presses the button again.

    Nurse Green to Room 2291!

    Nurse Green to Room 2291!

One minute goes by.

A flaxen-redhaired nurse comes in. Grey eyes, half black and white cat woman with a smile. She touches his forehead, pulls the covers down, takes his pulse. "If the nasty talkin' Sam Murphy hasn't risen from his grave." Puts the covers back up to his chest. "Your fever has come down." She checks his chart, writes in something, and sticks the pen in her hair that's up in a bun. "Now, Mr. Murphy, what can I get you?" Both hands stuck on her hips.

He feels his rib muscles tighten with the pain in his head. "Just aspirin and water."

"I got something better than that, a shot of Demerol. Now this will help you sleep good." A needle appears in her fingers. She feels for his hip and sticks it right in the upper butt area.

Wincing with the squeeze of the sheets balled in his fist. "Uhhhhh! I hope you a good shooter." A tear trickles from the corner of his right eye. "Feel like a mule kicked me."

"No. A six-inch blade kicked you in the side." She sticks a straw in his mouth. "Here's your water." She wipes his lips. "Slow… slow."

He stops. "What day is it?" He looks around at the antiseptic light blue room, window out to the sky, an IV and a vase of roses.

"Monday." She rolls the sheets back up to his chest again. "Now you sleep… That painkiller will take care of you for awhile." She wraps up the needle, sticks his chart back at the end of his bed.

He watches her leave. The door closes. He feels the pain slowly swim from his head and side. But his vision blurs with the white blue lights of the room. He feels his hearing deaden as his day eases off.

• • •

Land of Day, Night of a Boy:

A clapboard, small brick house between other small brick houses… opens its doors to a family of children and women, sitting, talking through a small black-and-white TV. A room brings a family together in the middle of the day, under a sky full of trees and planes… circling, circling. Sirens ring. Lights roll around in the neighborhood. People gather to watch two men fight. Black soup bone heads sparkle the day. The circle surrounds him of aunts, cousins, mother, grandmother, grandfathers, father, brother. Oxtail people soak up the sun… dance, clap, fight in a circle. A wedding of people strut down the street. All take part, drift in the dust bowl winds. Eat, cry, die, go to funerals. Love, have babies, fight, die, cry, see each other shiver in the cold. Cold, blue, mouths chat in the dust, the sun, the winds. All laugh. Whip and spank each other's kids. Lie, cheat, steal, beg under the shadows of the night. Church on Sunday, Monday. Bridge on Tuesday, bingo on Wednesday, fish fry on Thursday, get drunk and pay on Friday. All eat hot dogs and beans on a Saturday. Love on a Sunday with the devil man behind you. Hide your sins away. See the reverend scoot over your grandmother's body. Pray, beg God to take her, him, them. Pray God to take everybody this day. Play the ball game with your little friends. Swing! Swing! Through a thousand dreams in a day.

In a wallflower-papered room he looks at his mother, in a rocking chair by a window. White, blue crystal snow falls. Green, white colors as she shivers in a room with no heat. No food. A baby wrapped. His brother, about seven or eight, bounces a red, white, blue ball over the couch, not paying attention to the mother or the baby. But he just keeps bouncing, skipping after the ball.

No others around.

Sam tries to go to her, but his feet won't move. He can only watch another man, his father, come in the room. They kiss. Hug. Laugh, play with the baby by the snow-filled picture window. His brother keeps bouncing the ball. His mother pulls out her breast, feeds it to the child. Sam can only watch, from an invisible clear wall. His feet still don't move. He watches his father reach in his long, grey wool coat. Buttons open as a knife emerges. He starts to stab her in the face, neck, arms, chest. But he keeps saying,

"I love you! I love you!" No blood comes forth. Sam keeps banging on the clear window, until the mother, the brother, the baby are silenced by the father with the knife.

No others around.

His hands scratch, fall to his side as his screams are unheard. He watches this man, his father, button back his coat and leave out the cold snow room. He drops to his knees begging God for mercy. Begging God to spare his brother, his mother, the baby's life. He stares at the bodies. He looks at the horror of losing his family in the cold snow-room.

14

Tuesday morning, 10 a.m.

Ray comes in with some magazines under his arm. "Hey, man, how you feeling?"

All Sam wanted to know, "Did you get the bastards?" Pushes up from the bed.

Ray laid the magazines on Sam's stomach. "One. " Stuck a finger up. "The other got away. "Ray wanted to hug him, but he knew from being stuck himself that Sam didn't want no pawing over him. "I'm glad to see you up."

Sam plays it off. "This?" He looks at the IV. "Just a little stiff in the side."

"They were Haitian," Ray says. "Um! Somebody's in love with that woman to send two top-ranking military men to do a job on you."

"Yeah. Born and trained in the good ol' USA." Sam looks at the magazines. Browses over *Playboy*, *Players*, *Ebony*, *Jet*, *Sports Illustrated* swimsuit edition 1984, the *Post*, and *Washington Times*.

Ray looks for the pitcher of water. "You want some?"

"Yeah. The Demerol can make your throat dry."

He sticks the straw in his mouth. Sam sucks, pulls back. "Thanks."

"You know that was a warning?" Ray reminds him. "And they got diplomatic immunity." He looks at him to see if he was getting the picture yet.

"So?"

Frustrated, he gets out the chair. "They not getting locked up."

Sam opens up the *Jet*. "I know that."

He points down at him. "You need to rethink your priorities, man."

"I need to take my truck through the front door. of the embassy." He peeks at the centerfold, five- six from Arkansas. She likes to swim and dance.

Ray rubs his eyes. He's sleepy and tired of talking to his brother already, but damn glad he's alive. "Well, I see you feeling better again." He winks. "Let me get home and get some sleep. Mabel and Pete and the rest of the gang be by here later."

The nurse comes in with a tray of needles. Ray says, "I see it's time for you to bend over."

"Nurse Green, this is my brother Ray."

"Good morning, Mr. Murphy. You want a shot too?"

He looks at the clean silver needles. "Noooo! I had enough of that... Time for me to leave." He walks bacwards to the door. "See you later."

Sam uses his right hand to push up the gown. "Okay. Thanks for the magazines."

Ray smiles. "Give him two shots." He goes out the door.

Sam watches her concentrate on the milligrams of dope. Small dosages of Demerol drain up in the needle.

"You ready, Mr. Murphy?"

"As always." He turns on his side, grits his teeth from the bite of the needle. "Uhh!"

She pulls it from his hip and wipes it down with an alcohol pad. "There!" She lays the sheets back over him. "You have a lot of friends."

Rests his head back. "Why you say that?"

"The phone's been ringing for you since you been here. " She gives him some sips of apple juice, lets him finish his fill. "Especially women."

He watches her face darken with this statement. "You jealous?"

"Go to sleep." She turns around, straightens up the magazines. "You want to see the game?" Crosses her arms over a man with a hard rock face and soft caring brown eyes.

He sticks an arm behind his head. "Yeah, sure."

She picks up the remote, pushes the button. "Yuk! Baseball."

"You not a fan, huh?"

"I'm into basketball… "

"Knicks?"

"I'm a Laker girl."

"You look like one too," he says.

The blush comes over the freckled cheeks. A piece of hair falls down her neck from under the duckbill white cap. "I see you later. " Picks up the tray in her hand.

"For another shot?"

"No! For some of my favorite split pea soup." She leaves the room with a nice perfume smell following behind.

Sam closes his eyes to drift under the voice of the announcer leaving Cal Ripken on first base.

• • •

Demerol Devils at your feet:

Driving on Main Street the steering wheel taking him wherever he wants to go, Sam's mind is just speeding, like a racoon looking for a wet log, to familiar streets in Sweet Loaf. Places long dead, reconstructed into another hamburger joint, now lay in the path of homes he was once born around. Familiar dead faces of Miss Jones across the street, selling liquor to tired, old, runaway, train men, hiding from their wives and children. Drunken Mr. Bobby Lee sleeps on someone's steps for the night. Mrs. Makepeace tells everyone's business she can. Starburst fruit faces with open mouths. People point right at him in his old red truck. Children from six to eleven jump on the flat, raggedy wood back for a free-wheeling fun ride, down Vessup Place, around the corner to Jefferson Avenue, where they shot Frank Taylor just the other night. He is shocked to see his first sweetheart, Freda Pearl. The fourteen-year-old, four-eyed gal, with a big butt and size two waist, stands in front of Mr. Saperstein's grocery store. She throws him a kiss, turns her back on him, pulls up her dress and pats her ass at him, and runs in the store. She always was a tease, never gave him none. The truck takes him by lions, tigers, bears into some ghetto ruins of the Wizard of Oz. Ridiculous, grinning Black men with humps in their backs, Steppin' Fetchit style in butler suits. He tries to get to the edge of Sweet Loaf, an invisible line between Jordan, Hollis, Cambridge, Annapolis and Washington, D.C., but El, Zorro just stalls and goes into reverse.

Mabel is on Zane Grey Street at the bus stop. He stops, pulls over, and opens the door. She doesn't say anything, just treats him like a bug that should have been stepped on a long time ago.

"Fuck you, bitch!" He closes the door and shifts into second, until he reaches another bus stop on Henry Miller Drive.

Loretta Stevens is standing reading a *Jive* magazine. Old girlfriend, she was a stoic, sophisticated schoolteacher, a bisexual whore from the underworld, a doctor's daughter that would give you bed lice in a minute if you touched her. She wants to get in but he hits the locks on the door. "Sam, you a son of a bitch!"

He drives on till he finds Richard Wright's Garden Apartments. He spots Madge Johnson. She's a lovely black woman with East African features, high cheekbones, the Grace Jones look. He left her knocked up in San Francisco before he jumped off to Vietnam. A purse on her shoulder, she smiles. "Hey, Sam! Come on, give me a lift!"

He opens up. She pulls a gun out of the purse and starts firing. "I told your baby you was dead. Now, mutherfucker, I'm going to make that true!"

He ducks and steps on the gas pedal, speeding past the murderous woman. On Paradiso Street he slows down to the edge of a corner house. On the porch he sees Jeanette McKinna in a chair, rocking. He robbed her of her heart, her dignity, destroyed them in a rain storm. Brown, pine cone hair rolling down both sides of her face, she's crying, babbling something from her mouth. In her jeans pocket, she takes out a knife. She starts to slit her left wrist over and over again. He starts to cry as he drives off the street. She was a church girl with church parents who protected her from men like him.

He went to the Lord's House to get her, find her, knock that holy sanctity shit out of her. He had her hollering the first night. And it wasn't God she was hollering to. She was crying, pleading for him to do it to her again. She would come to his door at all hours of the night, crying for him to do it to her again... from the back, always from the back... on her knees, always on her knees. But her mouth was always on God. He said this. He said that. She chastised him for smoking, drinking, but he didn't want to hear her silky speech on this psalm or this verse. King David, my ass. He kicked her out of his apartment in a cool wet night, butt naked... shamed her. He had enough of her. He said to her, "B. B. King is God, and baby, the thrill is gone!" When he was putting her out, she went in the kitchen for a knife to stab him. He had to watch them church girls after that rainy night in Sweet Loaf.

Sam's truck took him down Girard Street, Fourteenth and Vanity Avenue, Tenth and D., Buchanan Road and the back end of Melville Place. Then back to a one-way street of rice fields with a street sign blinking off and on, Poe Avenue. Familiar noises of men hollering, mortar shells going off around him. Sunken faces of Vietnamese children begging to go to America. America! America! He sighs, looks away from their rice cake tan faces. Watches men in a flank spread out in the wet fields, shifting for better cover from the air. "Charlie up the right flank! Charlie up the right flank! Captain Savage, I can't get through to D Troop! I can't get through to D Troop!" Corporal Price was the radio man, good friend from New Jersey, had the receiver at his ear, M-16 in his left hand. Ten men duck crawl behind water buffaloes and tall grasses of wheat, water up to your chest. Rounds go off! Rounds go off! Sam buries his head behind his steering wheel, watching his buddies die in the sun.

He is in the village of Phu Bai, one hundred miles from Hell. No way in, no way out. His wife Luc Tran is kneeling, giving their son sweet milk from her breast, then places the baby on the mat. Blesses the bowls of rice, prayers from a soft flower woman. Long hair down her back, a face that showed love for him, the baby, her people. In this village her family rest, work, sleep, pray over the rice fields. Pray for the war to stop, pray for their children to sleep in peace. She waits. She waits for him like so many others.

The baby pulls at the sweet sugar apple nipples.

Viet Cong come. Roust the old people, split their heads one at a time with rocks, knives. He tries again to get out of the truck. He kicks the windows. He kicks and kicks. But the truck windows will not smash open. His wife kneels under the feet of the men with rifles. She keeps her head down. Nestling the baby gently as the men speak to her. Drag her by her hair and take the baby from her. She pleads to them. She begs. Opens her jacket, lets them see her

141

body under the sun. They rip at her clothes. Sucking, digging. Strangling her and the baby with fishing net when they had a full drink of her.

Sam's stomach meets his throat.

El, Zorro takes him from the village.

· · ·

1:30 pm. Visiting hours.

"Petey Pete!" Sam smiles up in the thin face of his partner. "Mutherfucker, don't bring no flowers in here. I ain't dead yet." Slaps him five. "And none of that bullshitting poetry either."

Pete grins. "They couldn't kill your hard rock ass anyway." Lifts up a box from behind his back. "Try these on."

"A gift?" He takes the ribbon from the gold box. "Pajamas!"

He sits down. "We all pitched in and bought you some nice silk ones."

Sam rubs some sleep from his eyes. "You tell the gang thanks for me."

"They will be here… We just trying to let you get your rest for now." Pete looks him over, unshaven, grey black face. His face is sort of stiff, not much emotion or juice coming from his lips. Cracked paper tiger man. He keeps a strong appearance, brave brother after losing a couple of pints of blood. "You know who they were?"

Sam winces. "Yeah. The guards from the embassy." He gets his cup of water. It's empty. Pete grabs the pitcher for him, pours. "Thirsty a lot, huh?"

He sips, nods. "It's the Demerol. Whew!" Sips again. "It's a hell of a drug." Pulls his right leg up, moves his arm some with the IV in it. "I'm having a bunch of crazy dreams with it too."

Pete leans forward. "I guess it's just part of the healing process."

Sam looks up at the globe light over his head. "Get a note to her." He puts the cup on the side table, and stares at Pete to see some hesitation in his eyes. "Just take some of that glue to her." Licks his lips. Closes, opens his eyes. "Okay?"

Pete pats his hand. "Okay, Sam."

"Thanks, man." Sam asks, "Who's driving my truck?"

"Nobody."

"Nobody?"

"That's what I said… Uh, Mike said we wait for you to get back." Pete rubs the back of his neck. "They might as well give it to you… Nobody else can drive it anyway." He grins. "The clutch sticks, the radio cracks, it smells up the street with exhaust fumes… Lucky you haven't got a ticket yet, and the windshield wiper blades don't come on."

"That's strange." Sam frowns. "That don't happen when I drive it."

He agrees. "I know."

Sam scratches his neck. "Who you driving with, Pete?"

"Bob Seal."

"Ohhhh! How he treatin' you?"

"Betta than you… you cheap mutherfucker!"

"Haaa haaaa," Sam says. "No kiddin."

"Shiiiiit, man, but I'm waiting for you to get back." Pete glances down towards his ribs. "When will that be, Sam?"

"I'll be ready in September." He sings, "On the road again…"

"I'll be waiting for you."

"Good, because we got some business to take care of." Sam yawns. He blinks up at the globe light that looks like a space ship over his head, buzzing. "Pete, I think about her most the time in this condition. " He licks his bottom lip. "If it wasn't for them pain killers, she would be the only thing." He gets mad, clutches the steel bedframe with his hand. "Sons of bitches!"

"Take it easy, Sam." Pats his shoulder. "We'll get her." Watches a tear swell up in his eye, grabs some tissues, hands them to him. "Just take it easy and enjoy those blue silk pajamas."

He rubs his eyes and lays his head back. "I will, buddy." Sam asks, "Now how about some of that shitty poetry?"

Pete reaches in his back pocket, unfolds a piece of paper. "Okay, okay, Sam."

• • •

Myrthe stands at the rose bushes, pruning, thinking of the tall man with the eyes that make her want to live again. This man has the face of a falcon and nose of a baby deer. She wipes a tear from her cheek when the sun comes out, unclogging the day of ten in the morning. Her hours are full with the other women in the house, their children, with the chores of cooking Haitian meals: *Konsomin, Bouillon pied boeuf, Diri ak poua Kongo, Gombo kala lou ak aran sel, Tasso Kabrit, Griot ak banan 'peze', poisson frit, salaise aran so',* and *Pin patat.* One day she will cook for him. One day she will make love to him… kiss him, bathe him, serve him beer. Watch American football with him. One day, one day. She just keeps clipping the branches from the bushes, waiting, watching all sorts of cars go by. She thinks she hears the motor of a truck, a truck like Sam's? It's green. But this man comes out… his friend, the thin man, carrying a can of glue to her.

"Ummm! Um, excuse me, ma'am… "

"I didn't call for any more glue… " She closes the clippers. "Where is Sam?"

"Myrthe," he puts the can down, "Sam is in the hospital."

She drops the clippers as a gloved hand comes over her mouth.

"He's okay." He lifts up the can. "I have a note for you." It's rolled up like a receipt. He hands it to her, pulls a pencil from behind his ear. "Just sign."

A guard is coming their way. She signs, then gets the can from him and the note in her hand.

He walks away from the woman standing by the rose bushes in a large straw hat. The guard and the dog pace behind him to make sure he gets in the truck. "Come on, let's go before we get shot."

Bob Seal drives off.

15

In her Keeping Room Myrthe kneels by her bedside, note in hand of Sam's. Unable to see from the tears in her eyes. The white magnolia hues of her bedroom splash cool sun across the pictures of her mother, two brothers on the table. Blessed Mother Mary statue is beside this picture frame. She reads it again to feel his words relieve her from her prison room.

Dear Myrthe,

From the mountains of Kenskoff you appeared. Sweet Jesus have given us time to reflect, to wash ourselves under the white moonlight. Dear, dear Myrthe, don't worry about me. I'm okay! Just a little scratch from the Colonel's cats. You just believe... I will be there. I will be there.

Love, Sam.

She folds the note. Bastard! Bastard! Sticks it under her bed mattress. She looks at the statue of Mary... chipped face of the mother. She feels scared, dead, robbed of a man's love, his touch. Untouched, robbed, raped by another, isolated in a birdcage thousands of miles from home. Home, she remembers the flowers from her mother's garden, her father riding on the donkey to school in the morning, her brothers playing with sticks and cans. But men in dark glasses shattered her world under the mountains. She digs under the bed for the note. She sticks it down her bust. He will find it there too. No place to hide from this man. Bastard! Bastard! She gets on her knees, grabs the statue in her hands, looks at the chipped face that has been through so much. So much as a reflection of hurricanes, earthquakes, hunger, beatings, rapings, murder, love, graves. Ceremonies of dark strangers dancing in the woods. To come to America! Come to America as a caged bird, to be let out to fly, play with children, talk to people. To read English, French, Creole, Spanish. To speak, from unknown tongues. To taste snow from New York, rain from Paris, feel the winds of Washington shape and shift leaves into a circle. Her head spins, spins as a little girl taken away from home. Maybe never, ever see the mountains of Kenskoff. Maybe never, ever, see the grave of her mother again. Bastard! Bastard! Her pharaoh keeps her under him. To serve him from a shutter room of wicker, French doors, grey-pink walls. Brass hood on granite fireplaces around the world. A foyer of smart-rich evil people from the seven-foot-wide entry hallways. She strolls the full length of mansion estates, serving him her breasts, her stomach, her thighs. She kisses the chipped porcelain face of Mother Mary, rubs her face against the cold face of Mother Mary. Crawls up on her bed in her Keeping Room and imagines Sam lying beside her under the whirlpool etched tray ceiling. She places the statue down on the table, rubs at the tears from her eyes. Bastard! Bastard! She turns over on her stomach to go to sleep.

Myrthe awakes with her familiar headache whenever she takes a nap. Her head throbs with thumbnail shots of pain in her right temple. Suspended, dress down, stiff neck, a growling belly. Sighs of relief, evening shadows of gold come from her closed shutters. Passes a hand over her face and eyes from the light turning into darkness, focuses on wall pictures of faces of the Haitian men working in the fields. Colorful red, yellow, brown, black men are bending over in the sugarcane fields, machete in hand. Her back feels like their backs. Wet between her legs. She opens up. Sticky, stale, day-old smells of moist bread. Her time has come. Her time has come. She leans up, stares at the pink bedspread. Blood under her ass. "Nooo!"

She gets up for the door, hollers at the top of the stairs for a woman-friend. She leans over the winding banisters and listens for mother-friend's voice. "Mrs. Prosper! Mrs. Prosper!"

A sweet, caring voice comes up the stairs. "Myrthe, coming!"

She goes back to her room, starts to pulling the sheets off the bed. Cussing under her tongue this deep sleep that has her period coming before its time. Her man is in the hospital, hurt. She tears the sweaty pillowcases off, flings everything to the floor. Stomping, stepping on the sheets in the corner by the closet door. Mad, ashamed of the cleansing, unexpected messy cleansing of the day in her deep, deep, sleep.

"Myrthe, what's wrong?" Mrs. Prosper comes in the door, worried as she stands watching her friend kicking, slapping the sheets. "What's wrong?"

She stops, and starts to cry in the middle of the bloody pile of sheets. Mrs. Prosper goes to calm her. "Shhhh, child... shhh!"

Myrthe uncontrollably pleads to her. "He must... he must die!" Squeezes her hand.

Mrs. Prosper pulls her hand away. "Who, Myrthe?"

"You know! You know!"

Mrs. Prosper looks in the wet eyes. "I know." Hugs her.

Myrthe chokes on the question for help. "Mrs. Prosper, how long?"

She tells her with conviction, "Not long... not long, Myrthe."

She shakes with chills. "Uh, something he could drink... something he likes to drink."

"I am his cook... He trusts me... I will handle this."

She becomes hesitant, but asks, "By... by September?"

Mrs. Prosper thinks. "The moon is full then. It is a dragon... waving its tail as quick as a flash over the earth's ash."

Myrthe rubs her brow. "It is read that the God Lekba will open the gates for the colonel to come."

Mrs. Prosper reaches out, touches the tears from her face. "Yes. He treats our songbird very badly. Yes... this shall be done." Crosses her hand over her heart. "But you must pray... You must pray every day to our Lord's mother."

She glances at the statue on the table. "Yes. I will… I will."

· · ·

Trees glisten over a triangle edge. In the middle of sun, of leaves, military men march in different colored uniforms with flags of many nations. Men come from many lands, books, maps, charts under their arms. Languages are spoken under hushed tones from Peru, Mexico, Saudi Arabia, Mozambique, Somalia, Nigeria, Senegal, Brazil, United States, France, and Spain. They are men in pressed khakis, pressed faces, pressed lips, no smiles. They run, walk, march into ivy-covered, two-storied buildings made of bricks, with white window ledges. Old cannons sit, musket balls frozen on the ground from past revolutions, past battles, won and lost in the fields. Men ghosts walk these green lawns, these sacred hollow grounds of war, not peace… death, not living. Soldiers walk now under the flag of liberty on how to do battle for the modern ages, battle that will continue to kill, cripple, and win or lose in the fields of blood… win or lose for whatever cause you deem, upon the heads of children.

Building #37:

Colonel Labossier sits at a desk, listening, engulfed in a stimulating, analytical seminar by driven men. A West Point graduate himself, the speaker's thesis was on "The Effects of Oppression in Emerging Third World Countries." The Colonel is interested in education and chaos… selective, defensive strategies to control the poor populace that wants simple things,

150

like freedom and democracy. He takes notes from Professor Ryder of the Army War College.

The paunchy, silver-bearded man bangs his thin baton on the blackboard at the words:

ACCESS
DEFENSE STYLES
INTEGRATIVE
BIOCHEMICAL
REVIEW
INTELLIGENCE
EXPERIENTIAL FACTORS
CAUSALLY LINKED

"Infiltration of political groups are maintained in three particular cell functions... one, contact; two, community; and three, information." He writes these three words on the board. "It is imperative that you men undergo a covert transformation of getting rid of the past. Cut the heads off anything or anyone that could hurt your future, which is what we are really talking about when it comes to winning against the battalions of socialism. Transformation comes from here," he points to his head. "Sources of comfort... friends, family, wives, girlfriends, trinkets of pictures, old relics of baseball gloves, model toys... must lose their hold on you. Nothing, once you are set up in another region of a country, should have any value, but the new. Your past is erased. Erased! You are apart, but not apart. You are wandering, trying to find answers. Gather intelligence. Intelligence!" He snaps the baton at this word on the board. He loosens his tie, and glares at the faces of the soldiers. "Gentlemen! Newman in nineteen eighty used the term *disinhibition* to refer to behavioral syndromes of impulsiveness, psychopathy, adolescent antisocial behavior, which is modified by differential experiences... Behavioral changes can and will affect all of you. Some of you will be lost in these groups. Some of you will come out okay... Those are the ones that will bring back the prize... and that prize, gentlemen, is intelligence... Yes, Captain Cruz?" He points at the thick-gaunt face of the officer from Peru.

The man's English is slow, third-gradish. "Doctor Ryda... dese are *problemos* in my country... by the Merilitos from the mountains. It is dangerous... to get close to dem."

The speaker squints to decipher the English. "Uhhh, yes. Dangerous and difficult, yes." He says, "Men, you must remember that patience will bring in this information. Infiltration into a single particular group cell could take many years. Covert operations into close familiar settings require a steady dose of training. That's why we have you men all here in the United States... to learn body mannerisms, dialect, cultural awareness, adaptability, and a love for the evolutionary process. In the sixties, our law enforcement agencies went undercover into many Liberation groups. A bunch of the groups were just harmless fraternities, but a few were very, very menacing. Now, from that experience we shall teach you to open the door to the psychopathy of our target groups and their leaders... such as the Merilitos." He scratches his nose. "We will use private voluntary organizations as a key to entering the door to such groups in your countries." He writes out on the board: "Interpeace Health Organization."

Colonel Labossier yawns, and drifts over the purple dry lips and words of this man, and his other tasks for the day. A meeting at the White House, a Congressional drink at the Capitol, meet the envoy Georges Oliphant from Belgium, write a letter home to his wife JouJou, send off the Barbie doll to his little girl Mercedes, read more lesson plans on the psychology of priests and the role they play in government. Then later he will enjoy a drink of red wine and paté with other officers: Colonel Benezar of Chile, Captain Z from Nigeria, Major Raman Abdul, the Saudi prince, Captain Bastillo, head of the Security Police of Panama, and Mr. Henry Thompson from McLean, Virginia, his U.S. liaison who brought him to Washington, D.C. for these exercises.

By twelve p.m., he will be finished with the day. Fifteen minutes pass, and he will be finished with her. He has lessons to teach, lessons that will make her hear the bells of the night, lessons that will be etched in her mind to never see this man again. He has lessons for both of them... and for his countrymen, for his wife and child. His truth is on the blackboard... his purple dialect, prose of torture, fear... have you twist in a chair... make you shout to your Catholic God for redemption. His truth is to look into your heart and see your pain, your hunger, your emptiness. Listen to the wind, the birds, the trees that break from a strong wind. Listen to him, listen to him. The pencil snaps in his fingers.

•   •   •

Second week in May a gathering occurrs:
Crisp, clean women sit around on stools in the kitchen of the embassy, frying plantains, baking pork

153

griot. Mrs. Prosper, Myrthe and Evaline's hands move over the papaya and orange peels, smooth over a dessert for the colonel. They play records from home, singing, humming, as they peel off potatoes and yams in a large silver bowl. A song from home has lyrics that narrow the time between a man and a woman, by Gerard Duperville. The words of a sweet tongue Haitian man sing out Choubouloute!:

Mrs. Prosper smiles into the clear brown eyes of Myrthe after they finish singing one of their songs from home. She had once been in love. She had once felt the tug of refrain from another man she wanted so very, very much. But suffering over the past isn't good. It can make you have a heart that breaks into a thousand pieces of stone. She doesn't think Myrthe, her friend, would survive. This sugar-brown Haitian woman is pretty, a delicate cinnamon rose. She comes from good parents of the mountains. It's up to her to see this lovely young woman pass on to a good man.

She takes a small knife and starts to shave her fingernails off into the papaya and orange peels. "If Napoleon could go this way, well, then, now surely our dear, dear Colonel can meet up with the Little Emperor one day."

16

Hymns, songs, chants, chimes and visitors awaken Sam back to health. Mix that up with drinking Nurse Green's fine pea soup, and you got crazy-ass Sam Murphy… up joking, pinching and kicking. Shit! Less Demerol and less valium in week three of your stay at Sweet Loaf Park City Hospital. He uses some hand weights Posie brought by to get his wrists stronger. Next, to get up. Up! Walk around on crutches. He will have Nurse Green give him the guided tour of the hospital physical therapy unit. He wiggles his toes underneath the sheets. Flowers spray his room from old girlfriends who want to see him dead, but they just aren't ready for him to go yet… not yet. Hell, he loved them all. He thinks International Woman's Day in March is a day made just for him. He chews on a toothpick. IV is out of his arm. He's ready for meat and potatoes now, food for a hardworking man that throws eighty-eight-pound rugs over his shoulder and goes up five flights of stairs. The wound is healing fine. The bow-legged doctor with a gunslinger's face, Doc Wyatt, told him he can leave here by next week. But he will have to stay away from work another two weeks and then take it slow after that. And Sam is ready to do what he has to do. He's ready to listen, wait, learn, plan... wait for the moment to take his Myrthe from the embassy gates. He yawns, bored, and feels the strength coming back in his long root legs. He handles a lot of weight from the rugs on his legs, they are his moneymaker. He slaps his thighs, slowly touches the bandage at his left side. "Um." He takes a deep breath, rests his head back on the pillows, twists the toothpick over and under his tongue. It helps him think. Cool, cool.

A knock at the door, it's probably Ray. "Come in." He sits up.

·　·　·

A visit from the Gargoyle:

"Hi, Dad." Sam is shocked as the old man tips on his cane. "Chair right in front of you."

His father hits it, pulls it back, and sits down. "I heard you was in the hospital... so I come by to see you." His long nails curl down. "That pussy going to kill you yet!"

Sam watches the wings, skinny arms of his father rest over the back of the chair. "Dad, why you here?" He picks up a *Time* magazine. "I'm in no condition for that."

The blind man's voice sprays the smell of liquor. "I'm not here to gloat. I could do that at home in my underwear." He picks his nose. "A blind man can see you in no condition."

Sam rolls his eyes. "What do you want, Pop?" He closes the magazine up.

A stupid grin comes under his dark glasses. He searches the room for the answer. "I want to see my angry, angry son."

"Out," Sam moves his legs up, "of love?"

His long ears flap. "Yes!...out of love." He leans forward on his cane. "I once told your momma that you was strong... that you just may reach fifty one of these days."

"What," Sam asks as some pain shoots through his side, "she say?"

A faint smile comes to his lips as he thinks about his wife. "She told me I was drunk, and go back to sleep."

"Ha ha ha! that sounds like Mom." He watches his blind father sit in the chair quietly. A hairy, brown, baggy sweater wraps around his small frame; turned-over pair of penny loafers. His face has a three-day beard of white coarse hair sprout from dark brown cheeks. Huge floppy ears, wings jut out from a pale dying coarse skin. He's shedding over the poor quality of a red hospital brick tile floor. Shedding his skin, his last dying words, his voice comes to a quiet boom of warning and caring doom to a son who is trying to heal, trying to pray in the silence of a room of flowers.

The hospital paging system rings through the room: "Nurse Key to Respiratory! Nurse Key to Respiratory!"

"So, how you healing?"

"I'm all right, Dad… I be out of here in another week."

"You lucky," his wings stretch, "you know that?"

"Dad," Sam looks from the gargoyle, "I live another day."

" You," he shakes his ears. "simple, and I'm going senile." He points at him. "My daddy once told me… you might have a college degree… you might have a Ph.D., but if you don't have common sense you ain't got shit!" fire spits. "Son, you got a death wish."

"Since I came out of the jungles of Vietnam… I had a death wish. Ain't nothin' new to me or thousands of other dudes out here walking the streets."

"What you looking for in the streets?"

"Peace, man, that's all."

"This woman is the answer?"

"You know about that," Sam scratch his brow, " huh?"

He sniffs, digs out a handkerchief from his back pocket. "I talks to your brother." He wipes his nose, and blows flames. "Awwww!"

"Ray talks too much."

"He always care about you."

"He's my other daddy!"

"He loves you, you know dat."

Sam doesn't want another man in his business. "Pop, I think it's time for you to go."

"Kick me out," his iguana eyes and long claws face Sam, "that's good, boy! You don't sound like you going to die to me." He gets smart. "That's good. You still can kick a blind man's ass!" He shakes a finger at him. "Just the other day, I heard two boys playing under my window. They were playing the way

158

you and your brother use to play with balls, sticks, broken toys from Christmas. You know that's an age when you haven't had a taste... not even on your mind. Don't even know what it is yet." Nods, crosses his legs. "But you grow up, get that first taste of a woman, and nobody can talk to you after that."

Sam says, "But that's a good taste."

His father's long tongue slashes out. "Um, um!" adjusts dark eyeglasses on his nose. "It's not funny."

"I know it's not," Sam says to him. "I've tasted flavors all over this world... but this is one flavor that makes me... makes me want to stick with it." He looks at the flowers, the jug of water, the magazines, the old gargoyle with the cane. "Now, if me and her ever get the chance to get together... you better believe my playing days are over."

"Well, she must be something... because you gave that Mabel up to your brother." Scratches his nose. "You boys acting like you living in some Greek tragedy... or is this something for the Oprah Winfrey Show?" Shakes his head. "Goddamn!"

"You always were good at pushing buttons... You good at that, if nothing else." Sam rises up on his pillows. He's ready to push the button to get him out of his room. He closes his eyes for a second. "Dad, why don't you go home and listen to the baseball game. The O's are losing, as usual."

"I ought to slap you with my cane. I tell you what... look around you. This woman got your ass in this bed." He twitches his left cheek. "You got my sympathy." Tips his head. "I admit we don't get along. But you still going to listen to me. Love can be bad for you too." He feels the sun on his face. "Once it's all said and done… we all in some kind of conspiracy to do harm to each other. We all got the cough! Spitting up shit to deal with one another… I know you ain't coming to my funeral… That's all right. But you going to remember what I taught you about dealing out here. I want you to understand the risks… the rewards, of getting the woman you want. You think!… You think that once you got her, it's going to make your headache go away. But son, you just replacing one headache with another."

"And that's what you think about love, right Pop?" Sam smiles away. "And I guess I got that from you." Rubs his fingers over his lips. "No wonder I'm fucked up!" He pours some water from the pitcher. "Dad, Myrthe's the headache I want." He chews on some ice.

"You betta take a good pill for it." He gets up. "Just remember what I tell you, Sam. It's good to be alive."

"Pop, you a fucking coward," Sam tells him. "Now get the fuck out of here!"

He rolls back the chair from his way, and straightens up with a smug grin on his lips. "Don't sound like you ready to die, to me boy. Looks like you going to be at my funeral first! Ha ha ha!" He taps the cane towards the door. He goes out whistling a tune from the movie, *The Sound of Music.*

Jim Murphy wants his son to live. He taps on down the hall, ears pitched for the sound of the elevator. Tick, tap, raps his cane from side to side. He did what he had to do. Upset him, make sure the fight is in him to live, not die in some hospital bed. Yeah, he did what he had to do. He keeps on down the hall towards the tingling quick sound for the elevator bell.

He makes a sharp right. Tick, tap, rap. A sharp, soft voice asks him, "Lobby, sir?"

"Yes, lobby... thank you." He stands and waits.

•   •   •

"In Guatemala, we use electric cattle prods to keep our students in line, provided by the U.S. government." He leans on his elbows, stares across the table at Colonel Labossier.

"Ahaaa! Cattle prods are too delicate a method, Major Berrios." He pats Myrthe's red-nailed fingers besides his at the lace cloth table, but he doesn't look at her. "We just pull them from their homes, day or night, and shoot them in front of their weeping mothers," he tries to win this debate on keeping the populace in line, "with weapons provided by Uncle Sam." He nods with triumph, and cuts into his stuffed potato and chives.

Myrthe eats slowly. In a voice of schoolgirl charm and amenity, she whispers to a skinny, size two, terrorized Mrs. Berrios, a bleached blonde with light green eyes that never move from her third glass of wine. She's the toy wife of a blood-sucking modern-day vampire, a chicken-eating husband three times her senior. The devils are at the dinner table.

"The major looks very well this evening."

"He is a jack rabbit that dodges bad health very well, Myrthe." She gives a smile around the other seven guests at the long table of gold candles, foods and flowers, a table of officers, businessmen, the Congress and international arms dealers. There's a woman on each man's arm, bought, stolen, and bartered, as a prize of peace for a job well done in crushing your enemies, and to enjoy the ambience of a good meal of expensive wine, bread, and cheese. She dabs her small red lips. "At Gstaad they have herbal remedies you take that will send you to the bathroom five times a day."

"Sounds like an exhausting regimen for good health."

"Yes. You must pay a dear, dear price if you want to stay alive for many years." She sips then uses a spoon to tap the side of her glass for the tall, grey waiter to serve her more.

He slides down from the corner of the door with the bottle in his gloved hand. She lifts her glass. He pours.

Myrthe is gracious in asking, after he returns to his corner, "Have you found the Swiss to be leaders in this field of herbal nutrition?" She feels the colonel's sticky, long, black fingers roaming over her knee, his steely fingers patting up her thighs. She dares not move. She dares not act out of sorts.

Mrs. Berrios' eyes fill with delight as she becomes in tune with this question. "The Dutch are also one of the leaders in this field of herbology. There is a doctor in Copenhagen... Um, I believe his—" She clutches her glass, and sips quickly, "... I believe his name is Dr. Hans Haaj in Copenhagen, who is crowned the best in the field of eating for life."

Major Berrios sits back to have more wine for his glass. "We do not bend to the demands of students the way some other countries do." He holds his hand up, and waves the waiter off.

The French envoy, Monsieur Maurice, was interrupted from his spoon of beef broth. "France is a true democracy... Anarchy is free!" He dabs at his purple mustachioed lips. "You little boys offend me over my broth."

Labossier applauds the envoy. Lifts his drink up to him. "Your democracy is a woman, Monsieur Maurice. Our democracy is a man. " He gulps, stops, and licks his lips. "It has balls!"

The guests laugh all around the table. Monsieur Maurice laughs too. But he points down the table at him. "You should never forget your father, who gave you the balls to interrupt his supper."

Mrs. Berrios speaks under the men. "My husband is mischief tonight." She waves for the waiter to come back over. "We met when he came to my village on the river of dandelions. At thirteen I disappeared into his world of guns and brass... I became a woman." The waiter serves her a full glass, then gets away from her bitter, soft voice. "At fifteen I became a mother."

Myrthe takes a glass of water to drink. His hand is back again. "We are both girls from a village." She puts the glass down.

"We have a lot in common then. I am from the village of dandelions, San Miguel de la Flora." She asks, "And you, Myrthe?"

"I'm from a village under the mountains of Kenskoff... Gressier."

"It's a delight to meet a new friend." Her words rob her slowly. Her vision circles the pigeon-colored faces laughing at her drinking too much. Her husband's eyes turn away from hers. He doesn't like her this way. She flicks some hair back over her left ear. She claps a gloved hand for the waiter to come again. The tiara on her head starts to tip to the left.

Capitol Hill parties, politicians meet drinking whiskey and whores in the deep woods, Washington heroes, grave robbers of children and women. There is a supple array of more jokes, basking in the fiendish displays of men wiping their back hands over their mouths of wisdom, and fuckin' your black whore in these woods. Myrthe nods back to the woman with the drunken, scared smiles. She listens to the others around the table. She sniffs up the perfumes of Giorgio, Yves St. Laurent and Crystal Passion cologne. Colonel Labossier's square jaw juts forward as he pokes out his mustached mouth at Major Berrios, to score a point over battlefield tactics.in countries that have little wars in arms smuggling, gasoline hoarding or drug trafficking for their governments.

She sips her water, listens to Donizetti playing in her head, closes her ears away from the noise of voices ringing from men's hungry lips. She smiles across the table at Mrs. Berrios. False hope for the village child from a Guatemalan Death Squad, trying so desperately not to commit suicide in front of the guests, on wine and raw oysters drenched in hot sauce, on Embassy Row.

17

Sam feels good enough on a Saturday evening to go for his first ride. He laughs at Ray and Mabel fussing over him. They treat him with the care of a three-day-old baby. He doesn't mind. It's weird to have his brother and ex-girlfriend know the way he likes to do things. He pulls up his pajama shirt collar, and ties a double knot around his bathrobe waist. He's hungry for some food, and he's lost a few pounds on some of this mush in here. Mabel kneels down, sticks the slippers on his feet.

"Darlin, you didn't do that when we were going together." He winks up at Ray.

Ray winces when he hears this out of Sam's mouth.

She gets up. "Keep it up!" Reminds him, "You didn't learn the first time not to mess with me?" She sticks her hands on her hips. "Now get in this wheelchair."

Ray turns it around for him. "Come on! You ready?"

He gets quiet and takes a deep breath.

"Sam, what's the matter?" Mabel asks him. "You don't look too pleased to be going on your first ride." She looks at Ray, but his face has no answers.

"I feel like a baby getting on my first Big Wheel... scared."

"Aiiiee, mannn!" Ray tries to pump him up. "You remember when I first taught you to ride your bicycle? How easy it was?"

Sam pulls on his ear. "I remember falling off at least ten times."

Mabel shakes her head. "I understand, Sam. But you know there's a pretty girl out there waiting for you." She grabs his hand. "We going to make sure you get to see her again."

He agrees, bites his bottom lip, stares at the wheelchair and the door knob, his freedom out of here and his first steps to Myrthe. He slaps the handles. "Okay! Let's go for that ride."

Ray takes the handles. "Great! there you go, little brother. Choooo! choooo!"

"Don't," Mabel scolds, "don't get carried away, Ray you in a hospital."

They grab each arm, then sit him down easy. Sam runs his hands around the large wheels. "It's not so bad."

Nurse Green comes in with an orange sponge and towel. "Oh! Am I disturbing something here?" She smiles down into his face, "And where are you going, Mr. Murphy?"

"I am," Sam slaps the wheels, "going on my first ride."

She rubs his shoulder. "You be on your best behavior." She winks, "Don't pinch none of the nurses. I was going to give you a sponge bath, but I'll be back. Bye!" She turns and walks out.

Ray winks at Mabel. "Sponge bath?"

Mabel opens the door. "Such dedication."

"You two stop that. " He grins like the wolf that ate the three pigs.

Ray hunches. "What?" He pushes the chair. "Choooo choooo!"

"Ray, if you don't stop that I'm going to hit you with my pocketbook."

Sam directs, "Yeah, Ray, get me to the cafeteria so I can get a cheeseburger."

"Yuckkkk! Hospital food."

"Haaaaa haaaa!" Ray laughs. "Mabel! I bet it's full of soybeans."

They all leave out the door.

•   •   •

He's alive. Sam wished him dead and dreamed of his father as a winged monster he would kill. He was afraid of him. He wanted him to die soon. Sam rolls past the battling art show of visitors weeping, carrying flowers to their loved ones. He remembers: a mother crying, fighting her son on the shiny, linoleum, black and white checkered floor. Blood. They won't let her see the corpse of her husband. Not yet. Not yet. He holds his head down, and musters up a smile with his paper plate cheeseburger in his hand, as Ray rolls him out on the cafeteria patio. Ray pushes him under the giant blue umbrella. They all sit down for hamburgers, coke, fries, food for a fast-free genera-tion that's ready to die any minute for anything... any second. Mabel dips her fries in some catsup. "You enjoying your burger, Sam?"

"Hell!" his mouth is full, "yeah."

Ray puts a hand over his mouth. "Mannnn! You act like you haven't ate in weeks." He takes a sip of Coke.

Sam swallows. "Let them put your ass on a bunch of drugs, and see how much you eat." He wipes his mouth with a napkin, then takes a handful of fries.

Mabel shakes her head. "It's good you hungry." She looks at Ray. "You leave him alone... Look like you almost finished yours." She takes a bite. "Not bad."

Sam says, chewing, "If they were, I couldn't tell."

"You always were a pig," Ray says to his face.

Sam throws a balled up napkin at him and keeps eating. "Ummmm!"

"Sam, you want me to get you another one?" Ray asks.

Sam licks his fingers. "No thanks, I just wanted a taste of home again."

Mabel takes her straw out of her mouth. "Home. I wanted to talk to you about that. Me and your brother discussed this, and we can take turns getting you back on your feet when you get out of here."

Sam put his hamburger down, looks at both of them. "Hell no! I ain't no charity case."

Ray gets mad at him. "Nobody said you was."

Mabel looks at him like he's stupid. "Who's going to take care of you then?"

"Look, I know yaw mean well… but I want you two to go on with your life." He leans forward on his elbows. "But I am going to need a favor from you, Mabel, when I get back on my feet."

Ray sits back. "Little brother… I ain't going to let shit happen to you. So you can talk all you want." He shakes a finger in his face.

Mabel doesn't want to hear any arguing. "Come on, Ray, leave him alone… Sam, what do you want me to do for you?"

"Once I take Myrthe out of that gate, we going to need a place to lay low for awhile."

Mabel waves a fly from her face. "Okay. I know what you need… No problem."

He leans and kisses her on the cheek. "Thanks." He picks up his burger. "Now back to you." He watches Ray sit there not looking at him. "I need your help, Ray. I'm not going to lie to you. But I need some questions answered too."

Ray asks, biting into a fry, "What's the question?"

He digs in his right ear. "Was anything about the shooting in the papers?"

"You didn't miss nothing, because it wasn't there."

He scratches his head. "That means I'm on my own once I take her out of there."

"That's right… That's what it means. " He crosses his arms, shakes his left foot. "You can't forget about her… can you?" and he knows the answer.

"Forget about what?" Sam asks. "The woman I love? Hell no!" He leans back, rubs his stomach. "Ray, I think I'm ready for some dessert now." He winks over at Mabel.

Ray looks over to Mabel. "Okay, what you want?" He wants to strangle Sam. But since he's using this "I'm sick" routine like a two-year-old, he decides to go along with the game.

"Pie and ice cream." Sam sticks up his fingers. "Two scoops of vanilla."

Ray stands up. "Be right back." He leaves them.

Mabel looks at Sam sitting low in the wheelchair. "This must be some lady... She sure turned you around."

Sam looks into those brown eyes that stared at him for so many years, while he robbed her of any stability of being with him. But she paid him back. "A lot of things changed after me and you."

"Um! I'll say."

But a tone of triumph comes in her words. "Hey, I'm glad some lady can tie you down." She sticks the last French fry in her mouth. "But I'm concerned about you."

"You and the whole fucking world." He pulls the straw out of the Coke cup. Frustration is a wave coming up in his chest. "I'm tired of waiting and I know... I know Myrthe's tired too." He slaps the straw on the table, and hunches up to let the sun warm him. Other patients are all around him, kidnaped by loved ones with the removal of body parts that leave a void of despair from your forehead down to a borrowed heart, lung or kidney. It's a great day for him to just smell the salt on a French fry or grease on a burger. There's a clear sign of life, and other faceless people like him are painting the time of inches... to fight or just take one more step again. To even hold the threat of nuclear war is a pleasant thought.

She sees the desperate fight in his eyes for this woman. "I waited for you; now I wait for your… your brother." She crosses her legs under her cotton skirt. "When a woman waits for the man she loves… a man she knows will love her back forever, she never regrets waiting. The wounds Myrthe suffers, and the rest of us suffer, heal slowly. But Sam, you got to remember they do heal." She places her hand over his.

• • •

Sunday after two p.m.

Myrthe bites into the thread over her Singer sewing machine. She weaves a yellow, green, gold tapestry summer dress of painted warm Caribbean flowers that remind her of home. The pedal under her foot closes in the stitches. She breathes slowly over the creation that gives her comfort, peace. She hides into the cloth world of yarn, needle thread. She dreams of a little girl dancing in a peach dress, dresses she never had the chance to wear as a child, too poor, on the road with the goats and jugs of milk for the others on the mountain.

In this sewing room she can see the face of her mother, Aida sitting on a stool right under the papaya tree, big breasts dangling, feeding milk to her brother Guy. She was the little mother trapped in the world of a child… no time to play with the children on the mountain… no time to laugh or be scared at the tall stick man, Mardi Gras Mort. She pushes aside a curly long piece of hair over her eyes, and ties her hair back into a ponytail with a rubber band. Picks the pins from her mouth into the dress, steps on the

171

pedal, and she lets the stitches roll along between her thumb and finger. Mother Aida, Aunt Jou Jou taught her how to sew, and make thick, black coffee for her father, Georges.

Mrs. Prosper comes upstairs in the low ceiling attic, her voice an impressive, high, shrill pitch. She has a dark black chubby face with two wings of fat around her neck, a big box woman with a face of calm that would make every creature on the planet come to an orgasm. A short, long-dress style woman does her business of cooking for Colonel Labossier for over twenty years, big city woman from Port au Prince and the mother-Madonna figure of the Washington, D.C. Haitian embassy. When she claps her spoons, people stop speaking and wait for her to have her say. She comes into the blue wallpaper sewing room of storage bank boxes. Settled old dust mixes in with the day's sun coming in a round shutter window over the top of Myrthe's head. The thin, curly-haired woman is in her element of yellow, white sun, dazzling long figure of a woman with long curly, wavy hair. Myrthe's eyes burn to see a lovely creation in the silence of the room, under the roar of a sewing machine. She is undisturbed by the dirty hands of Labossier, undisturbed by the darkness of her nights with a man leaving marks that can never be seen, except for small teeth marks on the lower left side of her neck.

"Oh, Myrthe, I see you got your hands on some fine cotton material from the attic." She touches the gold, green flower designs hanging down from the table.

Myrthe touches her nose. "I have a gift for sniffing out old things in dusty attics."

"My little songbird, you seem so lost in so lovely a fabric." She looks over her shoulder, and hugs her around the neck.

She leans back, and pats Mrs. Prosper's arms around her. "This is my time, now, while the colonel is gone." She fingers the cloth. "I can get lost in this Haitian cotton of green and gold leaves." She gazes up in the round, dark, butter face of the woman who makes her feel safer in her flabby fat arms... the way a mother would hold its child for the very first time. "I have been with you many years, Mrs. Prosper, traveling everywhere." Myrthe feels the woman's arms leave her neck. "Do you ever tire of me?"

"Hush, Myrthe." She softly pats the top of her wavy hair. "You are my daughter... just the same as Tiyi and Verdi." She uses a hand like a wand over Myrthe's hair. "We found each other when there was none." She bends, kisses the top of her head. "But I bring you good news!"

Myrthe bites the corner of her lip, pulls the material from under the needle. "It would be a gift from God to have such." She pops out the bobbin to refill.

Mrs. Prosper searches down in her apron, "Here," hands her a letter. "Now, I did read it."

She shrugs. "That's okay." She takes out a card. "It's an invitation... to go shopping with Mrs. Berrios." She pops open a tin full of sewing thread, and begins to wind a spool onto the bobbin with the machine. "She is a nice lady, isn't she?" Myrthe slides the full bobbin back in, and closes the small door on the machine.

"Yes, she is," Mrs. Prosper replies. "And the colonel approved."

Myrthe lets this sink in, then she jumps up and grabs Mrs. Prosper around the waist. "Ohhhh, I am free for at least an evening! I am free! I am free!" Then she swings the older woman around into a salsa dance step. "Hahahahaaaa."

Mrs. Prosper steps back, and watches her daughter-friend dance alone in the tall mirror leaning against the cobwebbed attic wall. It's delightful to see her laughing for just a few moments a day as a thin ray of sun comes upon them in the shade of the deep brown oak of the stale sewing room. It feels good to see Myrthe's craziness in the mirror… the little girl she taught how to read, pray to God, and love the meanness in the big blue world.

• • •

"You are a mistress, I am a mother. I guess I should want to scratch your eyes out, but I really like you," Mrs. Berrios and Myrthe sit in the middle of an eclectic dining room of French wine in a cozy castle, Chez Gerard in northwest Washington D.C.. They're one block from the White House, a million miles from both their homes. "Haaa haaa! Look at us." She taps her glass against Myrthe's. "Two poor peasant girls."

In the spacious intimacy of waiters and sauces, Myrthe is on her second drink. Mrs. Berrios has bypassed the rest of the world on the plane of drunkenness, but she holds her grapes well, with dignity and quite a foul mouth of her husband and his lovers. Myrthe can't say much but just keeps her eyes and ears open for the juice of rumor and military liaison secrets from a woman who has been around the circus of military baboons and stupid politicians. But after a credit card run on buying five pairs of shoes, four dresses, scarves and perfume from the Georgetown box stores, Myrthe is willing to listen to anything her doting, sad puppy friend says. To reassure her of an ear, that's all any woman wants, just a person to talk to... while your husband gambles with his medals and the lives of others. Getting drunk isn't a grave idea. It's the only thing a woman or wife can count on being able to control, in this city of policy and the eternal flame of J.F.K..

"Mrs. Berrios, we have so much at our fingertips," Myrthe says to her. "Except I am the invisible one, because you are always in the papers, and I am not." She runs a long nail around the glass rim.

Mrs. Berrios gets quiet, pulls at her ear. "Myrthe, sounds like you got the better of the deal." She flicks some strands of bangs from her forehead. "But nevertheless, we are both whores."

Myrthe sighs. "Ah, whores." She looks at the couples whispering in yellow candlelight, touching their faces, their noses, mouths, eyes, tasting cold soup. "At fifteen I watched my brother beat, jailed, and my father and mother shot in the streets, my little legs trying to run from the murders." She points at the pearls around her neck. "I was picked up by the Ton Ton Macoute, jailed with others in a cell." She feels the tears come up... coughs, dabs the corner of her eyes. "But, it so happened that one of the guards who kept the key to my cell and others, was Major Labossier." She drinks, clears the thick spit clogged up with tears in her throat. "He was God... yes, yes

God… That's who he was. He decided who lived." Chokes back tears. "Who lived or died." Her gloved hand comes across her face indicating the horizon. "His hand was a magical wand." She drifts into the story. "One night he came to my cell… I ran to a dirty corner like a scared mouse from a cat's claws. But he pushed through the sound of praying hands and begging voices." She gazes into the unmoving, non-threatening eyes of Mrs. Berrios. "He picked me up in his arms and carried me out of this cell… to become the official whore of Major Alfred Charlemagne Labossier." She feels drained, as if a crowd had spit in her face for not choosing death.

Mrs. Berrios lifts her hand, snaps her fingers. "You have angels watching over you, my dear." The pimpled, blonde, boyish face waiter comes over. "Yes, madame?"

"Garçon! We like another glass of burgundy, please."

"Yes, madame." The waiter opens up another bottle of the LaFitte Rothschild sixty-seven, wiping the sweat from the sides. He takes his time, gently allowing the wine in the glasses.

Mrs. Berrios moves her seat out, peeps at Myrthe, as she admires his butt. "Thank you." She lifts her glass. "A toast for… survival!"

Myrthe reaches for her glass. "To survival." She sniffs. "Um." She lets the warmth of the clear burgundy settle her back.

It's a little after four. Two waiters march in the room with flower arrangements in their hands, placing the vases at different tables in the pink and brass restaurant. Myrthe nervously slips a toe in and out of

176

her heel. "Mrs. Berrios, thanks again for inviting me to go shopping with you."

"We have to do this again, but it doesn't have to be over yet." Mrs. Berrios has that mischief twinkle in her eyes that tells Myrthe she needs a friend, a playmate.

Myrthe sidesteps this with a question. "But the colonel?"

"The colonel knows you are with me." She takes Myrthe's hands, and squeezes them in hers. "I called him." She smiles up in the face of a young woman who could try out for the Miss World Contest, if she so chooses. "When you was busy trying on them Italian pumps."

"Wheww!" Myrthe prays up at the almighty face of Labossier.

"Darling, I wouldn't put you in jeopardy with the colonel. I have my hands full... with the major." She opens up her alligator hide handbag. "Now where is my compact?" Searching through keys, pictures, money, credit cards, she finds it. "I need a favor from you, my dear."

Myrthe becomes anxious. "What is it, Mrs. Berrios?"

"Pleassssssse! Stop calling me Mrs. Berrios... My name is Galiana Marita Benita Guzman Berrios." She pats her warm hand. "You just call me Gail."

Myrthe plops a chocolate-covered strawberry in her mouth. "Um." Swallows. "Ummm! Okay, Gail." She nudges the bowl toward her, as the walls of mother and mistress crumble all over the white cloth table of champagne, strawberries, and flowers.

18

God is funny with the imprisonment and death of her family. He has taken Myrthe and swung her into a Mad Hatter world of frog men, bunny face women, politics, money, parties... of bondage with a cord around your neck. She becomes the angel of the misbegotten night, landing her into the mushroom, humid-soaked days of Washington, D.C.. Breaking her up, down to pray at her bedside, she's awash in the world of the colonel's fingers, lips, tongue, opening up her soft petal wounds to his hardness. Purple star night, purple star day. God is funny this way. He laughs, tickles you into tears. She becomes the tight thread, the babysitter to Gail Berrios. It's such sweet refrain from the prison of his touch, his smell... purple star day, purple soft night into the red brick bowels of Georgetown clubs.

· · ·

Cool, long faces of Mick Jagger look-alikes lounge in the West Indian Club, with its sandalwood bar, and a narrow, long hallway, into deep basement dimensions. It's off the main strip, with a side alley entrance, fifteen to sixteen feet down.

On many nights Myrthe has to rescue Gail from the blue face men. Boys want the South American princess of torture and pain, to use her as a cowboy would ride and break a horse from the Nevada prairie. Her white-shell face full of shrimp cocktail, blood-stained lips, covered up with thick lipstick, is bitten by two or three men at a time. She sniffs up lines of cocaine with the senator from some north, south, east, west state, no cameras, please. She belongs to me, the woman and the dope, as he unzips his pants, to let her grab a bit of American history. She screams at another, throws a glass of wine at his head. A crowd buzzes around more silver trays of Panama red dope. Who knows but the Bugaloo.

In her sari dress of gold and yellow flowers, Myrthe sits beside Gail in the booth next to the back entrance. Lights of yellow, red, blue flash over a group coming in the door, men in tuxedos, arms out to the gloves of the women, strutting in all their American glory.

She asks, "Is that President Reagan's top aide?"

Gail snaps her head up from the tray, wipes her nose, "Aw, I think so." She moves her hair from her left eye, "Myrthe, I'm sorry to drag you through all of this." She blows the smoke of the joint in Myrthe's face. "You don't smoke, you barely drink... What vices do you have, my dear?"

Myrthe swallows some of her sherry, "What do you think they are?"

Gail sticks her head back down to the tray, sniffs, pulls back. "Must be a man."

"Must be," Myrthe said. She spots a man coming over to her, his shirt open. His brown eyes fasten hold of her face. She wets her lips for anything tonight. Release, release into his arms.

He asks, "Would you like to dance?"

She looks at Mrs. Berrios to see if she's all right.

Gail slaps her nose, "Go ahead, my little brown doll baby. I'll be right here."

Myrthe takes his hand, and lets him lead her to the dance floor. A black box of music takes her into a spinning, twirling world of beats. She shakes, sways with her hands, shoulders and arms. She doesn't look in his eyes, but feels the lights go inside her. Whirling, whirling, her head bops. She swings against the back of another man, then another, unseen, as she twirls around into the womb of her mother. Myrthe closes out the faces of the men, women, just listening, pushing her hair back from her eyes, for the lights! The lights. Who knows but the Bugaloo.

God is funny. He makes you laugh, he makes you sing, he makes you do that thing. He has you doing the James Brown, spins, spins, spins you around. Myrthe shakes, twists into the words as her hips do the Lucy-Loo, belly shakes closer to the man with the hazardous brown eyes. She stares, rubs him up and down, lets her hair fly into the "Don't lynch me Mr. Charlie" blues voice. All the while, in the background, you know this man loves Jesus. He loves Jesus.

Horns spit out fire from heaven and hell. She circles the man, circles in the air. Above the crowd she soars, hair flinging, slinging over her eyes… only colors of the red, blue, yellow lights blinding her into James' screams.

Shoulders cover her up. She scans back through the tables to her seat, but Gail isn't there. She dances back some from the man's hand, pushes her hair from her face, sticking from the heat of the place and the heat of her body. Gail isn't there. She runs off the floor, back to the table of leftover ashes and warm drinks. She looks over to the men's and women's bathrooms, and spots a man dragging her in the door. She takes a beer bottle off the table, runs, pushes through the crowd of dancing clowns.

Just in the bathroom, the man is over her, pawing through her blouse, ripping, slapping her in the face.

She comes down with the bottle on the blond head of hair. His lights go out.

Gail starts hollering after pieces of glass and blood drop on her. She desperately struggles to get the cologne dog off of her.

Myrthe almost hurts her back when she rolls him off of her. The fright of a weak poodle is in Gail's eyes, she's icy cold, damn near raped, and high as a pissy skunk. She can only crawl towards the woman who saved her ass.

Myrthe starts cussing. "You stupid bitch! You stupid bitch!" She pulls her up from a ripped collar, drags her by her arm. "Enough, enough!" Myrthe pulls the knob. "You stupid bitch!" Others run in, step out of the women's way.

．　．　．

"Two cups of coffee, please." Cigarettes spill from a gold embroidered holder. Gail's eyes clear up from the fog in a twenty-four hour, two o'clock diner, three blocks from the club and a half-ass whipping. Tears slide down cold popsicle cheeks as a warm night rain runs over a front glass window. A few people linger. Dice eyes roam down bikers' leather backs. Nobody gives a penny to heaven when the party is over, it's just over. And all anybody wants to do is spend the night with a dream.

Myrthe collapses onto her seat, exhausted, trying not to show the slow burn in her eyes to Gail Berrios. She drinks a strong, black, bitter cup, and waves away the cigarette smoke, one teaspoon of sugar in, just a boost for the night air. In front of the dripping window, the limousine sits parked. She watches the tight, greasy jeans of the bikers mill around in their chairs. Quarters in a juke box suck in the heat, and blow out some of that blue belly, country-collard green singing from Johnny Cash's lips… down home. Bearded, cut face men swing their chicks around in the place. This makes the bubble-gum, seventeen-year-old counter girl uneasy. You can tell she's still a virgin child at home with Momma and Daddy by the way she keeps back from the counter, afraid of their tattoos and nasty talk from their lips. Myrthe rolls her teaspoon on the table, eighty percent still mad at her pale Spanish friend, sorry face of a woman who needs to be with a family. She licks the back of her teaspoon. In her sweet baby voice that's a whisper, instead of a scream, she gives her a warning. "The Americans have a saying… "

Gail touches the corner of her lip with some ice. "Ohhhhh!" Drops it in her coffee, "My dear girl, what do they say?"

"I believe it is… " searches her thoughts, "read… the writing on the wall."

"Myrthe, what does the writing say?" Gail is tired, hungry for the night rain. She squints at Myrthe's two faces, "My vision is just a little blurred right now." She's crashing down from the cocaine, thirty thousand-feet sky.

"It says love yourself." Myrthe's right hand goes up, as if to write something on this invisible wall, "Love yourself."

Gail says, "I need a second cup of coffee." She pushes the hair from her face, nods at the counter girl. "I don't need this Psychology 101 from a Creole whore."

Myrthe blurts out, "Imbecile!" She reaches across, snatches her wrist. "Next time, you will be raped!" But a strange silence comes in her eyes. "You've already been raped."

Gail spits this answer back in Myrthe's face, "I'm raped every night, the same as you!" She fumbles with her cigarette pack, drops some to the floor.

The bikers turn, scoot up, holler, "You tell her, darlin', because I'll get her right now! Looks like a piece of liver to me! I luvs liver! Shhhhiiiitttt, honey gal! I'll do the honors right now, if you don't mind!" One walks up to the table, grabs his crotch.

Myrthe rises out her seat, ready to throw a coffee cup. "Get away, you fucking pig!"

He jumps back, covers up. The other men laugh, point, go back to their beers and girlfriends, shaking

their asses to some of that hillybilly, jive fiddlin'
playing.

The counter girl's long ponytail jumps when one
of the bikers sticks a tongue out at her as she's going
to the table with the coffee. She darts out of the path
of his two hundred and fifty-pound box frame.

Gail keeps her voice low, "Myrthe, don't look at
them… They are dead already."

Myrthe glances around at the pink, pork faces of
men who have nothing but bad manners, a hole to
live out of, and a woman to beat, because they know
nothing else.

"Being with you has bought us to this… I, as a
friend, will come to your funeral with expensive
flowers." She points in her face, "Right, I am a whore!
But I am not a dumb whore." She rubs her sleepy
eyes, "Nothing worse than a woman who shows herself." Wags a finger in her face, "I… I survive with…,"
she looks at her cup for the word, "dignity!"

They walk in the rain with God this night, as the
limousine trails behind them. Clouds float, cool them
off as they hug up on one another. They aren't ready
to stop for the red light, yellow either, not ready to go
back to the coarse hands of men who use their soft bodies up like cotton swab pieces. They are finished, wax
women, broken, thrown away, covered in some trash
basket for others to step on. The walk will do them
good. The walk will let them define the way, the time,
the place, to tell if it's right to leave yet. Scarves cover
their soft hair, sunglasses cover up their tears. Black
skies surrender, let loose the rain from His hands, cool
them off, cool them off. They march, clap, take note at
window mannequins, what they're going to buy for the

next Congressional function at the Rayburn Building. Walk on girl! Walk on! Myrthe and Gail laugh at some of the drunks, point at the fools whistling at them in the four o'clock morning. They pat their butts, jump over puddles, twist an umbrella around their heads as sirens make their way up Western Avenue. They don't care. The sky has fallen upon their heads. Cool, chill rains release them into His hands… release them for the Saturday night till Sunday morning break of maids, cleaning, gowns, getting an Embassy Row mansion in order to receive a cutthroat asshole from the Republic of Lynch-Them-Before-They-Lynch-You States. Cool them off, God. Cool them off. They talk about love, they talk about freedom, they talk about parties, they talk about their families, they talk about their bleeding… a scar, a lump, a pair of shoes from South Africa to Belgium. Their families are still left behind in some thick, wooded jungle, dying, starving for a song, or just a bowl of rice and beans. God! Give them a bowl of rice and beans.

It's okay. It's okay. Myrthe hugs Gail around the shoulders in front of a country western boutique, takes her wet face in her hands. "He hears us… He hears us." Myrthe smiles, her pretty grey-greenish eyes fading into sadness. "Never, never question that."

Gail sighs, "Myrthe, you are so nice… and shy and stupid." She closes the umbrella, and glances at the limousine. "Our… chariot awaits."

Myrthe looks down at the rain coming over the headlights. "It's time?"

Gail pulls her arm, "I'm sleepy and you're sleepy… It's time to go back."

185

The chauffeur gets out, opens the door. They get in, and lay their heads together. The car slowly pulls away from the curb. Gail grabs Myrthe's hands, "Let me do something for you." Gail's voice is a triumphant plea, "Let me do something for you."

Myrthe rests back, scratches her wet head. "No. No. It's too dangerous."

"Is it him?" Gail moves closer with a whisper, "Is it him you want to be with?"

Myrthe gazes in the face of a hung-over angel, "Yes. It's him I want to be with."

·   ·   ·

Coffee black, two sugars.

In a cotton long robe, briefs and slippers, Sam sits at the end of his orange and brown-pillowed wicker couch. Tuesday morning, home a couple of days from the hospital, it will take some time to get used to the smells of his apartment. Flowers brought home from the hospital are stuck in the bedroom, living room, and the dining room, sectioned-off by a Japanese print screen. Sun comes in, and knocks the morning around in his head... awake at the sound of banging doors, neighbors going to work. It isn't time for him yet. He has to work out with the ten-pound weights on the carpet. He has to sit, watch soap operas, read the papers, listen to the kids in the neighborhood cry and fall off of their Big Wheels. He reaches over and raises the blinds over the couch, and pushes off the couch to get his sax. Afraid, he draws back from the nozzle at this strange circling instrument. He grabs a rag off the table, and sits down to bring the shine back. Sam flicks his lips in the nozzle as if he was kissing a tit, and rubs it across the side of his face. He closes his eyes, relieved to be alive, to feel the hard brass frame. He can't play yet. He isn't ready to go inside himself to see the devil break rocks over his head... or sit and watch the angels play basketball in his head. He isn't ready to rest upon the beach and hear himself mumble about the ocean, or talk to the fish swimming between the dead ships on the sea floor. He isn't ready to trip-out, trip over, trip in, or taste or feel or long for her. He isn't ready to cry, to feel selfish in his pain in not having her or another woman right now. He's only ready to puke up his fucking guts and heal from the stitches in his side.

He drinks, lets the coffee pull him up.

Sam licks his lips. He wants so badly to kill something. Catching a roach trying to get away, he steps on it. This makes him feel better, squashing something black, anything black. Strangling the fuck out of a many-legged, infested piece of shit... makes him feel again. Next he will kill a man, man who is a piece of slime, made, built by a green machine. His dreams take him to this man, this black man that he wants to squash, kill, under his foot. He scrubs the sax down, licks the side, all the way up to the keys. This is her stomach. He wants to bite, nibble at her. Rubs the side of the sax... this is her long, wide, African-black ass... sweet aroma of her pussy in his face. He kisses the keys, this is her ears, pleasure tunnels that listen to him tell her, "I love you."

Coffee steam rises as her ghost walks in front of him.

He reaches out, tries to grab at her long white dress waving. He drops back as the sax rests across his chest. The phone rings. He doesn't want to talk, he doesn't want to listen. He just wants to sit down, take a bath. The phone rings again, he looks at it resting by the lamp. He can't get up to move, he doesn't want to listen to no sympathy… I-help-you-out shit. He just wants to throw the cane in the garbage, walk to El, Zorro and take off to Embassy Row. He wants to kill something, he wants to kill something, anything that looks like a cockroach. He steps on another one.

He hears a soft knock at the door, not a man's. He raises up, spots the bolt and chain off. "Come on in!"

It creaks open.

Sam doesn't care if it's an enemy. "Nurse Green! You make house calls too?"

She closes the door. "No, I don't. I just come by to see if you needed anything." She sits on the couch. She rubs the sax beside him, and scans his place of old books, African paintings on the wall of Zulu warriors, women and children. "And call me CeCe."

"CeCe, huh?" He rubs his chin. Checks out the jeans, blue V-neck sweater, tied back dirt-red hair… eyes of the devil, red lips of a witch that he wants to kiss.

She leans down and tongues the side of the sax. "Yeah, CeCe." She moves closer up in his face.

Sam rubs his thumb across her soft bottom red lip. "I don't want this."

She says, "That bitch from your drugged dreams not coming back to you." She searches around the apartment for any signs of her. "I'm the one who took care of you, not her."

He's tired, doesn't want to get nasty with the red angel that nursed his ass back to some sort of trivia game life. "You right. She's not around… and you not either. Now get out. Next time call."

She uncurls her legs from under her. "I did. But you wouldn't answer."

He holds down his voice, "Meaning what?"

She grabs her purse. "I know, I know." Rushing towards the door. "Bastard! You living with a fucking ghost!" Bangs the door behind her.

Sam fingers the keys of the sax. He starts to play something, anything that will wash the pain from his ribs and chest. Not seeing the ghost of her shadows, not seeing her big brown eyes engulfed in a stream of waters from the fountain in the back of the mansion, not seeing the floppy straw hat on her head, how funny, cute bunny rabbit she looked as she swung a child around and around. He plays, searching to find her face in the melodies.

19

Last Monday in May, Memorial Day.

Sixth and Juniper Streets in Sweet Loaf are packed to the rim with shoppers. Children cry in shopping carts. Five-and-dime stores' doors are open to families. Desperate long nails grab for the sale on bras, sneakers, blouses, Lee jeans, cosmetics, mood rings, kitchen utensils, Barbie dolls, curling irons. Summer clothes are made in Taiwan, counterfeit Gucci handbags from the boot shores of Little Italy, New York. Mothers laugh with their girlfriends as a stilted clown bends down, passing out lollipops and balloons to their scared children. Fathers test the weight of a rake, weeder, lawnmower for their beginning days of grass-cutting. Boys finger roll, then drop the Julius Ervin basketball on the floor. Dribbling, bounce and stop when the tired, bifocal-wearing store manager eyes them to buy or leave it alone. People speak with a smile on this somber, fast-selling day. Familiar faces of the rainbow fan around counter tops, potato chip racks, cheese doodle stares from the ironing board stand. Unfamiliar nosy folks glare from five blocks over,. to five blocks under the south-side train tracks.

Mr. Murphy walks down this street with his oldest boy on his arm. Slow steps, guiding him along for a blind man's stroll as the neighbors bark at both of them.

"How you doing, Mr. Murphy? I see you got your eldest with you!"

"Ray! You and your daddy look good together!"

"Hey, Mr. Murphy! How you doing there?"

"Shopping today for dem Memorial Day sales, Mr. Murphy?"

"Hey, Officer Murphy," the vendor waves a Timex. "Check out my watches!"

"Mr. Murphy! Mr. Murphy! I got fresh slabs of ribs on sale!"

A woman comes up to the father and son. "You remember me, Mr. Murphy? I'm Lulu." She grabs his hand. "I'm DeeDee's daughter!"

Ray looks at his father trying to remember. He taps his cane against a sign post, the bus stop. He smiles down at the snaggle-toothed woman with two kids on her hip.

Mr. Murphy raises his head up. "DeeDee's daughter! Why, child, how's your mother doing?"

She smacks the little girl's leg. "Hold still, child… She's doing okay. They just cut her right leg off… them goddamn diabetes."

Mr. Murphy says, "I gots to come and see her. She still live up on Orleans Avenue?"

"Sure do!"

"Well, you tell her I'll be by there to holler at her."

191

"I sure will. How's Sam doing?" She smacks the little boy in his mouth. "Keep still, boy! I hear he was hurt in some fight or something?"

Ray nods. "He's all right. Me and Pop walking up to the park right now to hear him play with his little band for Memorial Day."

She starts grinning. "Uhhh, up at Malcolm X Park?"

"Yeah, picnic and everything." Ray pats the boy on his zip head. "Bring the kids."

"Okay, I'll be up there... Yaw save a plate for me!"

"We sure will, child," Mr. Murphy said.

"And I tell Momma you'll be by to visit her. Bye now!" She smacks both of them. The bus comes, she lets the two kids on first. "Go on, get yaw ass on that bus... and sit down too!"

When the bus leaves, they keep walking, both of them, Mutt and Jeff types in colorful Hawaiian short-sleeve shirts, two-three buttons open at the neck. Ray slaps a handkerchief across his forehead. "Whewww! Pop, it's hot as fire out here. Why didn't you let me drive you to the park?"

Mr. Murphy says, "Need time to think, son... Just slow walk it down, that's all you gots to do." Taps a fire hydrant. "You just keep walking straight ahead."

Ray stops at the corner. "Pop, you should have let me buy you that dog years ago." He shakes his head, getting mad at his stubborn father. "Don't treat me like your dog!" Light jumps to green.

"I'm sorry. I'm sorry Ray... I didn't mean to offend you none. I just wanted you to guide me right." He picks his head up higher. "What street we at now?"

Ray looks up. "Oh, ah, we at Studebaker Avenue."

"Studebaker, huh?"

"Yeah, Pop." Ray scans the nice woman with red heels and tight jeans passing. "Why? Why you want to know?"

He shrugs, keeps walking in the dark. "Oh, nothing much. This just the street where I took your momma to our first date." His hand rises. "Use to be a little coffee shop where us Black folks use to go to, Daisy's Coffee House."

Ray becomes melancholy remembering his mother's smile, her black butterfly eyes as golden as the night rain. "I see you miss her?"

"Sometimes, sometimes I do." He moves his feet to a quicker shuffle. "It's certain men out here who like to hurt women... you different than Sam and me. Smarter. I don't want you to hurt this pretty Mabel girl. Ohhhhh, I know she put on a good front, but you have to remember, he did hurt her. He hurt her for a lot of years, the same way I hurt your momma."

Ray understands that this is his father's way of saying he's proud of him. "Yeah! I'm smart enough, old man."

"Don't get cute, boy, because I'm going to give you a test."

"Test? What kind of a test?"

A crooked smile comes under his dark glasses. "Who got the diamonds?... You like jazz so much... you tell me who got the diamonds."

Ray scratches his hot face as he thinks about this question. "Ummm, that's a good one, Pop." They pass some more vendors on the corner of Fifth and Lexington. They're selling some African prints, books about Third World peoples and their problems, trinkets back to the white man. "I don't know."

Mr. Murphy messes with him. "Well, son, you betta get back to school when you find out who got the diamonds."

Another pretty, brown, butter woman goes by, pushing a baby in a carriage. "Pop, you can make me mad as hell sometimes. I know what Sam means now."

Mr. Murphy grins. "Oh, don't quote him. He don't have the answers. All he know about is driving some truck, playing a sax and chasing a dream."

"Pop, you crazy. You know that?" Ray slaps an arm over his shoulder, kisses his sweaty forehead.

"Yeah, I know that. Just don't you walk me into no cars."

"Dad, I'm not going to walk you into no cars. I ain't ready to see you go yet." Ray holds on his arm.

"Oh, no. Your brother is." He moves the cane from side to side. "Now that's between you and Sam." He reaches up, pinches his ear.

"Ouchhhhhh! Pop! What the hell you doing?" Ray grabs his finger off his ear. Some people stop to watch the blind man and his son.

He reminds him. "Ray, you just remember I'm not your enemy… I'm your father. Don' t you ever forget that!" He taps his stick. "You keep a lot of shit to yourself… but don't you forget I can still see what's in your heart, son."

Ray says, "Pop, what's wrong with you?" He rubs his earlobe. "Why you embarrassing me out here in the streets like this?" Shakes a finger. "Keep it up! I'm going to leave your ass right here!"

The blind man dares him. "Ahaahaa! Shiiit!"

Ray looks up at the sky for patience. "Come on! Let's get your ass to this park."

He stumbles up on the curve. "Don't walk me into no cars, boy."

Ray gives him a stern warning. "I'm going to get you back for that. I'm going to get you a seeing-eye dog."

"Shit! You betta get your own dog." He gets smug. "I ain't blind!"

There's silence between them. One block away, Malcolm X Park.

The park comes up from a small concrete incline. Benches, trees, diamond grass lawns come up, basketball, tennis, volleyball courts in the horizon. Kids and kites flying as some barking dogs try and chase the thin string flaps in the air. They pass people, picnic baskets, blankets, vendors selling T- shirts, barbecues and potato salad slapped down on plates. Nice music... it's sweet reggae, rhythm, jazz and soul from a stage of red, white and blue banners. Men walk around with medals on their chests, strutting pride, tears and war wounds for this day.

Ray searches the crowd for Mabel. "All right, steady now, Dad."

Mr. Murphy can hear and see in his heart all the people and fun going around him in the place. "You see Sam?"

Ray keeps looking. "Not yet. Here comes Mabel."

"Hey, Ray! Ray!" Mabel and Kathy run up to them. Kathy grabs Mr. Murphy's arm. Mabel plants a kiss on both their noses. Mabel hugs Mr. Murphy around the neck. Mabel takes his arm. "You come with me, Mr. Murphy. We got your plate all ready."

He asks again, "Where is Sam?"

Kathy looks around in the crowd of people. "He's here, Mr. Murphy... He's going to play some nice music for all of us this Memorial Day."

"Yeah, I likes to hear my son play."

Ray walks behind the women and his father. Shakes hands, kisses some of the women friends in the crowd. "Hey, Buddy, watch yourself."

Buddy hollers back at him. "Hey, mannnnn! Come on and get a plate of some of my corn on the cob and cornbread."

"I'll be over there, Buddy... Let me get Pop settled!" He points. "Hey, Mabel! Kathy! Don't ya' get Pop all excited. He's too old for you young things!"

Mabel looks back over her shoulder. "Shiiiiit! Your pop ain't dead yet, baby!"

"Did," Jim Murphy asks, " ya pick up my woman, Mabel?"

Mabel leads Jim over to Earlene cooking the chicken and ribs under the umbrella-shaped oak. "Earlene! your man asking about you." She takes him right over to her.

Earlene pats the sauce over the chicken, rests the stick back in the sauce. "Hi, baby!" She hugs him. "Now, you let my man go, Mabel Friday... he belongs to me."

"He's all yours." Mabel smiles, leaves him with his girlfriend by the picnic table. "You need anything else, Earlene... you just let me know."

Earlene pulls him over, sits him down near the bench in a nice lawn chair. "Okay, Mabel. Thanks."

She pats his face, kisses him on the lips. "I start to worry about you, baby, took you and Ray so long getting here."

His head rolls. "We just took the long way… Just getting to know one of my sons."

She takes his cane, lays it on the grass beside him. "Glad you here. You want a beer, soda pop or something? Ribs almost ready!"

He listens to the shower of noises all around. "Just give me a beer."

She goes to the bench, opens up the cooler, and digs under the ice. "Here's a nice cold one for you." She pops the top, hands it to him.

"I'll be all right. You just go on back and cook those ribs up for me."

Earlene pushes her grey hair over her shoulders. "I'm right here if you need anything."

He nods, takes a sip, and shakes his rubber sole toes to some of the D.J. music in the park. "Hey, Earlene!" Brushes a fly from his face.

She looks up from the grill. "Yeah, baby?"

"Have you seen Sam yet? He ain't played yet, has he?" He turns the beer can around in his hand. "Gots to hear my boy play now… even if he don't talk to me."

She comes over, wiping her hands on her red and white checkerboard apron. "He was just here a few minutes ago… him and some of the guys in the band. I saw him with Posie, Ralph, and Bobby Love… They must have gone on in back of the stage." She bends down by him. "But he ain't played yet." Pats his hard, wrinkled hand. "We got to hear a bunch of speeches before they play."

He drinks. "That means Reverend Patrick going to have to say something before this thing can really kick off." Twists his neck around. "But it's a nice Memorial Day for some good music and friends, and even old enemies."

She leans over, pushes her nose into his neck. "Now Jim. Ain't nothin' but your friends and family here." She kisses his face. "You just rest back and enjoy the day." She stands. "Let me get back to dem ribs."

Ray comes over and drops a football in his father's lap. "Here, Dad, I'm going to run all over their asses today!"

"Shit! Football... dem young boys going to hurt you out there." Sticks his beer can between his legs, acts like he wants to throw the ball. "Yeah, I use to throw this pill myself."

"You just let your son do it for you now... You know me and Sam, we a hell of a team against them assholes from the Ninth Precinct."

"Ahaaa haaa." Gives him the ball back. "You just have a nice time and don't get hurt."

Ray flips the ball in each hand. "Pop, I ain't no kid."

"Don't have me pinch your ears again, because you and Sam will always be my kids."

Ray doesn't want to argue; he wants to play ball. "Okay, Pop!" He throws it to one of his teammates, Charlie Frazer. "Save me some of them ribs." He runs off through the tables.

Reverend Patrick comes on stage with Bible in hand; taps the mike. "Uh, everybody, before we get the festivities started, I would like to say a prayer for

198

all of us here at this lovely green park, dedicated to a man that was also a soldier, a warrior for justice.

"Heavenly Father, we gather with you on this sad, but momentous day of heroes who have fought in many, many, wars in this nation and across the seas… For liberty. Oh Lord! They must know that they did not fight in vain, they did not fight for a frivolous cause. Their families that stand with us today at this picnic of food, fun, and music must also understand… if you want freedom, democracy, a right to say what's on your mind and to even pray in your own homes and churches, that this will take a great deal of sacrifice by us and our boys who are living and dead. Oh Lord, we give thanks, we give praise and remembrance of men who have fought for such cause." He raises his hand, gives the sign of the cross. "Yes! This is a great day of life and death!" He spreads his arms out over the people on the lawn. "Now, ladies and gentlemen, let's rejoice!" He hops down.

A red, white and blue colored curtain swings open.

Music of horns blasts out at the crowd. Sam is leading the charge with his sax from the nice little combo he put together about five years ago. They are greeted with a thunderous roar from the crowd, hoots and hollering. Drum riffs, a bass sings like Miss Holiday… shooting out a hopping, down-home piece that has you thinking you are swinging on a star. You know, makes you believe you are in church.

Posie's on bass, Rob Lee on the drums, Tony Gathers on trumpet… men upon a rock, upon the sea. They start to get comfortable and sit on the phrasing to twinkle the crowd's heavy hearts, all the way to the ribs and chicken bones in your belly. People nod their heads to the sweet jazz from the band. It's pork-fried-up jazz… cool, sixties-like stuff when Mingus and Trane was around.

Ray is beside Mabel, "Geeeezzzzuss! I see Sam's been practicing on that sax!" Snaps his fingers to the notes going over his head.

Mabel sticks her arm through his. "I see he made you put that football down." She scans the faces of the other people at the picnic tables. "He got their attention too." She urges him on. "Blow it, Sam! Blow it!"

The crowd starts to clap, whistle at the jumpy tune playing. Ray grins, takes a pull of gin from his cup. "Hell! If I sat at home for almost a month… I could play that damn good too!"

Mabel rolls her eyes at him. "Sounds like that gin talking."

"Naw! I'm proud of him. After the shit he's been through… all them stitches in his rib cage… I'm glad he got his wind back to play that good." Ray scratches the top of his head, and hugs her closer to him. "Sounding good, Sam! All right now, little bro'!" He closes his eyes, and listens to his brother play as if the day was the day for all the world to end. "Play it, baby! Play it!" He checks out his father sitting in the lawn chair, head rolling, and a grin under those dark eyeglasses, with his girlfriend scooted right up between his legs.

Mabel watches the men working out a Yankee Doodle Dandy riff that makes you smile at the notes rocking you back and forth on your feet. "They put a nice little tune together for Memorial Day."

Ray finishes his gin. "But he's not playing for us."

She keeps wiggling. "Well, who is he playing for?"

He swishes the ice around in his mouth. "He's playing for her, baby... He's playing for her." He gets behind Mabel, and hugs her up in his arms. In the middle of the music, he can feel something not right. If the men are in Sweet Loaf to take his brother out... and they didn't do their job... the devil will be back again. He spots the faces in the crowd, sees smiles, laughter, talking, eating. There's a group of men playing chess, another playing cards, others just under trees with their families. He knows they're still watching, still waiting.

20

I am thy father's spirit,
Doom'd for a certain time to walk the night.
—SHAKESPEARE, HAMLET, 1, 5

A hallway leads to a barrel vault study on the second floor with an archway off to the left. Down three flights of stairs is a library in three dimensions of a man. Colonel Labossier studies reports, maps, little lines that at night, give him peace beneath a cozy windowsill looking at the Capital. He drinks scotch. He rubs the rich Costa Rican wood furniture. Behind him, the room holds red and gold carpet, king size bed, flasks of sherry and liquor, throw pillows, white lacquer, and still breaths of a night. Still breaths of a man float over pictures of home, pictures of the mountains, the people selling their wares in the Port au Prince slums... her home. His fears of who will kill him are in his still breaths of the night, as he sits down in his hole that makes him comfortable. A guard outside the door? Drunk... he whacks away the night with a machete of thoughts, prayers, memories of him and her playing in warm waves, hugs in the Washington, D.C. snow, the first snow battle for both of them. And then there are memories of his wife, his children back home in Jacmel. His wife doesn't smile, she just bleeds out love in silence and devotion. Gilberté just gives out, casts him to his mission, his duty. Nevertheless, nevertheless, Myrthe keeps him from blowing his brains out with his gun. Still breaths of the room... he rubs his eyes, yawns. He's ready to go to her, but there's still a lot of work to do, for his mission is never complete... never finished. The pen wants to slip away in his fingers, fall to the floor and spill ink from his lips. It is good that he's working. It keeps him in place, at peace, under the windowsill. At peace with his mission, his target, he studies maps of Haiti as a Telex machine beeps under a green glowing lamp by the roll top desk, sending him a message from home:

UP. 12.P.A.P. VSC. 14:40. RPT
CAP HAITIAN... Objective ... seen to target... effectively... Georges Jolibois.
End Message

The list of people is getting longer. He looks at his dirty fingernails. The pen starts to shake in his hands. He lets it drop to the paper. Yawning again, he wipes the dreaded sleep from his eyes. He takes a drink of cognac. He gets a headache from anything else at this time of night. Names, faces of people he went to school with... old friends... they drift through his mind. He picks up his pen, and crosses out this name. George Jolibois wants something that he can't give... a taste of a ripe mango, a taste of fresh air, a taste of a sugar apple, a taste of this sweet word. Dare not speak. Shhhh! Quiet. Quiet from such sweet words... the exact words, shhhh, quiet, quiet. Such sweet words, shhhh! Unspeakable sweet sugar apple words. It has always been this way, always unspeakable words... no changes, even though Papa Doc is gone. Still, you cannot speak to have that sweet sugar apple in your mouth. Juicy ripe words. Shhhh, shhhh! He blinks, yawns, and listens for the Telex to bring more names.

Letters, codes, targets. Shhh! Baby Doc may hear him think. Shhhh! No! Oh, no! The guard outside the door may hear him think about the sweet sugar apple that he wants to taste. Shadows breathe under the windowsill. Over his shoulder they watch for the next leader of his country, the man who will take them to a beautiful beach and drown them all. Secret men are giving out orders, money, guns, commands. We all have our orders to carry out, waiting for us, our own jail cell... awaits, awaits for him. He opens the middle desk drawer, and stares at the .38 Police Special to take out something black. Maybe him or Corporal Francois outside the door, who are listening, listening. His hand shakes as he lifts out the paper with the names:

UP. 12.P.A.P. VSC. 14:47 RPT
Jacmel; School Principle: Albert Bellamie
Petionville, Canape-Vert; Gislaine Boudouin: Nurse
Port au Prince; Irma Mirrille: Dance Company
Cap Haitian; Georges Jolibois: Accountant
Belladere; Roger Montasse: Captain, Military

Kenskoff; Hubert Lefranc: Law School Student
Leogane; Father Roland Loiseaux: Priest
Laselle; Jean-Marie Mathurin: Musician
End Message

His kill list... he wipes his hand across his lips. He crosses out Jolibois' name again. He drinks more, lets the heat slide down his throat. He tastes more, and closes his eyes at the puppet people dancing in his think tank brain. He wants to holler. Scream! Scream! Shhhh! Shhhh! Baby Doc will hear you outside the door. He watched the men push poison down his brother's throat. He saw hungry dogs gnaw, drag and nip at his father's carcass on the street. His hand shakes, quivers for another drink... just another taste of her, his Myrthe, his sweet, dear Myrthe. Men pulled his mother out of the house in the night, and raped her with a wine bottle, a beer bottle, a stick, a knife... anything dark, sharp, until she screamed for God no more. He ran away from this, this family that gave him love and shelter. He ran away and hid under truck tires at the age of eleven. He ran away from the men, the ghosts of the Canzo. He wasn't going to let the spirits feed on him. He wasn't going to let the spirits eat at his sweet, young, boy flesh. He ran across the border to the Dominican Republic. He let the sugarcane have him, feed him into becoming a man.

Honey, yellow flames from the fireplace in the cold, dark brown, wood room... flames in the rot of his thoughts, loud, clear, beating the drum in his head. A marching band of men in green fatigues parades down Port au Prince streets showing off their World War II rifles, grenades, pistols on their hips.

They are braver than the men they really are, less brave than the starving dog in the streets, trying to feed its newborn pup. In the rot of the room, the rot of his thoughts, he has to talk, see another face just as black as his. He scratches his chin, rubs his hazel brown sleepy eyes. He is afraid, afraid of ghosts, afraid to die like his father. He goes to the door, and pulls the knob. "Come in, Corporal Francois, and join me for a drink."

He snaps to attention. "Yes sir!" He takes his cap off, follows him. Puzzled, he plays the mouse automatically to his superior, not knowing, afraid and wondering all at the same time. He sits in a wingback, rose flower chair. He keeps his eyes up, as the colonel pours, and sits in the same kind of chair next to him, with two glasses, half full.

The colonel's eyes are sharp, unbroken over the young clean face. "Don't be afraid, I just want to talk." He hands him his glass. "Enjoy."

The corporal looks in, tastes, and sits back with his cap in his lap... licks, sips again.

"I wouldn't poison the man who is trying to protect me from my enemies," the colonel tells him. He drinks. "Ahhhh! All the way from Paris, France." His nose sniffs in the glass. "It is my understanding, Corporal Francois, that we have some new names on the horizon." He rolls a thumb around the rim of the glass.

Stupidly, he stutters, honored to answer back. "Our arm is long. It... we, never lack names to monitor for the cause of the Haitian people."

He raises his glass, taps it for a toast. "One step ahead, one step ahead."

The corporal hits his against the colonel's.

Silence. Colonel Labossier thirsts for the cognac, it's smooth, warm. It takes him lower into his chair. He presses his lips together, feels the cool, wooden taste burn his palate. He's relaxed again, with the young, scared soldier across from him. He's ready to take his place, if he ever falls to the hands of the grave. It's a place of guns and chaos, freedom. He grins. All voices ring together, so you can't hear the right... torture, whip across your back... direction, directives, a line drawn between them and us, more kill lists, Napoleon's unspeakable democracy. Haiti and the U.S. join as friends. We continue to torture fathers, mothers and children to stay in line. The young corporal is a donkey looking for a piece of sugar apple too. "You have waited long outside my door."

He raises his head. "Yes sir, I have."

The colonel is polite. "Good, good." He rubs a hand down his itchy, scratch razor bump neck. "Do you like Washington, D.C., Corporal Francois?"

"It's, it has a lot of dead heroes, just like home."

"Ahhhhhaaaa, ahhhhhasaa!" He rubs his eyes, to stop the tears from his full-hearted, crazy laugh. "Dead heroes, dead heroes... Son, they are not dead heroes... They are dead butchers!"

Corporal Francois respects this answer and stupid, insipid laughter in silence, swishes some ice in his mouth.

The colonel pours him another. "Yes. They are a lot like us." He asks, "When was the last time you were home?"

"It's been three years, sir."

207

He says, "When you been home away that long... every place seems to have the flavors of your town." He leans closer, and slaps him on the shoulder. "It's time for you to go home."

The colonel looks in his eyes, eyes that have seen so much and show it with dark rings under them. He is a professional player in this game of the spider. "But not until I finish my assignment here."

The colonel rolls up his khaki shirt sleeves. "Is my Ms. Presumé on the track or off the track, because if she is—"

"Sir, she's on the track again, sir." He sniffs up the wooden smoke aroma of the cognac through his nose. "Except for side trips with Major Berrios' wife to New York on her wild trysts." He rubs a finger across his bottom lip. "She seems to give Mrs. Berrios great comfort at fundraisers and parties at the Guatemalan embassy."

He stretches out his left leg; it stiffens from a bad knee. "That's good. Her days are not spent gathering dust. Her role continues to be this tall, slim butterfly on her knees to the United States," his finger points down. "That we are for a democracy, but there is no need to disturb our precious customs to do so... She is good at this." His voice is stern, but soft. "Please continue to see that she stays on this track."

"Yes sir, I will." He watches the man across from him, taps his right toe nervously, stops, then starts up again whenever he has a question for him.

"Maybe you will be able to go home soon. What town is that?"

"Raboteau, sir."

He nods. "In Gonaives."

"Yes sir."

Colonel Labossier knows then that he had grown up in a slum., that he wanted the taste of the sugar apple finally. He wants to speak, eat, house his family, and the only way to do it is to squash this fever of wanting the sugar apple so quickly. Silence, only silence, you will dream about this sweet fruit. "I would like to thank you for having this drink with me, and you are relieved of your duties for tonight."

Corporal Francois gets up. "Goodnight, sir." He gives him the empty glass and leaves out of the room of books, maps, and names of the country's enemies.

Colonel Labossier walks to the large picture window. He brushes back the gold embroidered curtains made in Ghent, and then gazes out, up at the dark summer sky, where stars blink. He can hear her snores in her bedroom. He wants to be with her, hold her, beg her to love him again. He relaxes, not worried much anymore about their life together. He leans on the wall overlooking the huge, dark lawns of the mansion.

He arrived back in Haiti and joined up with the Army. He vowed to carry the goat as a sacrifice at the head of the Verve. A fire glowed. He took his knife, and plunged it in the middle of its head. Blood drips on him from the Coui. She marked the signs of the cross on his forehead with the goat blood. A fire glowed in him. She walked with a hot poker in front of his face, shaking her breasts. He felt the fire in her belly rub against his stomach. Sweat dropped from both of them, as drums sang, as drums robbed them of all vestiges of this world. The Ougan cut with a

209

knife across his chest, and held a cup under to feed the spirits with his blood.

Still breaths of the night, still breaths from the room. A green lamp glows on his desk, as the Telex delivers a message from home.

•   •   •

On June the fifth, Myrthe turns twenty-seven.

She's surrounded by women from Embassy Row, these women with presents for her in their world of African, Caribbean, South American politics. And from around the world, her friends give her gifts in the affairs of state... women's gossip, giggles, parades and tea parties at different functions of the globe. The Colonel has made sure she will get any and everything she needs while he's back in Haiti with his own family. She's happy she isn't in his box.

In the grassy, circled garden, salsa music lifts from a band on a stage that overlooks a crowd of Myrthe's guests, dancing to music from the Caribbean seas. Under white globe lanterns, people clap and sing along with the men. The band is dressed in bright orange suits, skinny black ties, with black pointed-toe shoes. The lead singer's mouth twists as he reaches out to the women.

Myrthe sits at a table right in front of the stage with some of her friends. She is delighted, but bashful when the singer gets off the stage, and pulls her up to dance with him. She kisses him on the cheek when he takes her back to her seat. She feels good, with friends from all over the world, good people she met while traveling with Colonel Labossier.

Lillia Nbotosui from Kenya, tall woman with a face of the cosmic night, Carmen Perez-Vicardi, a saleswoman with a chemical company, Joyce Tucker, a dear friend with the city government of Oakland… all here for her. Joyce comes to wish her a happy birthday before she flies off to New York City. Here is Marita Desanges, a doctor from the island of La Gonave. Josiene Georges, a businesswoman from French Guinea, has left in the middle of negotiations on the city tax structure, to dance with her friend on this special day.

Myrthe's hair is pulled up and down in a French braid. She's dressed in a yellow velvet pajama pants suit with her toes in gold strap slingshot heels. A thin gold chain shines around her neck, the crucifix. She is amazed at the friends who traveled so far to be with her this evening… all with miles of adventures and stories to tell of their lives, leaving behind misdirected lovers and husbands. The Central American crustaceous Generals and government finger-painters from U.S.A.I.D write more checks. Her girlfriends are all passed around to strangers on a beach, on a street, with a shop or on-the-job, or forgetting the birthdays with the names and faces of different lovers. Political favors… business… rich girls grow up to be whores too. They are all accomplished, buried under a man with children, extinct, lost-letter women, slaves, tied in rich colorful ribbons, under a pillow of happy tears.

The onion breath singer cradles the mike. On his knees, he croons to the group of women as they gulp down glasses of pink champagne:

Angel wings brought you to these shores
On the way to my doorsteps of love

For many years to dream
For many years to love!
That bonds us on the way
To the skies of our love!
Angel wings bring you to my doors
As I pray that you will
Never leave me
Never leave me!

After Carlos' singing is finished, the horns, bon-gos and marimba carry on for the night. Myrthe walks around to mingle in the crowd, hugging, shaking, kissing familiar long faces of people she hasn't seen in ages... old, young, children, babies from her friends' bellies who have grown up through the missed years. She dances with men with grey hair, faces with age of time and the rivers from Jordan, men who befriended her, men who kept in touch with this once-little peasant girl from the streets of Haiti.

Mrs. Prosper serves the guests meals, but a Caribbean favorite that most like is goat water stew. People come up to the short, stumpy matriarch who cooks and cleans the mansion, compliment her and ask for the recipe. Myrthe takes her mother-friend around and has her greet and talk to the many faces of people they have met over the years. Mrs. Prosper is over sixty, ready to retire. Some of the people she did remember, some she never did forget.

Mrs. Prosper says, "Good evening, Mrs. Vanderpoole."

Mrs. Vanderpoole is a tall, aristocratic woman from Rhode Island. "Mrs. Prosper!" They hug. "Darling, you still around?" She places an arm over her shoulder.

Mrs. Prosper is giddy. "Charlotte, dear, I'm not leaving this earth until you leave."

Mrs. Prosper's friend's husband is the senator from Rhode Island. She's a woman who loves to play gin rummy and drink her scotch and water, an ex-dancer from Kansas, a woman with guts and brains, and not afraid, in her snobbish way, to have a good time. "Fine, dear. I'll call you. We can have another game of gin rummy before we both kick off." She pecks Myrthe on each cheek, wishing her happy birthday. "Bonne fete, Myrthe!"

"Thank you, Mrs. Vanderpoole." She smiles. "Have you had enough to eat? Enough to drink?"

"Yes, yes, my dear." She peeks over her blue pearl eyeglasses into the crowd. "I haven't seen Charles at the party tonight."

Myrthe answers her quietly, acting as if she is sad from his absence, "Colonel Labossier had to go back to Haiti on some business."

Mrs. Vanderpoole replies as she takes a glass of champagne off the tray going by them, "Men! Men and their work. Never ceases till the day they die."

Mrs. Prosper interrupts with a tragic remark. "But we must see to it that they die with smiles on their faces, Mrs. Vanderpoole."

Myrthe listens to the two elder women, the tall bird woman, a sunflower in a sparkling red gown, and the short dark one in a long silver dress with a tunic covering her hair. They sparkle, they erupt in laughter and speak of their old husbands who are dancing to the salsa music with younger women at the party.

Mrs. Berrios comes between them with her husband on her arm. They kiss around, shake hands at seeing each other again. Gail Berrios is an orchid made up for tonight, a box in her hand, wrapped in silver-colored paper and bow. "Happy birthday, Myrthe!" She hands it to her. "I hope you like it."

Myrthe playfully shakes it up to her ear.

Mrs. Vanderpoole gets excited. "It's not a bomb, so open it!"

The people nearby carry the drunken request on. "OPEN IT! OPEN IT! OPEN IT! OPEN IT!"

Myrthe covers her ears, throws up her hands. "Awwww! All right, all right!" She desperately rips the bow and paper to a cardboard box. Inside is a small, hand-made boat with two little stick figures of a man and woman sailing, in colors of red and blue.

Mrs. Prosper gazes at the small, twisted rope figures. "It's made in the colors of our flag."

"It's an exquisite gift, Myrthe," Mrs. Vanderpoole says, peering down closer at the figurines. "Very tasteful, but simple… a sign of the times, my dear."

Myrthe says to Gail, "I will always treasure it," and kisses her on the cheek. "I will always keep it close to me. Thanks, Mrs. Berrios." Myrthe smiles at the sculptured figures. "But who are the two people on this boat?"

"Myrthe, that's for you to figure out… I had to go all the way to Haiti to get it."

People laugh. Carlos joins the band again, singing, urging all of them to dance. Mrs. Prosper grabs her husband's hand, and takes him to the dance floor. Mrs. Vanderpoole pulls her husband by the tie, snatching him from a curly-haired blonde woman.

Myrthe walks alone through her dancing friends with the boat in her hand. Mrs. Berrios comes up behind her. "I'm glad you like it, Myrthe."

Myrthe can't stop the tears from her eyes.

Mrs. Berrios takes her off, away from the crowd. "Don't cry on your birthday, dear." She pats her on the shoulder. She wants her friend to stay strong under the merriment of her birthday, to have fun, to dance, get drunk, eat plenty of chocolate, raspberry cake this night.

Water from the fountain falls, loud, splashing out the sounds of helplessness from Myrthe's voice. "God dammit! God dammit! I can't go on like this! Not without him."

"Myrthe, who do the two figures in the boat remind you of?" Gail shakes her under the music of a Latin lover. "Keep thinking about your dream… Keep dreaming about your man."

She wipes the tears from her eyes. "They remind me…" She holds the gift gently up in the red and blue lights from the fountain waters. "They remind me of Sam and me."

Gail Berrios gives her friend comfort in her arms, as the salsa singer gives them another song about love between two people, in a never ending circle:

> Our love will never die!
> It will never waste away
> Our time will come
> We shall hold each other
> Till another day!
> We shall see our love to the end!
> Oh, darling, never stop!
> Dreaming on
> Dreaming on
> Dreaming on!

Monday 5:45 a.m.. All sold out on wolf tickets to WGSV talk radio.

Sam gets back to work with a whistle in his throat. Yellow globe ball of a sun coming up over the I-95 horizon. Speedway traffic; spilt coffee stains on a dress, tie, pants. Excited, palms sweaty going back to his truck, buddies who like to shoot craps, hustle for some extra shag, Arabian carpets. Sam is glad to smell the gas fumes, dead squirrels, anti-freeze air, suffocating hot black leather seats of his car. His ribs are tight; muscled up with some forty-pound weights every morning after he has his coffee and Raisin Bran. He still can't put that cigarette away. Waxed-polished down his car, tuned up, brake job, yellow and black snake-eyed dice hang behind the rearview mirror.

Uptown:

6:20 a.m. in D.C. on Fifth and Buchanan.

Black part of town, picking up his riding partner Petey-Pete. Hits his horn in front of a small, dirty red brick house; two plastic flamingos are in the center of the yard.

Front door opens up. He spots Petey Pete's short frame tiptoeing up, kissing his tall wife at the door.

Sam leans over the passenger side, hits the horn again. "Petey Pete! Bring your ass on here, man!"

Pete grabs a brown paper lunch bag from her hand. He runs to the car in shorts, muddy boots. Cut off at the sleeves T-shirt with a red bandana tied around his neck.

Sam shoves the door open. A big window grin comes up in Pete's face. Sam sticks his hand out. "Give me five, brother!"

Slaps his hand. "Sam, my man! Good to see you back!"

Sam steps on the gas, getting away from the two pink flamingos.

Petey nods at his friend's marshmallow chocolate face, pencil mustache trimmed all up. He was still a lost little boy in the woods, but in another woman's heart. He knows Sam is nervous, not quite sure of his place with the gang back at the warehouse. "Sam, I just want you to know, man, things ain't been right since you been gone." He plucks a Camel out of the pack, offers him one. "Just remember you gots nothin' to prove."

Sam understands. "Pete!" Takes the cigarette, sticks it in his mouth; leans over at the red light as he strikes the match. He bends down, sucks, coughs. Blows the smoke out his nose that makes him slow down. He doesn't want to run over a good-looking woman on his first day back on the J.O.B.

"Yeah, Sam?" Scratches his neck.

"Shut up!" He peeks over at him. "You still writing that shitty poetry?"

Pete scrunches down in the seat. "I'm still writing it."

"Good!" He asks, "Now tell me... how is business in the warehouse?"

Pete could see the light of interest in his eyes. "Money still flowing... We got a new contract with the Department of Navy." Lights his cigarette. Puffs.

"Over at the Navy Yard." Flings the match out the window of no breeze, sticky 90-degree morning.

Sam's lips go down with the air of a man who knows everything. "Them admirals likes nice carpets... They got enough money to blow on women all over the seven seas. Why not blow some on us!" Plucks ash out the window.

"White boy Mike doing us right... He got the big boys upstairs bidding on contracts in every federal agency in D.C." Knocks some sweat off his brow. "Even got us some contracts to lay carpet with the city of Sweet Loaf. We had to put on two new drivers to help us with the extra work."

Sam gets nervous quick. "What about my truck?"

Pete spots the look of a little boy losing his toy in Sam's eyes. "I told you before, man! Nobody can drive that piece of shit like you can." Peeks in his sandwich bag. "I told that bitch! Turkey, not pastrami!" He drops the bag to the floor. "Damn!" Picks it back up.

Sam throws the smoke out the window. "I've had El, Zorro a long time, over ten years now." A fondness of the piece of GMC metal comes up in his voice. He missed the road with that piece of shit. Yeah, he loved the hell out of that red truck.

Pete takes two fast puffs off his, throws it out. "You might as well buy the damn truck."

He drives around a few men digging up the street, one waves an orange flag for him to slow down. He did. "Maybe I will buy it one day." Gravel, hot tar rocks kick up under his car. "I see you like women bigger than you?"

Pete answers him with a Tarzan he-man grin coming from his chest. "Little guys always got to prove something. Nothing but the best, plenty of legs to get lost in."

"How did you meet her?"

"Sara, she's my third wife... in a disco bar, late seventies. I was sitting there over my drink. She was talking to some other guy. I was listening, you know. When I heard her tell him that she didn't want to dance... Hey, it wasn't me. She was a pretty, tall black Statue of Liberty sister. Whenever I get tired I start talking plenty of shit! Then all of a sudden she asked me, 'What you going to do... you little short mutherfucker?' I told her I was going to take her home with me. Next thing I knew... " hunches, "... she was in my jeep going home with me." Scratches his raggedy beard. "After that first night she never left my side."

Sam checks him out of the corner of his eye with a compliment. "That was smooth, Petey." He slaps his hand. "You all right, Petey-Pete."

Pete thought of the Haitian songbird. "How you holding up, Sam?... I want to see you happy too. That wrong type of sandwich thing."

Sam laughs, pushes his golf cap back on his head. "Doing the best I can from knocking down that gate with my car on Embassy Row."

• • •

6:45 a.m.

Narrow concrete alley passage. Wooden power poles holding up people's phones and wet clothing on the lines. It was okay. He took a deep breath as his car cruises past a cop's car right in the path of dogs scampering out from garbage cans. A wine head or two trying to scrounge up some coins for a bottle of Thunderbird or Mad Dog 2020. It was okay as he came out the other end to the loading docks of trucks. Men leaning around on cars waiting for the iron doors to roll up.

Joe Buck damn near choked on his Egg McMuffin when he saw Sam pull up by the rest of them. "Well! If it ain't the sax man coming home!" He rushes up to the car door with Duck, Kenny, Bobby King, Mark, Bob Seal, Junior, Jesse and Darnell. They were excited as children seeing their mothers coming home from a shopping trip, faces waiting to hug, jab handshake him right out of the car.

Sam was smothered by their usual morning doings of cups of coffee, sausage and biscuit sandwiches, jars of orange juice mixed with vodka, cigarette, cigar, pipe smoking. Policy street numbers of paper slip from fingers, box; eight-three-nine for me this morning, man. Couple of early morning beer drinkers threw their empty bottles in trash can baskets. He heard the rattle, the noise of hoarse, husky, squeaky, religious, sheepish, climbing, tones of his road buddies. Voices of storms, drift desert winds. Sad renderings as they jab at his chin. He ducks, feint, weave, bob with Mark. Hugs Bob Seal as they both finger point at Petey-Pete.

"Man, that son of a bitch went to sleep on me in Annapolis," Bob said. "Here I am driving and talking and the son of a bitch went to sleep on me in Annapolis." Shakes his head. "Sam, I don't know how you can put up with that little man." He grabs Pete around the neck, rubs some knuckles in on top of his head.

Sam stood leaning back on his truck. "As soon as he nods, I slap him right on the nose." Laughing with a wink at his partner. "He just a little puppy."

Pete pulls his head away, throws his hands at all of them. "Fuck all of ya!" Pete pats the front bumper grille. He snatches the vodka and orange juice jar from Bob.

Sam turns, checks on his truck tires. Duck spits his cigarette butt out to the ground. "We cleaned her down and everything for you." He walks up behind him. "Welcome back, Sam."

· · ·

7:00 a.m.

Doors roll up in front of the drivers.

Mike Milano unhinges the pulley ropes, peers down at the sun brown-black faces of the men. In the small crowd he saw a long ago face of Sam. He jumps off the dock down in the alley. "Sam the man!" They shake hands amongst the cheers. Mike asks him outright, "You ready to ride?"

Sam nods back, rolls up his denim shirt sleeves. "I'm ready!"

Mike nods up over to Pete. "You got your partner with you. He'll show you the new sites we got for the company." Sticks some gum in his mouth. "All right, you men! Come on in and get your assignments."

Joe Buck slaps Sam on the back. "Let's go, big man."

Sam walks with them through the side doors into the cool darkness of the warehouse. Smells of new fibers of silk, bear, sheep, polyester, shag, llama, row up seven to ten feet high. He felt cold as the men bundled up at the office door. Familiar faces of friends playing, joking, cussing each other. Hyena laughing from Junior over beating out a foreman over some extra floor carpet for himself, selling him the less quality piece from the back of his truck. Road games again would see him on his way down the I-95 South white stripe. He just wanted to catch his breath again from her image, just get lost one more hour, one more day on the highway.

21

At the end of the week:

Friday was a sanctified retreat for Sam to get the tough week over from the bumpy rides, heavy lifting. Girl watch-lusting, bullshitting. Just whistling at you, Momma! Baby! Darlin'! He just wanted to shower away the uncompromising back pain blues. His empty apartment without any woman's sweet leg smells was a coffin. A sacrificial sin, a piece of celibacy of corner dust. Spiders on his books, Nigger Bible, Mama black widow. All iceberg. Kill a White man now.

He reaches on top of his refrigerator, uncaps a bottle of scotch. He shakes down ice cubes out of the tray from a place as cold and unforgiving as his tired ass about now. He falls on his couch, drinks down the scotch, unbuttons his shirt, kicks his mud working sole boots off his onion fried feet. It hurt, it hurt so damn much. He drank up, felt his tongue swell away the pain in his mouth, not having her in his arms.

Never having her in his arms. It hurt, it cut through the right side of his chest like a butcher's knife, the knife Mabel was afraid of all her Black-ass life.

He looks around his place. A silence, afternoon, evening noise of children. Mothers coming home with bags, boxes, hollering in the halls. He unzips his pants, stands, rips them off his ass. He falls back on the couch, reaches for his drink. *Penthouse* magazine pages of some bare-tit Amazon poking out her lips in strawberry lipstick. He starts to sweat, turns the pages to a Chester Himes short story.

A couple of knocks on his door:

"Who the fuck is it?" He's mad. "Who the fuck is it?" Should he put his pants on for the stranger? Hell no.

"Mutherfucker! Your brother Ray! Open up, Sam!" Bangs his fist on the door like he was going to raid the place with a pickax.

He flings the magazine to the floor. "Coming!" He walks over, pops the chain lock off the green door. "Well, if it ain't the goddamn pig!"

"Let me in, man!" Ray hugs him around the neck. "That's right, I'm making a house call. Checking on my little brother."

He backs up to let him in. "Have a drink." He walks over towards the refrigerator, reaches for the bottle. Dirty glass from the sink, rinses it.

Ray sits on the couch. "All right! I'm through too for today… I'll have a little one with you."

Sam pours, plops some cubes in.

Ray looks around at the place. Books, magazines, sax, a couple of stinking socks. A small dining room table, shirt and pants on the floor, over top the boots.

Rubs his hands together, takes the drink from him. "Finished up your first week?"

Sam stretches, sits next to him, picks up his drink. "Yep, and I'm sore as shit!" He drinks, gets back up, makes him another one. "How's Mabel doing?"

"That's why I'm by." He's eager. "I got her doing some detective work for me, over at State."

"Like what?" Sam is interested, stirs his ice cubes with his finger.

"Checking up on our Haitian brothers over at the embassy."

"What you got her checking on?"

Ray wipes his hot forehead. "The players."

Sam pulls his earlobe. "The colonel and his boys?" He scratches the side of his face, he needed a shave. "No surprises."

"What you mean?" Ray asks him like he was stupid or something, not politically hip.

Sam hunches, "It's like jazz. If you playing and making money in this country... you's connected."

Ray gives him a shameless wink. "Little brother, it's free money everywhere and as long as you can get away with it. Without," points at him, "and I mean without getting popped, you a free man."

Sam raises the glass up to his lips. "Well, I'm black and poor."

"We all are," Ray says. "But that don't stop you from doing your thing."

Sam responds back quick. "My thing... I really don't give a fuck about politics... I just want this pretty black Creole woman in my life."

Ray spits out some of the ice back in the glass. "They watching you." He wants to shake him by his thick neck. "That woman is going to come at a high price... It's about magic, man, magic!"

"That voodoo shit!" Sam slaps his hand in the air. "Like Red Foxx use to say... you show me a ghost... I'm going to cut him." He scratches his chest. "Ray, I'm sitting up here scratching my head, scratching my ass, thinking about one thing and that's Myrthe... Now all I need is you and some of my boys to block this so-called puppet colonel mutherfucker and all that voodoo shit. I'll do the rest." He rubs his chest. "In the war the V.C. got all hopped up on some dope and came after us in the day and in the night. They were screaming, yelling, killing a-plenty. But one thing they never forgot. And we lost the war, but they got a good ass-whipping!" He bangs his fist on the coffee table." I didn't die there... and I'm glad I didn't, because it wasn't my fucking war... But one thing I know." He points down at the floor. "Them black bastards on my soil now." He slurps his drink. "A little colonel and a little country with a few rifles been fucked left and right by every white man in the world... ain't going to come over here and tell me I can't have the woman I want. They got just enough to keep poor people in check. I'm sure them high-yellow niggers kicking black people in the ass because of the color of their skin. I tell you what: I will die right here today for this woman because she's enslaved by her own people!" He rests his arm on his chin. He becomes solemn. "Now I found somebody that I stopped all my partying for; her voice made me look into my own heart. Her tears have made me see my pain. Her smell has made me realize life's fragrance on a cold and warm summer day." He points at himself. "She has given me life."

Ray listens to his brother's fire. The time bomb of words coming from his heart, his soul. "All for love, right, Sam?"

Sam answers him. "That's right, Ray. All for love."

Ray reaches inside his sports coat pocket. "Happy birthday, man!"

Sam was shaken by the envelope. "It's June the tenth?" He takes it. "Huh?" Rubs his fingers through his hair. "I forgot... "

"I know." Ray pats him on the shoulder. "I know."

"Shit!" He felt like a bug, out of his hole into the light looking to find a crumb, a piece of life again. "Damn!"

"Open it up." Ray grins. "Something me and Mabel got you."

He rips the envelope. A card; picture of a man fishing on the dock. Pipe, straw hat, toes sticking up. Pole in one hand, sitting in a lounge chair, can of beer beside him:

> Waiting for the fish to come in
> The world waits with you
> On this very special day
> You can be a pain sometimes
> But you can also be a clown
> Don't worry you won't drown
> Happy Birthday!

Two airline tickets fall out. He picks them off the rug. "I'm going on a trip?"

"They for your honeymoon." Ray finishes his scotch. He got thirsty for another one. "You know. For you and Myrthe."

227

Sam looks in his brother's clean-shaven face. Unspoken words. Nothing had to be said. Enough was said. He believed him. Convinced him that he wasn't going crazy, didn't have to be locked up again. No, he wasn't crazy, not even on his birthday.

22

A few days later Sam was driving on Twenty-first Street near the campus of George Washington University. He felt as if he was melting in the wet, hot, humid air of a warm rain. Traffic slowed in the afternoon amongst red, grey mausoleum offices cascading down from Thirteenth to Twenty-third. Cobble, slick-black streets made a path towards people waiting for the rain to end. Some just kept walking as if the tide would never change. Under Haagen Dazs lights they hold on to their precious newspapers, magazines, briefcases, Styrofoam cups. Local book stores shed comfort for the wet, tired GS-7 clerk. Pictorial movie special blazes from an adult book store: Christy Balloons coming your way in a few days. Army, Navy surplus, Marine flak jackets on sale today. While the shop next door had all sold out on Ronald Reagan dolls. Sterile glass people in sterile glass storefronts drink coffee or espresso over a cheese Danish. Lies from their lips on Mayor Robinson: a new house in

P.G. County. Window washing a wife and a girlfriend at the same time, trips to Atlantic City. Bus ride cost you fifteen bucks. Throw in lost dogs, lost children snatched by their mothers for a welfare check and you will always find street people ready to jump right in the headlights of his truck. He bangs the horn. "God dammit! Get out the way!"

On a government coffee break he met Mabel at the Foggy Bottom park across from the State Department. She had on a red African wrap around her head. Long braids fell down to her shoulders, accenting a moon, sunny brown face. Small gold earrings, short sleeve gold top, long brownish-gold dress straight down to her ankles. Gold watch on her arm, gold bracelet on the other. Brown pumps on her small, delicate feet. yes of light blue shadow. A mile of a smile. A kiss on the cheek for him as she spoke in her hourglass soft, sleepy voice. "Hey, baby! How you doing?" She wanted him to smile and mean it. She didn't want him to look at the pigeons, the drunk on the bench, the squirrels at their feet looking for a nut to kill. She wanted him to feel the sunshine coming back out over the sleepy willow trees. She knew when he was acting phony, he would give her a short hunch of his shoulders. Patient man but stared in space at other planets.

He wondered about that. "All right, I guess?" Scratches his chin.

She looks over his shoulder. "Where is Petey?"

Points at the truck a few feet away. "In the truck, sleeping, dreaming as usual."

She takes his hand, guides him to a bench. "That what makes the world go round, Sam. Leave him alone… Just let him dream."

Sam crosses his leg. "You called me. Now I'm here." He was matter of fact in his attitude with her. "Ray told me you was doing some detective work for him?"

She knew he was a nasty man when it took him too long to get what he wanted. She guessed that was because he was the baby in the family. The last one born, the last one to get all the cuddling, gifts, petting and sucking from his momma. "You always told me,you gots to know what you dealing with out here in the streets."

"That's terrible! You mean to tell me you remember some crap I said to you over a hundred years ago?" Shakes his head. "Whew! I see a lot of things come back to haunt me."

"Even me?"

"Yeah, even you." He pulls out a pack of cigarettes. Coughs, strikes a match to one of them. "You want one?" Puts the pack back in his shirt pocket.

"No, I quit." She opens up her black leather strap purse.

He thought how Ray was a success story for her. He couldn't make her stop. Lord! It took the other brother to bring her health back. He was bad for her. They were bad for each other, two bad apples sitting on the bench, relaxing under the burnt trees. Praying for more rain. He looks at some reports, gold seal of the bald eagle. "What you got there?" he asked.

"Study these… Know what you dealing with."

He snatches them. "Shit! You can get locked up for this." He peers around the greenery of the park scene. Mothers strolling with lovers, suits walking fast to some meeting, cops driving by. Scared pigeons strutting, looking for a crumb to kill. He sticks the papers in his back pocket. Uncrosses his leg, frowns. "Um!"

She shrugs. "It doesn't matter to me, especially when it comes to saving a man I use to care very, very much about. " She rolls her eyes. "Fuck those white people with all their secrets against us."

He pats his pocket. "What are they?" Puffs, knocks ash to the ground. Rests his eyes over her valentine heart-shaped face with those eyelashes of teddy bear qualities.

"Architect plans." Closes her purse. Snuggles closer. "They have plenty of secret doors in that place… I figure you need to know some of them."

A rain cloud trails over. Exclusive stop-action motion used up between their tornado love affair. Dropping down from the sky, black, twisting. But leaving the two of them with others. He finds her hand. "Will she, will she still be there when I go after her?"

Mabel clutches tight. "I'll see for you."

He pulls on the front of his cap with a simple grin. "If they fire you for this, you can always work on the truck." Kisses her on the cheek. "Be good."

"I will." She watches him walk away with a swagger in his steps. Bad left foot from marching, dodging bullets. Tall, hunched man. All she could notice was his solid concrete stubbornness and his love for riding on a Ferris wheel in the backwoods of Sweet Loaf during an August moon. He hops up in the truck. She waves as he drives off, felt cool drops of rain tap her arm. She rises, bends her head, catches some on her face. Shoulders her purse back to her job.

• • •

A few days later Mabel carried a handful of files to take back to the Haitian Desk Division. Grey and black tile floors scuffed by loafers. On the heels of diplomats, strangled by their suspenders. Run towards the fire of different wreckages. Democracy in chaos across the spinning twilight globe. Diplomacy seeking jungles; doors emblazoned in plaques: South Africa, Colombia, Eastern Europe, Asian under-secretary. Pictures of the primal elite from George Bush to George Schultz, throw in Ralph Bunche and a bag full of Harvard cryptic-speak fools. Add Jean Kirkpatrick and you will have a full house of queens beating down the door in flag-waving drag.

Communications Division was in the basement. Men with bat faces slept over monitors, copiers, spaceship WATS phone lines. Maps on the walls blink in green, red or yellow, hot, warm, cool spots in the world. Sunbathe in the south of France or get a bullet-riddled suit in El Salvador. That was life, and it was cool, as she wore a tight-fitting, black, short leather skirt, spiked heels to offset her long legs and wiggle. A white cotton blouse with the collar unbut-toned for the man she preyed upon. Happy, pleasant smile, put on her foreign affair charm to get a favor from a man. She didn't consider herself a glamour queen, but she could surprise the pants off a fish if his tail was served up on a plate. This fish is Othello Azmery.

Haitian Creole man, hair falling out, in his fif-ties. Walked fast, slammed his fist on desks when his files weren't ready to be delivered to the embassies.

He was a stickler for detail and never got shit out on time himself, but he was a part of the scheme to control the world. His Uncle-Tom French-sounding voice was always interrupted by a consistent cough, that made you want to give him a cough drop or tell him to take a few days off. Now, now, don't be afraid, Mr. Azmery. The man's not going to kick you out on your ass if you not here to deliver the messages to our beer drinking friends today.

Nervous palms. She knocks on the door to his office. Cough. "Come in."

She opens it, a file drops. His eyes pop, mouth drops, closes his lips in a purple grin. "Ms. Friday!" He gets up, rushes to pick up the file. Coughs, hands her the jacket. "Dese iz a pleasant surprise."

Mabel fumbles with the stack. "Mr. Altman told me to tell you that there is a rush on to get these files..." pushes them up to her chin, "... to get these files to the Haitian embassy by twelve... Something about a fiscal year fourth quarter deadline of private voluntary payments to the government."

He takes the files from her. "*Du soleil, un ange est tombé a mes pieds.*"

She blinks. "Excuse me?"

He looks into her eyes, fights to keep his view from her ample chest. "Nothing. Something I couldn't stop myself from saying in French. 'From the sun an angel falls to my feet.'"

"Ah, that's pretty."

"*Oui*, you are very pretty."

She crosses her arms, watching him place the files on the desk. Bald patches of his hair combed to the left, combed to the right to cover the barren earth of his head. Nervous man, ready to die in a hurry. He sat down at the desk, moves the files to the side.

"But the real reason I am here is because I am taking an interior designing course at night." She leans over slightly above his globed, patched head.

He taps the eraser of a pencil on his desk calendar. He wanted to grab her by her braids, take her right on the desk. "What school iz dis, Ms. Friday?" He watches the tight skirt pose, squeeze her hips. Imprint of her nipples, departed from her soft cotton blouse. He draws circles to take him from her face of watermelon lipstick.

"Eastern Shore College." She walks around, parades, pushes some braids back over her left ear. Essence of a smile, a dimple. She baits the hook in the waters, she won't let him nibble yet. "I hear the Haitian embassy has gone under some renovations recently and I would like to take a look… take some notes." She was kittenish, but humble. Wets her bottom lip.

He sits back, rolls the chair away from the desk to look at her high heels, legs going up to the mini skirt. He was aglow. He started to bite his nails. "Yes, of course! Of course, education iz a most powerful medicine." He stood, came back around the desk, walks up to her to gaze at a picture locket around her neck. "I would be glad to take you there." Peeps at the V design of her breasts pushed together. He points. "That is lovely."

She touches it. "It's a picture of my family; my mother, aunt and uncle."

He straightens up. "Be… ready by eleven."

She puts on a girlish, grateful act. "Thank you, Mr. Azmery! Thank you."

He opens the door with a smile and a cold sweat. "Just be ready at eleven."

She leaves out with that hip-shaking walk of triumph at snagging her man, passing men who twist in the halls—wanting to fall at the feet of a sun angel.

· · ·

At the Haitian embassy Mabel found the beauty of the gold mansion eclectic, cool, smart, in classical French motifs. Two-story foyer flanked by a giant dining room and a blue embroidered formal living room with plants and mirrors. Employees worked from offices on the first floor with files, papers, boxes. Spoke low on telephones at a front desk and greeted Mr. Azmery with a handshake and a smile. She gazes down at the cherry wooden floors; six tall marble columns divide them from a reception area. She became relaxed and tried to watch to see if she saw Myrthe. Maybe it was the one with dimples, hair in braids? The woman with a nice smile that greeted them at the desk? Could it be the one who walked with a vase of red roses? She stood patiently as large windows bring in the afternoon sunshine from the reception room.

A thick-neck, squat guard greeted Azmery in a blue shirt and pants, kissed him on both sides of the cheeks. They spoke in French as they hugged each other.

He turns and introduces her. "Ms. Friday, this is Major Cabaret." Hands him the files. "He is very grateful for these documents."

Mabel shakes his hand. He has an old scar over his left eye. "You are very welcome, sir." She gives a compliment. "It is such a lovely place."

"And I also mentioned to him that you are doing a paper for your college."

Major Cabaret interrupts. "Mademoiselle," he takes her hand, "we will be most delighted to answer any questions you have of our renovations." He looks around, taps his chin. "I will get one of the ladies who have helped us a great deal in finishing some of the grueling work in the embassy." He touches Mr. Azmery's arm. "I'll be right back." He leaves them to go to one of the people at the front desk.

Mr. Azmery was delighted in having her by his side, but he didn't have time for sightseeing. He checked his watch. "You pleased?"

She smiles as she strains to see the fireplace. "Ah, yes." She saw him check his watch twice already. "Look, you go on back. I know you have a lot to do." She just gave him a Lauren Bacall whisper. "Thanks, Mr. Azmery."

He nods, drags his feet like a playful deer in love in the woods for the first time. He has to ask, "Should I come back to pick you up?" Sticks his small finger in his mouth, bites his nail. Coughs, steps away from her face as he suspects the morning tryst was over.

"No." She gives him that look that lets him know that she's through with him. She has used him up for her purposes. Lets him sniff the perfume from her neck, she pleasantly let him touch the locket on her breast. This was her warning to him that could make a lion stand still in front of a she-wolf.

He became numb. "Fine! I'll see you later… "

"I'll see you later." She turns her back.

He says goodbye to his friends, walks out of her purple life of flowers, sardines, saltine crackers and a blank stare towards the paintings on the walls.

Mabel became a voyeur in the art of a people.

Artists on the walls: wood carvings of masks of voodoo gods by St. Aimie, sugarcane cutter paintings splashed in the yellow of the sun and river of stars by a guy named Lauselle. Marketplace, fishermen on the wharf, Hippolyte's hands were thick and dreaming in blues and green of the seas. Just women walking or sitting with baskets on their heads, faint from the sun and flies, by a man named St. Clair. Battle scenes by Antoine; revolutions long ago, show Napoleon the way.

Checks her watch, almost twelve thirty.

A guard walks a German shepherd dog through the entrance. Trained to attack, not to piss on the rugs. She became nervous amongst smiling people answering phones, greeting others in the reception area. Some were turned away, some were asked to be seated. Friends or enemies of a state, the tiger watches everyone.

Just that moment she sees her coming down the winding stairs with Major Cabaret. Tall, elegant, a Diane Carroll look-alike. It's her, it has to be her. Her neck thin, carries a bunch of long hair down her back. Dressed in a traditional outfit of red, white, blue lace that comes down over her smooth, brown golden shoulders. Sam told her she had a lot to do with decorating the place.

Major Cabaret was a mole to this tall black swan.

Mabel waits, heart pumps faster. Glad to still see her here in Washington, D.C. for Sam's heart-tugging sake. Her lines are of a model, about five-nine with the curves of the African woman in her hips, champagne glass breasts. Evidently a woman of many languages: French, Creole, Spanish and English. A woman with only one focus, and that's to be with a dirty, hard-drinking, drunk driver.

Major Cabaret introduces her. "Ms. Friday, I would like for you to meet our charming lady of the mansion, Mademoiselle Presumé."

They shake hands.

Myrthe spoke slowly in halting French inflections. "Come... diz way... please." She leads her towards the veranda of three sets of French doors. "Let's... show you the gardens first." Myrthe notices that the woman doesn't have a pencil or pen to take notes. "Do you need... pad... pen?"

Mabel follows her out the door. "No, just talk... Just talk."

Myrthe frowns. "Major Cabaret tells me you... are student?" She stops at the balcony overlooking the trimmed hedges. Rose bushes were being cut for the foyer. She didn't have time for nonsense with this strange woman with her tight butt, poked-out mini-skirt on.

"I am taking a night course in interior designing."

"And... " Myrthe's hands wrap around the white steel awning fence. "You work where?" She watches as the men clip, cut, snap the thorns off the roses. She stares at the woman with the mascara eyes, butter brown plump cheeks. "I don't believe you."

Mabel can hear the water falling into a crescendo of noise over the emerald blue grass. "Show me the grounds some more. I would like to see up closer what Sam Murphy saw in this garden."

In a voice of joy Myrthe said, "Sam!" Anxiously she asks, "You a friend of his, aren't you?" She closes her eyes to imagine seeing that silly little cap on his head with his shirt collar opened, showing hair sprinkled up from his chest.

They start to stroll down the steps towards the gardeners, maintenance workers, guards roaming in circles, men up ladders. Fixing light bulbs, tulip bulbs, terminating bugs. Other women bring out Hefty bags of trash from last evening's affair of state; some roll down the giant umbrellas over the tables.

Mabel lets her mask of pretension fall. "Yes, I am a friend of his." Takes her by the hand. "Come on, Myrthe, show me the fountain's waters."

23

Ten steps up to Sacred Heart Church for Sunday mass as Catholic rites circle around upper 16th Street from the Washington, D.C. sidewalks. Traffic floats, cars, buses cruise lazily to the eight a.m. show. Myrthe takes these steps to see Jesus on the cross, enters the oak doors with others. She kneels, crosses her heart, prays to die with the lamb, up on her feet. She sits in the pews watching Father Boudreaux in his flowing red and white robes read passages of prayer. "*Benedi camus Domino. Deo Gratias.*" Two sleepy faces of thirteen-year-old altar boys follow behind him with their hands clasped together. Prayers, citations ring, songs in offerings to the Virgin Mary. Myrthe prays with him in a white scarf, white dress, gloves. She becomes the lamb beside him to sacrifice. Candles flicker, flowers sit behind this tall, white-haired man, eyes of smoke blue, hands frail, unromantic to see. He blesses the body. He blesses the blood.

She rises, follows others, kneels in front of him. Her head goes back, lets him slip it in her mouth, tastes the salt, bitterness of his body. Father Boudreaux speaks:

>Our Father who art in Heaven
>Hallowed be Thy name
>Thy kingdom come
>Thy will be done...

He blesses her with the sign. She gets up, walks back to her seat, basks in the tunnel-high gold ceilings of the church, cold, broken brick floors. Cracked-vein old people wait for their heads to be chopped off. Saints pray with the sinners, sing with the angels, dance with the devils. Calm down the crying babies; breast-feed them in front of God. See them through, see them through the storms. Help them grow, to be slaves of bondage to the King of Rock and Roll. Feed them cream white milk from a mother's breasts, keep them quiet in the pews.

She stands, kneels, grabs hold of an old woman's hand. She must have ten, twelve babies, be a good Catholic wife as a bullet ricochets off your skull, for God's sake. Myrthe looks at Jesus on the cross, soaked in blood. Her sins washed away down a sink as she sleeps with a man who tortures her in a chair at night, blindfolded, gagged, gun to her head, knife at her throat. He licks the baby's breast milk from her tits. She prays, kneels, listens to the dead words of Father Boudreaux strangle her to submission.

Marble-white columns hold up the placid Sistine tabernacle. Windows in red, blue, green, cut-glass figures of angels, crying, smiling, playing with us on earth. The blood of slavery rings out from choir high falsetto voices. Songs dance, roam in the giant halls of giants. Pages of a man who wanted to share life with her, plant seeds for a people. Love! Love! Love! She lets the frail, dark woman's hand loose, lets it drop, fall in prayer. The woman's face was a bottle of swollen pox splotches. She stood in an alcoholic slump of smells, eyes fading over the canvas of the crucifix. She prays with her for release. Let me go, Lord! Let me go! In a long blackish-grey, drab dress she kneels, shorter than her, five-foot-two, elfish with straw hair in a bun, probably used to be a healthy woman of parties, flowers, picnics. Now she prays beside her for a man, always a man, a dog. A world that didn't care about her pain in her ribs, her chest, a lump of cancer eating at her breasts. A pill-box woman that dripped with the leaking faucet of prayers. A man on the cross cries with the guy who watches football, baseball, basketball, hockey, soccer games... and sucks beers. A man, always a man who drinks cheap, twelve-ounce beer and fucks her at night. A man who died on the cross. A man who bleeds for her this Sunday, was not afraid to die again.

They both drank blood red wine. White pearl-framed eyeglasses cover those eyes as the shawl of lace and time over her shoulders. It must be the same piece of cloth she wore the night she married her husband in some small country town. Maybe the night she had her second child, that died in her arms from complications of stress? Precious baby-boy-child. Daddy wasn't home. He had gone to sleep with some White, Latino, Black, Italian, Irish pickled woman just before the baby came that night. The night the dogs howled for a baby, a man, a God.

Myrthe grabs her hand, both of them afraid—afraid to love ever again. Myrthe looks at her without smiling. She watches tears travel down cheeks of brown dry cotton. This is her daily reward of life with voodoo prayers from Mrs. Prosper's tongue. Her voice mixed up confusion, that was just a figment of a thumb print from French missionary hands.

She whispers back a prayer for God to hear... just God to hear.

. . .

It was Tuesday, almost midnight, in Mrs. Prosper's bedroom of green walls. White light from the quarter moon comes through lace curtains. Fourth floor, back room, nestled away from the rest in the mansion. Closet long enough for three seven-foot coffins. A place for a ceremony of skulls with three dark women praying at the altar, never forgetting their African gods, wrapped up in the arms of sweet Jesus.

Rum bottles, black face dolls, one of a man, one of a woman. Two bare-breasted women stand behind Mrs. Prosper with their heads tied up. All wearing white. Low, soft charming hums, hymns come from their lips, not to wake up the guests, workers or even the mouse. Flickering flames glow on top the mantle. Flickering flames waver in the night darkness of the coffin-shaped closet. A snake lay twisting beside the many bottles of rum, twisting its tail nicely over the skull, in front of the crucifix of Jesus. Sweet, dear Jesus.

Mrs. Prosper grabs the back of its head; its mouth opens. Sticks the Host in its mouth, the body of Jesus, sweet Jesus. She shimmers, waves under a soft, delicate whisper with the other two women a song in Creole:

  Diab la mandé tra vay!
  Apre Dié gadem pa pe peson oh!
  Diyo mrin la ro sou kre ya manyin mrin
  Manyin mrin sou kre ya manyin Choual sila
  Ma rele gadem pa pe peson oh!

African women of Dambala; God of the snakes. Come forth! See! See my mystery.

The women shake their hips, jut their asses. Mrs. Prosper's hands go up, she holds the snake above her head. Spins around and around in the aroma of rum and smoke flaming candles. She lashes out with the snake as one of the women falls to the floor on her back.

Mrs. Prosper holds the snake over top of her. Pushes it. Pulls it back from her face, neck, over the skirt rising above her yellow hot hips. The loa; Dambala and Jesus enters her. She rips the buttons from her dress. Eyes roll back in her head. Mrs. Prosper jumps on top of her, the snake licks at her lips, making her taste the wine of Dambala. The meat of the sacrifice to him with the sweet Jesus. Arm in arm over this woman of Africa. This woman of the earth, trees, stars, this mother of the Diaspora. All strip-butt naked in the flames and smoke of Dambala. The other woman sings a hymn standing still in one place. No shoes or sandals, nipples puffed, swollen. Their bodies pouring with sweat as Mrs. Prosper and the woman kiss each other in front of the altar of skulls and oil lamp flames.

White dresses with broad shoulders wrap around their ankles. Mrs. Prosper pours rum on the woman on the floor. All three become a circle in this room, this night, this day to give praise. All thanks to Father Boudreaux for the rosary beads.

Mrs. Prosper looks down at the woman still shaking on the floor. She lays the snake on the woman's belly., lets it roam over her stomach, breasts, thighs. Until it finds the entrance way up her heart-shaped hole of love. Hole of feast. Hole of birth. Hole of death, all for Legba.

She jerks, shakes, grits her teeth, pushes her hips up for the snake to get in deeper. Shuts her eyes tight, to be fucked, to be loved by Dambala and Jesus. Mrs. Prosper grabs its tail, gulps down the bottle of rum, passes it to the other girl. She dances over top of the humping woman, pulls the snake slowly out. All the while chanting a song underneath her breath:

> *Grand Bois ro!*
> *Grand Bois moute bra! la le!*
> *Oh! adie Bou die…*
>
> *Kongo l'azil oh!*
> *Kongo makout odan!*
> *Anye! anye! laaaaaa! odan*
> *Nou!*
> *Grand moun*
> *Ohhhhhhh!*

Not long after this night Mrs. Prosper started to bring about spells from the aloe plant in her duties of giving Myrthe her freedom from Colonel Labossier. She had the forethought to cut out this rotten root of a man from the crust of Myrthe's soul. Around the mansion she had to be careful not to get caught, for in the history of her people, Mother Africa had

246

remained with all its spells and magic. Stories, remedies passed down from the first slave landing on the island of Hispaniola. Columbus had done the new world no good by bringing the mother of the earth here. But with all the instincts and survival skills of a cat landing on its paws the first time out of its mother's womb, so did the African survive war, disease and hatred for his race. It comes a time when women of the earth, the first born shall reap the harvest of a field, full it up in her basket, stick it on top of her head and walk down the road to take care of her man. Mother Prosper knew, and did this to three husbands. The fourth one, Mr. Prosper, died in her arms after she planted a spell on him to live in this plant that now sat tall and strong by her bedside.

•　　•　　•

Sunday, last day in July, limited edition of a hot cliche coming up for air at the beginning of summer August days. Mrs. Prosper in her white-cotton dress, white head tie, plump waist of an old woman. Energetic enough to tend to the plants and tend to the colonel and his guests from the Florida Keys.

She serves them ice tea on the veranda. Sugar, lemon for the husband with a raccoon toupee that waited for a breeze to blow the tight grease from his bumpy black Grecian Formula sideburns. His wife a blonde that acted like the last whore on the streets of Washington, D.C.. She smelled like the dog taking a piss in front of the White House in her wraparound red mini skirt. Sparkling diamonds around her neck and a voice that was of a little girl in her first year of

247

high school, about to fail in everything except fuck-ing the lab teacher behind the Bunsen burner for a B. They were a nouveau riche mess. He smokes a cigar. She pops gum in between gulps of the tea.

He leans over the bowl of lemons. "This is our last day in Washington." They shake each other's hands. "I want to thank you for your fine hospitality, Charles." He plays with a diamond ring on his finger. "You just make sure you come and visit me and my Elthel anytime." Pats down the back of hair that he paid almost a thousand dollars for. "Honey, pass me some of them sugar cubes."

Colonel Labossier gets them for him. "I'll be delighted, Mr. Venuzzi." Hands him the bowl. "Maybe sometime in September."

Mr. Venuzzi picks up one, plops it in his drink. He reaches for another one. Mrs. Venuzzi plucks his knuckles with a spoon. "That's enough, Joe."

He smiles at her. "Heavens, dear! Heavens!" Stirs, "I'm glad we had this chance to meet and talk about our special project." He dabs his forehead with a napkin.

"I don't want you to worry about anything, sir. Your shipments will be well guarded in Haiti before coming to Key West." He crosses his leg. "We will be in touch by Telex… if there are any problems in September."

Mr. Venuzzi drinks. "I know you like to fish… so you just come on down whenever you are ready." He puts his glass down. "We have some great marlin fish-ing in the Keys."

Colonel Labossier stirs his ice tea, but his right hand starts to twitch. It felt as if some mosquitoes were stinging his thumb and knuckles. Drops his spoon, scratches at his hand.

"Charles, are you okay?" Mrs. Venuzzi asks. She reaches down, places the spoon back by his tall glass.

It stops itching. He watches Mrs. Prosper ordering one of the maids to move the plants into the sun. "I'm fine… " Shrugs. "Just some ants trying to get the sugar from my fingers."

"I am sorry we didn't get the chance to meet your wife," Mrs. Venuzzi said.

"Um, she didn't come this trip… She doesn't like Washington, D.C."

Mrs. Venuzzi twists another lemon peel in her drink. "May I ask why?"

He smiles, plays with his mustache. "She says I never have time for her or the children here… " He frowns. "Something about too much business going on."

Mr. Venuzzi agrees. "It is a company town." Pulls on his ear. "No place for families… Just ants trying to get the sugar from your fingers."

They all laugh. Clap their glasses together.

24

Laughter from flies underneath her bare feet.

Myrthe stood watching the immaculate, vindictive puppet colonel and his guests from Key West under her balcony of finger-stretching ivy. Twisting leaves roam up to her room as she watches his business dealings without her around. Haiti was just a small, black-ass country street whore to the highest bidder.

She knew he sold their land, their home, pieces of people to fill his pockets fat with dollar bills. She knew her country would always be a street whore of a long ago revolution, selling its freedom to drug merchants. Haiti was a rotten piece of apple, mango, pear or plum for the picking at the barrel of a gun, with her father, the street urchin, always trying to push the cart up a mountain.

She closed her shutters at the sickening laughter.

Knocks on her door. She walks away from the sound of flies to let Mother Prosper in. Hugs her tight. Locks the door behind with chain up. Latch bolted across from this man who kept her enclosed in a world of brick, glass, ivy of brutal forced love. She was afraid and trained by his fingers to beg on her knees for more of his tongue licks over her chocolate milk flesh.

"Mother Prosper, would you like to help me finish doing the curtains for your room now?" She pushes some hair from the side of her left eye.

Mother Prosper guides her to sit on the side of the bed. "I want to show you a new stitch on your sewing machine." She pulls out a piece of cloth. "We call this the Black Widow stitch."

Myrthe handles a piece of white cloth. "The stitch is done into the shape of a small spider."

Mother Prosper answers her. "You see, it's right in the hem of the cloth."

Myrthe sees that the light in Mother Prosper's face isn't there… It has sort of disappeared into an overcast cloud coming to cool off the hot August day. A storm of silence is brewing inside this old friend. "Mother Prosper, teach me to make this stitch."

She sticks it back in her dress pocket. "This stitch is only done before the day of the full September moon." She crosses her legs, places both her hands in her lap. "This stitch is done when you have the worries of the earth on your mind. Before birth, before a death." She touches Myrthe's hands. "It is a stitch that you teach to another woman who meant a lot to you over the years… such as a sister-friend."

Myrthe asks anxiously, "Like me?" She wants the love of this woman who has given her the strength to hold her head up high, to never be afraid of the shadows in the night.

"Yes, child, like you."

"I must do it before I leave, then… " Myrthe says this under her breath. She still hears the stupid, drunken laughing of the colonel below her window. Goose bumps travel up her arm, she rubs them away.

Mrs. Prosper reassures her about the future. "Your footprints in the sand shall wash up one day on the shores of our country… We are shadows roaming the world, without a home or place. But your love for this man will teach you patience, and he will give you strength after me." She looks away from her eyes, then back to her again. "Your heart is up there." She points towards the ceiling of gold with a whirling fan spinning around for some cool air. "With the stars… " Closes her eyes for a few seconds. "I sense the spirit of your mother with you, beside you. In your trials of love you shall never forget the shores of Haiti."

Myrthe listens to the soft words coming from her lips. "Mrs. Prosper, why you say such things?"

"I talk like this, Myrthe, because you must know the winds are about to take me away from you… but you must not be afraid. This man Sam… this mountain of a man will fight to keep you close to him and keep the night shadows away from your dreams. He is a good man… He is a good man."

Myrthe reaches out, hugs the old woman around the neck. Smells the spices of chili powder, bay leaves in her hair and neck. This made her think about her own mother in this bedroom.

Mrs. Prosper said to her, "You must not cry… I have seen nights of many stars, and one night soon…

I shall be with them." She grabs her apron, pulls it up to Myrthe's face, dabs some tears away.

Myrthe slaps her eyes. "Our colonel seems to be very relaxed underneath us."

Mrs. Prosper's eyes became a saucer of laughter. "Dear, dear, it's not a good time for him right now." Shakes her head, trying to keep her voice down from the shutter windows.

Myrthe pulls her arm. "Let's sew!"

Mrs. Prosper stood. "My mother taught me how to make this stitch."

Myrthe nods. "Your mother taught you everything."

She unbolts, unlatches, opens and closes the door behind them. She looks up at the woman with the eyes of the moon, as black sunlight came in her hair all the way down her back. "Yes she did, Myrthe… and remember that."

Myrthe goes along with this. "I will, Mrs. Prosper."

Winks up at her with a sly grin of a curse. "One day… you'll have a little girl too." Points at her with a long nail. "One day… you'll see… " She lifts her long dress to measure the stairs. "Now, let's get up these stairs."

Myrthe holds her by the arm. They take slow steps up to the attic, to the sewing room. One stitch at a time with her mother-friend. One step would be more.

• • •

Different points of view on a Wednesday afternoon as Mrs. Berrios plays with her Andy Warhol costume jewelry of popcorn necklaces, bulb blue,

253

red earrings, snake bangles around the wrists, silver charm bracelet of the African elephants from her box of goodies. Campbell soup cans, Marilyn Monroe, the Beatles, pictures on pink walls. She loves to show off her American icons. Romantic woman from the South American jungles gets all she can from this culture of silliness and violence. She learns their hip, jive, slick language from the halls of Congress to the El Salvadoran neighborhoods on Columbia Road. She displays her love for this country with tributes to the gaudy tinsel minds of a lazy people calling themselves artists. But she knows they are really media entertainers, becoming rich over what is hip today, tonight and tomorrow.

She slips an elephant charm bracelet around her left wrist, admires her Ruby Tuesday sunglasses on her eyes. Only she can see rainbow faces in her rainbow world as Myrthe sits behind her on a fat pink love seat sofa trying not to giggle at this silly show. In this private gallery of Pollock and Warhol paintings of stripes and American icons, she is comfortable under the bright lights and cool, refrigerated central air. But this display does make her thirst for more traditional paintings of Renoir, Matisse, Cezanne. But Gail isn't about the past, she lives for today, and that's all that is ever exposed.

"You need some Van Gogh on the walls," Myrthe says with the crossing of her legs in her short denim skirt that rises up to reveal her thighs.

"I don't want a man who cut off his ear on my wall," Gail answers. "It makes me think of blood dripping all around me in this room." She picks around in the box.

"But that's art!"

"That's bullshit from a crazy man."

Myrthe pinches her ear. "They are all crazy... destructive pieces of shit."

"Yes, they are, but I still don't want this man's blood on my walls." She spins around, picks up the bracelet. "I like these elephants... don't you?"

"No, I don't." Myrthe goes to the mirror. "I like these." She pulls up some round silver earrings with ivory stones in each one.

Gail rolls her eyes. "Oh! They boring!"

Myrthe looks at her. "Just like me?"

"Yes, just like you." She twists the bracelet off.

"Whore!" Myrthe calls out, sticks the earrings in.

Gail snatches the brush off the dresser. "Beetch!"

They both laugh in the mirror at each other. Black face, olive-white face. See each other to smile at their gifts of being women. Playing in their little girl world of lipstick, doing their nails, trying on each other's shoes, dresses. Not much to do except get prepared for fall parties. House guests from Nigeria and Sweden are to arrive soon. They have time to call each other bitch, whore, slut, and laugh as they throw makeup, powder, lipstick. Make their own body pictures on each other's faces-butts. Mess up their hair to go to the shop in Georgetown later on. Nothing much to do but to beat the shit out of each other.

Myrthe accuses her, "You play games... just like them Americans!" She jumps on the sofa in her bare feet.

Gail is ready to throw a brush at her. "I got a surprise for you!"

Laughing at her, "What? What is it?" She hops down. "Another game... right?"

255

Gail is tired of chasing her. She sits down, pats the spot next to her. "I'm going to order some carpets this week while the major is on his trip... Do you know the name of a place to acquire such items?"

Myrthe scoots closer. "I know a great place!" Throws the pillow at her. "Whore!"

Gail knocks it down with the brush. "Beetch!"

. . .

Sweet Loaf Carpets warehouse on a Thursday morning. This dark box is hot, stuffy. Columns of shag white, broadloom, beige, brown, teal, blue, green, plush wheat brown. Twelve-foot-high rows along the side of dusty racks, all wrapped up in brown paper, thick ropes. Dust odors make you want to puke up last night's dinner with the cheap bottle of Napoleon brandy. Mike Malone's stomach pops out just like he handed out the delivery orders at the band of men waiting by the office.

"Duck and Kenny, heads up!" He waves the clipboard. "Rayburn Building... Congress. Don't make no deals for me." He hands the papers down to them.

"Bobby King and Junior!" He searches through the papers. "Tysons Corner... the mall... Get a couple of them commercial carpets on the rack." Winks down. "And don't go shopping."

"Mike! Bob! You two men going to... Pentagon." He yawns, hands them the papers. "Buy me a couple of them grenades for my neighbor's dog for keeping me up last night."

He flips through the orders. Sam! Sweet Sam Murphy!" He searches for him amongst the black, sleepy faces.

Petey-Pete nods up. Nudges him. "Sam."

Sam hollers up, "Here, Mike!" He was in the back, leaning on a row of flatbed trucks.

"Embassy Row!"

He walks through the arms. Doesn't care about them hollering at him and he damn sure doesn't care where he is going. He is already in hell waiting to see his Myrthe. He takes the orders.

Mike leans down. "You been requested." Points at him. Don't get in no trouble, Sam, with them high class women in D.C.." He cares. "Just bring your ass back to Sweet Loaf after you make them runs."

Sam walks back to read through the list of places:

     Guatemalan Embassy
     Swedish Consulate
     AMES Construction Company
     Army Research Institute
     Washington, Navy Yard
     Hawkins High School
     All Saints Hospital

Petey tries to look over his shoulder. Sam hollers at him, "Mannn, get in the fucking truck!"

Petey moves away, warns him, "All right. Just watch yourself."

Sam argues, walking behind him. "It says Guatemala, not Haiti."

The others follow them out. Picking up their rolls on hand trucks, dollies, lifting, grunting, cussing at the carpets on the back of their twenty-footers. All of them hollering. instigating, talking up plenty of shit before driving off.

Jesse picks up his hook bill knife. Slaps the dry grey glue off onto his pants leg. "Hey Petey-Pete, give me a cigarette, man!"

Pete opens up his door, turns. "Get your own, mutherfucker! You owe me a pack now!"

Kenny asks Duck, picking up some cans of glue, "What you do last night, man? Kiss your ol' lady's ass again when she came in late?"

Duck spins his Redskin cap on the back of his head. "Naw, man. I beat her... then fucked her... Is that awwwright with you?"

That satisfied him. "Yeah! That's coooool."

Bob Seal smashes an empty can of Schlitz in his hand. "Did you read the *Post* this morning?" he asked Junior, opening up a pack of cigarettes.

Junior lit up his cigarette. "Naw! man...," sucks, puffs out the smoke from his nose.

"The robbery!"

"Robbery?"

"Yeah, man, somebody stuck up the First Baptist Church."

Junior leans on the front grille of the truck. "Goddamn!" Plucks the ashes by his boot. "A church?" He scratches the bald spot coming in the back of his head.

"Shot Preacher Browne dead too."

All the men gather closer together when they hear this. Some look up at the sky. Some keep their heads down or just rub their chins, trying to figure the world out early in the morning.

Sam calls out, asking the men, "They didn't have to shoot him, did they?"

None of them answer in the silence of the morning.

Mike comes out the back door, wondering what's going on with the men. His arms go up as if to start flying like Superman. "Is there a problem out here?"

They snap out of the death of the preacher man. All of them move towards their red, black, green, yellow, white, brown trucks.

Darnell slaps Kenny on the back. Sam throws a thumbs-up to Mike. Opens the door, hops in. Petey-Pete snatches his red and white polka dot bandana from his back pocket, ties it around his head.

Bobby King, behind the wheel with his partner Joe Buck, said, "Man! I can't wait till Friday." He turns the key. "I have to see if Mike got any extra carpet to throw my way… I got a nice deal on some shag over in Marlboro."

"Mike always got extra carpet to throw your way if you need it."

Jesse hollers at Pete again before he gets in. "Give me a cigarette, man!"

Pete shakes his head. "Man, why you got to fuck with me? Go ask somebody else… Mutherfucker, are you drunk? Go ask Junior."

"I'm going to pay you back Friday, man."

Pete gets in the truck, slams the door. "Jesse… Friday ain't never here with you."

"Fuck you!" He walks away from the truck staggering.

Sam starts the truck up. "Pete, let's go man." He snatches the brake loose. "And he is drunk." He pushes his foot down, cruising out the alley as barking dogs start their vicious wag-a-tail dance around the wheels.

25

He chews on two Tums and excuses the shoe-lace figure traffic trailing in the donut of Dupont Circle. Back down to U Street. Sam takes the short-cut to Irving and Fourteenth, crosses Massachusetts Avenue over to Rock Creek Park. Under the rock bridges police motorcycles park on side roads for a coffee break before hitting a driver up for a stupid-ass speeding ticket or a twenty-dollar bribe. School buses roll behind him through the acres of dead Indian ghosts. Graves of a new age. Red brick homes up embankments; scaling high over the Watergate vestiges of Nixon's shoulders.

He drives up to a tall gate with a red phone. No guard or dog. He gets out, picks it up and speaks. "Mornin'."

A voice buzzes, "Guatemalan Embassy. May we help you?"

"Sweet Loaf Carpets."

"You may enter."

He walks back to the truck, pulls his cap off, slaps Pete in the face with it. "Wake up! We here." He smiles at the small pup face of his partner. "Mannn, why don't you get some sleep at night?"

Petey yawns. "Okay, Sam." Stretches his arms out, digs his fist in his eyes. He sits up, checks out the dome of the mansion. "Wow! This is nice."

Sam glides the truck through the gate. Drives up towards the circle entrance way, towards the fountain in the middle. A butler with a fat neck, skinny body, directs him around the back.

He shrugs. "Of course, for the servants." He gazes around at the Colonial siding of the manor of the man from the Guatemalan plantation. Trees sprinkled around an acre of lawn. Wood and stone mansion of the state dictatorship from South America. He throws the brake, pushes the clutch into neutral. "Shit! We here. Let's get this carpet off the back." Throws his cap back on his head. Sticks his gloves on his fingers, balls up his fists.

He goes to the red back door, knocks on a golden door knob. This cute blonde opened up. He smelled whiskey on her. Hair bobbed back, a cracked face, but with some mystery to it. A ponytail, little ass in a tight pair of jeans. Low-cut black blouse, spike heels. Sam greets her. "Good morning, ma'am…. We from Sweet Loaf Carpets."

She leans on the door, peers up at this six-two frame. About two hundred pounds and a nice chin she would like to bite on, but he wasn't her man. Didn't look like he had a brain in his head, just in his pants. "And I am, gentlemen, Mrs. Galiano Berrios." Sweeps an arm out towards the fields of grass, trees, flowers of purple and gold. "I am the lady of this dump."

"Uh, we here to bring you some shag... shag carpet." Pete asks, "Where you want it at?"

She plays with the top button on her blouse. "It's so early and muggy." Fans her hand across her face. The short one was slim with a wide chest. Face of a ruby, eyes bright, brown, spaced wide apart as if to see the universe for the very first time. "Bring it through here, gentlemen... the kitchen."

"Yes, ma'am," Sam said. He pulls Petey from the door. "Come on."

She watches them walk away. The big one has seen the universe a little too much for her taste. She warms up to this game and the surprise awaiting Sam. This crazy fool in love with another crazy fool in love. She watches the men fight with the rug off the truck. She calls out for the butler, "Rolande! Guide these men to my playroom!"

He comes in, bows as his voice answered like a church bell that scared you into God's arms. "Yes, Mrs. Berrios."

.   .   .

Winding stairs and a seven-foot hallway lead them to cascading, hanging curtains, painted with pink doves. A room with a gallery of pictures, circle furniture and a soft pink love seat sofa. A crystal rock bar, mirrors around with a large window for a view over the garden. A large framed Marilyn Monroe hangs over the fireplace. She damn sure didn't smile at the goddamn world. Giant Campbell Soup can portrait made you afraid to sip another spoon of soup. All this pink furniture stuff made Sam believe he was a character out of Alice in Wonderland. He wondered where was the Mad Hatter? He drops his end of the white shag to the floor, and bends up to see Petey-Pete walking away with Mrs. Berrios.

She stops, blows a kiss back at him. He wants to catch it, but he can't believe his partner is ready to take this old blonde vulture down in another room. Over his shoulder a voice calls him. "Sam."

He looks towards the curtain breezes to see Myrthe. Opens his eyes, arms, as she runs to him.

She kisses him over his face of rock, eyes of black stones. He is mighty surprised. She can tell this by the way his arms shake. She laughs, tightens her grip around his waist. She holds her treasure. Close to the end of the line for them both as she feels his fingers nuzzle into her waist. She pushes her hair from her left eye. She pushes her hips tighter into his hips, grabs hold of his back pockets. Pushes her lips on his lips. She has her tongue dance with his as she cries in his arms.

"Mabel told me you were still here," he says. He pulls her over to the couch. "You tricked me!" He nuzzles his nose down into her neck. "That's your friend." He points his thumb at the closed door. He sniffs the lilac of roses from her raven black hair.

She thinks he's going to say something smart about the woman who just brought them together. "Yes." She curls up in his hairy arms.

He throws his cap on the floor. "Thank her for me, will you?" He pulls the gloves off his fingers, flings them over his shoulders.

She sees that he's inspecting her slim body. Touching her stomach, down to her thighs in her one-piece jumpsuit of white cotton, stringed top opening that accents the coconut curves of her breasts. Just a peek.

"How do you say quickie in Creole?" he asks.

She knew what he meant. Not much time to breathe. Especially not enough time to have him on this small sofa. The floor? She rests back, pulls down his zipper. "There is no such thing in Creole, but we do have a saying about two humps. It is... *de' fouape*."

He rubs a thumb over her breasts. "*De' fouape*!"

She laughs at his pronunciation. Unstrings the top for him. He takes her up in his arms. "*De' fouape! De' fouape*!"

She pushes him back. Hops on his lap. Lets her sandals fall off her feet as her hair drops upon his cheek.

He whispers in her ear. "*De' fouape*."

•   •   •

Myrthe continues her mission of waiting off the shores of military-ambassadorial receptions with the colonel. Eleventh hour efforts of cocktail parties. Casualties of French champagne. Ongoing Hollywood Bob Mackie invasion of three thousand-dollar dresses parade through her days and nights. Honorable guests from bloody countries pass by: Israel, Egypt, China, Bolivia, Belgium, France, Germany. She shares a toast with them; it tastes too sweet. New parties. New regimes. New fools adhering to stock market fatalities with their corrupt smiles, waiting in the wings for the prices of rifles and dope to go up, up, up.

She plans to leave September 19th, to renew their morning under the pink crepe curtains. Sweat dripped from his face. New white shag rug spread over the floor. It was a week ago; seemed like yesterday. Sam's tongue still in her mouth. The scent of Tamarisk cologne still on her hands.

She was stronger in his arms, arms that took her away from the colonel, from Mrs. Prosper. A place to hide, cover up in. Grounded in his chest, neck, throat of a paper-tar black face. Moth-eaten from hot, cold winds. A face that made her laugh, giggle. Kiss heat based arms. Legs move in. First time to unwrap the lollipop brown chest, suck the hardness, softness of his petals. Black stars on a morning's wings. Wait, sit, wait. Caress into a galaxy of one, two, three strokes. Just in time for him to make his next delivery.

She works in the kitchen with her mermaid-water girlfriends who have been with her for over ten years. Young women coming from the slums of Haiti as contraband to work in embassies all over the world. She's going to leave them, make this her home, but she can't say goodbye. She asks Yolande if she needs any help in the kitchen on a Tuesday morning. They are all sweet, vindictive, petty, loving women of an afternoon storm.

Dressed in yellow polka dots, Rose-Marie does the laundry. Blue, roundtop dress of crepe cotton, Anita the wash-woman battles stains with some bleach. Yolande has on a crinkled black and red peasant skirt, dicing carrots. Jocelyn, the house cleaner, stands tall in her floral print dress of red roses, eating a big peach while shoving trash down a Hefty garbage bag. Hips as wide as their mouths; between twenty-two and thirty-five, for raising children. All honey-bee buzzing women with silk wings. They will set you straight and turn a man up and down if you don't treat them right. She misses being with them and faces their birdsong gossip this morning. She wants to remember the rich street French-African language of Creole from home.

"Myrthe, don't put too much cayenne pepper in the soup," Yolande cautions her as she grates the cassava. "You eat too much spice."

"You don't eat enough." She puts it down. "How long will it take?"

"Just keep stirring."

"You want a bite?" Jocelyn pushes a peach in Anita's face. "It's sweet and sour."

Anita knocks the juice from the side of her mouth. "Ummmm!" She swallows. "It's good."

Yolande makes a bold statement about somebody in the group. "People go out with their money and don't spend it."

"Who?" Myrthe looks up from the pot.

Yolande's chin points. "Anita! You finish with the ginger root?" She keeps grating. "You finish with my dress?"

Rose-Marie sits at the table with an Army fatigue shirt in her hand, picking the lint off. "You too intense." She asks, "Sebastian didn't give you none last night?"

Yolande points the cassava her way. "My little coquette, you shut your mouth before I have the colonel send you back to your hole in Port Au Prince."

"Myrthe, you want some?" Jocelyn pushes the peach in her face.

"No, I had enough."

Anita sticks her nose up. "You mountain girls always had enough."

Myrthe knocks her off balance by humming and stirring up the fragrances of black pepper, scallions, green onions with the sea.

Rose-Marie didn't like her smart mouth. "Jocelyn, you need to finish your chores." She walks over to the ironing board, turns the iron on.

Jocelyn throws the seed in the trash bag.

"I have to send money home to my mother," Yolande said.

"We all do." Rose-Marie starts ironing a purple blouse. "My sister is pregnant and I have to send some money to her."

"Where is her husband?" Myrthe asks.

"In Belgium with his other wife."

Anita rinses off some socks under the kitchen faucet. "Give them what they need." She slaps them against the sink. "We are fortunate… Give what we can as long as we are here to help."

"I testify to that," Yolande says, sounding like a preacher's kid. "My daddy use to beat me in the name of the Lord when I was a little girl. Now he's in a wheelchair with both his legs cut off… I can't ignore that." She cuts up some scallions for the soup. "I give him what I can… while the flies wait on him to eat his shit."

"Strangers are not as kind." Myrthe said this with sadness in her voice. Longing to have her mother still with her. But she knows that will never be. No, never be.

Yolande watches Myrthe's peaceful decorum over the steaming pot. A face of good sense on her side. "You right, Myrthe. Strangers are not as kind."

Jocelyn takes Myrthe's hand. "Did Colonel Labossier give you this ring?"

"Yes." She gazes at it over the pot. "You want it?"

Jocelyn got dumb. "Ha?" Scans the faces of the other women in the kitchen. "Yes." Puts her hand on her hip, testing her.

Myrthe takes it off. "It's yours." She goes back to her stirring. Hears the women whispering, gawking at the ring. She takes a spoon, dips it in and tastes. "It's too spicy."

26

On September the 18th, before it was time for her to leave, Myrthe's back aches from sitting up in the wooden chair. Above the emerald garden of fountain and stone, she sews the Black Widow stitch in the white China silk. She didn't know what to make, but Mrs. Prosper's instructions were to let the needle do the sewing. She would be the vessel to carry the water to the lake. She would be the hostess to carry the wine for him to drink. She would be the maid to take him her lips to kiss before he went to sleep at night.

She hears the lawn mower churning up the wet grass. Sweet potato pie smells come up the stairs to the sewing room. She licks her bottom lip for the taste of the sweet pie. But she doesn't budge; she has to finish—The Shawl.

Myrthe is scared, her fingers stop pushing the material through. She stands up, gazes out the window. Gardeners in large straw hats, women wearing long white dresses, scarves of yellow, red, blues tied up around their heads. Almost for a moment she thinks she is back home as they bend over to pull up weeds.

She moves back to the sewing machine, steps on the pedal. She gets up the nerve to continue when she closes her eyes and sees the face of Sam in his light blue golf cap. He is funny, strong, makes her laugh. He makes silly mistakes when he tries too hard. Opening the door for her, pouring her a glass of water. Buttoning up her dress in the back. He would miss a string, a button or two. Spill some water on her hands and arms. He was a nervous man, ready to die to be in her company. She needs that and wants that for the rest of her days, a man who will treat her like a piece of silk cloth from the Great Wall of China.

She finishes it, inspects it, holds it up to the last hours of orange sunlight. Drapes it over her shoulders, smooths her hand down over the white silk. Two black spiders lay on each of the sides. She lights candles and incense. One black, one white. She lays a silver necklace crucifix with some rosary beads between the two candles. In front of them she says a prayer. "I come to you, Father, this day… I come to you, Lord. I come to seek your forgiveness. I come to sing. I come to dance… to be with you in the sun and the moonlight… on September the 19th. This day I shall be born again."

She holds both her hands together. "Oh Lord, release me from this man of hatred and injustice. I beg you for his freedom… for you to let me walk… run… crawl away in the night with the one I truly love.

Oh, Lord, listen to my pleas. I want a husband... a family... a little boy... a little girl. Take this man away from me with these spiders that I have made... Take him back to the hell from which he has came." She trembles. Eyes still closed. "Oh, Lord Jesus, Father... let me see my family, my mother, my father... For if I can't be with Sam... oh, Lord, let me be with them."

After this prayer, a vision comes between the two flames. The smart, brown face of her mother appears. She trembles with joy at the woman in a flowing white robe. In the vision her arms open to her. Myrthe tries to touch her hand, but reaches through the smoky-grey rays of her mother's hand. Blue, white light comes from her eyes. Her hair is as if fire is in it. Flames rise all around. Red hot coals under her feet burn as if to be just in space, time, the galaxy of white stars. Black stars rise. In the vision behind her are trees, misshapen, but as if blowing in the wind, near a black, flowing river, near a bed of flowers. In grey. No colors.

Dogs, goats, chickens, children chase each other. Men, women dancing at a party. Drum music from Africa makes her heart stop, hop, jump, pump. She starts to sway to the sounds of Coupe' Cloure-Trio Select.

Her village appears with the mountains overhead. Her brother sits on a bench in front of their small white house, carving out African masks with a knife, hammer, chisel. He is whistling in tattered pants, shirt. Chest open to the sun, winds, mountain waters of Kenskoff. In the vision, her father is sitting at his rocking chair in front of the radio. After dinner, listening to a speech by the great president, Papa Doc.

271

Rocking, speaking to other men, telling them little jokes as he puffs on his pipe.

Mrs. Prosper is under a tree rocking, pointing to a wrecked ship on the beach. Waves splash up as the sand crab hides from the water's white foam.

Myrthe wants to go to them but her mother's hand rises to stop her. Waves her back to nod with a smile, a tear. She fades away, up over the black river edge.

Both the candle flames go out. She opens her eyes; they burn from the vision of her family. Tired, she sits back down in the chair. Lays her head on her arms on the table.

· · ·

The dream becomes a man:

Mother Prosper stands over her pots in the kitchen this night. The mansion is quiet. Not one party going on. It is time to cook. She rests a hand on her shapely, soft, round hips. Wooden spoon in her hand, cooking the colonel's sperm up.

Drying it up over the flames. Lets it almost burn the spoon. She sticks it in a cool place. Hums some home-grown Creole songs under her breath.

Tastes it, then lets it cool off right under the corner of the windowsill near her potted aloe plants on the patio that night.

She comes back at about a quarter to two. Pushes the spoon in the dirt of the plant, upside down, then placing some of his military ribbons in the dirt with ground-up pieces of his toenails.

· · ·

On the night of Myrthe's departure:

Sam gets the men together in front of his apartment building. Ray is quiet, concerned. Petey-Pete is talkative, wanting to bet on the horses with Jesse the next morning. He isn't worried about getting hacked or shot at. Sam doesn't care either, as long as he has his .45 like the rest of the men. It's a little after eleven. Blackness, quiet summer breezes. Good night weather that makes you want to put on the blanket with your woman.

Ray drives with another cop, Big Bob McKay, in an unmarked car. Petey, Duck, Kenny, Jesse are packed in a station wagon. All of them strapped down with enough pieces to blow up a lot of shit on Embassy Row. Nobody is nervous. If they have to go in to get her, they will. But either way… she is coming out.

Before Sam gets in the truck, Ray gets in his face to ask him just one thing. He wants to see the madness in his eyes, the sweat beads pop on his forehead. The cool chill blow through his nose. They had both seen a lot of men die in the war. He knew if they were ready to die. "You ready, bro'?" Ray asks. He spits the stump of a cigarette out of his mouth to the sidewalk in front of Sam's apartment. Steps on the fire.

Sam smiles. "Yeah." Pats his chest under the short black leather jacket. "Ain't got to worry about me… I'm going to kill something Black."

Ray shakes his hand. "You just follow me in… When I hit the siren, all shit's going to stop… " He says, "If the colonel comes out… we take care of him for you."

Sam made sure he understood that he wanted him to be patient. "Just wait for me… I got the plans to go around the back first… She should be at the gate entrance to the garden."

"Okay, I give you ten minutes, then we coming in… "

Sam plucks the cigarette from his mouth. Steps up in his truck. He starts the engine, follows right behind his big brother to Embassy Row.

•   •   •

Colonel Labossier is going to use his Academy cufflinks for the evening out with Myrthe. He is ready for a night on the town with his Myrthe… A late dinner at the Sans Souci. A toast of champagne after the Kennedy Center with the ambassador from Bali. Taste a yummy piece of night with his lovely mistress on the town of Washington, D.C. is all he needs. He was so tired lately. The doctor just told him it was fatigue. Maybe a touch of malaria flaring up. His trip to Nigeria in seventy-six didn't do him one bit of good. He rubs some grease through his hair, stands in front of the dresser mirror, brushes the waves in his hair. Slips on his silk monogrammed shirt, knots his Brooks Brothers black and gold tie given to him by an aide to George Bush. He grabs his face. It starts itching, burning.

He just can't believe this as the fear comes up in his chest. The mirror flashes before him spiders. Crawling, roaming over his face, hair, eyes. He slaps them off. He stops itching after a few minutes. Peers back in the mirror but nothing is there. He sits on his bed, tries to calm down. Wrestles with his thoughts and comes up with one answer. He jumps to the door for his men. "*Garde! Garde!*"

He takes two other men with him, kicks down Mother Prosper's door with a clapping thunder of a man's life in the fever of a fire.

She is standing right in front of him, a few feet back in a chalk-drawn circle. No clothes on, her body blue, plump. Wrinkled arms out to hug him.

He jumps back. "You witch! You voodoo witch!" he screams. Afraid of the woman but he can't stop asking, "Why? Why you do this to me?"

Dancing, shaking. She hollers, curses in a fast pace Creole tongue in the circle. Pointing, spitting at him and the men. "You hurt the moon, sun, the stars... Let them go... Let go of the universe in my Myrthe." She spits at him. "You will set her free."

He grabs a scared soldier in the collar. "Shoot that witch! I order you to shoot her!" He pulls him to face her. "She's a fraud!"

The soldier is unable to move, to believe the unreality of welcoming himself to her room and her fat arms. He shakes his head. "No, Colonel, no!"

But the other soldier isn't afraid of her magic. He shoots her right in the middle of the chest.

She dangles, hop-scotch in mid stride. Laughs out as if the house is in a giant horn. She falls back, eyes still open like a child's laughter. Blood squirts out of her like a strawberry soda pop fountain.

He steps closer to the circle. Kicks her foot. He suddenly starts to feel the burn come back in his stomach, chest, throat. He finds the spiders crawling back over his face, hair, eyes.

The two soldiers move back. Nothing is there as they watch their beloved colonel fighting off some sort of invisible creatures. Digging his finger in his

275

ears, nose, mouth. "See? See them? See them?" He grabs the gun from the scared one, rushing around in the room, still fighting the cursed spiders. He raises it. "Do you see them? Do you see them?"

The soldiers run from the quick-pop of the gun going off. They go back in to find the colonel on the floor beside the old woman.

• • •

Sam, Ray, Petey-Pete and the others get to the seventy-seven hundred block of Massachusetts Avenue to find red, blue, yellow lights on top of police cars, and ambulances all over the place. The street is blocked off. People are running straight to the embassy in the night to see the carnage of two body bags being rolled out the front door.

Sam runs up in the crowd to find Myrthe. He doesn't want God to play games with him right now. He watches Ray go up to one of the cops holding the crowd back.

Ray flashes his badge. "What's the problem, officer?"

The cop gives him the respect and tells him real fast. "Two dead... Just the rest scared."

Sam is right behind his brother. "Who ? Who ?"

Ray has to ask him, to calm his brother down. "Was there a young woman in there, officer?"

The cop gets peeved. "Officer Murphy, I don't know." He shoves him back into the crowd. Another cop pulls out yellow tape to let you know that this was where you would stand to gawk at a murder scene.

Sam tells Petey-Pete beside him, "We going to check around the back to the garden."

"Okay, Sam." He pushes his way out of this hot scene with the men.

Reporters from the *Washington Post*, the *Times*, walk up in the crowd with their cameras peeping. Earplugs hanging. Mikes ready to be shoved in a dog's face if he could bark out a few answers right now. Sam stares at the people. Long, small, fat, veined, blue, brown, grey, black eyes all stare back at him. All mischief elves of gossip. Embassy workers shiver in sweaters, jackets, stand around being questioned by detectives. One of the guards does the interpretation. The cop is not believing any of the stuff he's hearing. He shakes his head. Yawns over his cup of coffee, pencil and pad.

Sam feels a tap on his shoulder, thinking it's Ray. He turns around. "Myrthe! Myrthe!" Picks her up strong in his arms. He doesn't care about the world right now. "Baby, you all right?"

She holds him. "Sam… take me… away." Squeezes him.

He sees the reflection of red police car lights circling around in her big deer eyes. He sees the fear up in her face of almost dying in some fucked-up dream through a night that doesn't make much damn sense. He kisses her cheeks to get rid of this monster. "Okay baby, I'm going to take you home."

Myrthe takes his hand, walks away from the madness of lights rolling over the crowd at the gates. Her mother once told her, "Never look back, always look up at the stars. You will find me there." She looks up at the stars.

27

July 20, 1991:

Sam has to get off the road. He has enough memories in him to last till the day they would throw dirt in his face. He calls them up-front memories of the guys on the construction sites. Along with all the many ladies on the balconies: nurses, secretaries, school teachers, barmaids, wives, doctors, lawyers. He calls them shortbread-women on a hotsauce Saturday night.

On the bus. A fool's fingers search for riches, going for butt-pockets as the human cycles of rage come up in a man's voice. "Mista! You betta get your hands out of my goddamn pockets!"

He runs between shoulders, backs, arms. He kicks open the back door. Jumps down in the middle of cars, trucks, bums, bushwhackers and bicyclists. Scrambling all over like a hard fried egg in the streets.

Sam checks his watch. It's almost eight and he is getting a headache. He's stuck up by his eighty-eight

Dodge Dart. He calls the car El, Zorro too. She just didn't want to get up this morning. He can't much blame the car. He feels the same on his wife's soft, spongy back that made him sink into a dream of being in a jungle with nothing but naked black women. He's a Lucky Strike man, for every night he drowns between the breasts of a French-African woman.

He's still a hardworking man. With a heart as big as the growing town of Sweet Loaf on a Monday morning. Green, red, yellow lights tell tales of a crowd missing their time capsules. Mostly po' Black folks that gave blood first in three wars. The first town to even elect a Black man mayor on Maryland's eastern shore. He guessed you would call it some civil rights deal that brought in the pork chops during the last election of 1988.

Narrow-minded man, Sam only gives a damn about one thing anyway: his wife, Myrthe, and a chocolate lollipop daughter, Zara. She's five and talks so much you think she will be a lawyer, business-woman or con artist. Pick any job title and his little girl will charm the ice cream and cake right out of the refrigerator.

He dozes off and on. Lets the bus rock him into a pink cloud. Until he smells up this light perfume. He wakes up quick to notice a nice woman sitting across from him that has him thinking of creamy Amaretto honey. He just wants to stick his finger in her jar and taste it. Is she a model? She has on them black stockings. Bank teller? A smart blue blazer business suit with gold buttons. Or just for sale? She wears a grey plaid, pleated skirt. Black pumps, with long, brown, frizzy hair that looks like she just got out of the shower to dance, sing, or just do that thing. She is down with that African-American, Annie Hall look.

Bell time. Sam stands up, pulls on the red cord. He jumps off the back steps. Lands on Fourth and Kennedy Avenue. He walks two blocks down to the Hotel Hennesson. Another war, a different day. This is the real thing. Fighting laundry bags at a dry cleaners.

He enters the hot, French fry stale-smelling lobby. Ugly 1960s blue shag carpets, bellhops hustling from one grey-haired blue lady to the other, a Congressman or two stopping by to fuck his secretary off I-95 southbound from the Capitol rotunda. Wasn't a reporter going to catch them or even care about them messing around in Sweet Loaf.

He walks to the exit sign doors. Down a couple of flights to the basement where a few janitors are shooting up craps underneath the stairwell. "Morning, Timmy! Joe! Buddy-Love!"

None of their heads come up but they answer back, "Morning, Sam!" Just before he gets to his glass cage world of hundred-watt lights blinking TROJAN CLEANERS, spots his boss counting at the cash register. "Morning, Nick!"

"Morning, Sam!" Scratches his bald head. Keeps counting the tens and twenties. Flicks some ash off the giant cigar from his lips. Grumbles under his breath.

Sam keeps going, ducks under the counter top. Nick always grumbled. This man had a beef about ants on a sunny day. He had a bad stomach, either constipated or farting. Didn't nothing much really please him. Sam guessed he was waiting for the New York Jets to win another Super Bowl.

He goes to the back room, undresses at the lockers. Sits on the bench, kicks off his penny loafers. Opens a locker up, throws in a couple of ham sandwiches, chips, grape soda pop that his wife fixed for him. He slips on a pair of blue overalls, muddy Chuck Taylor sneakers. They have gone up at least fifty dollars by now, or was it eighty?

Well, you know. The world has been fair to him. According on the man upstairs plan. His knees are stiffening up lately, back kind of sore. Cut down his liquor drinking and dope smoking after he married his Myrthe. Still had some bad dreams now and then when the Redskins would lose to the Dallas Cowboys. But the world's been fair to him. He bought a house by his brother on the lake. Used up his G.I. Bill and some of his wife's gold as a down payment. Uncle Sam didn't kill him. He was doing fine on his own. Life would always be a nasty whore that looked good to any man. She worked you hard and butt-fucked-licked you down. Till you couldn't come no more.

He took any job as long as it wasn't on the road. It was harder to fight dem temptations. Myrthe is still all the planets and his little girl all the stars. Sam didn't much mind, because the world's been fair to him. He buttons up, turns the radio on to WJZZ-FM to some nice jazz.

Nick comes to the back room while he's sweeping the floor. "Sam, I got more plastic bags for you here." He throws him the box.

Sam drops the broom. "Thanks, Nick." Catches it.

"Has Tony came in yet?" Nick checks his watch on his hairy arm.

Sam places the box on the bench. "Not yet." Opens it up with his penknife.

"You call me when he gets his ass in here." Nick walks out of the back room like a fat-ass Groucho Marx.

Sam knows he's pissed, but that isn't going to get the work done around the cleaners. Loading, unloading wrinkled pieces of clothing. Pops his fingers to some horn. Dizzy plays, AH-LEU-CHA for the morning. He stopped playing so much after having Zara. This little girl took a lot of energy out of him. After working all day, fighting traffic to get home, he had to give his little girl time. Don't even mention his wife. She had enough to do around the house. Most of it didn't include him. She was into everything in the neighborhood. It was cool. He was into doing a lot of fishing on the lake. Listening to some old jazz cuts: Miles, Dizzy, Trane. Thumbing through some books on art, religion, Black-Caribbean literature. Watching his Redskins kick some butt every now and then. He kept up on D.C. and small town politics of Sweet Loaf. He only cared about Black folks. You know. And watching over his family like a lion from the jungles of Zaire.

Mabel, who was now his sister-in-law, had his Myrthe involved in church bake sales, raffle fundraisers for the Children's Hospital, even a golf tournament for Black golfers wanting to get the young'uns in this sport. She worked part-time at Zara's elementary school, a French language course to the third graders. She was the right woman that took his heart and his balls all at the same time.

In the alley he heard the laundry van pull up. He turns the music down. "Nick, Tony's here!"

Tony comes in the back door, slamming it, shaking his hips to some cha cha music playing in his head for only him. "Morning, Mr. Murphy!" Slaps him five. "Where is the old fart at?" He keeps moving his hips like he has some woman in his arms.

"Who?"

"You know who. My brother."

"Up front with a customer." Pulls out the giant plastic bags.

"Good." He picks a comb out of his shirt pocket. "I had a great weekend, Sammy. Oooo!" Combs his wet-black hair to the side. "How was yours?"

Sam didn't want to talk to a half-wit who thought Donald Duck and Bugs Bunny cartoons meant they were the thirty-seventh and thirty-eight presidents of the United States, or thought Mississippi was in Eastern Europe. But he was the boss, so Sam gave him a chump change piece of respect. "Fine, I guess." He snaps open a bag, stuffs the shirts, pants, suits in. Sticks a red tag on it with the number 625, one customer at a time. Staples it together.

Tony puts the comb back in his top shirt pocket. "Shit! Mine wasn't too good."

"Why was that?"

"My girlfriend wounded me."

Sam stops bagging. "Where?"

Tony points to his crotch. "Right here." He laughs, bends over, slaps the air. "Aw, man! I can't believe you fell for that one… Have another cup of coffee on me." Flips him a dollar.

"Tony, go to hell!"

"Shit, man. I'm already there." He picks up the dollar.

Sam scratches behind his neck. "You sick and you late too."

This was a warning. Right after he says it Nick runs back there with a baseball bat in his hands. Points the bat and a finger in his younger brother's face. "You the baby? You the baby! I should spank you with this bat!"

Tony grins, crosses his arms. "Get the bat out my face, and your finger, Nick."

Nick calls him hard. "You goddamn asshole!"

Tony wants to hit him with a right, but he does think about that bat first. "Man, fuck you all right!" Backs up to the door. "What momma going to say?" He laughs. This is his shield. "If you put me in the hospital?" He waves the comb like a sword, slicks his hair back slow with it. "For being a whole hour late."

Nick drops the bat. "Just get your ass to work, baby!" He walks away from murdering his brother over some time arrangement.

Sam wants to pick up the bat. "Boss."

Tony scowls at the funk of life. "What?"

"One day momma gonna die… Then your ass going to be dead."

"Shut up!" Sticks the greasy comb in his back pocket. "Keep stuffing them suits." Tony walks away. "I'm going to the bathroom and read the sports page."

Sam calls this his daily routine with the Trojan brothers. Asshole Greeks with plenty of money, in

284

the steam business. It's madness between them two. Hollering grown men talking about telling an old, crusty-ass, eighty-year-old woman in a Seacrest Old Folks Home about their fights. They're grown clowns; fun to be around. One day he might get to see them kill each other as the spectator. Popcorn in the stands, as the two olive-hairy beasts fight over time and a dry cleaning bag.

When Tony finishes with the sports page, Sam has all the clothes bagged, ready to go to the factory to be cleaned up. This is their other operation across town, getting the clothes dry cleaned by a bunch of illegals: Nicaraguans, Vietnamese, Africans, Irish, and throw in just po' folks. Mostly women, eating dirt, boots, cats, corn flakes for a living. In America for fifty cents on the dollar, God bless you all!

Sam didn't worry about the brothers. They weren't mad at him. They were into their own shit of "Momma spanked the hell out of you the most" vibe. He worked the customers. He liked some of them. Some didn't like him, but it was cool. He handed out receipts, prices, dates. He even rang up the cash register while Nick was busy playing the street numbers, horses and baseball games. He was into the fever of handing out receipts, prices, cash, dates to his bookies in D.C..

One of the customers comes in around ten. Mr. Howell is in his seventies, on a cane, face resembling a skeleton. He has the old nerves to still drive his sixty-four Mercedes around the block to the cleaners. He has to be half blind and out of his mind. But he would speak to Sam before he spoke to Nick.

Sam jokes with him. "Did you get a piece last night, Mr. Howell?"

In his feeble, slow voice. "Let me see... Sam..." He gives him the answer in weakened decibels. "I think I patted it." He hands him seven dollars.

Sam laughs at his triple chicken neck. "That's fine enough for me, sir." He bangs the cash register. "Have a nice day." Closes it.

Mr. Howell sticks his hand out. "Where is my change, young... man?"

"Oh! I'm sorry." Sam hits the cash register again. "I'm sorry, sir." He gives him twenty cents back. "Uh, your answer threw me off." Digs in his ear.

"I know, son. My answers throw a lot of people off." He slips his thumb in the clothes hook. Hunched, his cane under him. He whistles out the glass doors past another customer, his pants over his left arm.

Nick came up. "The old fart stinks."

Sam was matter-of-fact. "Let's just say... some like me, some like you." He wipes sweat from his brow. "He's something else."

Nick slaps his hand. "We a great team."

They can hear Tony hitting the horn from the alley. Nick doesn't want to see him. "Sam, go see what he wants." He looks over his shoulder to the back. "I don't want to see him right now."

Sam swings two bags over each shoulder. "I'll take 'im these... This should keep him busy up till lunch."

Nick lights up a cigar. "Good." He blows smoke in a customer's face. "Can I help you, Mr. Lui?"

"Hey, I got something for you!" Sam shouts.

Tony,s getting from behind the wheel. Finger-popping to more soundless music that only he can hear. He looks up, slides the doors open. "Right here." Claps his hands.

Sam slings one bag over his shoulder at him.

He catches it, throws it in. Then a second one comes in his arms. "Thanks." He closes the doors back. "I'm sorry about this morning, Sam."

Sam sees that he is trying to apologize in his own Elvis-looking way. "I think you betta be talking to Nick right now." He's ready to go back in. "He's your brother... I'm just the help."

Tony leans back on the side panel of the van. "Maybe later." Rubs a thumb over his top lip. Unloosens a red handkerchief from around his neck. "I guess you just a little sick of all this arguing between us?" Sticks it in his back pocket.

Sam shrugs. "Hey, me and my brother do the same." He looks at the face of a young man, not knowing what he was going to do in this three-hundred and sixty-five degree underworld. "Uh, Tony... "

"Huh?"

"I just want to tell you... no matter what you do. Just do your job. And the day you can't do that, just move on. It's a big world out there. Your dream don't have to be the same dream as your brother's."

Tony liked Sam; didn't never tell him. A man that made things come in line. When there was nothing else to be said. "Okay." He hops back up in the van. "See you quitting time." He drives off from the back door.

Sam gets back to Nick to catch him meditating on a mustard stain from Mrs. Bronya's navy blue skirt.

"Sam, bag up these slacks and shirts for me of Mr. Lui's."

"Got you!" Sam replies. He lifts them from the counter. Tags, stuffs in the bag.

Mrs. Bronya was a blonde from the Baltic Sea. In her fifties with a face that was slowly wrinkling around the corners of her mouth. Kind of looked like she had a pencil mustache growing around the corners of her thin, pink lips. In the hotel they called her the dictator with a pussy. "I vant my… skurt beck by Vednesday."

Nick scratches the side of his neck. 'They'll be back by Vednesday, ma'am."

"And pressed!" She doesn't like his comment in trying to hand her back her bad English. "You smart… little mon… you lose my biznus if you keeps that up."

Nick pushes the skirt down to Sam. "It will be ready Wednesday, ma'am." He wants to hit her in her prune-squeezed face. But he forgets sometimes it's business in pleasing an exiled Communist-wombat. "Yes, ma'am. Sorry, ma'am."

She snatches the ticket from his hand, starts to leave.

Nick lifts the counter top, runs up behind her.

She jumps, scared he's going to attack. "Ahhhh!"

But he opens the door. "Have a nice day, ma'am." Bows.

She almost drops her shopping bag. "Dank you… Dank you." She can't hold her panties up fast enough to get out of there.

Nick laughs so hard, his false bottom teeth almost fall out.

"Nick, I don't know how you stay in business." Sam shakes his head in disgust at what he just did to the dictator with a pussy.

"What?" Raising his hands. "I love everybody."

• • •

Ray comes in the cleaners around four o'clock. He's on his way home from his government job in D.C.. He surprises Sam, hugs him up over the counter. He fakes a left hook at his little brother's chin. "Hey, man, where's my grey pinstripe?"

Sam can't believe this. "I ain't seen you in three weeks, and you come back asking for a cheap suit. Ain't this some shit!" He turns to the round rack of clothes in the plastic bags. Finds his suit, hooks it up on the hangers by the cash register. "Ray, how was your trip?"

"Boring as hell! Chicago, New York, Detroit... " Rests his elbows on the counter.

"Sounds like some swinging towns to me, Ray," Nick says, twisting the cigar in his mouth.

"Maybe another time, but this was business." Rolls his hand through his hair. "But I got a few days off to be with my family."

"I'm sure Mabel's glad to hear that," Sam said, reading the ticket.

He's tired, just wants to see her and the boy. "Yeah. She'll be glad to hear that." He peeps over to the ticket. "Uh, how much?"

"Twelve."

Ray pulls his wallet from his back pocket, thumbs for the money. "Here."

Sam takes the money, sticks it in the cash register. "This is a good surprise, bro'." He gives him the suit from the rack. "Here you go."

"I knew it would be." Points at him. "You, Myrthe and Zara come on by later. Check out this new train set I got for Ray Junior." He takes the suit. "Something from the Wild West."

"You mean for you," Sam says. He knows his brother always liked them cowboy shoot-'em-up movies. One of them John Wayne freaks.

"For your favorite nephew."

"Okay. We come by later."

"Not too late." Pulls on his ear. "I gots me some making up to do."

"I know you can handle it," Sam says. He didn't want him to worry about anything. Mabel might fuss but he knew it was because she was worried about the funny little things he could get into out there on the streets.

"See you, Nick."

"Say hello to Mabel for me."

"Okay." He looks at Sam. "Tonight."

"Later." He waves him off.

Ray walks out of the neon lights of the Trojan Cleaners. Steam, pressed air of fine suits, pants, jackets, dresses. Smelling like you were in a Irish spring day just before the IRA blew up a red brick school house of Protestant first-graders. You could call it innocent-heat.

He was glad to see Sam. Loved the hell out of the knuckle-head. Not with the wives, children around. They always seem to make it difficult. Secrets of pillow-love. Women chatted too much sometimes. Kept their man smothered under their dresses with the pubic hairs in your mouth. You couldn't talk around them.

Men seem to be happiest under the tree. He unlocks the door to his blue and silver grey Z. On the field, under a car, just sitting on the porch drinking a beer. Talking about killing somebody or just running the fuck over another man.

Sam is relieved to see him. That's his brother, his limb that's rooted in his past. This man knows where the hell he came from. Under a tree, a rock, a Gargoyle. Between Cindy Lou's legs on her thirteenth birthday. Where is she at now? He watches the clock. He's ready to leave at five. Glad to see that great black shark grin on Ray's face. He remembers: "Nick, did you find Mr. Steptoe's gabardines?"

Nick looks up from a pile of clothes. "Got 'em right here... I would hate having to pay that son of bitch thirty dollars."

"Good." Sam takes pride in his work. He knows the place doesn't belong to him. But he knows everybody has a boss. You have to answer to somebody. We all seem to need to want to answer to someone or something. He snaps another ticket on a plastic bag. Measures the slow time-dying. The customers fading away or rushing to get in before the doors close. The constant ringing, thunderstorm of money coming in and out of the cash register. Just another day. A matter of time before the war ended.

28

Trip on home.

Between a rock and quitting time he gets back on the bus with coffee stains, cheeseburger smells from passengers breaths. Riding, pushing, shoving, humping on backs, shoulders, butts, breasts. Three-piece Slim Fast suits. Cotton in, polyester out. Workers trying to find a job. Got a job. Jockeying for another one if you have the right look. Jazz on the bus; stretching out. Don't Cough On Me Blues. Sam doesn't miss playing that much. Sometimes he goes into his basement, plays to his Zara. She digs her tired old father with the grey over the ridges of his ears. He plays for her only. He bumps into a Milk of Magnesia stomach, burping up the ham and cheese sandwich from lunch. Faces in the crowd, pick at a scowl. Blue, Red Cross lovers try to be sanctified. Hold each other's hands at the edge of a lake. At the edge of sanity they are all going insane on this Metro bus ride back home to the anchors of love.

He jerks, shakes. Sits next to a fat-ass blonde bigger than his six-foot frame. Damn, he had put on twenty. But this woman could whip his ass if he told her to move the *Cosmopolitan* out of his face. He was into *Vogue* himself. Long-legged white girls with crying eyes. Starving for a ham sandwich to choke on, for a million dollars worth of bullshit to wear for the faggots of Paris or New York.

He rocks. Dreams about some jazz riffs. Dreams about his honeymoon on St. Sebastian a hundred years ago. Longer than the hundred years war. He was in love with his long-legged, brown-eyed, model-looking wife. Hair curled down her back. Legs twisting over his stomach on crystal beige beaches. Blue waters sweet enough to lick salt, get sick and die between her legs. Eat her mango tits for breakfast, lunch and dinner.

Hold each other over the six o'clock morning white dove sky. From green hills of their balcony windows they point at the orange, chocolate horizon. She sucks his fingers with the strawberries. He pulls up her lace cotton dress above the waist. Kisses her in the grass with the goats sucking on their mothers' tits. He finishes. Pulls her dress back down before the seven o'clock rain. Remote caverns of his love. He takes her high in the hills. No one can see. No one cares about them in this world of the islands. Papaya trees blush, drip juice into their mouths. Myrthe's breasts are just as sweet. He wakes up.

Bells, whistles. Screams. "Hold the damn bus!"

Sam watches the man float over the crowd of the Crocker Landing bus. Patch-walks around butts, backs, saying, "Excuse me. Excuse me. Excuse me."

He watches the cows graze. Horses stand by fences, trees blaze their green colors of God's hands. They are a masterpiece in making this earth so plain, uncompleted. We do the other rotten things to ourselves. The woman's knee rubs against his knee. It's her move to make. She wants a Black man for supper. He flashes his wedding band across his other arm. Dozes some more against the breeze of the pages. Nowadays this Woman's Lib thing says, "Hey, I don't give a fuck if you are married... I just want a little bit."

He trembles at the freedom. Death takes a holiday and buys thin plastic, elastic condoms in a window for sale. Large, medium, small. He trembles at the view of the countryside burning with the graceful neck of AIDS watching over the highway of people. He trembles at the beat of the road. Lost in the black pavement of Never-Never Land. He's holding Myrthe's hand, afraid to let go. Because if he does, he will surely be dead like this squirrel they just ran over. He trembles in her arms at night. She holds him. Rocks him inside of her tree limb legs. Tells him a story in French. He doesn't know what she's saying. He doesn't care. It sounds nice. Nice enough to put him in a blue sleep with the angels. His mother is there in the dreams of her voice. He knows she's there watching him make love to his wife. With confidence her wings push him on.

Childish hot, yellow, blue evening starts to fade. Cut-out candy wrappers three blocks from his home. A small community of grassy knolls. Enough to kill a president of the highest order. But wasn't no presidents on this street. Just boats, wives, children, dogs.

Sometimes barking all at once. Picnics on barbecue grills burning. Chicken, ribs, hotdogs. Neighbors around flirting with a good time. Before somebody pushes a button or takes a telephone call to kick someone else's ass in the world.

Hell, he needed a rubdown tonight. His back tightens the closer he gets to the white picket fence. Flowers of spring. His little girl Zara runs out the screen door, plaits jumping in the air. Plaid dress flying as her mother stands at the door with a wooden spoon. Bowl in her arms, whipping up something.

Hops up in her father's arms. "Daddy! Daddy! Daddy!" Smooches his rusty cheek.

"Hi, baby." Sam tickles his nose against hers. "Where's Mommie?"

"Right there, Daddy!" She tells about her day. "Mommie's bad."

"Mommie's bad?" He gave her a startled look.

"Yes, Daddy."

"Why, Zara?" He puts her on the ground. "Tell Daddy."

"Zara," Myrthe says, "tell Daddy why Mommie is bad."

"It's my lollipop, Daddy... That Uncle... Uncle Ray gave me."

Myrthe knows her daughter is playing the game of little girl police officer with her father. She watches her husband melt into a piece of cheese at her dimples rolling, puffy from her sugar cookie face. He was a sucker, chump for her. She has to keep her daughter in line most of the time. He knows the rules. She has to tell him many nights to watch the dimples. Watch the dimples.

He's tired, but gets the energy to play. "Now, Zara," he bends down to her level, "are you going to tell Daddy you want your lollipop before eating your dinner?" He touches her shoulder.

She sulks and gets up the nerve. "Yes, Daddy." Bats her eyes up at her mother in triumph. She touches his salt, pepper beard. "Daddy, may I? May I, Daddy?"

He stands straight. "Only after dinner." Pats her head. "Mother's word is law."

"Law." She takes him by the thumb. "What's law, Daddy?"

He goes up the three stairs. "Follow me… "

"You deserve a kiss for that," Myrthe says, pushing the door with her knee.

He hugs her. Kisses her cheek poking out. He asks about the spoon in the bowl. "Ah! What you making?" Slips an arm around her waist.

"Peanut butter cookies." She watches Zara following behind him. "Little girl, you set the table. Get the spoons and forks out of the kitchen cabinet. Let your Poppie breathe for a few minutes."

Zara skips off to the kitchen.

Sam runs upstairs to the bathroom. Closes the door, takes his piss. Washes his hands. He gazes at his face in the mirror… tired, half-dead eyes. Greying up. Restless man. He's glad to be able to sit, eat, watch the six o'clock news. Listen to his little girl and wife fuss over cartoons, alphabets, math games, dinosaur puzzles. He heads to the bedroom, kicks off his penny loafers, takes off his khaki pants. Throws his watch and wallet on the dresser. Unbuttons the blue button-down-collar shirt. Puts on his Lee jeans, that were born from the sixty-eight riots, after Malcolm's last words. They dragged his ass off to a war he didn't give a Gook-fuck about. Damn sure didn't know about an M-16. Not until Captain J. J. Johnson got finished with him in that foxhole. Stretch marks on his body in the dresser mirror. Long shoulders, thick neck, wet, curly chest hairs. His stomach is getting a pouch. He always had skinny hairy legs. Uncorks two aspirins, swallows.

A face, a mask of a man who has been in plenty of trouble. Now he's in plenty of love with a little girl and a sweet-butt wife. Who speaks three languages in cooking up something nice in the kitchen. The smells walk up to the sea green-blue bedroom of mirrors, rugs, pillows, lights. He tries to guess: roti, goat stew, fish soup, with a lettuce, tomato salad? He slips on his Redskins T-shirt. He places the leather calfskin slippers on his toes. Hunger pulls him down, down the steps of ginger-curry spices.

"Peanut butter spoon, Daddy." Zara licks the spoon like it's the drippings from the fountain of youth at the dinner table. She doesn't look down at the plate of curried chicken, rice, mixed carrots, potatoes, string beans under her chin.

Myrthe is beat, more tired than a jackass pulling a cart of bricks up a dirt road in Haiti. This little girl with the brown-cotton mushroom eyes, Zara's face bubbles over with rainbows after a spring storm. The child had cried to taste the spoon, after she stuck the cookies in the oven to take over to Uncle Ray's house after they ate dinner.

Sam can see his wife is whipped by the five-year-old. "Baby, did Mr. Petersen of Alco Garage come check on the car?"

"He came," she said, scooping some of the vegetables over on his plate.

"And?" Sam didn't want to catch that bus of thieves another day.

"Just the battery." She picks up the casserole bowl of chicken and rice. "Little girl, is that all you going to eat?"

"Ummmm!" Her mouth was stuck; her plaits wiggled up and down. "Ummm!"

In silence Myrthe begs him to talk to her at the table. Bargain with the little girl who is tearing up the peanut butter spoon with no vegetables on the side.

"Zara," Sam quietly calls to her over his plate of food.

"Yes, Daddy." Her tongue dances.

He leans on one elbow. "If..." he points at the food on her plate, "... you don't eat some of this nice dinner Mommie cooked for us... you not going to get the lollipop Uncle Ray gave you today." With the patience of an elephant about to charge he was ready for the brown-sea change of decision coming in a moon-face of cheeks and valentine lips. Sam made sure not to look at her dimples.

She stops. Looks at the spoon as if it was a lost relative about to go away again. She sees that she has lost an ally in this war against her mother. She puts the spoon on a napkin. "Daddy, I'll eat some chicken."

"And don't forget some of your vegetables." Myrthe lets her know the world is about giving and taking. "Just think of that lollipop Uncle Ray gave you." She smiles over to her husband.

Zara chews some of the chicken. Closes her eyes, dreams of that peanut butter spoon. She stabs at the heart of the vegetables, placing them in her mouth.

"That's very good," Myrthe applauds. "Now another one for Daddy."

"Ohhhhh, Mommie." She squints from the taste. Swallows, rocks in the chair. She reaches out for her father's forked hand. "Daddyyyy!"

"Go ahead, baby, it's good for you… It will make a tall, beautiful brown swan out of you. Just like your mother."

"*Oie du lac*," Myrthe said quietly. "Swan of the lake." She was proud to give her a French lesson at any moment or time of the day.

"Mommie's a swan, Daddy?" Zara asks her father, twisting the fork in her little hand, waiting for this magical answer.

Sam isn't going to disappoint her. "Yes she is, baby. Now eat all your food so we can visit Ray Junior." He picks up a fork full of rice and chicken. Morsels of delicious peanut butter float under his nose; cookies being baked from the kitchen. He looks over to his wife, who sits under the picture of the castle. On top of the mountain with rocky high seas splashing up, trying to get to it. She has a seventy-watt aura around her head and face from the blue lampshade behind her on the corner table of *Sports Illustrated* and *Essence* magazines. She is a true resemblance to pictures he has seen of the Black Madonna.

"Sam, you all right?" Myrthe asks him after catching him looking at her.

"Back acting up again." He scratches his brow, sticks food in his mouth.

299

"We don't have to visit your brother and Mabel this evening if you are tired, honey." She looks at his face. It becomes longer as if ink is being poured from his eyes. She wants him to feel good all the time, every day. The same way he feels about her in this cold, bloody-ass world of hate, war, racism, poverty and not one damn day of peace for a Black man with a family. Oh, yes, they were lucky because she had enough goddamn sense to save the gold and diamonds. After she sold her body and soul to a madman so many years.

"No, let's go. When we come back home… " He gave her a foxy grin. "You just going to have to give me one of those special rubdowns." He spots her blushing. She puts her hand up over her mouth. He plays peek-a-boo with her. "I see you."

"Mommie will kiss it and make it better for you later." She pokes her kissable lips at him across the table. It's all about her favorite tongue bath.

She gets serious with her daughter. "Zara, drink your milk."

Zara reaches over her plate for her glass of milk. Drinks, then takes quick glances of her mother and father batting their eyes at each other at the table. She shakes her head, not knowing what the grown-ups were plotting against her next.

29

I t's almost seven-thirty when they arrive at his
brother Ray's place. All they had to do was walk a
couple of houses down the block. Under a summer-
warm, black cloak night, the three of them hold each
other's hands. Crystal midnight blue water below
them a hundred and fifty yards down a grassy slope is
going to sleep. Search lights drift. Fog horns slip from
boats as they white dot the water's shores. Stars nod,
drift off like newborns. Houses of white frame, shin-
gled, green aluminum-sided shutters. Evening lights
come out in front windows. Dogs bark. Cats scream.
Men's strong voices drift up from the deep black lake
of the night. Down by the landing, cargo comes off
to waiting trucks picking up the night's produce of
shrimp, trout, seaweed, Chinese mushrooms and
other bits of delicacies from a man's hook. Neighbors
sit on their front steps talking. You can hear some of
them laughing at silly summer reruns of "Jeffersons,"

"Smoky and the Bandit" or a Clint Eastwood whistle for "Three Dollars More."

Sam lifts Zara up to ring the bell to house number two-eighty-two.

The door opens up as Mabel and Ray greet them. "Well, look who's here."

Mabel bends down in Zara's face. "Who does this cute gingerbread child belong to?"

"Zara, tell Auntie Mabel... you Mommie's and Daddy's little girl," Myrthe says.

"I am Mommie's and Daddy's little girl." Her bright eyes speak as her arms go up to hug her aunt around the neck.

"Aw, isn't that nice." Mabel kisses her. She acts surprised at the gift in Myrthe's hand. "Cookies! They can't be for me!" She peeps down. "Ray!" She closes her eyes. "Take them out of my sight."

Ray gets the plate. "Yaw come on in!"

Sam closes the door behind him. "They for Big Ray and Little Ray." Myrthe messes with her. "Your butt too big to eat these."

"Yeah, honey, but my man likes it." She pats her hips. "Ray Junior, come say hi to Zara."

He comes from behind his mother's long denim skirt. He takes her by the hand, pulls her into the living room.

"Ahhhhh! Isn't that cute," Myrthe said as her heart warms up over the kids. They follow the children into the peach-painted living room. It's breezy with green flower couches, fireplace. Two pillowed rocking chairs full of toys: Barney, Super Grover dolls, stuffed bears. A bat, ball. Three-wheel tricycle on the floor. His and hers bedroom slippers lying around.

With Ray's pipe in a round glass ashtray on a side table, about to burn out next to a vase of red roses.

"Now let's get to the root of this cookie mystery." Sam smells up the aroma coming off the plate. Ray put them on the ottoman coffee table.

"Peanut butter, Uncle Ray." Zara tells the secret. "Mommie made dem."

"And I bet you licked the whole spoon?" Mabel quizzes her.

"Yeaaaahhhhh!" She shakes her head; plaits jump from the good thoughts of licking a peanut butter spoon. "Ummmmm!" Zara prances. "It was goooodddd!"

"She sure did." Myrthe sits down beside her husband on the couch. "She's debated me for days to get that spoon."

"You haven't said a thing," Ray said pointing at his son in his cute suspender jeans outfit. Captain Kangaroo logo on the front. A Baby Hero badge pinned to the suspenders. Ray Junior had Zara on the floor playing with some building blocks of houses. A Farmer Brown's play kit with some sheep, cows, chickens. He has problems in putting them together. This has him crack up into a heavy summer shower of tears, flat on his back.

"He's so handsome, even when he's mad," Myrthe says. "Such large black eyes. He could be one of those television children selling Ovaltine Chocolate Milk."

"Yeah, he's a little movie star with temper tantrums," Sam laughs.

Mabel picks him up. "Baby, stop crying." She kisses his cheek of tears. "Here's a cookie." She puts it in his little fingers. "There you go."

He stops crying quick, as soon as he gets it in his hand.

"He's all right now," Ray says, looking up to the ceiling. "Saved by the cookie."

"Daddy, look!" Chewing, he shows off the cookie.

"I see it, son… Just don't eat them all up." He tickles him. "Save some for Daddy now." He laughs at his son's butter popcorn brown face. All cooked at a pleasant age of two, going on a hard-count of three.

"Here, Zara," Mabel says, handing her one. She's playing with a dinosaur puzzle on the floor, pieces of teeth and green tail under her shoes, knees, blue jean bottoms. She eats the cookie and tries to figure out parts to the years the creatures roamed the swamps of the District of Columbia. "She's a smart child… I can see that… Just like her mother."

"Hey, what about me?" Sam questions her. "Didn't I have something to do about that too?"

"Yeah, right. Two beers and seven minutes." Ray laughs, shakes his head at his brother. "She takes after Myrthe." Ray rubs his son's head. "Now him! He takes after you. This head is hard as a rock!"

"Don't say that about my baby." Mabel hugs him tight. "He does what Daddy says… after he drinks his Chocolate Ovaltine."

Myrthe tells them in a gentle voice for the future, "Looks like he's going to be tall, just like his uncle and papa."

"He does have some big feet," Ray says. "Come on, bro'. When I was in New York I got some new cuts by this dude, name Dubi-O."

Sam gets up, tugs on his pants legs. Peeps down his wife's turquoise blouse. He smiles at what he likes. "Never heard of 'im." He follows Ray out of the room, down the hall to his left. Another door, a flight of steps to the basement.

It's quiet, covered in wood. Bar with dusty liquor bottles. Mirror with small lights circling it. Three chairs lined up. A hard, brown-tiled floor, black leather couch. An old bumpy, soft chair right across from it. A couple of rooms in the back of the washer, dryer, baby crib. Dead broken toys and a stuffed Teddy bear on the floor. Golf clubs in the corner. On the left side of the wall is the stereo component set. Two floor speakers, naked woofers, tweeters. Busted screen door, shut closed with a bolt across. A refuge for a summer, winter, fall night. Underground dive of beer cans and paint-by-the-numbers pictures of green valleys leaning on the floor.

Old sweaters rolled up on the couch. Beach balls, lawn mower, a rake. Too small little boys' clothes. Music, music, everywhere, albums on the floor in front of the stereo set. Picture over the couch, in red cloth felt of an African King. A woman at his feet, spear in his right hand. A baby in her arms. Certificates on the wall. Heroic past of training academy courses from Quantico, Virginia, Fort Bragg, North Carolina. Weapons and small arms training. On a mantel to the right, Ray had won a couple of softball championships. Mabel had her degree in business education tacked under an old grey statue of the bald eagle.

Ray steps behind the bar. "Get your favorite spot… because we getting ready to jam on some nice new sounds."

Sam sits in the corner of the couch, close to the speakers. Kicks his penny loafers up on the coffee table. "Now, who's this Dubi-O?"

"Brother's from the jungle... Trumpet man." Ray unscrews the top off some brandy. He takes two small glasses from the back rack. He sets them in front of Sam. "This coworker-buddy of mines hip me to him." He picks the cassette off the table. "Check this out, he's out of South Africa."

"Maybe I ought to call Myrthe down here to hear him. She likes international music." Sam says this, knowing his brother's answer coming up. No women allowed.

"Don't even try it... If you like it... you can take it home." He flips down the door to the cassette player and pushes the power button. "Now, check this out."

Sam sticks a toothpick in his mouth. "Let him play!" He sits back, listens to the trumpet of this man. It sounds like a cat, an angry, angry cat. But some of the instruments have him hunched over, feeling a breeze. A heat. A rain come down his neck. He watches Ray fix the drinks. The music is good. Cold, icy. Just like that brandy his brother is pouring in the glasses. A Napoleon thing. Short, hard-nose. A type of sound that would spit in your eye, and keep on pumping, jumping. Dubi-O didn't give a fuck as the drummer tapped for you to get out of his way. All African; calm-mean-cool.

"How you like 'im?" Ray asks. He sits his drink in front of him. He sits in the bumpy short chair across from his brother. He watches Sam, head turned, legs crossed.

"He's working for me." He listens, takes a drink. "Man, this is all you got, cheap Napoleon?" He put his glass back on the table. "Give me some of that expensive shit from Paris."

"You come down here to listen to some music, not drink up my liquor," Ray tells him, as the Dubi-O horn is telling a tale of Mandela in prison. It's sadder than a piece of shit on a three hundred-pound man's shoe. "Man, fuck you... I'll drink that shit at your funeral."

Sam rests back, finger up to his ear. Picks the glass back up with a toast to his brother. "To when I'm dead."

"When we both dead... drink the cheap shit!"

"Why is that, Ray?"

"Because our lives ain't worth a fuck in this country either... Man, I'm a cop.. and all because of how I look... I could get shot by another cop in the blink of an eye." A half-slice grin rises in his right cheek. "South Africa, shit! Dubi-O needs to play for me too."

"He is, Ray... He is." He taps a toe to somebody on the bass. "How was your trip?" Sam finishes his drink. "Pour me another."

Ray takes his glass. "It wasn't a pleasure trip." Pours the brandy, hands him the glass back.

"Never is for Superman."

"Fighting crime with a badge instead of an 'S' on my chest, now that's a real Superman." Ray turns his glass up to his lips. Brandy is cold-moist, just as his soul is getting warm-dry.

"It's the breakfast of champions—lead hollow-point bullets," Sam says.

Ray gets the bottle. "Ma said you always was the funny one." Fills up his glass.

"This dude sounds a lot like Hugh Masakela." Sam looks over at his brother concentrating on the music. Hunched, wide shoulders man, peeping into a crystal ball of sound. Trying to out-think the world and the animals in it.

"South African sound of shields and spears," Ray tells him, revealing the distinct flavor of a people on a horn-rich continent of war.

"Those some bad brothers. All praises due." Sam rubs his eye. Yawns. "When you going to stop working this job for Uncle Sam?"

"I don't know. Pay good... My life's cheap."

"How about us starting a business or something together?"

"Shit! You mad? We'll be just like those two... Trojan brothers you work for. But I would have to kill your ass the first day on the job."

Sam picks his nose. "I couldn't work with you either, but it beats stopping bullets with that silver badge of yours."

"That's okay." Ray's voice sounds sadly reluctant. "I'm not ready yet, bro'. I still get high off of busting corporate heads of state for being major players into our underground economy... Your drugs, dummy corporations, dictators, kings, queens, a rook here or there. With their long arms and noses in Swiss bank accounts... Shit that don't reach the papers."

"And you the fucking White Knight." Sam scratches his chin. Scared but proud of his brother and his noble cause that wasn't going to kill a fly. He knows Ray is a caring type of dude, with comic book ethics in his heart in being some fucking Superman. The flag, honor, justice is his thing. "I see your eyes and nose widen when you talk about it."

Ray looks at his brother in rock black face under the sounds of African jazz and a summer mosquito buzzing around his head. "No, I'm the Black Knight... The flame hasn't burned out in my belly yet."

"Now, yeah... I remember you did collect a lot of those Superman comic books."

"So what? You was into Batman... "

"But I didn't turn out to be some right-or-wrong freak!"

"Fuck you, Sam... " He didn't want to be analyzed today or tomorrow. "Listen to the music." Ray sips some. "You want me to make you a copy of this?"

"Yeah. He can cook. Make me a copy."

"Okay." Ray listens to Dubi-O. "When I was in Chicago I found out about a lot of things... I couldn't wipe the dirt off my shoes in what I saw. What I heard."

"Like what?" Sam asks. "I thought you knew about everything."

"Not really." He rubs a scar across his nose. "This shit I'm in... is a fucking joke... and if you ain't down with it, you going to get crushed."

"You becoming cynical now." Sam drinks the brandy. It hits him in the chest like a flame torch. It's getting good. He's getting high. "Don't worry about the shit, man... Get your paycheck and bring your ass home in one piece."

"Sometimes it's hard, you know." He shakes his head. "This world we live in is a big fat wallet. Just make sure you don't get your pockets picked... This drug war can't be whipped. Can't be licked, can't be sucked, can't be fucked... You can only make love to it. Whisper in its ear, make deals with it. Talk to it, kiss it, lick it soft. Try to keep it in bed with you... All around us." He points to the bolted door. "They bringing it in right now. Under our noses as we sit here and listen to some freedom jazz. They bringing it in right now at the landing from boats, ships, tourists, planes, military, captains, kings, queens, rooks and even... even White and Black Knights."

Sam knows this, but he wants his brother to stay calm. Cruise in the shit... reach an early retirement, come home to Mabel and Ray Jr. in one piece. "So you becoming more cynical... super cynical... Superman cynical... Just remember, Ray."

"Remember what, Sam?"

"Be cool... like this jazz you listening to." Sam leans over, opens his right palm.

Ray slaps him five. "Thanks, man. I needed that." He rubs his chin. "It's good to be back home with family."

"That's right, that's all you got, Ray. Family... We'll keep your head above water... if you ever need to know if you are doing right or wrong... Just go to me or Mabel. Even your little boy with those beautiful big brown eyes of his... will hug you around the neck and bring you back to reality. I was in the war. You was in the war. And baby, that wasn't real... It was a dream. A dream that never lets go. But you come back in one piece. A half of a piece, back to your family... for us to put all the pieces back together again..."

"I heard from Pop, Sam." Ray caught him in the corner. "He wants to see Zara... his granddaughter."

"Why did he call you and Mabel?" Sam asks. "He can talk to me anytime."

"Oh yeah? When was the last time you talk to him?"

Sam pulls his ear. "I don't remember. You tell me." Sam doesn't like these questions about seeing Pop. It's a bitter taste in his stomach. His hands get sweaty around the glass of brandy. "Like I said, he can talk to me anytime."

"Well, he wants to see Zara."

"No problem."

"You need to cut that shit out, man," Ray says, pointing a finger at him across the table. "You talking about family. You want the truth? You a fucking coward!"

"Coward! Coward about what? Pop?"

"I thought you had this settled a long time ago, man... Stop acting like a damn kid, Sam... Pop did wrong... did us all wrong! But he still your father and that means show him respect."

He checks his watch. It's almost eight-thirty. "I got to go... Make me a copy... Bring it by later." He grts up. He doesn't hear the music anymore.

"Sit down, Sam," Ray orders him, standing up with him.

"I gots to go. My little girl is sleepy... It's past her bedtime."

"This is about your little girl, Sam."

Sam stares; he's about to hit him. But he doesn't want this homecoming to be a mess in the basement. "Just tell Pop to call me."

"Okay, man... I tell him, but you can call him."

"I know... I know." He hugs Ray. "Welcome back." Sam walks back up the stairs to his wife and little

311

girl. This has his head spinning. When he reaches the light, Zara is running after Ray Jr.. Myrthe is sitting in the living room sipping tea, eating a cookie. Mabel is laughing about some old man chasing her down in the grocery store. Girl stuff. Friendly, warm, melted ice cream of words between two women.

He goes in the room to Myrthe. "Come on, baby, let's get ready to go."

Myrthe looks in his eyes, sees the drops of a mysterious disappointment. "Okay, Sam." She sets her cup on its plate. She knows her husband. When the smile dies in his face, she doesn't ask him any questions about him being uncomfortable. This isn't the time, this isn't the place to blow in his face. Even though she's having fun with Mabel and the children, it's time to go.

Mabel stands. She knows the look too. "Okay, well... I see you tomorrow, Myrthe." She looks around. "Zara! Come here and give me a big kiss before you go."

Zara runs to her, gives her a hug. A kiss.

Sam hugs Mabel. "Tell my brother I see him later."

"Okay, Sam." She walks them to the door with Ray Jr. in her arms. He starts to cry for his cousin. "Shhhhh, Ray... You'll see Zara tomorrow."

Myrthe kisses Little Ray on his warm, fat cheeks. "Bye, Little Ray... See you tomorrow." She kisses his little fingers.

Mabel bends down with him. "Give Zara a kiss goodbye."

"Ummmmm, mum!" Zara says to him. "Bye, Cousin Ray!"

He's better after the kisses. Waves his little fingers at Zara. "See you."

Sam takes his little girl by the hand out the door. Myrthe follows behind her husband and daughter in the white star night.

Mabel closes the door. She marches right back to the basement door. "Ray, Sam is gone." Pulling it open. "You brothers ought to cut that stuff out!" She slams it shut. With her little boy on her hip, she goes upstairs to bed.

30

Saturday morning after Bugs Bunny cartoons and "Soul Train," Zara plays in the screened-in front porch. Riding a red big wheel tricycle. Light yellow sun, her favorite color of the day. She rolls back and forth, screaming, laughing at her fast feet spinning on the pedals. Yellow dress up above her knees. Not a doggone care of her mother and father in the house, back in the kitchen discussing something. They can't be having more fun than her.

Sam pushes his thumb in his chest. "Don't tell me I don't love my father, Myrthe." He shakes his head like a crazy lion. "Don't you tell me I don't love my father!"

"You don't, Sam." She gives him a smirk. Not afraid of the big husband with tears of defiance swelling up in his eyes. "I... I don't want to hurt you, baby. But I will tell you the truth."

He paces the red and white checkerboard kitchen floor. Table, four chairs. He's ready to run out of the back door. He doesn't want to fight. He just wants to fish on the lake. But she won't back off. She has the strength of a wife that would stand up to a hoard of men. Her face robs him of his happy mask. Life was a plum. Mother dead. Don't think about a blind man, a Gargoyle that sits up in the dark eating hot summer flies. He's a shadow, behind him. A dream. A piece of paper that won't get off his shoe.

"You have lost control… *de'cu*! I don't want you bitter like this around our child… Bury the past, my Sam." She moves towards him. "*Blie sak fin passé.*"

Her Creole, French words sting him hard, harder than the American phrases of him being a bitter man. He's going to shove this back in her face. "I'm not bitter. I just want to go fishing."

"You Americans joke." She sticks her finger up in his face. "You Americans joke too much about old people, Black people, poor people, rich, young, smart, dumb… but our life is not a joke. Our little girl is not a joke. She is our flesh. our blood, Sam." She pulls his rolled-up shirt sleeve. Snatches his rock hard chin to her. "You hurt… Stop joking about dis."

He grabs her skinny wrist from his face. "Leave me alone."

She folds her arms. "You don't scare me… Zara shall see her grandfather."

"He wasn't there for me. Why should my little girl be there for him?"

"Because you want him to know… that you are not like him."

He looks down at the floor. "This is hard, this is hard." He feels his chest heaving heavily on his heart.

A sharp pain comes up in his arms, down in back of his legs.

"Sam, let it go... Let it go." She stands tall. "Dis is not right... Not."

Pots of rice boil.

He takes the hand that pinches, bites, kisses the inside palm. Pulls her to him, smells the honey, white rose perfume from her hair. Kisses her warm cheeks; they remind him of the summer blue lake. Fresh, brown starry eyes of his wife aren't going to let him drown, aren't going to let him fall to his busted-up knees. Sweat drips from her nose when she's mad. He made her lose that bourgeoisie attitude from the French. Made her more American-wild-Indian like. Upset her and made her cuss him out in three languages all at once. He loved the hell out of her. They could fight. They could fuss. He made her crazy for his love. He made her listen, think about being Black. She became a sister. Just like Mabel. He made her parade her love for him right in the streets, when they shop for toys, groceries. But she made him think. Shamed him to see his father, the Gargoyle, in a room licking hot summer flies and drinking a can of beer.

She runs to the stove as the hissing of steam breaks the silence between them in the kitchen of a red sun. He shrugs; no fishing today. Just fish for her love.

● ● ●

It's in November when the Gargoyle sings to thee:

316

Eyes closed tight, under dark, shaded eyeglasses. An old, blind, junkie beatnik from the fifties is just now to become an old magician as the aura of his days of magic fades over the red applesauce sky from his bedroom window. Behind curtains this man with long wings, claws, sits. Waits with his tongue licking out from under his broken nose from knife and fist fights. In the splotched, stained wallpaper room of his last days. He continues to sing the theme of "I Love Lucy" re-runs. Catchy tunes from the TV commercials dominate his days on the edge of a six-foot grave of diabetes, heart attacks, one stroke. Sores in his mouth. Puss dripping from his bowels. He smells up corn muffins and collards from the kitchen pots. Licks a fire-red tongue out to catch a fly. Muffles sounds of his heart. Picky, nagging sounds of Earlene shuffling in old brown slippers too big for her corn-husky feet. Cold shivers run down the back of his legs. He pulls a sweater up around his shoulders. Long green-hairy arms. Dirty khaki pants stained with mustard-catsup hot dogs from last night. Maybe he take a bath later? Maybe not? Post-partum breathing old man of sixty-seven. Coughs up thick phlegm. Spits it in a trash basket by his chair. Repeats, counts ten breaths. Blows his nose on his sleeve. Plays with his belly button. A mosquito circles his nose like he's a piece of shit stuck on a sidewalk for another man to walk on. Waits for him to die. Snaps, pops a finger. He feels life down his legs. He rocks from more jokes from Lucy's mouth. She was getting on Ricky's last Cuban nerve. If that was Castro, he would have shot her on the sidewalk, right in front of the other red-headed prostitutes on the streets of Havana.

317

He rocks. Curls his claws like a mountain lion about to eat a baby lamb on a Sunday afternoon just after the football game. He drifts back to the days of alien, shape-shifting, strawberry white women. He use to sale them off and on to the sailors coming in port. You had to pay him a dime a lick. A quarter a peek. Sea-salt tasty women. Sniff up their lemon-smelling hair in your nose. Soak a blood-stained right arm across their breasts after he shot up for the night. Long dreams of a day after leaving his wife home alone with the boys. He can't blame them for not wanting to see him for Thanksgiving. Hell, he always had plenty fun. He didn't need to see his granddaughter none. He got word that she was doing fine. He held her when she was just six pounds, seven ounces. He held his grandson when he was seven pounds, two ounces. Naw, he didn't need to see them. Hold them, kiss them. Wrestle with them, slip quarters in their sticky candy fingers. They were too busy chasing their dreams. The same way he used to chase that train of dope, women, wine.

He understood. He understood the fun of living, seeing. Kissing a pretty girl's belly. Licking it up. Kissing it down. He flaps his small wings, places his feet up on the cushy ottoman. He was just a little sad. Just a little bit.

Earlene pops her head in. "Jim, you okay?"

"I'm okay, baby... Lucy's not too funny today." He holds his head up in the empty space of a room. He can hear a mouse tearing at a piece of wood in the walls.

"Dinner be ready in a few."

"Call me when you ready." He scratches his hand that rested on his gold-handled cane across his lap. "Did we get a call from Sam or Ray today?... I know I dozed off 'round 'bout one."

"No, Jim. We didn't get a call today... You want me to turn the heater up some by your feet?" She felt sorry for his nasty ass. White hair still there, balding in the middle. She watches his head move towards her at the door. She loved him and gave him the time to soak up his existence in front of a TV tube.

"No! Don't come near me."

"Okay, I won't." She pulls her head back from the door and his bad ass ways when he didn't get his phone call. Let him keep his pride bottled up in "I Love Lucy" shows.

He brings his head up defiantly as if he was still the boss in his one-bedroom apartment of dust, plastic plants and a can of cockroach spray. "Fix me a pork chop too, Earlene."

"Doc Henry say, leave that pork alone."

"You and him both go to hell," he mumbles under his thick black lips. Flicks his right ear from a fly's mouth. "Give me a beer then."

She opens up the refrigerator of old bread, sardines, cat food, lettuce, lunch meat, eggs, turkey-bacon. Unfinished crab cake mix. Milk, water, juice, pressure pills, beer. "Jim, what kind? Schlitz or Budweiser?"

"Earlene, you know what I like. I'm a Bud man."

She laughs from the kitchen. "You a fucking commercial!" She gets the beer, takes a glass from the rack. "You need to stop watching TV so much." She takes it to him, snaps the top, pours it in the glass for him. "Here you go."

He takes it from her fingers. "Thank you."

She turns. He slaps her butt. She spins around grinning. "Nasty old man!"

"I'm still half alive and don't you forget it!"

• • •

After dinner a couple of his buddies come over his apartment. Slick, grey-dog Hal Jackson. Ex-boxer, junkie. Railroad man from Meridian Mississippi. Has a brown bag under his arm, probably a fifth of Cutty Sark. Billy Buffalo is with him. Hunchback, sewed-up cut down his right cheek. Older than a horse's bad knees. Always carried a pair of dice with him. He got shot in the stomach once over some gambling thing. He's been walking with a cane and the same pair of dice in his pockets from this incident over twenty-five years. They are his friends. Men who laugh, cry with him. Listened to some of that dizzy, crazy bebop jazz shit during World War II. Old boys. Part of the underground that hid from the volunteer, draft thing. You know. Get your black ass shot at in order to save the race.

They both sit on a dirty brown couch across from him. It's almost seven. "The Price Is Right" is just coming on. He doesn't know if he feels up to dealing with these skeletons tonight. Their voices in his ear sound like an off-beat jingle bell. One horse sleigh thing for the holidays.

They're drunk and cheery. "So, Jim, we thought we come by to see your old dead ass," Hal says. Winks at his blind friend in the chair. "Take that shawl shit from around your shoulders. Stop acting like you 'bouts to die or something like that."

"I'm under the weather."

"Mutherfucker! You ain't under the weather... Just tell your girl...," Billy Buffalo scratches his face. "Uhhhh, what's her name?"

"Earlene," Jim answers him, but it makes him mad. "You boys don't disrespect my home."

"I'm sorry, Jim." Billy Buffalo stands up, slaps him on the shoulder. "Just dat you ain't been out in the streets with us in a long time."

"Just tell us what's the matter," Hal asks him with the hunch of his square shoulders. "We ain't blind like you... We just wants you to know we are here for you."

He leans on his arm some. "I guess it's just the holiday season... you know, families all around."

Billy Buffalo glances at Hal. They know he's getting weak on them. Lonely, times are crossing over his shoulders. Rocking chair friend. A man who stood by them, stayed with them, damn sure drank with and ran women right behind them. They wanted to keep partying around Sweet Loaf, D.C., even Virginia. Old con men didn't want to feel the shadow of loneliness over their shoulders. Didn't want to hear the voice ticking off in their heads telling them it was time to go to bed or even an early grave. Boys from the fields of Georgia, Mississippi, and South Carolina who came up from the old school chasing that train, ten inches from the Klan whip to get up so-called North. Land of honey, land of fading into green, grey jungles of buildings. Piss-shit jobs of sweeping, driving school buses, hustling women, shooting craps, shooting good dope in your arms on a yellow Sunday summer afternoon. Beating a woman like a bitch dog back in the forties-fifties. Marlon Brando style. Holler out the bitch name in the street. She hollering back at you to leave that other bitch alone. Wasn't no Black Revolution thing back than. Naw, sure wasn't.

"When you last seen your boys?" Hal asks him.

"Why you ask me that?" He rocks some. "Huh?"

"Looks like it's eatin' at you." Hal isn't going to back down from him. He's a man who would try to fix anything, but he needs answers first.

Jim picks his cane off his legs. "It's kind of eating at me."

"Why don't you call them?" Buffalo asks. "If it's bothering you."

Jim moves his shoulders towards the left, then to the right. "That's not my place." He adjusts the dark glasses. "You don't bother your children."

"Even I seen your grandchildren," Hal says to him straight.

Earlene comes in. Stands right by him. "Hal, Buffalo, you want something to drink?" She wipes her hands on a paper towel. "We got beer."

Jim answers for them. "They had enough to drink." His voice becomes tense, tired. "They not staying long… They wanted me to go out with them but I'm tired." He reaches for her hand. Pats it. "Just too tired… You know I'm expecting a call soon."

Buffalo doesn't give a damn. "Leave him alone. Go on, watch your TV set and crawl in it… so I can turn it off."

He wants to swing his cane at the harsh, hoarse words of Buffalo. He raises his head up toward Earlene. He knows she's about to charge him for being stupid, stubborn over two grown men that have gone on with their own lives and lies. He's gone inside an inner tube of hot wires and electric shock waves. Mannnn, he's out of it.

"Jim, I'm going to say this in front of your friends… Don't do this to yourself. You get your ass on out of here and have a good time… Go have some young thang or something." She kisses him on top of his head. "Whatever you old men do."

"Now that's an understanding lady you got there," Hal says. He peeks up at Earlene, grinning like he was a calico. "You betta watch her."

Jim responds in kind. "Like a hawk." Laughs up at her. He can't see her but he knows she's thick-honey Black woman. He has for many years. She always washed his clothes, cooked his food and made sure he took his medicine on time. She kept him in line with a stern, soft tongue that didn't make him upset. She was a good woman. A woman that added sugar and cream to his last days in a black world of voices, smells, tastes. With blue note music passed along for a good time between her legs twice a month.

She takes him out of the chair. "Now you come on, get washed and dressed for your evening out on the town with your friends."

"You boys wait for me… I'll be right with you." He follows her as if she was a big old stuffed mommie bear.

31

"Shoot the ball, man!" Ray's hands were in Sam's face.

"Here's a jumper in your eyes!" Sam's right wrist flexes. The ball sails in the air in the basket over the top of Ray's head. "All net!"

Ray gets the rebound. "It's basketball and football season." Bouncing right up in Sam's chest, faking, dodging, shaking his shoulders. "And I could always beat you at one." He holds up his finger. "That was this one!" He drives his shoulder into Sam, knocking him to the concrete. Slams. Dunks.

Sam gets up. "Foul! Foul!" In his face. He grabs the ball. "You cheatin', man!"

"This ain't no sissy game, little bro'." Ray gets down lower. Scoots his pants up. Checks, weaves, bobs his head with the ball. "I'm going to take it from you, little bro'."

Sam points, dribbles at the same time in his face. "Take what?" Jump shoots. The ball travels, backboard, banks, goes right in. "I got a lot riding on this game."

Ray hustles for the ball before it goes out of bounds by the trash can. "You damn sure do, little bro'." He feints his head left, a shoulder right. Steps back, dribbles, pumps the ball, dribbles around him for a lay-up. "Haaaaahhhhh!" Points at him. "Hahahaaa!" he throws the ball at his chest. "I'm coming again!" Sweat with cold steam coming from his nose. "I'm coming again!"

Sam slows his dribble, fakes a shot. Spins, moves around him. Shoots. The ball bounces off the rim, but not in. "Shit!"

Ray grabs the rebound with his hips and elbows. "Basketball season's mines." He shoots. It banks in the net. "Football season is yours, stay with your sorry Redskins… I'll take the Cowboys any time!"

Sam bounces the ball at him, driving real hard.

Ray slaps at it. Misses. "Almost! Almost!"

Sam dribbles quicker to his left, right. Stops, backs up on his right pivot toe. Dribbles, jumps. "That's in!" All net.

Ray grabs it coming out. "I'm not playing with you no more, little bro'." He dribbles. Shoots a sweet Oscar Robinson jumper.

Sam shakes his head. "Lucky shot!" Wipes the sweat from his neck.

"Luck, my ass!"

Sam dribbles right at him. Head fake. Slams a shoulder right into Ray's chest, makes a lay-up off the back board.

Ray bends over for air. "Awww! man! Little bro' getting nasty."

Sam bounces the ball back at him. "Come on, let's go." He hunches down in his stance, backing up as Ray comes at him with that stupid head fake. Tongue out via Michael Jordan imitation-down. Legs go up for another slam dunk.

The ball comes down hard on the edge of the rim. Misses the hoop, popping up and off in the air for Ray's sticky fingers.

He snatches it with a hard stare. Swiveling, focusing in on Sam to teach him a lesson on who's the king of the back court. "I'm going to take you to the hoop and slam dunk you, punk!"

"Punk! Punk!" Sam hollers up in his face, swatting at the ball. Banging his knees against his brother's. Shoving, fingers flying at the ball as it dodges from his sneaky advances.

Ray zips it through his legs. Still steadily moving towards the basket, turns his back, pushing him back ten feet under the basket.

Sam gets up on his back legs. Hands out in front of his chest. He tries to keep his brother from moving any closer. "I'm not going easy! I'm not going easy, Ray!"

"Shit, you can go hard!" Ray goes up with a left-handed hook.

Sam's fingertips missing the ridges. "Ahhhhhhhhh! Ahhhhhh! Noooo! Noooo! Noooooo!"

They both watch the ball loop to touch just net.

Ray jumps high, pumping, kicking the thin cold air. "Awwwwwwww! Awwwwwww!" He takes a bow to the invisible crowd. "Thank you! Thank you! Thank you!" He watches his brother bending over between his legs, looking for his tail.

Sam huffs, puffs, coughs, spits. Leans against the garage door. Shakes sweat from his face to catch the blur of his brother doing a war dance.

The wives, children come out back with cups of hot cocoa. "Who won?" Myrthe asks, giving the cup to Sam.

Sam points his head. "The fool doing the war dance and laughing at his little brother over there."

Myrthe goes to her husband. "My baby." Pecks his forehead. "I'm glad you lost." She smiles. Pinches his nose. "You lost a good bet… a bet that will make our holiday right… a silly bet… but that was the only way you could be persuaded to see your father."

He scratches his head. Picks Zara up in his arms. "You feel sorry for Daddy, don't you, baby?" He smirks at Myrthe. "Tell Mommie."

"No, Daddy. I want to see Grandpa."

He rolls his eyes. "Ummm, just like your mother." Puts her down. Drinks his cocoa.

"Get cleaned up, man." Ray bounces the ball back. "See you in half an hour." He takes the cup from his wife. "This is good." Sticks an arm over her shoulder. "Sweet taste of winning." Ray Junior follows behind his parents with a small football under his arms.

"I'll call you… Let me go sit on the king's head." Mabel raises her fist. "Victory!"

"Okay!" Myrthe balls her fist back to her. "Victory!"

• • •

Victory marches both the brothers to their father on a Saturday afternoon around six. Marches them

327

three flights up in brownstone off of Sixth and Jefferson South. Cobwebs spray over their heads the first flight. Little Spanish girls play with a Harlem Globetrotter basketball on the second flight. A black-white sheepdog pisses in the stairwell on the third floor. His master is drunk asleep on the steps. Mouth open. Pockets empty in the cold hallways of their father's home.

Two knocks. A surprise for the Gatekeeper of the Gargoyle, Earlene Johnston.

She looks them over, hugs Ray. Shakes Sam's hand. He's Sir Lancelot coming to rescue his father. Look for the Holy piece of Grail under beds, behind curtains. She doesn't give much for him. He damn sure doesn't a duck's tail for her. But respect is all there ever was between them; they kept their thoughts to themselves. Their words down their throats.

He looks at her as a standard old whore who used to drink a lot of scotch. Chased married men around with a pitchfork. Stuck their asses in the fire until she latched on the one she really wanted, that was his dad. She established her place, spot in life, with the green-skin old man. His eyes closed to the super highway world as he took a dose of acid in the face for her.

A patient, consuming, large woman. She wouldn't go to anyone's funeral. She just waited for her own. Older than his father, three grown kids of her own. By three different men. One Jamaican, one country, one from Philly. The one from the country threw the acid in his father's face.

She greets them with a thick, whirling, blue-grey wig on her head. Smudged orange bathrobe. Brown

328

socks on her feet. With a cigarette hanging down to her large, elongated tits. Her voice is rough, as if to tell any man or woman: I will fuck all of you if you get in my bed.

"Where is Pop?" Ray asks. "Is he asleep?"

"He's back in the bedroom... watching his 'Gunsmoke'."

"Come on, Sam... Let's surprise him."

Sam follows Ray to the back bedroom. Ray opens the door. "Hi, Pop."

"Ray, is that you?" His voice is suspicious.

"Yeah, Pop, it's me." Ray leans, hugs him.

The blind man pats his back. Sniffs the air. "Is Sam with you?"

Sam bends down, pats his father on the shoulder. "Hey, Dad... how you know it was me?"

"You wear the same kind of cologne I wear."

"What's that, Pop?" Ray asks, looking at his brother.

He scoots over on the bed. "Old Spice." Slaps the spot for them to sit.

"That's right, Dad." He sits at the foot of the bed.

Ray goes around, sits on the other side. He rubs his father's legs under the blankets of gold and army grey-green. "How you been doing, Dad?"

He coughs. Unfolds some Kleenex in his fist. Spits. "Awright!" Hoarse, raspy voice has him almost talking in a whisper. "Just a little cold, but I'll be awright... Don't you boys fuss over me."

Sam gazes around the room. Picture of a white Jesus Christ over the bed. Papers, dirty books on the side Earlene slept on. Couple of pillows puffed up behind his long green head. Dark glasses on. Matt

Dillon talking to Miss Kitty. "You boys still listening to dat jazz?"

Sam grins. "Yeah, Dad."

"Where yaw always know… Monk's my man."

"Yeah, the timekeeper," Ray replied. "Nineteen thirty-nine was your year."

"Damn good one, too." He laughs. "You boys want a drink?" Touches his glasses up to the bridge of his nose. "Huh?"

Pop always told them, no man never likes to drink alone.

"Yeah, Dad… we'll have a taste." Sam nods at Ray.

He squints. "For the holidays. Hey, Earlene! Get my boys here a drink. Some of that Bristol Cream."

Earlene's voice come back at them. "Okay, be right there!"

Sam catches his father's knee shake some, then stop.

Ray looks at the black face of his father smile, listen, smell creep into their thoughts. He watches his father's hands pop with thick veins. Black skin of a hard life that circled the globe of jail, beatings, cold-turkey fuckings on a Cold Turkey afternoon in some yellow gal's house. Police, dealers, women, babies all after you. He was over fifty. Now he could die in peace in a warm water bedroom with a seventy-watt light bulb. A woman by his side. Ray guessed that's all any man wanted when he died. A woman by your side. Didn't matter if she was ugly with hair a thumb long. Just a female voice taking care of you and get-ting your medicine on time. Just like your momma used to do. He sees the contentment in his face. He doesn't see the bitterness in his cheeks. He's just a sick man ready to go when the Devil calls.

Earlene brings the drinks to the bedroom. "Dad, you not drinking?" Sam asks, takes his glass from Earlene. She shakes her head a bit as if to say, don't ask, and goes back out the room.

Jim hunches. "Sometimes, son... I just want to stay dry..."

Sam drinks the sherry. "I understand that... Thanks for the drink."

"You welcome, son." He asks, "How's my granddaughter?"

"All right, Dad... She's doing fine."

"Good." He turns to Ray. "You awfully quiet, boy... How's Ray Junior doing?"

"Just watching TV." Matt Dillon ducks from a bullet at his badge. "He's doing fine. He's going to be big, just like the Murphys."

"That's good and fine with me, son... You boys got good genes." He laughs with a tickle and a cough in his throat. "Can't keep those Black Irish down!" Scratches his hair.

"Pop, it's time for you to get a haircut," Sam said. "You want me to come over next week and shape you up?"

"That's all right, son... Earlene's my barber," Jim says to him with pride. "That's the secret of us staying together for so long... Can't get rid of your barber."

They all laugh around the bed. They don't have to fish for words to say to each other. The holiday season makes them catch up on things that haven't been said in a while. Bitterness comes out. Words of wisdom come in.

"I'm glad you boys came over here." His right leg shakes under the covers. "But what I want to know is... why?" The leg stops.

331

"What you mean, Pop?" Ray acts like his father is seeing boogey-men.

"Why now, boys?" Shakes his head. "Doc told you something? Earlene call you up about me?" His hands go up in the air. "Somebody dead?"

"Pop, we don't know what you talking 'bout... We just want to see you." Sam looks at him straight in the face of dark glasses.

"You lie, boy. I can hear it in your voice... Don't play games with me, Sam and Ray." He reaches for his cane. "I got something to get the truth out of you."

Sam puts his hand up. "Aww! Awwwwright, Dad. It was a game."

"A game?" His dark glasses move up his nose.

"You see... I wasn't coming to see you." Sam doesn't mind telling him. "I was busy."

Ray attempts to soften these words from Sam. "Pop, it was nothing... A game."

"Shut up, Ray! You ain't gots to defend me or your brother... Don't bother me none." He hunches. "I see you won!"

"Yeah Pop, I won," Ray answers. He wants to keep peace, some respect amongst them. "Pop, I made him come... The wives too."

"The wives too?" He frowns, places the cane back on the side. "What was the game?"

"Huh?" Sam blinks when Matt Dillon gets injured under a tree.

"Basketball," Ray repeats. "Basketball, Pop."

"Dat ain't your game, Sam."

"I know, Dad." Sam smiles at the Gargoyle in the bed. He's shrinking, shivering under the covers. Scales turning grey. "Dad, you okay?"

He pulls the covers up. "Time for my medication." He growls out, "Earlene! Earlene!"

Earlene hollers from under a tree lamp; reading *Redbook*. "Coming, baby!" She gets up from a comfortable, high-back chair to the refrigerator, taking his bottle of pressure pills. She's getting tired of them both being sick most of the long days of their beginning winter dream. Both of them smelling up with Vicks rub, alcohol rub with a dash of Florida mineral water rubbed over their legs before they go to sleep. Pills for his pressure. Pills for her heart.

She pours a glass of water from the bottle. Shuts the door. "What's going on in here?" When she gets in the room his leg is jumping.

He takes the pill, drinks the water. "Nothing, Earlene. Just get out."

"Earlene, before you go, I want to ask you and Dad to have Thanksgiving dinner with us this year over my place." Sam wants them both over his house. "Please come and be with us and the kids."

"Come on, Pop." Ray acknowledges Sam's plea.

She looks at Jim's face. He has a smile on wider than his belly full of invisible turkey and grandchildren. "If it's okay with your daddy… it's okay with me."

"That's fine with me… I'll eat both my sons' shit to be with my grandchildren."

"Pop, it ain't got to be like that," Ray says to him. "It's family."

"Well, it ain't got to be… but it is." Jim's voice cracks with shame. "I know the wrong I done to your momma and you boys."

Earlene looks at the three of them. All of them with big heads, long shoulders. Bright brown, polar lodestone eyes. Men of pride, that stand with heavy weights of keeping their dignity intact. All three Billy-Dee-looking men who love the hell out of each other but would never say it in public. Maybe behind closed doors. "We'll be there, Sam." She leaves the room with the three talking to the TV set in the bedroom.

"Matt Dillon's a bad man," Jim says to his sons.

"You right, Pop… he's a badddd man… Got shot three times, ain't died yet!" Ray laughs at the marshal dodging more bullets under the tree.

32

December 15, 1991:

Sam watches the Gargoyle play with the children in the winter of gold leaves down by the lake. In a winter as shiny yellow and green around Santa Claus's nose. Under the contentment of watching his little girl chase behind a blind man of the magnitude of being six feet with wings. Fire-breathing. Long arms, a cane. Sunglasses wrapped around his thick, fleshy face. He watches his father—tender, soft melody moments—swing his little Zara playfully in the air as if she was a brown cotton ball. Ray Junior cries to his mother for everything. He's afraid of green Gargoyle of 1939 Swing. He watches his father give them his time. Eat his turkey at the dinner table. Talk politics, sing songs with Myrthe, Mabel, Ray at an old piano. He still plays a little blues, Chicago style. Once dreamed of being a blues man, leaving them for the road of music instead of dope and women. He watches his father and Earlene playfully touch, bob, jab each other with insults. But yet still tenderly end up leaving together in the evening. Tucked away as if two angels had kept them hidden under an oyster shell in the lake.

He's brought home the tree. Zara is sucking her thumb, reading a children's book in a fluffy chair by the burned-out stone fireplace. A story of knights, princesses, a dragon that looked like her grandfather.

He can't wait to open the presents this year. He has gotten his father a leather shaving kit. Very expensive, with all the toys of cutting your throat and smelling good at the same time.

"Zara! Go help your father dress the tree." Myrthe's hands are on her hips. "Are you just going to read that book all night, without preparing for Santa?"

"Okay, Mom." She jumps out of the chair. "It's a good story, Daddy."

"That's my girl. Now dig in those bags and get those bulbs and lights out of the bag," Sam says. He pats her on the head of twisted plaits. "Mommie, you going to help us?" He pushes the tree log in the red-round stand.

"I'm in the kitchen baking your favorite banana nut bread for tomorrow." She slaps her hands on her apron. "I think you and Zara can handle... the Christmas tree... As soon as I put the bread in, I'll be right there."

Sam loves the way his wife tells him how she's going to handle things for him. She took charge of the house. Kept his life in order, made sure they ate good foods for your bowel movement. Oats, grains, rice, cheese. She kept his clothes clean, pressed. Her ass even bled on time. But she did get tired; she was Superwoman with a period. She always had her period around Christmas time. But she kept going. He made sure she took her naps by not calling her much when he was at work.

"Daddy! I want dese on the tree." Zara's voice is excited like a ringing fire engine truck. She has plucked up some blue and gold crystal bulbs from the bag.

"Ummm, they are pretty." Sam bends to her three-foot height. "They will make the tree the best one on the lake this year." He straightens up to pull out the branches evenly. "Your mother likes green and red, you like blue and gold and I like yellow and red." He hugs her. "I promise you, Zara... you going to have a nice Christmas with your grandfather." He walks over to the bag. "Now, what else is in this bag?" He picks out long strands of gold wreaths.

She takes her time with the different color lights. Unwrapping them out of the boxes. Tongue in her cheek as she pulls herself onto the sofa to do this task of creating a Christmas for all of them. He sees his daughter become a mother to the tree. He moves around the tree, throwing icicles on the limbs, up, down, around, and the back. She takes little toy ornaments of stars, elves, reindeers, Santa Clauses, and the angels of prayer around the bottom limbs. He helps her with the top limbs.

About fifteen minutes later Myrthe comes back to the living room. Apron off, hands clean. She watches them work like the elves of Christmas around the tree with the lights. She goes over to the bag. Plucks out the giant gold star that will sit on top.

"Ohhhhh, Mommie," Zara says. "That star is so pretty."

"I see you two are having a Wambe… so I want to join in too."

Zara is surprised at this strange word. "Wambay?"

"Yes, Zara, in Nigeria they call having a party this word, Wambe." Myrthe tickles her little chin. She turns to her husband. "Here, honey, take this beautiful star. Since you taller than all of us… you can hang it up."

"Ohhh, nooo. That's Zara's job." He picks her up.

"Here you go, baby." Myrthe puts it in her hand.

"Steady… steady… take your time." Sam lifts her higher at the tip.

She licks the corner of her lip, concentrating as she places the opening on the top branch. "I did it! I did it! I did it, Mommie and Daddy!"

He pulls her back down to the floor. Both the parents look at their little girl glow in the living room around the tree. She has become one of the bright bulbs on the limbs. A small, wonderful part of life, blessing and kindness. Their daughter is a light. A bridge for the both of them. A summer song, a fall golden evening, a winter lake white snow upon them.

Zara yawns. Covers her mouth, shies back when her mother points a finger at her. "Mommie, no! I'm not sleepy yet." She is strong in her convictions that the sandman isn't going to take her away from her Christmas tree.

"Zara, now you know it's past your bedtime." It's after nine. "You have to go to school tomorrow to see Mrs. Jackson," Sam says, kneeling to her. "When you wake up, the tree will still be here."

"Come on, TiFi," Myrthe says. "Say night-night to your father."

"Dat means little girl. Right, Mommie?" Zara asks.

"Yes, Zara." Myrthe rolls her eyes over to Sam as the child is playfully wearing her out with the energy of a comet and the rapid questions of a Sherlock Holmes.

Sam kisses her on the forehead. "Night, baby."

"Night, Daddy."

Myrthe guides her by her hand to the staircase. "I'll be back for you," she says to Sam with a sexy grin and a finger pointing, warning.

. . .

When she comes back down the stairs, Sam is nuzzled up in the wingback, nodding off to sleep. She walks to the kitchen. Fixes two cups of hot chocolate, a marshmallow apiece. They talk about Christmas in Haiti. How her mother always made a squash soup during this time of year. All the family had to get up early in the morning to go to Mass. Nod off at Father Bertrand's words of Holy Father give the sheep a cool shade to lie down.

They put on their coats for a walk by the lake to watch the lights of Christmas under the orchid white moon of Crocker's Landing. Myrthe cuddles. Sam leans into her. Cocoa warming their flames. They both wear camelhair coats, which has them look like twins instead of husband and wife. Murky grey waters wash up near their shoes. Snowflakes float, follow them around the lake of benches; tall, hot lamp lights. Horizon of cold-stars above their head. Box-shaped homes around them with the colors of Christmas circling them. Other couples just strolling along at the dock. A sky of moon-shaped stars to the north greets them a Merry Christmas.

Cold winds pull them closer. Wraps them around gloved fingers. Rubbing, feeling each other's hips. Hugs, kisses. Slow steps as Sam listens to her little-girl French voice of light, gentle eruptions of love. He gazes up the embankment to the others' homes of Baby Jesus, three kings, and Santa's reindeer.

"You miss your high society friends around Embassy Row?" Sam asks her under the melody of barge lights down by the dock. The channel of night changes, shifts, with his voice becoming scared, afraid of losing her.

"I miss the champagne, caviar." She messes with him. "No. Sam, we been together over five years." She unleashes his hand. "Why you ask me this every Christmas?"

"I don't know." He looks at the peaceful lake. The fishermen wonder out loud about a flood further up north. "I don't want you to be without nothing... I can get caviar for you..."

"Stop it, Sam." She sticks her arm through his. "I'm happy... If I wasn't... I would have left you a long time ago." She gives him a reminder of the type of woman he has. "Don't forget, us Haitian women can turn their husbands into plants if they don't act right."

Ice drifts on the lake. He scratches his beard. "Fear is what keeps me with you?" Shakes his head. "Hell, fucking no." He takes her closer to him. "You giving me everything I ever wanted... I ever needed." He rubs her butt.

"Get your hands off of my ass… I know what you mean. And you get enough of that." She giggles. Does a stroll with him near some fishing boats.

"Oh, excuse me." His hands go up as if he was under arrest. "I thought I was Tarzan again."

"Sam, you a kidder… a big kidder."

"Myrthe, why you say that?"

"Because… " She hesitates. Stops at the railing.

"Because what?" He nudges her shoulder some.

A towboat dredges up smoke from its pipes. The smoke smells so bad, they have to close their mouths. They walk from the railing as it leaves.

"You lost a basketball game to Ray…"

"My brother."

"Yeah." She nods smartly back to him with the roll of her eyes. "Then you turn full circle to let your father into our lives." She's puzzled. She leans closer inside his coat to play with his big brown buttons. "A game, Sam?"

He turns away. Watches the fishing boats go out with their nets. "Ah, sure… Just needed an excuse."

"An excuse to show love to your father." She can't believe the sound of his voice under the horns, whistles, bells of the tugboats. It's one of mischief. A reprieve to do what was right by all of them.

Sam answers her forthrightly. "Yes." He kisses her slowly over the lips. "Now… is everything cool between us?"

"I guess it is." She pulls her hair back over her collar. She gets lost in his simple answer. He had the nerve to cover his feelings with a game. He knew wars could be solved from such games. Games to keep peace. Games to keep silence in the family. Games to talk about under a thousand years of bad blood washed into the lake. A game that would make his feelings melt. Dry up. Drift out like the fishing boats of the night. A game of basketball kept a father and son together. A little girl, the score over something much bigger than her. Death lights a fire, a game puts the flame out.

"What a pretty Lena Horne-looking sistuh like you doing with this old truck driver?" He acts like he's ready to box with her. "Pinch me!" he hollers up to the sky. "Is it a dream?"

"I'm going to let you act like a fool out here doubting yourself." She gets behind him. Grabs his butt. "Now!"

"Hey! Watch that." Sam jumps back. He's embarrassed as another couple is coming by. Pulls his coat in the back. She comes beside him, holds him around the waist. They keep walking, towards a fishing boat called *Centaurian*.

"No, I don't doubt myself," he says. "But God, I'm just so happy to be with you... I can't help it if I act like a big kid sometimes... Just thinking about coming home to you is like a lollipop before supper."

She tips up. Kisses him on the neck. "I love you."

"I love you too, baby." He looks at her seriously. "So what you want for Christmas?"

"You... Just you and my little girl under the tree. All wrapped up, smelling like a new prize present of Lalique crystal, costing a half million bucks from one of the finest stores in New York City."

"Okay, that's a bet." He sticks his pinky finger out. She hooks hers in his. Snatches it back out. They walk up to the *Centaurian*. Sam spots the skipper, a tall, skinny black man. A grinning Uncle Ben with a navy pea coat on, earring in his left ear.

"Shooter! Shooter!" Sam hollers up to him as he pulls some nets over the side.

He looks up. "Ahhhh! Merry Christmas, Sam. Merry Christmas, Myrthe. Where is that cute little girl of yaws?"

"She's asleep," Myrthe answers him. "Past her bedtime."

"I see yaw out for a little night air."

"We out to see the lights on the lake for Christmas." Sam asks him, "You going fishing tonight?"

"Yep. All the time," he says, looking down at the nice couple. "You can catch me and my boat out here looking for the big catch."

"It's always a big catch… huh, Shooter?" Myrthe asks, wrapping her arm around Sam's waist. Nuzzles up to him to keep the wind from feeling up her coat pockets.

"That's right, darlin'." He tips his tattered cap at her. "Always a big one." Scratches his nose. "I gots to beat out the competition on the *Morningstar* and the bellyaching first mate on the *Gypsy Rose Lee* early." He points his cap at the other boats down the landing. "We always got a good bet going on."

"And what you bringing in, Shooter?" Sam asks him.

"Mostly crab just out of the lake… twenty miles off of the Chesapeake… right under the Baltimore Harbor bridge."

Sam takes Myrthe's hands. "Well, Merry Christmas to you and your family, Shooter."

343

"Merry Christmas, Mr. and Mrs. Murphy." He waves.

Sam acts like he's about to fall, but he grabs her butt like it's an accident. "Baby, I'm sorry! I slipped!" He backs up from her with both his hands up.

"I'm going to get you for that… pig!" Myrthe hollers at him. She chases him around the benches and night lamps on the dock. He runs from her back up the wet, grassy hill.

33

"Mabel, leave my big toe alone!" Ray shakes the paper from his face. He sees her toenail clipper going at his left foot.

"Shhh! Keep still, Ray," she says. "Junior just went to sleep."

"I don't care. Let me read the paper… You go to sleep too." Ray hides his feet under the blanket. He's getting high on some J & B and reading about the twenty-ninth killing in the metro section.

Mabel doesn't give up her battle. She pushes the covers down. "Now don't you move." She grabs the toe. "I got to get it… They are snagging holes in your socks."

She knows he doesn't think of it like that. He's into his world of work, travel. Double-knot ties from Brooks Brothers. An ironed shirt, tailored suspenders to match the nonchalant grin on his face when he goes to work in the morning. A man of good taste in clothing, wines, secrets of police work for the federal-dog government. "What you reading?" She snips at his foot.

"More killings in D.C. over this drug thing."

"Why read it... when you live it?"

"You right." He closes the paper. "Now come here." He reaches down, grabs her from behind. "Come here, woman!"

"Stop! Ray!" She moves her hips but feels his strength. "Okay, what?" She turns over. Climbs on top of him. A big pink plastic curler falls from the side of her hair. She kisses him. "There! Is that what you want?"

"I want you to make me forget." He looks up at the ceiling like the master of the bottle and she's the genie.

"Forget what?"

"This fucking world... So many Black boys killing one another... The white man grinning in my face all the time... Marilyn Monroe... Madonna... Michael Jackson... and chocolate chip cookies."

"Haaa!" She rubs his belly. "The cookies, now that would be impossible." She sticks a finger in his dented chin in the figure of a small Y. "Don't get serious on me... Think of Santa Claus, our little boy, your father being alive, your brother, your cousins, your aunts in Pittsburgh, Mississippi, your friends still on the force. Us here in bed together." She rolls on her back beside him. "Just relax... Take a deep breath, close your eyes, Ray."

He looks into her eyes of glass stars. Indian, Pocohantas pudgy woman with soft, dark nipples peeking through thin green cotton pajamas. "You make a great hypnotist."

346

Curlers of a new hairdo. The shag look of a puppy dog, warm-cuddly woman on a white winter night. He reaches for his glass, not his gun, takes a gulp. He bends over her, unbuttons the pajamas. Rests his hands over her nipples of brown sea flowers.

"You want this?" She curls a finger over her lips. Kisses his left ear. "You want this?" She pulls his right ear as she feels his thumb rest beside her right nipple. She watches his face go down as the winter storm feels warm inside of her.

"You want this?" he asks her. Pulls her hand down to his stomach, lifting up his Dallas Cowboy T-shirt. He snuggles on top. In her ear his breath flicks a curler away.

"Yes," she said. "Give it to me."

"Come and get it."

"No."

He stops. "You jiving!"

She laughs. Pulls him to her. "I'm just playing with you." She lets her stomach push up to his. Her legs open, moist, clear smells of his cologne. Tender plucks of his flesh-bone-hips. Move, drift, shift. She tastes his lips of steam J&B. Desert island man. Alone, a husband in her arms. A brother inside her cry. She looks at the light. Opens her mouth to taste the wine. Arrows from cupid's bow to see them entwined.

After their carnival a two o'clock shadow rests over the bedpost. As they lay in each other's arms, the quarter moon shines on their wet black bodies. A husband and wife surrender into each other's' thoughts. Outspoken worlds of pain. Sadness, fun, silly childish dreams of castles, death. The night lays still, rests upon their windowsill. A child cries for a bottle. Little boy in the next room with big eyes soaking up the night. Their son begs for milk to grow into a man of the earth.

Mabel holds him in her arms, feeding him a cup of milk. The milk bottle long gone. He just wants milk, his mother. In bed beside her, Ray just wants to sleep, rest.

"Baby, you can't sleep? I'll take him in his room."

"No, it's okay." Ray looks over at his son's closed eyes. A face of a brown angel sleeping with the sheep. Engulfed in his mother's bare arms. As her breasts hang down from the clouds. A face of a doll. Sweet-salt moisture woman. Curlers all lost. He touches her face. "You are so beautiful."

"How can you see me in this darkness?"

"The moon shows me your beauty."

"Man, go to sleep."

"I can't."

"Why?" she asks, rocking the boy in her arms. She rests up on two pillows for her back. Holding him close. Kissing him on the forehead as he sleeps.

"This time of night, I always seem to think of my father."

"Why this time of night?"

"When he ever was around... 'bout this time of night when he thought we were all asleep in the house, he would beat and fuck my mother to death, then wrap her arm up with an electric extension cord to shoot dope in her." He looks to the moon, the frost on the window. "Always a party going on." He looks up at Mabel to get her reaction. "Huh?"

"I see why Sam got problems with him."

"Sam don't know about that part… He was too young."

"But he had seen enough."

"Yeah… he had seen enough."

"You two have been through a lot with that man." She places the child between them. "Some father…"

"I guess you can say he taught us about life real fast… especially the streets." He rubs his eyes, looks over to his son, sound asleep. "He's a handsome little dude."

"Just like his daddy." She fluffs the pillows up. "Now go to sleep, Ray… You got to get up early in the morning."

"Work, uh, yeah! Baby, I forgot to tell you something."

"What?" She strains to see him in the light of the moon. "What now?"

"They sending me on the road again." He knows she doesn't want to hear this. "After Christmas."

"Good. I'm glad you be here for that." She turns away. "You know I'm sick of this shit." Closes her eyes tight, rolls back over to him and the baby. "Where you going this time?"

"Key West."

"Okay." She turns away, a madwoman ready to dream of strangling him. "Now go to sleep…'Night."

"'Night, baby."

•   •   •

Sweet Loaf night, Christmas Eve lights blink in the small city by the lake. A bus, train, cars, church choir singing midnight mass. Music blasts from parties going on all over the place. Old people huddled up by the TV set watching Christmas miracle reruns over and over again. As the Gargoyle sings to thee.

Jim Murphy finishes his second beer. "Earlene! Bring me another!"

"Jim, you had enough... It's after twelve. Your sons be by early in the morning to pick us up. Daddy, put your cane away. Let me take you to bed now." Earlene stands in front of him, hands on her basketball hips, feeling tired. Beat after ironing his shirts all day. He couldn't even help her put up the small, white, fake Christmas tree in the living room just in front of the window.

"Go to hell." He sits there in his dirty, catsup-stained wing back. "Get me my medication... Then I'll go to sleep."

Earlene goes to the refrigerator, takes out the pills and gives him two with a glass of water. She watches him swallow. "There. Now time for bed."

He stands, cane under his arm like the maestro at a sleepy symphony you just paid forty dollars a ticket for. Gestures with the back of his hand. "Lead me, my guide dog."

"Foolish old man." She shakes her head, takes half-steps with him to the bedroom. "You got to get your rest, Jim."

"Devil say." He motions with his shoulders away from her. Falls hard to the bed. He looks up in the space of darkness towards her slurping-sweet, caring voice as she unbuttons his shirt. "Leave me alone, woman. I can do that."

"Okay. Get to it then… I'll be right back. I'm going to the bathroom."

He blinks. Finishes unbuttoning his shirt. Kicks off his thick rubber shoes, loosens his belt, unzips his pants. Leans back, kicks them off. Struggles in the mess of being half high. "Earlene! Earlene!"

She rushes back in. "Jim, you all right?" She stands watching him lying flat back on the bed, half undone, smelling like pieces of greasy fried chicken. Pants down around his ankles. "I thought you say you could do it yourself."

"Shut up!"

She finishes the job of attending to her blind lover. She smiles up at him. His face a black cloak of pride and sleepy wonder. Still handsome with all the grey in his hair if he'd stop dying it. She peels his pajama top from the bottom of the bed, under the blanket. "Stick this on you, and get your ass in bed."

"Um! Luv you when you mean to me."

"Shut up. I'm going to the bathroom to brush my teeth."

"Don't bother me none. I'm going to sleep."

"Good." She leaves the bedroom of unpainted closets, mouse traps, a bed small enough for a three-year-old that keeps them warm during this time. It was just too much during the summer. Small TV still on. The Mormon Tabernacle Choir is on, singing some fucking 'Jingle Bells' or something like that. She flips off the light switch.

• • •

He's awake. God is with him. His arms feel heavy, can barely breathe. It isn't him. It's her snoring. He can hear the birds; it has to be almost five. His left arm is limp, the arm he shot so much good and bad dope in over the years. He senses, hears his mother singing him a lullaby. He's dreaming, no. He's up, but he hears his mother singing him a lullaby. A warm rainfall comes down his face. Warm lips go over his chest. He can't reach for his cane. He can't even speak a word. But he feels the arms of God. Yes, the arms of God. They sweep over him like the ocean waters splashing on the beach of dead-old seashells. He sees his years in front of him. All the names he was called: Jamaica Man, Nigger! Fish! Pretty Eyes, Sweet Poppa, Daddy! Honey! Black Man! African Man! Stick! Jimbo!

Dope man trying to run away from the screams. Screams that make you bury yourself in the sands on this beach. Trumpets loud. Dead horns from Sonny Rollins rule the morning light as the birds chirp with Eric Dolphy. He wants a taste of that dope right now. Shoot it up. Sniff it up. Lick it up on her belly. To just forget who you are for a minute, an hour, a day. An evening, a night. Forget you are a Black man trying to catch the train at 8:40 p.m. Trying to make a date to get around the corner. You don't have much time. The fish are dying on the sand right along with your black ass as you thirst for your last hit of blow.

This bedroom, this morning, is his last stand. He will fight it off beside his sleeping Earlene. He isn't going to wake her up. Don't fucking cry in her arms anymore. He's tired. He wants to see the jail bars. Hell, fire, the ice black earth. His wife. All the babies he left behind. All grown, hating him. Wanting to eat him like a piece of raw, rotten fish. A voice, God, speaks. *It's okay. It's all right. Don't be afraid... I'm not going to hurt you.* He hears more horns. Classical jazz for a blind man. Mad that he can't see a goddamn thing in the bedroom. But he seeks out this world through the smells of sweet-bitter death. It smelled up the place with a symphony of lilting odors: Steak, fries with catsup. Coffee, tea, milk. Sour milk, tart lemons, cheeseburgers, fish sandwiches. Soul food dinners cooked up by the Second Baptist Church. Two-seventy-five a plate for all the ribs, potato salad and collard greens you can eat, and don't forget the cornbread by some of them fine brown sistuhs. Just before going to that choir practice. Pray for me, Lord! Pray for me! The evening blue-grey shades of day from love left over on bed sheets comes up in his nose. He remembers blood from a knife fight, wiped on his pants leg. Coffins float in the streets of old bop tunes from Miles' horn in the streets of Laredo Avenue.

He yawns; a blade of pain hits him in the chest. All he can see is a red light. All he can see is the sun. Just the sun. He knows he's dying. It's like a mint leaf in his mouth or a vanilla icing cupcake. He touches Earlene's sleeping buttermilk soft hips. He can say nothing. He nudges a knee of warmth from her leg but she won't awake from her paradise snores. Nuts, he shrugs. Blind man already a living death. He's gonna miss them "Gunsmoke" TV shows. Blind man already a piece of old shit on a Christmas day. Nuts, sweet taste of honeydew melon comes up in his throat. He can smell the smoke hambone aroma of hair between a woman's legs. Stinking good pussy. He does not feel his face. Eyes burn. He feels cold, remorseful not to have his Zara on his lap. Ray Junior bouncing on his knee. Winter calls as his boat goes gently out to sea. A bell rings twice. He watches his wife open her arms to him, asking him to come closer. Wings sprout out from his back towards the red-blue horizon. Outstretched he flies, as the Gargoyle sings to thee.

·   ·   ·

Sam notices his father had a lot of friends on the funeral ride down Charleston Avenue to the George Washington Highway cemetery. Mostly for Black folks. He walks with Myrthe, Ray, Mabel. The children all done up in smart black suits, patent leather shoes, ascot grey ties, white handkerchiefs. Dark fish nets hang down from large round hats over the women's eyes. Nothing to see but another dead Black man soaking up the worms in the earth. Two days after Christmas. Miles away from sainthood and falling on Joan of Arc's sword. He stands in silence next to his crying brother. He wishes he would stop. Big man so sensitive of death and the family. Cousins from Mississippi, two uncles from Chicago. Gus and Mike never liked their own brother either. One aunt from Pittsburgh with an arm and leg cut off. Wheelchair bound, Aunt Maureen Murphy. She still smokes two packs a day. In the Murphy family nobody cared about life. Nobody cared about a dream for the future. All his family was ready to walk in front of a car, truck or airplane for a better life. In a messed-up day of red carnations, freezing in a cold sun. Just under an X-rated-shaped willow tree.

He smiles at the coffin of his father. He wrestles with his life. His death under the disguise of really caring, giving a fuck about somebody who gave you hell for breakfast and shit for lunch. He holds his wife's hand. He knows his little girl doesn't know what it's all about in her Walt Disney way. She just keeps asking, "Where is Granddaddy? Will I see him again? Will I see him again, Daddy?"

Myrthe looks around at her husband's family. All smiles. Death wasn't a sad time for them. At least not for this man. Jim Murphy was the number-one bronco buster of men in Sweet Loaf. He broke a lot of hearts. Heads, asses, and especially his last girl-friend, Earlene, who fainted at least three times before they could even get to the cemetery. "Baby, what's gonna happen to me? What's gonna happen to me?" She slumps down over the bronze bullet-grey coffin. Pounding to get in.

Mabel shadows her husband. Keeps patting him in her arms like he's the thick baby in the family. She hands her son to the nurse in the crowd. Listens, tells Ray his father was a good, kind man. That the things he done to his mother were mistakes. Minor car accidents of love by a man who fucked the world, and women.

Yellow roses spread out on the coffin. The attend-ant with dirt gloves pushes the button. Earlene faints again. The nurse, two other old friends pick her up. Drag her back to the limousines. Soaked in tears, wet cold rain knocks her straw black hat off. Mabel looks back, away. She takes Ray's hand, tries to makes him understand that this is not the end for none of them. In his ear, she whispers her love. "Baby, I love you. Ray Junior loves you. He loved you…"

Solutions for them to get on with their lives. In raising the next generation of Murphys in Sweet Loaf. This isn't the end for her or him. She rubs his long black suit shoulders, picks his chin up. Kisses him, and pulls him back to the car.

Back on the highway to Sweet Loaf, they all follow each other in a twenty-five mile per hour cruise with police motorcycles in front. Sam rides with Ray and his family in the same limousine. The nurse with a cocktail waitress face of too many martinis, too many men at the Lizard Lounge, holds Ray's hand; Mabel holds his other hand. He's a midget between the two women in the car. Sam leans towards him. "It's over, Ray… He's dead. You just buried him."

"Fuck you, Sam."

Sam rests back in Myrthe's arms. Knocks the rebuke off his shoulders from his brother. He becomes afraid in front of the wives, children and the nurse-mother-woman with dyed red hair. He doesn't want to fight. So he looks out the warm car windows of a thirty-degree day. Away from his brother's pain. A badly painted picture of a wicked, barren earth. Frozen bones at the foot of everybody's headstones. The Murphy name grows in the wilderness on this lost day. I-95 South, please, get him out of this scene.

He sits his Zara on his lap. Little Ray is asleep in his mother's arms. That's good. He wishes he could sleep too. But he can't. The ghost of the Gargoyle will always sing to him. His father will always be there in his dreams with his mother. He tries not to think, blink, or care about the power this man had over him. But it's there. It's there in his TV watching, his battle to stay off the streets, his fight against jumping in another woman's bed,. even though you have a wife and child home. The adventure of life will always pull him to the edge of his father's grave. He sings to it. He dreams about it. Smoke dope, get high. Chase women. Shoot, cuss, slash at a face. Throw a left, right jab at another man's head. He's always there in his world of war. His world of peace. No tears for the dying. Only room for the living on the George Washington Cemetery this day. He won't look at Ray's simple ass; bawling like his own son. He can't look at the dry-ashy face. He's a piece of soft dough in Mabel's hands. She can handle him. He isn't a doll. And she's the Puppet Master. They are now just in-laws riding in a funeral car.

"Daddy, look!" Zara points out the window.

"Ohhhh, cows!" Sam spots them out on the farm. He looks at Myrthe wiping tears from her face. "You see them, baby?"

"Yes, Sam." She pulls a handkerchief out of her purse. "They eating some grass." She sticks her hand through his arm, lays her head on his shoulder. She dabs at her eyes.

"Mommie, I like cows," Zara says. "I want a cow, Daddy."

"No, Zara. I don't think you can have a cow where we live." He asks, "How about a cat?"

"Okay," she says. "A cat would be fine." She leans back on his chest. Knocks her shiny black shoes together, watching the highway whisk in front of her face like a colorful green kaleidoscope of roses and marshmallow pudding figures.

"We almost home," Sam says. "It's almost over." He licks his chapped lips. Tests his brother to see if he's ready to climb up from his father's grave.

"Yeah, it's over for you, mutherfucker!" Ray wants to stop the car and tackle a tree trunk. "Just when we were all coming together he passed away." He shakes his head.

"But he's not dead," Sam says back to him. "He lives in here." He points at his brother's chest. "And here…"

"You couldn't shed one fucking tear for him." Ray sticks up his finger.

Mabel gazes up to Myrthe holding on the shoulders of Sam. They keep quiet. Let the brothers wrestle with the pain of a father that killed everything they loved.

"For what?"

"Godammit!" Ray balls his fist. "He was our father."

The limousine hits a speed bump, shaking the whole family up from their seats.

"Fuck dat! The bastard killed our mother!"

"She killed herself!" Ray raises up in his face. "She killed herself."

Sam turns back to the car window to horses on a farm galloping along the fence with the funeral party as salty tears drop to his lips.

34

Into the glossy brown lake Sam tries to ease his mind. April spring thaw under TV waves of terrible-genocide news comes into his living room. Awful times of a people. His people dying all around him off the I-95 highway. He tries to close his ears. But he can't close his eyes to young men driving around in expensive foreign cars without an inkling of a high school diploma. Sneaker shops, Michael Jordan shoes make them fly high to the heavens under the ricocheting bullets on a city corner. He tries to read the sports news before stuffing laundry bags, but the news keeps popping in his view. Ten die in one week, twelve the next, twenty for the month. He tries to listen to his jazz, but the sixties awareness runs from the shadows of the nineties death threats of drugs. He cries in silence. Shakes his head at the view from his living room window to the boats. Men on the lake working for a buck, a dime, a quarter to bring food to the tables for their families. A job was enough for him, but the commercials from Madison Avenue had the young Black boys of America soaking up the lies of having a White, Black, tall trophy model on your arms and a gold shackle around your neck. In your mouth. A black-death tells them to get it now, because your momma, daddy can't afford it. Come on man, buy this gun for five dollars and get it, "Now! Now! Now!"

Sam drinks some brandy and takes two aspirins because he's a part of this shit. He bolts his door, tries to keep out the flies from his wife, his little girl. He turns off the television. Let Zara watch Walt Disney, adventure shows, "Sesame Street" in the evening, but he knows it's worthless to try and shield her from the black death around Crocker's Landing. It's stupid. Crazy, madness to see her come home and use words like Madonna, Prince, hip-hop, Fade, Philly, Cabbage Patch, Kool Moe Dee and even gang-bang. He popped her in the mouth when she used this one. Nothing but low-cal diet values. She wanted to collect gold chains, go on walks with her little friends to the corner. Play with little girls with no mommies or daddies around. As bums prowl the streets looking for a child-deer to molest or kill. He argues with Myrthe to make sure she never leaves the porch without him or her around. Watch out for that ice cream truck! So from Monday through Friday he bites his nails over laundry bags at the Trojan Cleaners, worrying about his Zara playing in a schoolyard.

Sam tries to calm his nerves with a beer after work. Read the funnies, listen to foul jokes from Eddie Murphy's mouth. Taste chocolate ice cream for dessert, and rent family movies on the weekends.

He does a big chunk to help Myrthe out when she has to run errands for some political campaign or volunteer work at the hospital. He takes Zara to the playground, watches over her and her little friends when there are no mommies or daddies around. But he's afraid. He's scared as shit when the boys from fifteen or twenty-five come to play some basketball. If a fight breaks out over some points, or a foul isn't called fast enough, a gun might do the talking for all of them. He's afraid to take his daughter to the playground when the headlines read:

GUN BATTLE ON FOURTEENTH STREET!
SHOOTOUT AT THE MOVIE THEATER!
TWO WOUNDED OVER BASKETBALL GAME!
THREE POLICE OFFICERS DOWN FROM RUN IN WITH DRUG GANG!
LITTLE BOY GUNNED DOWN IN PLAYGROUND!
TWO YOUTHS SLASHED AT SCHOOL TODAY!
FIGHT BREAKS OUT OVER TURF AT THE BLAIR PROJECTS!
MOTHER DEAD! BABY INJURED! CAUGHT IN DRUG CROSSFIRE!

Oh yeah, he's scared all right. Afraid of losing his little girl to America's twenty-first century terror. When there are no mommies or daddies around. He listenes to all the speeches: the deficits, the church-preachers, the Johnny Cake hustlers of Civil Rights Liberations. Past and present. But when it all means nothing, him and Myrthe get on their knees and pray by their sleeping child's bed at night. Pray the angels keep her safe when she leaves to go to school in her yellow school bus. They pray before breakfast, they pray during lunch, they pray during dinner and they damn sure pray at night over their Zara's six years of life. Especially when there are no mommies or daddies around.

He drinks a beer. Tries to cool off, listen to old jazz, new jazz. Some of it is cool. Leaves his old road buddies alone most of the time. He goes for walks with his little girl around the lake. Watches, points to her all the boats coming to the landing. Chases her, wrestles with her. Reads to her, holds her tight in his arms just as long as he can. He doesn't think too much about his father anymore. The Gargoyle is dead, left him alone now to have his own family. To learn the lessons of being a man. A Black man in a world that uses computers to keep you locked out of the system. He uses his wits. He keeps his mouth shut. He just talks to the TV and watches his wife and daughter cook in the kitchen or go shopping for new socks, denim dresses, purses, and groceries. He watches his long-haired wife carry on her life in Creole. Laugh at him when he doesn't know what the hell she and Zara are talking about. But he does know it sounds sexy. Sexy as an Eartha Kitt-kitten curled up at his feet at night in front of a fireplace.

Both of them bare-ass in love. She licks his ear. He digs in her ass, stomach, thighs, with his tongue. She swoons in unspoken tongues of lust. Desperate love from her red painted nails scratches his back up. As he prays over her body for more. Love, peace, silence. At the end of an hour, day, week.

Sam sometimes tries to blink away his mother's image of love and pain in the bathroom mirror when he shaves in the mornings. His mother's gaunt-golden face stares back at him. She asks him what he's doing today. He just shuts his eyes. She was a small tree in a land of charcoal Black men. Destined to love and die at the hands of one of them. Death was an innocent child to her. And he's glad she's dead; glad she doesn't have to suffer anymore from the shit in her body. The heroin painted white horse rode her hard. This white powder wiped her love off the earth and took her up, off in the clouds. This little boy-man sees her shadow. The face of a dead yellow-red sun that always seems to come to him at this time. The time of her death in a psychiatric-detox ward of Our Lady of Goddam Mercy General—for Black folks only—Hospital... Six-thirteen a.m.

He cuts his face, slams the Gillette razor down in the sink. He turns on cold water as her face disappears in the reflection of his blood. At five in the morning Myrthe and Zara sleep in their beds. Help him. Lord, help him. He is just a little boy all alone with a crazy woman throwing fits, gagging on her vomit. She is naked on the bed of sweaty-dirty sheets. An ambulance sounds in the far distant night. They are coming! Lord, they are coming as he holds her head in his little lap, wiping away the hair from her eyes.

He slaps some Vaseline on the nick. He closes the medicine cabinet and walks back to the bedroom to put his pants on. Buttons up his blue button-down collar shirt. Straps on his Timex. In the early morning smoke, gray light, he struggles to find his wife. Her head an unplugged mess of pink curlers. Her childish French lyrical voice asks him, "Sam, you going to work?" She reaches up to him. "Come back to bed."

"Myrthe, I wish I could." He sits on the bed. "Love you."

"Come here." She throws her arms around his neck. "Don't go."

"Myrthe, I gots to get to work this morning... Got a bunch of bags to stuff." He pulls his face from her lips.

"Call in sick," she teases him. Dares him. "Chicken."

"I called in sick last week... remember?" He kisses her nose. "You bad." He stands up.

"Call me later." She peeks at the clock, then folds back up like a tadpole under the sheets.

"I will." He leaves their bedroom of warm quilt. He's getting sick to even think about her stomach calling him back. But he has to make that money. It's Wednesday, hump day. Doesn't look right if he stays home today. Just two more days, just two more days. He stops in his daughter's room. Her plaits drift down over the white sheets, blue wool covers. Her small face is like old black and white photos of daughters beside their mothers. Eyes closed before the flash went off. At peace, at rest before they wake up making volcanic noises. Surrounded by ancient African secrets for the first time. He bends down. Kisses her cheek, picks the covers over her plaits, and thanks God that she has a mommie and daddy around.

Sam Murphy doesn't play around when it's time to go to work, fish or drink a few cans of beer with his friends from them old warehouse days. He takes his life on the lake as a lucky privilege. All just from meeting a Black swan Haitian princess. He cuddles up in her life of giving back to a country that needs kindness from the many.

Myrthe has left the flashy world of Embassy Row parties but she still keeps her index finger in the cherry pie whenever she needs a favor of charity from Gail Berrios, who is now divorced from the major of Guatemalan death squads. Mrs. Berrios has now become Mrs. Steighauser. The high priestess of Aryan shame and amnesia of German death camps. Forget the burning flesh of a Jew and live forever with a rich Volkswagen industrialist on the cobblestone streets of Georgetown.

Myrthe talks to her friend on the phone every three or four months. She misses the life of champagne and cherries one percent enough to get money for charities or political campaign parties for the city of Sweet Loaf. She uses the people by tugging on their cold-golden hearts for poor Black, Spanish, White folks of the city. Nobody wants to see more families becoming evicted from their homes or the loss of a proud man's job after he becomes paralyzed from a fall on a construction site. Nobody wants to talk about how a proud woman or man has to come to poverty agencies, charity relief funds to get a free meal, a turkey sandwich, a break to pay his rent and keep the winter-wolves away from his door. People are being thrown out of their homes, apartments, their skins for being unemployed. People are crying. Crying at the American shame of watching "Dynasty" along with the soap operas of Erica Caine; drinking down champagne and fucking ten men at the same time to stay rich and cruel. People are crying at doors of a city fire escape. Asking for somebody to throw them a net so they can jump out the window. Commercials of get-rich-quick, two-minute blasts rammed up your ass by pickpocket con men robbing you of the dream to survive from someone else's caring hands. *Sava-me! Sava-me!* Myrthe remembered this in the mountains of Haiti as she cried tears over a plate of rice her father finally decided to give her. After she finished, he beat her with a rope for having hunger pains.

Sam sticks his chest out every morning and feels like a man who is lucky to have this woman beside him in his bed at night. He buys her red carnations damn near every day. They last longer. She makes him a strong man. She makes him ready to take shit from a land of the selfish two million dollar baseball player free skies. Who have the nerve to go on strike. He shrugs, turns off the kitchen light, with his ham sandwiches under his arm. He whistles a bebop tune by a funny little piano player, Thelonious Monk. A piece that keeps him on his toes through D.C. Beltway traffic called: Straight, No Chaser.

Clock radio alarm awakes Myrthe to a Billy Graham sermon. She slaps the seven o'clock voice of God. Zara is still asleep. Pushes up. Scratches her claws over her puffy-crust, pumpkin pie shell face. She dreams in Creole. Back home to the mountains. Always the mountains. Her man is gone. She has to get her baby-girl off to school. Pushes up. She slips out of the electric-white-warm kingbed sheets and stumbles to Zara's bedroom. She speaks in Creole for her to get up, "*Leve, Cherie! Li le pou al lekol.*"

Zara twists under the covers.

"Wake up… Time to go to school." She wipes a hand down the side of her daughter's face of black rope plaits. "You want pancakes?"

"Mommie, I don't want to go to school," she pleads. Her arms reach out to cover her mother's resistance. Hugs her. "No, Mommie. I want Daddy."

Myrthe is in agreement with her. "I want Daddy too, but he's gone to work… You going to school, and I have to do some volunteer work at the hospital today." She lifts her by the arm. Her daughter is turning into a tall young little girl with long feet. A face of brown marshmallow sand dunes. Star eyes closed. A yawn that pulls her arms up over her head.

"Mommmmie!" She opens her eyes to her mother's face.

"Come on, baby. All your little friends are going to be waiting for you at the bus stop… Don't you want to see Celine, Vanessa, Rahim, and Jacob?"

"No!"

Myrthe uncovers her. "Ohhhhh, don't be like that, Zara." She asks her again, "You want pancakes?" Waves a hand down her hair. "Come on, let's go to the bathroom… brush those teeth of yours."

"Ohhhhhh, Mommmieeee!" Her head falls back in protest as Myrthe pulls her slowly from the bed.

"Shhhh, Zara. I want to cry too, but we have work to do." She takes her in the bathroom by the sink, turns on the faucets. Pulls her dinosaur pajamas off, runs the hot-cold water. Washes her down with soap. Awakes a pretty child of winter orchids, plaits, feathers, and peaches. She's a daughter with funny dreams of lizards, Uncle Ray, her father, her friends pushing her in a tire swing. A park of rabbits, giraffes, gold fishes all talking to her by some rainbow pink-blue pond.

"Mommie! I called Mr. Fish to play with me. Den I met Mr. Bird singing on a tree. A pig ran by me... Porky! Porky Pig, Mommie!"

"You did, Zara!" She asks, "Did Daddy catch the pig?"

"No, Mommie. The pig... Mr. Porky was too fast for Daddy... But granddaddy caught 'im."

"He did!" Myrthe towels her off. She flashes the red toothbrush. "Okay, now... let me put the tooth-paste on for you."

"Okay, Mommie," Zara says with a voice that sounds like Second Street Baptist church bells. She takes the toothbrush and tries to master this task of getting the back teeth.

Myrthe helpes her out. Washes her face, combs her hair back. Tied up two plaits, with red ribbons that match red Mickey Mouse pants and white blouse with puffy short sleeve shoulders. Black buck-led shoes, white socks. She sees Sam's chin dimple. A familiar small, wide nose. Lots of legs just like her momma. She kisses Zara's nose, cups the sunflower face with both hands. "Now it looks like you don't want pancakes... Looks like you ready for a hot bowl of Quaker Oats this morning."

"Yuccckkk!" Zara says with a cringe.

"Quaker Oats with honey, cinnamon and lots of butter." Myrthe tries to bargain like a good Haitian mother would do with a wise street vendor in Port au Prince. She takes her by the hand to the steps. "Let's hurry so we can get the bus with the others at the corner."

"I don't want no oatmeal, Mommie."

Myrthe takes her down the steps. She measures the silence of the morning with the life of the seventy-year-old house. She sniffs up the aroma of the fresh bread morning from the walls. Tastes the sunlight licking through the rose-colored curtains. She feels the creaks of the wood stairs under their feet. She hears the tires of cars coming under the doors of the house when they get to the bottom. Afraid to let her go out in the world. Hesitant mother-lion. Myrthe holds her daughter's hand tight. "I know... Grits with lots of butter."

"Okay, Mommie, grits!" She smiles up in her mother's eyes. Jumps off the last step.

35

He snatched the thunderbolt from heaven, the scepter from tyrants.
– A. R. J. Turgot, Inscription for Houdon's bust, 1778

Four days before Easter in the basement of a silver building in downtown Washington, D.C.. Beasts with hairy backs, ghosts with hair in their ears, demons touch up their makeup in ordinary smudged mirrors. Men with dinosaur arms pack small guns behind their backs at the District Court . Name change; to shine behind men and women fighting a war behind desks. Clocks in different time zones. No credit card for a life that's just been shot down out of a helicopter over a South American jungle. And now the first morning hour at nine. Coffee time.

Ray takes advantage of his second hot cup of black coffee, he use to make for his grandma every morning, no cream, one cube of sugar. Reggae music plays on a secretary's desk. Space-time continuum of a freaky life that got you looking down a nine millimeter in the morning. Unshaven, dragon faces crowd around the coffee pot. More coffee. We almost out. Some hip hop come on the Black D.C. radio station. This music gets the cowboys for the streets. It's the only way to die for the things they got to do out here.

Ray and his fellow compadres have to be hip. Old, young, cocky monsters, not afraid to die tomorrow, today or later on down the road. They have a mission. The mission is to save the children—make it hard for the young girls and boys to get this cocaine up their noses or in their veins. Ray isn't afraid to die. He dies every day before going home to Mabel and his little boy. The life his father and mother lived affected him. He's a psychotic Superman behind a badge.

His world is closed in with hip talk. Police shit-talking men from the streets with spots of the leopard on their lapel buttons. They belong to a team, a gang called the Spotted Leopards. Jungle men trained in the art of operations and everyday family lives of going home nine to five. Take a business trip, here, there… to do vital research of population growth. Sail ash trays in a briefcase around the United States. Some of the men take excursions to Copenhagen, Sweden, Germany on secret hashish raids in the guise of researching maps of people fourteen miles from the Russian border. Ray's office is closed-in, without a window. One file cabinet, a desk with no papers, just a Rolodex with names of other bureaucrats, from the Pentagon to the embassies around the D.C. streets. His other information is kept in a locked vault; taken

371

out to remember names, faces, places, people on a drug run dying, over a million dollars to save a South American world that was dying with a rock of cocaine stuck in its heart.

Ray's co-workers are tight in three-piece Brooks Brothers suits, colorful suspenders to hold up their dicks, with their André Rossi silk ties. Everything they need in holding on to a world and an agency that has gone fucking mad. When a man loves money, ain't no stopping him but keeping his lust in check. Each agency around the Beltway is spying on another. But Mr. CIA has its dick up a lot of little dresses all over the world. They kill every fucking body for that good as sweet dollar bill. Always fresh, always courteous. The devil wears three-piece suits, drinks dry red wines from France. Smokes cigars and Bang! Bang! Bang! The ladies run right to them for more fucking on the French Riviera, jungles in Nigeria, Paloma, Spain, New York City. Casanova, Bossa Nova, Columbia, South America, L.A., and don't forget the Romans. Hunting down a piece of dope in the homes of an Arab, asshole sheik is fire in your thighs. Ain't no stopping this big-headed monster. Who gives a shit?

Ray's boss is out of Harvard in the fifties, a "Leave It To Beaver" mutherfucker with a black spot on his heart. Ex-colonel, in the closet-gay, Marine Corps. Old fart with a patched leather face. He coughs a lot in his middle office looking out over the city with a big picture window that keeps him from fucking the president anytime he wants to. Baxter Walters is a scrappy bastard, good with a gun. Plays rounds of tennis in his private CIA country club on the Potomac, and keeps his secrets soaked in vodka. Super spy, gay guy.

Ray gets the call to come to his office. He stands at that window coughing. Crossing-uncrossing his skinny silk shirt arms. He sits down as soon as Ray comes in. "Have a seat, Mr. Murphy," he says, sounding as if this is just another day in a baby-spoiled world of Egg McMuffins and Calvin Klein jeans.

"Yes sir."

He closes up a folder on his desk. "Reading position papers."

"Position papers, sir?" Ray scratches the stubble on the side of his neck, crosses his legs in the chair. Pad, pen ready to jot down notes. Or does he want to talk about Ray's red sports car?

"The Venuzzis. You ever heard of them?"

"Yes… I heard of them."

He scratches his long nose. "Pappa Venuzzi just became the mayor of Key West." He pushes the folder towards Ray. "Read this later."

"People buy anything for a jingle." Ray lifts it off the desk.

"Now it seems like he's going to work the small town circuit." He lights up a cigar. Smoke, fire comes from the black leaves out of his mouth. "Home boy, can't seem to stay home."

Ray wants to smile when he hears this white man talk street slick. He opens the folder. "That means he'll be here soon." He closes the folder. "You know the places?"

"The mules will be coming to Bellview, Virginia, Roseville, Maryland, Lynden, West Virginia,

Andersonville, Virginia." He says the last one with a touch of hesitance. "And Sweet Loaf."

"My home?" Ray stares at him. "Where I live?"

"You... me," he says. "We can't hide from this, Mr. Murphy." He looks at him with bittersweet sadness. "We all got families. We all got kids and we all ain't never seen a war like this one. Commercials with sex, cigarette signs with a cool camel on a billboard, alcohol pleasing to a baby's taste." He thumbs his red neck tie. "Soap operas of men, women, jumping in each other's beds. It's cool to be rich, it's cool to be hip and no morals, it's cool to beat the shit out of your wife, kids. While the rest of the world looks up to you like a god on Mount Olympus." He pulls on his ear. "I've been with this agency for almost twenty years...I used to just spy on agents having extramarital affairs or selling secrets to some goddamn Bulgarian national. Now I'm watching drug sells by other agents. My country selling its ass to the highest bidder to protect one drug lord over another drug lord. Put a spin on dope going to your kids and mine in the streets. Killing themselves until they can't take it anymore. Genocide... homicide... legalize the shit so we can't get rich no more." He points at his chest and starts to cough. He covers a handkerchief over his mouth. "Go on." He wipes the film from his lips. "Just do your job, Mr. Murphy." He walks back to the spotless windows looking out over the gray buildings on Pennsylvania Avenue.

"Okay, sir." Ray gets up and takes the folder, closes the door behind him.

Back in his office, Ray flips the switch on his computer. Unloosens his necktie. Rolls up his shirt sleeves. Feels his heart pumping over the faces, places, names of the mules in and out of prisons from all over the world. Aliens, citizens, John Does. Who knows? Who cares? False names, passports, birth certificates. Husbands, wives teaming up to carry packages of dope, money. All points in Florida, Haiti, Mexico, Texas, Canada, California, New York, New Orleans, New Jersey, New Mexico, New Rochelle, New Finland, Copenhagen. New vestiges of new wealth. New men, new women with new born-again names. New preachers, new politicians, new cars, new homes, new neighborhoods, new San Diego, new aliens, new illegals, new files, new faces, new cases, new places in Bombay India. New agents, new brand prison I.D. numbers, new offenders. New banks sprouting up on the borders of San Diego, new men, new women, new dummy corporations, new man-made islands. This, that. New fools, new prisons, new ice cream of the month, new perfume of the year, a new asshole star is born. New men, new women, new computers, new software, new high rises so high make you want to leap off fifty floors and be in a new Disneyland in new America. He presses the buttons-arrow keys. Names, faces, more places until. Until he finds the face that may come to Sweet Loaf.

•　•　•

Happy hour; after five. Ray goes to the Top Crab Raw Bar around the corner from his job. Sun going down like a woman's red skirt that is accidentally swept up by a stiff breeze; slowly. Soak him up, tired of the shit. Thirsty, has a taste for scotch on the rocks with a twist of lemon. A headache, eyes weak from the blue computer screen.

He walks past white faces, frozen-cold to the apple's core. Black faces angry at the day of "Brother, you lost your job again?" And suicidal red-yellow faces between the city streets and a village they left under freedom bullets and grenades. Doesn't nobody belong here. He bumps, slashes, cuts between the shoulders of light wool jackets, dresses, suits. As golden rain drops fall from Crocker's Landing to the streets of Washington D.C. He feels helpless and sticks a left hand down in his pants pocket. He pushes the revolving doors open to the bar. His lips tighten when he watches the blondes of Pennsylvania Avenue wink at his lying smile. He keeps going past the dining tables straight to some red curtains. Tasteful, classy place of brass spittoons with cigar smoke floating amongst framed pencil prints of Pollock, Hobbs and Picasso. Music plays from horns and soft drum brush strokes as if a baby is about to go to sleep.

Other agents, bureaucrats, business people drink down their own blood before going back to their wives, kids, girlfriends or to an empty room. Doesn't nobody belong here. Shadowy images of people stand or sit in front of seven-foot mirrors behind the bartender. Low-golden lights fall down on heads like the rain drops from Crocker's Landing. Salty-brown, white men and flag-waving women speak to each other holding on to their glasses of beer, water, whiskey or rye. A buxom-pale woman dances on a stage. Bending over, slapping her cheeks. Winks back, drops her pink robe down on the stage floor. She humps on a lion-long pole imitating a vampire in heat as her

Irish red hair falls loosely over her left eye. She jiggles her breasts under the golden raindrops of light and piano music as men dare to stare.

His co-worker, Llosa Perez, is sitting at the bar. Legs crossed, tucked up in a frilly white blouse. She wears a two-piece gray business suit, black high heels. Her long black hair pulled back in a bun. Men want to pay for her. She flashes a badge instead. In her late thirties; some know, some don't know, that she is out of Spanish Harlem with a law degree from Yale. Story has it that she catches her drug lords with a pearl-handled twenty-two in a thigh holster. She's a sexy-subtle woman with brains. Llosa can talk your pants off in three, maybe four languages. But she's all business when she's drinking or playing catch-a-dope-dealer at the office. She can grab your balls and tell you a joke about masturbation at the same time. A second-degree black belt who likes to bird watch in the Hamptons and bet on the New York Knicks losing the big one again. She's looking up in the mirror at the dancer and chewing on ice cubes from a glass of scotch.

"Well, Ms. Perez." He pecks her on the cheek. "I see you checking out the show." Sniffs up some of that nice perfume from her ear. "Um."

"The bitch ain't got no ass." She lifts a finger at the bartender. "What you drinking, Ray?"

"I'll have the same." He sits beside her. Unbuttons his blue blazer sport coat. "How you feeling today?"

"Tired as usual… Ready to quit."

"I know what you mean, but when the alarm bell goes off at six the next morning I'm ready to get back to the trail again."

"I'm the same… At the strike of the bell… come out fighting," she says.

The bartender comes over, places the scotch in front of him.

"Got to keep going." He tastes, freezes when the scotch burns his tongue.

"Here's to 'got to keep going'." Taps her glass against his.

Some other agents come over. Slap them on the back. But they move down a few seats. They're folding up in a cocoon in this place you don't have to take off your gun. A place where nothing but the same come to have a drink. Die a thousand deaths under the golden raindrops of piano music and a naked woman that won't go away.

Llosa pulls the pins from her hair; it falls like the showers outside. Another man comes up to her. Ray pushes him away. He watches her face glisten in the lights of the woman's movements. He watches her eyes stare under the spell of the scotch. "I got some bad news today."

"News you can't tell your wife?"

"What you think?" He rubs his face, takes another drink. "Can't get the public nervous."

"What is it?" She understands that sometimes a man or a woman needs that strange face to talk to. A face that doesn't really care. But a face that understands what's heaven and a personal private hell you and them are going through at the same time. Golden faces of light become wet in the truth of the day. A wink under the dry, hot sun as the hot stops and maybe the last face you see before somebody blowing your good-time ass away.

"We getting visitors soon."

"The mules from Key West?"

"Yeah, the mules from Key West."

"They coming your way?"

"Yep."

"If you need me… you know my number." She says this like a Hispanic Lauren Bacall about to jump Mr. Bogart for a cigarette. She reaches down in her suit pocket, pulls out her own pack. Waves it. The bartender comes over, lights it. She puffs, "Thank you."

"I like to see you dance one day." Ray says this with an edge in his throat as the scotch is making him ready to go home to his Mabel.

"Ray, you a family man with a hard on…You just fantasizing." She pats him on his back. She blows out the smoke, watches it float across the mirror over the crystal bottles of bourbons and brandies.

"One day when you settle down and get that white picket fence just like me and have some babies, you'll be fantasizing too." He gives her a warning and pats her on the back. "You see this ring on my finger?"

"What about it?" She peeks at his finger.

"That's about will power… Just because you got that ring don't mean you stop begging for love, lust and anything else."

"So you telling me… now that you got a drink in you, you begging me and that no ass whore up on the stage for some love?"

"No. That means I'm begging for will power right now."

"Men." She finishes her drink, crushes out the cigarette.

"Women," he says, ordering another round for both of them. "Where you be at for Easter? Because…"

"Hold it, Ray… Are you trying to invite me over to fix me up with another blind date from your pool of lonesome police buddies?" She glares at him pretentiously. "After the last knucklehead who wanted me to read fairy tales to him and tie him up in a rocking chair… I think I pass."

"Marvin wasn't that bad." Ray laughs. "Just a little kinky… But he had the face of Tom Selleck and the body of Mr. America."

"The man's crazy as hell," she says. "So forget Easter dinner… I'll visit my grandmother in Hoboken instead." She runs a hand through her hair that needs to have something done with it. "Now your brother Sam…"

"I can't help you there, honey."

"I know. I know. But if he ever leaves that wife of his… I'll be first in line to soothe his soul." She gets happy just thinking about Sweet Sam Murphy. She shakes her shoulders to the Cinderella monkey-grind music. "The bitch doesn't have an ass."

"But she got tits." Ray turns towards the stage, holding his drink.

"Fool! They not hers. They belong to a chemistry lab."

"Here's to chemistry." Ray holds his glass up at the dancer humping to the show tune of "Ain't Misbehavin'."

36

Sam goes back to his old neighborhood to get a haircut. The sign in the barber shop window announces: "Easter Haircuts! $2.00 Special!" Newspapers flap in the corner of the shop as a fan rolls out air over peppercorn-head men lounging under the barbers' hands. Sweet Loaf City talcum powder breezes on this quiet Friday. Clippers, scissors, razor-strops pop, yank at the black, brown, red moss-covered hair flakes of the men in the chairs. Bulldog, lamb faces going to their final slaughter to get that hair off for a Sunday best showing for God, momma, girlfriend and wife. A little boy about nine squints, squirms in the chair as his father looks on with a pride full of revenge.

Ernie, Leroy, Ty and Little Mo are still at this job of yapping, talking up a bunch of hot sauce full of shit: wives, politics, girlfriends, sports legends and that old time question on where the party's at this weekend. A cruise, trip over to Atlantic City, new club opening uptown Saturday night, or just somebody's giving a cookout, house party type thing for some mother, father, sister, brother, aunt, uncle, cousin. Whatever's going on in Sweet Loaf, they know about it. Especially when it involves Black folks in this small city, about two hours drive from D.C..

Sam sits there listening to all the shit-talk, waiting for Little Mo to finish cookin' up those ham hocks in the back.

Little Mo sticks his head out. "Sam, you want a plate?"

Sam: "Naw, man! I want a haircut."

Little Mo: "Nigger! Dats got to wait until I finish these ham hocks!"

Sam shakes his head. "Gone, man! Finish eatin'." Slaps his hand back at him.

Little Mo closes the curtain back.

Sam sits back to watch a thirteen-inch TV stuck up on a table. He takes all the commercials in. Dozing off into a wine cooler world of emergency gunshots, diabetes, instant coffee with Mike Tyson dying to get locked up again. Potato chip wars, fast-food burger joints, toys for molested tots to keep their mouths shut, Barney getting on everybody's goddamn nerves. Even the kids. A picture of Muhammad Ali, Joe Louis, Sugar Ray Leonard staring down at the men on chipped blue walls. Baby Jesus, Man-Jesus praying on a rock. Praying that a Black man won't get his daughter one day. A giant window plugged in front and under the big red signs of Little Mo's Barbershop. Girl watching. He turns his head at plenty of the sistuhs on Third and Taylor. Shit ain't changed. Young girls still having babies. Palms for the poor!

Spring thaw. Easter raw as Good Friday sunlight pilot over the barbershop crowd of men. Parked in corners of hairstyles. Plastic bag heads. Jerry-curl honey comb hairdos. Burning their scalps with a bunch of hot grease. Chuckles at the gripes of man and justice from Ty, the smooth-talking, bald barber discussing living with a woman today.

"You know something funny… A man is more of a dog when he has one woman than when he has two or three women. Now, take my cousin Red Jerry, for instance… Now here is a man who has been married over fifteen years. All because he got two mistresses. One on the east side of town and another on the west side." He spins the man and the chair around. "His big-ass wife Sadie is a fine woman. But a woman gets tired of being fucked day in and day out… She once told him, 'Man, you gots to give me a rest. Reds… go on… leave me alone now!' " He looks up at the men listening to him. All of them with a wink. Waiting for his next line. "'Jerry, you not going to use my ass up like a piece of hamburger… I got a white liver now!'" He spins the chair, tilts the head back. And keeps clipping. "So Jerry gots mad, tells her he's going to another woman… if she don't give him none." He waves the clippers like a baton. "She tells him, 'Go ahead… Gone give me a rest now. Come back in two weeks…' My poor cousin had no choice. He had no choice! So he zipped up his pants and found a horse-face gal and a dinosaur long-tail gal. His wife knew both of them, they all friends. Yaw! Just remember… a woman don't give a man a choice… but yaw remember dis… My cousin is still with his wife. He's still with his wife."

383

Little Mo comes from the curtain. "Come on, Sam, get your ass in dis chair."

Sam pops up, "Trim me all around and give me a shave too, Little Mo."

Little Mo spins him. Pumps the seat up. "Awright, Sam, just sit back and listen to the game on channel nine."

Sam asks, "Who's playing?"

Little Mo grabs his head. "Bulls... Mike Jordan!"

Sam closes his eyes. "That cube ball head mutherfucker from outer space."

Ernie studies the head of hair in his hand. "Shit! He is space."

Leroy pops his hot towel. "Next!"

Ty shakes his head, "That mutherfucker going to get all the money."

Sam grits when the clippers go over his right ear. "He's flying with his tongue out all the way to the bank."

Little Mo laughs. "Uptown! Nothing but bank!"

Leroy's ready to debate. "Shiiiittt! He is the bank!"

Ty looks at the others, agreeing. "Next! That be two dollars."

Little Mo asks Sam again, "Now, how you like yours cut?"

Sam tells him, "Just feather it out, not too much off the top."

Little Mo messes with him. "You don't want a new style, Sam, like these young'uns out here in the street?"

Sam answers him quick. "Don't make me over... and don't make me dumber."

Little Mo sticks his foot up. "I'm so sick of writing in their heads all kinds of bullshit, like, JIVE! LOVE! HIP HOP! RAP! MONEY! HATE! KILLER! JACK! TAP! RAT! JUDY! TRUDY! BRO', MAN! Pictures of Michael Jordan dunking a basketball. Swirls, whirls, feathers, tails of peacocks… and this shit costs, and you know where they gets the money!" He looks in his shop at some of the teenagers and faces of the young Black men. Staring up at the TV set of Michael Jordan flying in the air. "That's all they know—basketball, gold chains, two hundred dollar tennis shoes, guns, dope, BMWs, and knocked-up young girls they got pregnant this year… Oh, they know about killing another young man on the street corner selling dope to Jesus and the Devil." He touches Sam's left ear, pulls it back. Moves the clippers around it. "God is dead! God is dead! God is dead!" He hollers at the men sitting in the chairs waiting for him.

A couple of them flash gold teeth and gold chains, walk out of the shop.

Ernie points his chin at the back of the men leaving. "See, they know it!"

Sam squints up his left eye. "Crack is God."

Little Mo crawls his thumb under his chin. "You right, Sam. Crack is God on this Easter year."

Ty smiles up. "Shit carved all up in their heads. None of them ain't saying a goddamn thing. Hell, during the sixties we had a lot to say. A lot to go to jail and die for too. Riots, sit-ins, plenty of Mingus and Miles jazz shows up on the Avenue in D.C.. Marching all over the goddamn place. Black power! Umgawa! Say it loud! Brother James coming to D.C. pleading for us to stop burning down the city. White man

saying peace when we start to kick him in the ass...
Jesus is a Black man!" He nods around the room at
the men. "You hear me? Jesus is a Black man! Yaw be
proud of dat. Yaw stop killing each other for a bag of
white mans's dope... Ain't no cocaine fields up on the
avenue... Ain't no poppy fields around the corner...
Brothers, stop this mess, get a haircut with some
sense... Ain't none of you Mike Jordan... Niggers!
Can't even play basketball. All you got is this." He
taps the back of his head. "Use it!"

Little Mo spins Sam around. "Preach it, brother!
Preach it!"

Ernie joins up and keeps clipping a head. "Pray
for liberation from these goddamn commercials. Hell,
I'm so sick of looking at excellent Black actors getting
McDonald's commercials... Grinning when they take a
bite out of a piece of burger or chicken... I believe we
all gots to eat. Shit! Be a Barber... Have some dignity...
Stop working for the man. Stop working for the man!
Snorting up, shooting up that dope in your arms and
nose... We all done it... Ain't worth a fuck! Get you
killed quick. Pack your bodies up with this AIDS shit
going around. Pray for a job to take care of your families, children, sons. That's true liberation... Leave the
dope alone, bruthers! Leave that goddamn dope alone!"

Ty looks around, pops his towel. "Next!"

Little Mo walks around Sam's closed face. "Man,
I'm glad you come back through the neighborhood
every now and than. We need more bruthers like you...
You a good man. Don't forget where you come from."

Sam sighs under the long white sheet. "When
I got married to Myrthe I had to give up my truck,
El, Zorro, but I wasn't going to turn my back on the

streets where I grew up at. Shit! I can't get a good haircut on Crocker's Landing."

Ty stops clipping. "Haaaa ha aaaaah! They might put a bone in your nose. Huh, Sam?"

The men laugh at Ty making this racist crack.

Ernie shakes some powder down a neck. "Where is Ray? I think he forgot all about us down here in the ghet-to!"

Sam tightens his chin. "My brother? Naw, he might not come back here but the shit he's doing... would make a lot of you proud of him."

Little Mo nods over to Ernie. "That's good to hear as long as he don't make Black folks look bad. Because that's all they want to report in the first place.. a bunch of negative shit."

Sam says, "You'll be proud of him..."

Little Mo asks, "How's the wife and that pretty little girl of yours, Sam?"

Sam's face grins up like a big chocolate pie moon. "Wife is fine. Little Zara getting tall and beautiful like her momma."

Little Mo splashes the shaving cream on his face. "Awright. I'm going to give you a nice shave now for the Easter Bunny."

Sam holds on to the chair tight, waits for the razor to hit his throat. "How's your family, Mo?"

Mo stops the blade at his sideburns. "Bobby gone off to college down south."

Sam winces when the blade goes down his cheek. "That's good news. Congratulations!"

Little Mo's tongue flips in the left corner of his mouth. "I'm proud of him, but Harry just went off to jail..."

Sam licks his bottom lip. "For what?"

Little Mo's voice lowers. "Bank robbery, Sam."

Sam opens his eyes up. "Man, I'm sorry to hear that, Mo."

Little Mo shaves him slow. "Guess he just couldn't get it together."

Sam asks, "Is he your oldest?"

Mo tips his head up when another man walks in the shop. "Naw, my youngest."

Ernie hollers up, "Next! Come and get your Easter haircuts here! Just two dollars. We want yaw all to look clean for the Lord on Easter Sunday."

Ty hollers at him, "Man, stop clowning..."

Ernie pops his towel at him. "Shut up before I cut your head!"

Closed eyes. Sam feels Little Mo's breath tickle his left ear. Shouts from the men in the shop. "Dunk it! Dunk it!" He hears the street rap. Spit talking, rapid quick cadences of the young'uns on the streets. Cars whizzing, honking, gawking by the place. The door slams, greetings from the customers. Greetings from the men who cut heads. At the open door, young mothers holler. Teenagers run amok down the streets. Dope dealers flash. Hunch-pick pocket tens-five dollar bags of dope to potential customers. Noises of the African-USA south. His home that has gone from selling house liquor to house dope. One-block streets that he used to ride down in his truck so many miles, days, nights. Kids, dogs always chasing behind his wheels. So many miles, days, nights of gin drinking. Passing out, trying to forget the death of your youth in Vietnam. Picking up your ass from a green dream. Picking up the old and young women on the streets. Pulling them up in the cab. Getting them hot, bothered with some of his sweet licking words. Feel over their tits, thighs, ass. Rub up on their bellies. Hawk-dove, fly over the lonely-hearted women in the parks. Listen to their stories; kiss their tongues. Duck from the husbands. End up fighting, kicking ass, getting kicked. Pull a knife on another mutherfucker for cheating on the dice game. And slap a son of a bitch upside the head for stiffing you on your carpet money. Now everybody got a gun. Life was cheap, just like your momma.

He dreams of the pork chops and fried chicken cooking down the corner at Gracie's Grille. Maybe when he leaves the barber shop he'll go down there and buy a couple of South Carolina barbeque sandwiches. Palms for the poor! It's good to be with the people that know him—cuss him out anytime they want something or don't want something. His people are all cool, smooth African-White lilacs… with James Brown smiles and Michael Jackson moves. Love and chemical manufactured AIDS tries to kill them. Dope won't leave his people alone. Uh, mister, you got a job? A job so I can feed my family… even pay some child-support to Mr. Judge? Uh, mister, you got a job? More hollering. "Slam dunk it! Send him home crying to his momma! Mike! Palms for the poor! Mike! Mike!" Southern, Eastern, Caribbean, African flavors mixed all up with some collard greens, cornbread, beef patties and johnnycake. Palms for the poor! Slam dunk it! The TV watchers scream over Scottie Pippin's spin-move against Patrick Ewing.

Little Mo looks up from Sam's nose. "What's that Rastafarian mutherfucker coming in here for?... He don't needs no haircut."

Ty shrugs. "Shit! He looks familiar… nawww!"

"How yaw doing?" He walks in and greets the barbers. "Oh, yaw don't know me now?" He walks up to Little Mo at the chair.

"Should we?" Little Mo's asks him, takes the blade from Sam's nose. He's ready to cut the expensive Italian shoes off his feet.

"Sam, you know me, don't you?" He taps him on the shoulder.

"Huh?" Sam opens his eyes, stares up at a gaunt, burned face of beard and brown eyes that jives with the world on a bullshitting day. "Pete?" He sits up. "Petey-Pete!"

"Sweet Sam, the mannnn!" Pete shakes the large hand coming from under the sheet.

Little Mo jackknifes a stupid grin his way. "Alllllmannn! I was ready to cut you too, Pete. Welcome back! Have a seat… I'm almost finish with him."

Pete sits down in one of the chairs amongst the men of the barber shop. He squints up at the TV. Watches some of them nod off. Lime-onion smells rise over the place, take him back to the times him and Sam lived in the streets with these men. He now watches Sam under a sheet. Content to snooze off. Not waiting for some fool to come after him for some shit over a woman or money. Picture postcard gossip-talk about games being played on the streets and on the tube. He slaps some hands. Just the ones that know him. Just the ones that care to know if he's still riding mother earth in the saddle.

37

The curfew tolls the knell of parting day
— GRAY, ELEGY WRITTEN IN A COUNTRY
CHURCHYARD

Sam is delighted to see Pete back in Sweet Loaf. He now lives in Key West, Florida. They take a little walk down the street to Gracie's Grille after his shave and hair cutting by Little Mo. He gave him a five dollar tip; told him after, to visit his son in jail and to go to church, because he knew the sinners would definitely be there.

Razzle, dazzle; Petey-Pete is still inquisitive about the world and all the bullshit in it, briefcase of cat-alogues under his arm. He wears tan slacks, a thin white cotton shirt with bone-colored buttons from off an elephant's back in Africa. He has become a smart-ass peacock, looking like he just got out of a university prison system. He knows about some of the latest artists, musicians. The costs of drugs, the cost of Black power politics and the worthlessness of the Civil Rights Holy Grail Church. He has learned to speak French, Creole and Spanish, all because his wife; who was Haitian, had taught him and he listened. He isn't a typical Dodge City, fuck-your-culture American. He wants to know about it all. He even asks a bunch of questions to Sam on whether the Mets are going to hell or the Orioles will ever see those glory days again with Frank and Brooks Robinson brothers. Sam doesn't have the answers. He's just grooving on the sun. African princesses strolling in tuna can-size hats. Police sirens speed off down the streets. He's just grooving on the sounds of the men rolling in their chairs, sipping on icy bottled beers. Trying to pull young things in their cars. Just grooving on a woman in an African wrap with big hips licking on a chocolate ice cream Eskimo pie at the bus stop. He's reading the streets of his home like the letters off a cereal box. People mingling around shops buying dresses, suits, Sunday best for the Easter parade. He's just trying to groove on his friend with all the red, black and green colors elbowing out of the winter's confinements.

Pete's gaunt but well. He still chews on his soul and tail to keep his anger down. Things ain't got no better. Times change with the clothes. New people come in, old people move out from the streets of South Sweet Loaf. A place where just Black folks live, party, have babies, go on welfare, go to school or just die in the streets. Waiting an hour for an ambulance to come and pick them up.

They fly inside the Grille to Gracie, a dark, fat mermaid. Southern-fried nice gal with guts that can cook up a ten-course meal: ham, toast, hominy grits, gravy, fries, fried fish, bacon, steak, flapjacks, and eggs in half an hour. Her motto, "The faster you get it to dem, the faster you make the money." She greets her rainbow customers with potato salad, veggie burgers, Coke and fries for a luncheon special; all for $2.50. Palms on the wall over a picture of a white Jesus Christ.

Old women come in and sit on the stools and talk to her as her husband Baker is cooking up Sam's barbeque sandwich. Pete's having the veggie burger. He's into a health phase with the Rastas down in Key West: "SMOKE DOPE! PRAY TO GOD!" thing.

Gracie's getting noisy with some of them old bean-fried women wearing tattered straw hats on their heads, with their stockings rolled down just below their knees. Some of the men come in the place off the streets with cigarettes behind their ears; ordering steak and cheese sandwiches. Three teenage girls pop in the door wearing large hoop earrings from their drug-dealing boyfriends. In fake, long braided hair and nose rings hanging from their pearly brown faces. They're cussing like a machine-gun at a table: This bitch this! Dat nigger that! Sam shrugs. It's a part of the world today. Ain't no family or debutante balls on these streets. People are just fired all up on a sunny Easter weekend. Adventure of fun, laughter, jokes, and five people getting killed within twenty-fours hours of the day, with all the Sistuh Sadies going to church on Sunday praying to the good Lord to keep their families alive.

The young girls get louder. Gracie points a finger towards the door. The young girls leave, cussing her out as the door was closing in their venomous faces.

Pete bites his burger. "Ummmm! This is all right." He gives Gracie a thumbs-up. "Thank you, baby. This is good… Healthy too!"

She leans over the counter in a pink blouse with drooping big tits. "Don't you forget Gracie when you go back to Key West. You tell 'em all to come to Sweet Loaf for some of Gracie's veggie burgers!"

"I will, Gracie."

Sam grabs a napkin, swipes some of the barbeque sauce from his lips. "That's a damn good pig." Sips on his glass of Pepsi. "What's with the dreadlocks, Pete?" Sam wants to know. "You a true Rasta or are you just styling this week?"

"I saw Jesus in a dream." He dabs his mustache. "He was after me, man…"

"Yeah? That's cool… Now what kind of dope was you taking?"

"Dropping acid, but that ain't the point."

"The hell if it ain't the point… I saw Jesus when a mutherfucker stuck me up at the craps game when we were at Bennie's crib some years back. You remember that?" Sam holds his sandwich with both hands, chews to give Pete time to get his memory together.

"Yeah, I remember, but this was different."

"How?" Sam wants to know the difference. "I'm a fucking skeptic."

"It was real, and he was half black and half white."

Sam grins up in his bearded face. "That was some good acid, man…"

"He said something to me." Pete holds a French fry, sticks it in his mouth. "It scared the shit out of me too."

"What he say, Petey-Pete?"

"He told me Haile Selassie was on a train, and that I could meet him in Key West."

Sam almost chokes on his sandwich. He looks at him like he's a clown in a space suit. "So you left for Key West."

"Yeah. I left for Key West... Left my third wife, children, and got on that train straight for Key West." Sam listens to his voice as it trails off down that noisy rail on the Southern Blue Bird Express. "Got robbed, beat up as soon as I got there."

"Who saved you? Jesus Christ?... I don't think so." Sam laughs at this foolish man.

"No, some good Rastafarian brothers... You know, doctors, lawyers, engineers, all chillin' out in Key West... attending some reunion of the head of the clan from Jamaica." He reflects back like a child on his first pony. "It was meant for me to be there."

"Be where?"

"Sam, you laughing at me like I was some crazy-ass fool getting up and leaving my wife and children. The man touched me... just like I'm touching you now."

"What did Jesus tell you Pete?... To leave and put your family on welfare and leave your children without a father?" Sam frowns. "Did he tell you that, Pete?"

Pete stares at Sam's leather black face. "Mannnn! I didn't say what I did wasn't God-awful wrong..."

"Haile Selassie died in the seventies, Pete." Sam asks him, "Did you know that?"

"I knew that, but I was going to follow him anyway. And I was going to meet him there on that Freedom Train."

"You didn't find him." Sam shakes his cup of ice. "What did you find?"

"Another family."

"And the Rastas…"

"That's correct." Pete gives him a big grin, sausage smile. "My JuJu is a sweet little Haitian woman. We live on the estate of Mayor Venuzzi." Wipes his hands. "That's really the reason why I'm in Sweet Loaf… Bizness."

"You a shoe salesman, and you work for the mayor of Key West?" Sam is trite in Pete's new-found status.

"Mayor Venuzzi owns shoe factories. He still keeps his business going… You never know when his term may be over… so I work for him, and my wife is a maid in the mansion."

"What's your little girl's name?" Sam asks.

"Solangé."

"Solangé… That's pretty," Sam says . "Well, I tell you what, man… to each his own. It's good to see you again. Your story is crazy as shit. But you was always a little off. Writing all that poetry and reading all them books in El, Zorro." He grabs his hand. "Welcome back. You stay with me and my family over the weekend. Myrthe will be glad to see you again. Okay?"

"Thanks, Sam." He pulls out a brown pamphlet. "I got some of my old poems printed up. This is called 'Upon This Rock I'll Bleed for Thee'." He flips through some pages. "Here it is:

"Upon this rock
I'll bleed for thee
Rotten beast I will always be
Upon the skies I dream of you
Soaked in red wines off the seas

Velvet slick blue men talk-talk
Slow dancing blue velvet girls
Roam the dance hall world
In a spinning pirouette
I look for a face
Of a woman and a child
Inside the yellow eyes of the dead
Outside soaked love on the bed sheets
At an age where I can see no more
Upon this rock I'll bleed for thee
To find waves splashing
Over my body
With the rest of me."

"Bravo! For another shitty poem of yours, Pete!" Sam claps.

They slap each other five. Pete grins with pride. He grabs up his cup and swallows a piece of ice. "No hope, huh?" Crosses his arms on the table. His dreadlocks hang down over his face. "It's about my life man… That's all it's about."

"Well then, man, you got a shitty life." Sam likes it but he never will tell him. "Keep trying."

"I see we both changed a lot, huh?" Pete scratches his forehead. He watches the old women eating plates of potato salad and pigs' feet.

"You a Rasta and I became a Catholic."

Pete laughs. "Ahhhh, man! You more of an asshole than I am." He pushes his plate to the side. "Why did you leave the road, Sam?"

"Wife, a kid." Sam looks at him. "Why you on the road?"

"Wife, kid." Pete knocks his dreadlocks over his left shoulder. "You miss it?"

"Sometimes… sometimes." Sam thinks about the madness. The speed of faces zipping by on a gas-filled planet. Women and con games. A whole new day of hustling for a buck. Trying to get over and have some fun too. He taps the table with a spoon. "Knees gone now, steady job at a laundry." Sam's brow wrinkles up. He rubs it away. "Myrthe took all the steam out of my sails. She gives me everything… air, sea, sand." He became enchanted. "And fire."

"A pretty woman can do that to you," Pete says. "She can either put you on the road or keep you off the road."

Sam grabs up the bill, "Let me pay this." He opens his wallet, places a ten down on it.

"Awright, but I owe you."

"No problem." Sam shrugs. "You ready to go, or you got to take care of some more bizness with the mayor?"

"No, I'm finished," Pete replies. "I have to be back on the road to Florida. Monday morning in my car." He pushes his hair back over his ear. "I'll follow you."

"Let me take you to my home on the lake."

"House on the lake, huh?" Pete shoots a sly wink his way.

"Yeah, lake." Sam welcomes the smile. "Huh! You in a mansion!"

"After you, kind sir." Pete backs from the entrance with a bow.

They walk out of the Grille. Catch some old friends: Ginger, Bug, Monty, St. Claire and Freda talking at the bus stop.

Ginger is a cute chick with a short blonde Afro haircut. She checks out Petey-Pete. "Ohhh! You a

Rasta now! I didn't think they were into religion. I always see them riding bicycles, delivering newspapers, selling dope and jumping around to some of that Reggae music." Jabs a fist in the air. "Jamaica, mon! Marley, Pete Tosh, and the Wailers. I dig the music, man. But Petey-Pete, I think you trying to run a game on me and my peoples here."

Pete crosses his arms. Checks out her black mini and leather jacket. "Ginger, you the last one that needs to be talking about running some game on somebody. If you got God in your soul, sistuhhhh, we all going to hell! Jesus Christ was a Black man! Did you know that? Did you know that? Haile Selassie was his descendant... a Black man. A Black man!" Pete has to tell all of them, "We are all victims to the game. You walking around looking like a goddamn fool with a black face and a blonde afro. Ginger, the man dun drove you crazy!" He looks at them. "Give it up, brothers and sistuhhhhs! Madison Avenue dun drove us crazy. Baby, we from Africa... Take that bleach out your head."

"A Black man that left a bunch of his people starving in the streets," Ginger screams back at him. "Haile Selassie was a goddamn fraud!" She points at his face. "The same as you! And you know what? If you called him Black, he'd cut your throat!" She struts around the orange pole like Pocahontas as the bus comes up. "You need to take that shit back to Florida, man!" She gets on the bus. Sticks her head out of one of the back windows, throws out a dollar bill. "And get a haircut too! Have a happy Easter, Petey-Pete!"

"Fuck you, Ginger!" Pete sticks a finger up behind the trail of bus smoke.

399

"Ain't it great to be home?" Sam asks him... "Come on, follow me."

"Great." Pete's frustrated. "My people."

Sam agrees with him. "That's right, your people."

．　　．　　．

Pete drives past a large boulder on the road with white letters painted on it, "Crocker's Landing." He knows he's entered a world that is exclusive, cut off from the rest of the people of Sweet Loaf, if you can afford it. White broccoli, cabbage patch homes in a circle. Separated by the space of grass, fences, lamp posts, concrete-paved sidewalks. Colorful children in swings, chasing behind their parents or running past their parents. A warm wind flutters up off the blue lake of sailboats drifting in his view on the right.

He drives with Sam into the complex of middle class America, without their families' guts to starve with a smile. Don't fight a war. Kill the bastard quick attitude, so I can run out for Chinese food. He's amazed at the niceness of how the people greet Sam the man. This is his turf, just like the turf he had back in South Sweet Loaf. This is his people, too. Different shades. Refilled with lawn mowers and bottles of California wine, instead of the cheap stuff they used to drink on the corner, when they were on the road together selling carpet to some of the highest Pentagon bidders.

He parks his white, classic sixty-eight Mustang behind Sam in the driveway. Just as Sam gets out of the car, the door to his house opens. Pete watches Myrthe and their daughter come out to greet Sam.

He walks around the front of his car, leans back with a smile. She has a tight black mini dress on. Black belt with a gold buckle. She's still a ghost to him, a ghost he dreamed of having but couldn't obtain. She belongs to Sam… She's his ghost that went inside his skin and stayed there.

She doesn't recognize him except when he gets closer.

"Baby, look what I dragged in." Sam hugs her around the waist as he holds Zara up in his arm.

"It's… it's Peter! Pete! Petey-Pete!" Myrthe rushes to him, gives him a huge hug and a kiss on his face. "You here! You here!" She grabs his bearded face, inspects his long hair. "Why, you are a Rastafarian?" she asks in the bright brown eyes of a traveler coming back from a long journey.

He smiles up in her eyes of earth jewels. "Yeah, but I'm just here to see some of the government officials in Sweet Loaf this Easter weekend. I'll be heading on back to Key West Monday morning."

"Come, meet my little girl Zara."

"Hi, Zara." He takes her hand, kisses her fingers. "She's a princess, just like her mother." He peers up at both of them.

"Zara, you got to watch men like this and your father," Sam says. "Don't worry, baby… Daddy and Uncle Pete here will teach you." He winks at Myrthe.

They all laugh and go inside the house.

The house is filled with a puffy burgundy couch, gold shiny pillows of crepe designs. A bookcase on the right side of the fireplace. Eight small, cut-out windows on the left, with gold curtains drawn back to look out on the lake. Petey-Pete stretches out his legs on a gold and burgundy rug underneath a long glass coffee table that has an unfinished game of chess on top. Magazines of *Vogue, Essence, Paris Match* and *Sports Illustrated, Field and Stream* at the end. In the corners of the living room, wood carvings of Haitian women carrying bags of rice and baskets of fruits on their heads. Cinnamon-laced air with the aroma of chocolate chip cookies filtering in from the kitchen. He's in a world without many passengers coming off the streets. You have to know them, to be with them.

"Get comfortable, Peter, while I bring you and Sam a beer," Myrthe says. Zara follows her out of the room.

When she brings the beers, "*Merci,*" he says.

Surprised, she responds back, "*De rien.*" She leaves the room holding her daughter's hand. "Zara, come help Mommie sew."

"Myrthe, you like my haircut?" Sam asks, following right behind her.

Pete sees that Sam's woman is a piece of chocolate wrapped up in gold paper. She hugs the little girl up in her arms. Kisses her smiling M & M face. Holds the horses back on her husband as he cuddles up behind her in the dining room of French doors and white candles. Kittish, sexy speck of dust in a man's eyes. Sam's woman is a pail of running water splashing all over the floors of the house. A blessing of African voodoo magic, consisting of strawberry perfume, and a hot flame candle burning in the midnight. A thin piece of gold hangs around her neck of Jesus Christ on the cross. Sam's woman is a queen. A long river flowing down from north Africa, past Zaire into the mountains of South Africa; back across the Atlantic to the isle of Hispaniola soil. Gorgeous, no makeup. Large lips that shadow-box with her husband's. A woman of pride. Protecting her man, her home with a wish that came right off the top of the waters from the lake. He notices their love flows with the tide, the color, the passage of the sky in this living room. It's a good day, it's a good life for them. Sam's woman has suffered enough. She had endured the pain of rape, degradation, humiliation and lust from a rough man with no soul. Now she has a man with a soul, a kindness that will never end. They have saved each other and it shows in this room as he sits down and drinks his beer in a jelly glass of the Flintstones in the town of Bedrock. It shows in her face of kindness, an ease in the air that you can't cut. No tension here, just the sacrifice, of love.

38

"Somebody gots to stop him," Ray says. "Just because it's Saturday and the goddamn police and everybody are at some Easter parade, party or picnic, don't mean this wheel gots to stop." He looks at Llosa sitting across from him in a purple back swivel chair, clueless. Without a direction on her peach brown face of big red lips and a perm problem with her hair today.

"Ray, our man has already passed on the money to the people in Sweet Loaf... It's gone. Gone!" She smooths back her hair, crosses her legs in her tight, waist-high jeans. "We get him another time."

"Hell no!" Ray tightens his lips. He's about to jam his fist in the middle of the pile of papers on his desk, but he stops himself. "God is dead, but Ray Murphy is here to do his job for him this Easter weekend."

"Man, you loco!"

"I want to kiss you all over too, but I ain't loco... I'm just mad as hell!" He thinks that's like kissing a

404

shark with a .357 Magnum: dangerous. "We had too much time to get this asshole, and we let him just waltz in here and do his thing like he was some fucking James Brown." He shakes his toe in his sneakers. "Shit! What the fuck are we doing here?"

"Collecting statistics." She gives him a brave new world smile. "Watch out for the Hispanics, the Caribbeans, the Europeans, the Asians, and count bodies with a gun."

"Just in case they all get out of hand and start shooting at the president of the United States." He reaches across the desk for her cigarettes on the corner, ready to light up, but she slaps his hand. "Leave me alone, Llosa, before I blow your brains out!"

"Man, you are crazy." She laughs in his desperate face of a thousand hangovers curling up on his forehead. "Go ahead! I'll tell Mabel on you later."

"My faithful, watchful eye." He grabs the cigarette. Lights up, sucks.

"You just cool it and wait to hear from Baxter."

"We stuckkkkk… ahhhh ahhhhh!!" He spits out the smoke. Coughs, gags. "Awwww, shit!" He pushes the cigarette out in the ash tray. "I haven't smoked in three years. Shit!" Ray wipes hot tears from his blue face.

"You come to your senses." She thumbs through a folder. "This is your man?" She looks up from the file. "He sure had a lot of names over the years."

"I know him as Petey-Pete. Ray said, "he's always seen his own shadows. Some cats get a religious experience and think they are the Easter Bunny rolling eggs down the hill all the way to the White House door." He sadly looks at the dead cigarette. "He's a sharp tooth… very dangerous and we almost had him." He takes the file from her. "But he's not going to get away. He still got a lot of things he can talk about to us with his eyes closed."

"With his eyes closed," Llosa said, pointing a finger like a gun barrel right at Ray's head.

He's diplomatic with her playfulness. He backs away from her strange attractiveness, this Indian Aztec beauty. Desired by many men but dedicated to a force of good versus evil. He's glad to have her as his partner, friend; confident of being a part of his ego of righting the wrongs of many governments. He knows what she wants to do on Saturday morning. "You miss your cartoons this morning?"

"Porky Pig is on right now," she said, looking at her watch that said almost ten o'clock. "You know Mr. Sturdivant, don't you?"

He doesn't want to answer her as the phone rings. He jumps. Hesitates, picks up the receiver. "Morning."

"Mr. Murphy." Mr. Walters is in his robe and slippers. Practicing his golf swing.

"Yes sir."

"Pick 'im up Monday morning," he says. "Have a nice Easter."

"Yes sir."

The chief hangs up.

"I got what I wanted," Ray says to her.

"And what's that?"

"My man."

She nods. He's satisfied that he's the cat in the can of tuna fish again. "What's our next move?"

"Go to the Easter parade," he says with the face of a dirty little boy getting caught reading a *Playboy* magazine.

· · ·

Sam wipes his wet neck in the middle of a shoving parade. A gathering of colorful people on the sidewalks clapping at the floats. Turning heads, fighting with purses, elbows and knees. Room for one more between the bus stop poles, trash cans, police lines. He stands between hard-working families, all retreating between the markers of the past and lessons of laughter. Snatching up their kids, blowing their noses, pushing carriages, holding twins, or holding a plastic cup of beer. Suffering under the sun and pouring a water cup of ice on your head. Debating animal sneezes of hay fever sufferers. Tabloid headliners and talk show hosts talented enough to lead an Easter parade down the streets of Sweet Loaf.

Never mind. Sam's a part of this vacation craziness, a fight breaking out in the crowd as he stands with his wife and little girl, and Petey-Pete with his breached sons. They took a lost ride with their stolen boxcar father, lambasted in a crazy sax groove on a train ride and a spiritual tribal revelation. God, he's having a nice time with all the balloons and live music of bands. Show boats and majorettes down the streets of Easter bonnets. He's laid back with the imitated subhumans huddled under the KOOL ads. He points at the mayor, his wife and clown-face cronies. As simple as the day is blue. Waving, kissing for a vote, and stomach pains of liking people for a plantation buck.

Sam notices the mice droppings of clues from the mommies and daddies handling the affairs of a large outing. Eating the buffalo wings under the trees. Standing in the shadows of the Post Office and the Bureau of Licensing for some shade. Sam sees his friend Posie and his family. They grab each other, snatch reflections of each other's souls in their palms. They gaze into each other's' amusement park eyes. Marshmallow memories from men in a lost world, hangouts, bars, soup kitchens, women. Crying children watch their fathers act like tree branches, telling Dr. Seuss stories. The miles, the miles on the road, fog-wet truck stops. He's grayer, not afraid to be with his children as long as his wife handled them. Sam's glad to see him still alive in a world of sleep deprivation and Sweet Loaf ice cream trucks.

Praise the Lord! Praise the Lord! He has risen! He has risen! Let's be a family again in this crowd of marked faces; Whites and Blacks. Let's shed our values of hate for the day, the weekend. He watches the brass bands step past him and his family. He slaps a fly from his eyes. Slips his daughter on his shoulders above the crowd to watch the high-stilted clowns take long strides down the boulevard.

Hippie majorettes strut their young, fine tails. Chocolate and vanilla popsicle girls in size sixteen ages. Fathers gawk at their daughters' pretty thighs as they spin in the air with the batons, looking up to the heavens. One day his daughter will be stopping traffic with a stick. Seventy-sixer old men wishing, praying to get their hands up under their gold flapping dresses. Sam's knocked out when he sees historical old friends in the tuna can tight crowd. Mighty knights of the road, Round Table style: Duck with his high yellow wife and five kids; Joe Buck with his white girlfriend, Doris. Always with a smile; a saint with a black man. She's too nice for him. Kenny's fatter than two quarters, now suffering with diabetes. He walks on a cane as they hug. Jesse Jenkin is divorced. He has his boy and girl with him at the parade. As their lives changed the locks on the door, they opened up other screws and locks from their cowboy-road days. Desperate fathers buy a bite to eat and a T-shirt for their shared kids, to remember them, instead of Peter Pan.

Soap opera tastes of life. They still turn on the game shows. Still looking for that perfect burger. Still taking reconnaissance runs now and then on the I-95. They slap hands, give high fives. Watch out for the various degrees of gold chains around the young boys' necks. Gentle, soft smiles. All nod at each other in the Easter mess. The sun drifts hotter, washing over the straw, crumpled paper cups on the street. All break in to a germ-free Listerine song, "We Are the World." Children, wives, wrapped in each other's arms, snaked arm in arm with love. Sing-along with the markers of baskets, stuffed rabbits, eggs. Push-ups for the old truck-driving father trying to keep his chin up and gray hair away. Robby King flashes a smile at Sam's wife, but Sam reflects it with a wave back at him. Truck drivers searching, seeking the sunshine in another man's woman. The way he used to hang up the shingles in another man's house. Just dues for a new suburban country fool.

They were still dogs. He didn't get much sleep last night. He was too busy being a dog himself with his African-Creole wife. He remembers at two in the morning turning her over like a warm pillow to cuddle, to kiss and sweat into. He ate into her like she was a piece of Snickers bar, all sweet and gooey. He scoots behind her in the crowd with his Zara holding him around his neck. She was crushing his orange and black Baltimore Orioles baseball cap.

Myrthe stands beside Posie's wife Rose. Rose had once shown her how to cut out curtains in a nice crepe-blue fabric for the kitchen and bathroom. The women often talk on the phone about their pet-dog husbands, wooden shoe children in school, computer programs to keep the budget straight, shopping at some bargain hunter's wet dream store that was going out of business. Forever and ever, basking in the glow of Erica Cain killing another husband in bed or Jeffrey fathering his third black child on "The Young and the Restless." From picnics to group pony rides, they have been friends to just break the sky's black clouds of motherhood. Mystic seas in a world of clothes, sneakers, recipes from the Caribbean and the south. Rose's home was Springwater, North Carolina, just ten miles down Rocky Mount. Myrthe doesn't get to see that much of her. Last time was a month ago, but they had spoken on the phone to each other just last week. Sam's friends wandered into her life like a meteor crashing to the Sierra Nevada desert in her life. She laughs, points out the colorful rainbow zip-head children to Rose. Myrthe munches on some popcorn, while cursing her weight this weekend. Rose, plump neck, slips a tongue around and down a chocolate ice cream cone.

410

Myrthe tells her of the time she was in a parade in Haiti as a child. She was sitting in her classroom getting her lessons one morning when the police, the Ton Ton Macoute, drove up to the school door. They carried rifles, knives, grenades. Snake-purple men with no eyes, covered up by thick sunglasses. Tall-skinny, hot-bothered men holler to her and her class-mates to get up from their chairs. "*Leve sou chez la!*" They made all of the school children march in a parade for Papa Doc Duvalier. Myrthe thought it seemed such a long time ago, but it wasn't. No, it wasn't. Pain would always need a way to come back and remind you that freedom was a parade. A jolly parade to make the people forget that this world was a dragon with a long tail that slept this day. The mon-ster gave you a break to chew on its own ass when it might strike again. It was random, like a piece of trash flying across the street, sticking to a light pole. It was random, like a boss screaming at you in the face. All because their life was shit and they didn't want to see you in it. It was random, like a soccer player hitting a goal for his team or when a man would just slap his wife for no apparent reason. Maybe dinner wasn't on time or the sheets were too hard. Men made you march for Christ, for freedom, for the dead, to just keep the dragon asleep, away from the children for one more day.

Happy marathon children shout out at the array of white, brown, spotted ponies carrying asphalt cowboys down both sides of the lane. A troop of sharp jaw, explosive Marines snap up the show with bird light rifles, no bullets, please. Tossing, spinning the sentiments of where the skeletons of freedom

411

should lie in the graves of Arlington under ten feet of dirt. A series of good fathers look on. Cramped, stretching their necks over a thousand people. They substitute small chatter with their wives, for the satisfaction of getting them out of their full crop of deeds for today. Praying, maybe they can get to the bar later. Mawkish, masked presidents run down the street: Johnson, Reagan, Nixon, Lincoln. Horns spray the audience into a summer trance to fly Christian soldiers off to church on Sunday. As we listen to Mother Marie-Louise weep with a hip pocket of Irish whiskey in her purse as we pray to the Lion King.

Sam tightens up to Myrthe's back, their proving ground. He squeezes to smell the fresh Camay soap from her hair. Perfumed, animal rights woman. Sweat over him in the crowd. Travel thousands of miles from an island to be with his old crew of truck drivers. Innocent, sunny, significant day results in having an old friend beside him.

"Jonathan! Davey! There is the Sweet Loaf High marching band," Petey-Pete tells his sons on top of his feet in his Sanford wingtips.

"Daddy, I want to be in the band too," Davey says.

"You will." He asks, "What do you want to play?"

"I like the flute, Dad… It's cooool."

"I like the trumpet." Jonathan enters in the conversation.

"I buy you one for yaw birthday. Okay?"

"Okay, Dad."

Pete observes his two sons closely. Little signs of growth. Pain and rich gifts swollen, missing him. He rubs both their heads. "I love you and I miss you."

They both look at their father with the thick rope hair. They hug him back, not letting the day die between them. Just remember the herd of people and the weekend their father came back to take them to the Easter parade.

"Sam, do you see Ray and Mabel yet?" Myrthe asks, tightening herself to him.

"No, baby." He catches the pretty strawberry blonde with a butt the size of a pregnant elephant, shaking her nature down the street, flashing teeth, tits and three batons.

Myrthe calls him a pig. "*Cochon!*"

"Huh!" Sam shrugs this insult off with a grin. "I don't see 'em."

"Mommie, there goes Little Ray!" Zara waves through the heads. "Uncle Ray! Aunt Mabel! Over here!"

They guide them like a fish to a worm over a marsh of lemon grass. It was tight. A burned down barn, fitting in the landscape of friends, places and boxes of Captain Jack popcorn. Mabel moves straight to Myrthe, they hug each other, two feminine allies. Exhausting blue, red, yellow flames of motherhood having to drag their husbands to a happening of hot dogs, clowns and rabbits on Saturday morning. They blow back their permed heads of black-brown streaks of hair under bushel baskets of straw hats. Both of them feeling success in taking their men away from animal clutching baseball-basketball games, auto repairs, beer cans and fishing lines.

"Mabel, where you been?" Myrthe asks.

"I'm sorry." She gives Little Ray to his father. "Here!" Turns back to Myrthe. "Ray had to go to the office this morning." She shifts the blue diaper bag around her shoulder as if it was a third arm or leg. "That husband of mines is something else." She watches the float of the queens go by. "He don't eat, don't sleep, he just flat as a pancake in bed… Honey, I don't know what's wrong with him." She peeks over to her husband, Sam, Pete and his boys, Posie and his family behind her. "Child, who is that Rasta standing beside Sam?"

"That's Sam's old partner, Petey-Pete," Myrthe says. "You know him."

"Why, he sure has changed."

"Mabel, we all have changed…"

"I hope for the better," Mabel comments.

"I hope so too."

Ray puts Zara on his shoulder. Sam takes his nephew. Exchange of children like money for pawn tickets to a hot Ray Charles concert. "You remember Pete, man," Sam says. "He use to be on the truck with me a lot a few years back."

Ray examines the small face, long snake hair. "Shit, yeah!" He scratches the back of his neck. "How you doing, Pete?"

They shake hands. "Where you been, man?"

"Florida."

"Picking oranges?"

"Funny." Pete laughs. "Working for a shoe salesman."

"And the mayor of Key West," Sam says. "He's a big man now."

"That's good, Petey-Pete." Ray turns back to the parade. "Have a nice Easter."

"I will."

Sam cuddles Little Ray. "See the horses?"

Ray wraps Zara's legs around his neck. "See all the beautiful children marching in the parade." He points through the heads. "Ohhh! Is that the Easter Bunny?"

"Yeah, Uncle Ray!" Zara's voice sparkles. "See? The children marching with Easter bonnets on!"

"Myrthe! Sam! I use to be in this very parade," Mabel says to the couple. "See, Zara, I was one of those marching girls of Lincoln-Jefferson Junior High." She claps, points, hops up and down, loaded with sun and beer. "Get it, girls!"

"How many years ago was that, honey?" Ray asks with a mischief grin on his face. He shifts his cap. "Sorry, Zara, your aunt here is trying not to age herself in front of all of us." He stares at Sam with a Santa Claus wink.

"Go to hell, Ray!" She sticks her nose up at her husband. "Sam, you remember, don't you?"

"Yeah, Mabel. I remember your little mop Shirley Temple head bobbing on down the street... dropping your baton ten times before you got to the corner."

They all laugh. "Sam! Shut your lazy butt up. I remember you chasing behind that pony with the school patrol down the avenue too... looking goofy with those big Dumbo ears and skinny body... letting the wind take you every which way."

"Dumbo ears?" Myrthe said, inspecting his ears.

"Yeah, baby." He comes back at her. "But I was sharp too." Sam hugs his nephew. "Little Ray, your mother was a fine little thing then."

"Huh! I still am!" She rolls her honey bee eyes up.

"Pete, you coming back to my house for the bar-beque cookout?" Sam asks.

Petey-Pete straightens up over his sons. "Yeah, I be there… Let me take them home first."

"Bring them with you."

"Naw, man," he says with reluctance of having to give up his two boys for the rest of the time while he's in town. "Holli told me to get them back after the parade."

"Awright, man. No problem." Sam understands. "You just come on when you ready… I save a plate of ribs for you, okay?"

"Thanks, Sam." He grabs his sons' hands. "Come on, pumpkin heads, time to go." He takes them to Sam. "See you later, man."

Sam dips down with Little Ray. Shakes the boys' hands. "See yaw later, and have a nice Easter."

In sweet Vienna choir voices the boys wave, "Bye, Sam, Zara, Myrthe."

Myrthe throws a kiss to them as they squeeze through the crowd, touching shoulders, hands, backs to get out of the sleepy heat. Myrthe smiles back at the good-looking boys with a father that had just got off a space ship spouting poems, long hair, a beard, and asking for their love again. At least he did come back. At least he did care enough for his sons and the destiny of what he made in the past with another woman he had once handcuffed to his heart of love.

39

Sweet Loaf didn't change much. A couple of new burger joints. Strip joint on the west side. Pool hall on the east, a little feather in the cap for the City Council to say they fight crime while pocketing money in corner pockets.

Petey-Pete's third wife, Holli Jackson, has turned into a fat woman with little breasts and a cheerier disposition than when he was with her. Holli Jackson is still uncomfortable when she has to sit still for any long moments of time. Insipid Steven King thoughts would always creep up over her of her daddy being axed by another man down in redneck Macon, Georgia during her country girl days. Now her man is back.

She lives in a federal government rental apartment that all mothers usually get for the fireworks of making love in their lives to a Black man that has the blues done to him too. "Mr. Charlie going to lynch you some kind of way, boy!" He left her with the sons, and she was glad his ass was comically gone on that Freedom Train. Leaving her alone for the rest of her loving life. But Pete's like a herd of horses coming over a trail to get away from the cans of Alpo, dog food man. He's in her path again, but she's cool. Keeps a small pistol down in her robe. Won't ever get hit again, by no man.

Aretha Franklin sang in the background a sad sounding song, "Ain't No Way," as he sent the boys out of the house with ten dollars apiece in their hands. "Yaw gone out and play some basketball."

Holli Jackson puckers up. Whistles a smile and braves this man who left her to survive in the projects of Emery Corners. She hustles hard and doesn't faint when it gets too cold. Sells food stamps to the highest bidder. Bakes cakes, cookies at church bake-offs. Doesn't mind having Preacher Thompson slap her on the butt every now and then for some of those free chicken legs. She even makes African print dresses with the same designs. Crew neck, long back, past you knees. The material is tie-dyed in her bath tub. Tells the ladies it's from Ghana, Nigeria or Kenya. They buy it. They love her and even let her throw rent parties in their homes sometimes. They split the cash if it's a good party that night. She sticks the money down her bra and whistles again at a young boy to tap her on the ass for the night. She loves truck drivers. Big hands… big things in their pants. She had a thing for Pete, but he was special. He had hurt her too much and loved her too much. It was a frozen, wonderful weekend for her sons to see their father. It was a classic Greek idea of a woman suffering. Petey-Pete was pitiful but a strong thumb man that survived on that dreamy Freedom Train to come back to her and the boys.

Skip notes. Beats. Skip wives. He sits next to Holli. Tone deaf out Aretha's voice. He would always love her, always love them. Black-polish lips of her face that drowned in his memories. Cosmic eyes. Stone-love. Stone cold. His pain. He hurt so many years, years ago.

His ex-wife, his past. She fixes him a steak and French fries that crinkle. He misses her. He forgot about how lovely she was to him, until he drank, smoked a joint and listened to those black lips of cork chalk-screeching across a board of their pain. Of finding happiness in this world again. Job to job, truck to truck, bars to bars. He drinks up the red wine. Tastes, plays with her. Speaks of old jokes, old times when they did have fun. Before he left for a new wife, a new life, and become a Rastafarian-Revival. Now what is that? A man with pride. A man who knows his blackness. A rough edge to the planet. A man with a crown. The descendants of a lion. A manchild. A man. A boy. All grown up and dangerous because he knows who he is? And what he is? He now sits with pride in front of her at the dinner table, in fancy shoes, clothes that would pay ten weeks of rent to the government man.

He married her after he left Janet Victor with a boy and a girl. She taught him how to have fun, act silly, simple again. She taught him to feel the pain of a people dying of alcohol, drugs, childbirth. Wife-slap your wife abuse. Play a piccolo and feel the rain. She pushed him to get on that train. Going to get on that train! Going to get on that train in the morning, baby! I gots to get out of here. I gots to live one more day. Can't breathe. I gots to breathe! Gots to see that sunshine one more time. I love you. I love you... I love you.

Choooo! Chooooo!

She remembers. He remembers. The boys small, asleep, dreaming of Peter Pan, dinosaurs, Mickey Mouse, space men, boogey men. The darkness. The angel of the night watching over them. The angel watching over a husband and a wife. All sleep. Not afraid of the summer storms because all they knew was that Daddy was here. Mommy was here. In the day, in a lifetime.

"Holli, that was a good dinner... Now, what can I do for you?" He reaches in his back pocket.

In front of the catsup, butter, salt, pepper shakers. "Not money, Petey. You."

"Me." He flinches. "I got a wife, pretty little girl down in Key West... We can't get back together, Holli," he says. "Stop fucking with me, girl, and take this money for my boys."

"Why?"

"Because we hurt each other... that's why."

"Come on back home... to me... your sons."

"Baby, we doing awright without each other. Have you gone crazy? I'll be back in Sweet Loaf next month." He touches her hand. "Send the boys down to Key West later on."

"Your children." She moves the salt, pepper shakers between them.

"Baby, I got a new life... Don't mess it up. Don't mess it up." He gets up, walks over to the kitchen window to watch his sons play some of that round ball.

"They your sons." She walks up behind him. "They need you."

"No guilt trips." He turns. "I didn't come here for that."

"Really?" She's pissed at his calmness. "You one of those brave Rastafarian lions going around selling smoke from their bicycles... Don't expect shit to happen to you... Don't even expect to spit out your own guts from good vegetation ingested in your blood stream. Pete, you always was under my foot. Always going around thinking you betta than the next man, just because you spin some pretty words from a pencil, use your tongue to kiss all the ladies... still bright. I hate you. Don't nobody keep you, mister Petey-Pete. Don't nobody keep you unless you wants to be kept. Typical asshole brother. Shit talking, shit walking. With just a new game... That's all you got. Go on, run to that train now, man. You ain't shit!"

"Holli, why you actin' nasty like this?"

"Because I need you."

"No, you just need a man," he says with pity in his voice. "I'll stay the night."

"You right!" She tips up. Licks his juicy bearded lips. "I just want to look at it, feel it." Her hands spread down his pants.

He feels safe, in front of this dangerous great wall of her body that warms over him. "Stop."

"Don't pity me. Fuck me."

"Get out of my face." He gets away from her hand and goes out the back door to his sons playing under the open wooden basket. He doesn't look back at her. He looks at their faces. Treats of brown candies. He hugs them up. "I'm getting ready to go now... but I'll be sending for you, okay?"

Davey asks, "Dad, when you leaving?"

"Monday... Oh, here." He takes money out of his pocket, rolls it up tight. "Give this to your mother and have a nice Easter." He kisses them on their cheeks, shakes Jonathan's hand and walks past them out of the back yard. Pete can't look back, but he smiles when he hears the ball bounce again.

Pete arrives back at Sam's around about five. He drives up in front of a bunch of friends, egg-head neighbors and their kids stumbling around the side of the house with baskets, aluminum-wrapped platters of food for the cookout. He walks up on Duck and Kenny going in with their kids. Posie's holding one of his daughter's hands. His wife is fixing up bowls of potato salad in the kitchen, with Myrthe fixing fried plaintain, and Mabel getting together a platter of sea-food salad from a favorite recipe her Aunt Ivey gave her. He finds Sam sitting under a tree, talking, listening to old stories of the road. He hugs Sam around the neck.

"Welcome back." Sam asks him, "You all right?"

"Yeah, I'm okay... Give me a beer."

"You got it." Ray reaches in a cooler. "Here, Pete."

Sam spews out spit and shit to his buddies from the times they were on the road, coloring up the highway from the shores of Sweet Loaf to the northwest side of Washington, D.C.. Vocal loudmouth tales come up in their hoarse-hard throats. Men take their spotlight in talking about the times they were, and some still are, tending to their business in their trucks. Oh, the many tales they tell, full the days of beer, bourbon, wine and women. A humanities class on this Easter weekend. Walk tall across the stage and find them lying on each other as the rabbit-hopping couples jump to some of that Wicked Wilson Pickett gut-bucket music. It makes you sweat and throw your butt and dress up under the red, yellow, blue Chinese moon. Sam tells his story to the men under the old long-neck tree that holds a swing car tire for his little Zara:

"This is called. 'When a Man Drinks up a River of Bellies'."

Limpy McGee use to draw up straws to see if he was going to see his girl Sally Proctor during the days her husband was gone out of town. He was a scared ass, pit-dog-ugly truck driver that had just came up from the sticks of Mississippi to the city of Havensight, Connecticut. His sister, Dizzy Diana, begged him to come up from them fields to help her out around the house and to watch her little boy Tim when the boy didn't have a father around. Limpy didn't mind. He would find out what cartoons were playing on TV Saturday morning. Sit a bowl of rice-flakes in front of the eight-year-old and let him watch whatever he wanted. Just as long as the kid didn't disturb him. He'd call up his secret-sleeping mistress. Slip her in around the back way from the basement and have her stay with him while his sister was cleaning up an industrial waste plant in the next town of Millsap. They never said much to each other, but what they did say was something out of a comic book prehistoric cave magazine:

"Om!" he said.

"Eh!" she said.

"Om!" he said.

"Eh!" she said.

"Where is your husband?" he wanted to know, because he always kept a gun under his pillow.

"Chicago, I think. Uh!"

"Om! Om!" he said.

"Eh!"

He looks down in her strawberry flush cheeks. "Sally."

She bites his chin. "Eh?"

"Open your legs wider, baby, I'm trying to make conversation."

"Eh! Eh! Eh! Eh! Eh! Eh!!" She opens her eyes. "Is that better?"

"Yeah, baby."

The men crack up all around him. Tears come from some faces. Satisfied, a few of them search for their wives. They grab up plates of fish, chicken, hot dogs and burgers. Dance some more to that Sam Cooke asking them to grab their sugar before somebody else do, like his dead ass.

Duck drinks his wine. "Ah man, that was good! Here's one! Here's one!" He raises his hand for them to stop laughing. "Awright! Okay. It's called, 'Charlie Finch and Zoo Girl'."

Charlie Finch and Zoo Girl were a couple on the farm that stayed way out in the country on the edge of good-bye and on the line of having a third child.

Charlie Finch loved horses, and one of his favorites was a silver three-year-old gelding he

424

called Pookie Slim. Zoo Girl's real name is Zoey Turner, a veterinarian by profession. She had a pig she called Margie. The pig was a special piece of Visa Gold card to her and Charlie. A two hundred-pound piece of brown and white spotted pork that won prizes all over the countryside.

Zoo Girl is a good cook too. Now, Charlie Finch was getting old. Hitting that road leading to fifty. His hair was graying up on him and his belly was popping out as if it was a table around his waist. He was in a quiet crisis, meaning he wanted to feel his youth again.

There was this country girl about five miles down the road. One day Charlie gets in his yellow Ford pickup truck to Mary Lou Jacob's house to do some chores around the barn while her husband Bob was on maneuvers with the National Guard. You know, make a few bucks.

Mary Lou needed help all right. When she saw big handsome Charlie poking out at her, she thought of having her twenty-second birthday party with this turkey-size plate of a man. Charlie Finch picks up his pitchfork. Starts cleaning out the barn. She came in the barn with her cotton shirt off. Shows him her two planets of sweet dreams that blazed a trail straight to his tight zipper. They celebrated her days on this earth in the middle of bales of hay and chickens clucking.

Charlie got home late that night. Tired, he went right to sleep after he finished his postcard workout date with Mary Lou Jacobs.

Zoo girl had a sharp nose. In fact, she had a big nose and woke up in the middle of the night sniffing up a different perfume on her man. Plus she spots strands of brown hair and hay on his T-shirt. She was going to fix him a good breakfast in the morning for this.

Sunday morning when Charlie got up: "Zoo Girl, what's for breakfast?... I'm hungrier than a bull!"

"Breakfast be ready in a few, Charlie," Zoo Girl hollers up from the frying pan. "Wash your face and hands and come on to the table."

The children played at the table over bowls of hot oatmeal, spiced with lime zest and honey. When Charlie got to the table he had a whole spread laid out in front of him. Bacon, ham, eggs, steak, toast, flapjacks, melon, strawberries, coffee, juice, milk, even a few rainbow trout on the side.

Zoo Girl sent the two children out to play, knowing they didn't have time to eat. Just time to play in the field of rain and rainbows. She ate with him, watched him eat up everything on his plate. He had a smile of contentment that he was getting the loving and the food too. She knew how to get to her man. She knew what made him happy and it was food and a good woman sitting in front of him watching him devour a thick porterhouse steak in the morning. Smothered in catsup and onions.

"Honey, you want a beer with that?"

He burps. "Maybe for lunch." Wipes his mouth with the napkin. "Whew! That Mary Lou Jacobs had a lot of work to do on that farm of hers." He sticks some bacon in his mouth. "Um, um!"

"You enjoying your breakfast, Charlie?"

"Um, um!" he sleepily said, sipping his coffee.

"I figured you would be hungry this morning. I wanted to just tell you I love you by fixing you up a nice breakfast like this sometimes. You deserve it… after working around this place and other people's barns." She kissed his cheek. "And just bringing home the bacon around here." She rubs a thumb over his wedding band. "While I'm pregnant with our third child growing in my belly." She takes his hand, rubs it over her stomach. "That feels so good."

"Zoo Girl, I love you too," he said "My beloved."

Her voice became a night presentation. "Charlie, there is something else I want to tell you… I think you need to check on your horse."

"Pookie Slim!" He jumps up, runs to the barn to find the horse breathing hard on its side. He kneels down to see a river of blood coming from under his back legs. "I'll be a son of a…"

"That's right, Charlie." She was in the door. "That's what you be!"

He closed his eyes and stood up over his beautiful horse.

"Thanks for bringing home the bacon," she said. "And eating it too."

The men around the tree grab their crotches. Duck looks around at the fear on the men's faces. They all walk away from him.

"What I say?" Duck begs. "It's just a crotch story."

Sam gives him another cup of wine. "Yeah, and don't let the women hear that either… They all want to do that to us."

427

Kenny laughs. "Duck, you a spectacular fool."

"Come on, Sam, let's dance." Myrthe walks up to her husband. A chicken leg in her hand, she bites into the tender meat. Watches the pasta-smooth, bearded face of her husband surprised and happy to see her.

"Ah, baby." He takes her by the waist, spins her to some nice smooth music coming from Ray Charles' lips. "Georgia, Sweet Georgia."

"I see you drinking up your friends tonight," Myrthe says. She winks over to Mabel dancing with her husband as they do a little tango to words of love in the peach state.

Sam acts silly. "Before God arrives tomorrow."

"You must be drunk." She pinches his butt.

"Ouch!" He waves a finger at her. "I don't know when all my friends will be together again." He gets back to dancing with her. "I love you."

"I love you too, my Sweet Sam Murphy."

Ray's voice pushes out some spiritual soul. "See your ma. See your pa. I'm gonna take you back to Arkansas. Ahhhhh right! Heyyyyy! Heyyyyyyy!"

"Oh, Mabel invited us to visit her church."

He thought about a rousing sermon. "That be nice... to have some foot-stomping early Sunday morning."

"We'll bring Pete along."

"If he wants to come." Sam shines a smile down into her swan black eyes. Packing plump lips to kiss. "Key West and his type of lifestyle with the Rastafarians is far away from Crocker's Landing."

"The lake makes us seem far... but we not. We in a place that has long poles of hate and love. People from all walks of life come in and out of here like

428

the rocks upon the shores. No, Key West and the life he leads selling shoes, writing poetry… isn't far at all. It's just a stone's throw in the middle of the lake. Drop your fish line, and you will bring up all sorts of caca from its depths."

"I see Zara is having fun." He points with his chin.

She is a magical fairy dressed in denim overalls, sneakers, Barney T-shirt. Dances with the other children in the yard, plaits flap. She waves. "Hi, Mommie!"

Mabel and Ray pick her and Little Ray up. Dance with them as if they were toy grasshoppers and butterflies.

Neighbors clap. Start a circle around the children. Urging them on to jiggle their bodies to some of that fast music of Prince. "Little Red Corvette."

"Pete isn't dancing." Myrthe sees him standing under the tree with his beige tunic on, dreadlocks hanging over his eyes. Writing in a small black book, tapping his foot to the music, spaced out. He's gone in his little world of being, not being. Writing, observing the dance of coming back home.

Sam looks over to the bearded little man. "He hasn't changed, he was like that in the truck, too." Sam finger pops with the others. He shakes closer to his Myrthe in her tight jeans. The swan twists away from his hands as he looks over to see his daughter dancing with the poet under the tree.

40

Guests snuggle up to the last dance under the blue quarter moon. Steal pieces of ribs off the grill. Tell two more crotch jokes after finishing off bottles of blueberry wine. Wives pull their husbands by the ears. Chase down the last of the running children. Church meetings arranged under the African violet sky. Myrthe kisses Mabel down the street, hugs Ray around the neck, pats the baby goodnight. Off flies her apron. She licks a spoon full of potato salad and from the table... watches her husband and Pete under that old tree of red lights, shaking friends' hands. Bye, bye! See you around. See you in the next life. You dirty dog! What you say? Ah! Going down to Florida too in the fall. All going to see Pete with his Jab Rasta family, all of them holding that giant lion flag. Jump up to some of that good Reggae music, smoke good grass and talk to God on the beach.

Quotations, songs. Praises due to the chocolate face man with a beard and dreadlocks. A funny joke on all of them. The mystery, the riddle of him coming back to visit. Drop in from the sky on wings of soft orange Italian shoes, leather handbag. First born, last son seen on the winds of an Easter Sunday. Pete was mellow. Cool, thin man. Threw his arms around his buddy Sam, spoke with a drunk voice. Slurs of poems, unforgettable man. Somebody save them from drowning in their love for each other. Sits Pete down on the sofa in the middle with him and Myrthe, as Zara's head of plaits drifts on her mother's lap. Show off pictures of a family at the lake, Jones Beach, at the Sweet Loaf Carnival. Camera shots, good focus. Bad weather. Unclear smiles. Gray bright days under trees. Streets, waterfronts, birthday candles. Twenty-one days of pure holidays with a marriage born on the fourth of July. Myrthe in her wedding gown and Sam in front of the big red truck, El, Zorro, as he bends over giving the truck one last kiss.

"Do you miss the truck, Sam?" Pete challenges him. "Tell the truth."

Sam scratches his chin. "Sometimes."

"I knew it," Myrthe said. "I knew you did." She pecks his chin. "It's all right, kitten... We all miss something from our past that we had to give up."

"It's the craziness." He looks up from the picture with guilt on his wild, Sea World windy face that rages in amusement over the pictures from the past.

Pete pushes his hair back from his eyes. "Sam, you will always be a man of the road." He yawns. "That doesn't take anything away from wanting to be with your family... The truth will clean your biles out."

"Clean my biles out," Sam replied. "Man, shut up."

"The truth will set you free." Pete asks him, "You want to be free... don't you, Sam?"

"Honey." Myrthe hugs him around the shoulders. "You must know I miss that embassy life sometimes, too. All the traveling. The mansions in Rome, Paris, Milan. The mighty bullshit that goes around from a fairy tale brutal life of champagne, parties and designer dresses." She was honest with him a thousand times of sand castles in her heart of magic and love. "You feel better now?"

"Hell no!" He rubs his daughter's sleeping head of hair. "It hurts, man, that I would even think about leaving this sweet little girl and her mom." He pounds his chest with his finger. "And hit the road." He squints up, unbelieving that he would even think of this act. "It hurts that this monkey wants to get on my back. Whisper in my ear and tell me to get the fuck up, and get the fuck out of here from this suburban stuffed-shirt kind of life. I want to say 'Bye!' When shit gets heavy between me and you, sometimes I holler! You holler about some bullshit... After work, after stuffing laundry bags at some goddamn cleaners. Yeah! Yeah! I want to get the fuck up and leave out of here sometimes. Tell Oprah that shit! Travel like Pete here. In the heartland, wetlands of America with the Latinos, Haitians, Irish, Redneck Bobs all wanting to kill my black ass in America. I want to travel in that lifetime achievement award of our American culture and say fuck it all! It hurts that I don't want to see my little girl grow up into a fine woman like her mom here." He hugs her back.

"Sam... you can't be like me," Pete tells him. "We each got a calling."

432

"You right, Pete, and this is mines." He smiles back at Myrthe.

"Come on, baby... it's time for us to go to bed," Myrthe says. "Pete, good night." She wags a finger at him. "Be ready for church in the morning."

They get up from the couch. Sam picks up his daughter like a sack of potatoes on his shoulder going to the market. "See you in the morning, man."

"Night, Sam." Pete nods. "Morning."

Myrthe kisses him on the cheek. Pete watches them go up the stairs, like compact disks. Take their marching orders like the parade he saw today. They're working well together. He's glad Sam is finally able to go to sleep at night with this woman being his medicine and the child his cup of warm milk.

He makes a phone call home to his wife. "Hi, baby, it's me. Did I wake you?"

"No."

"Miss you..."

"Miss you too, Pete... my love."

"I'll be home Monday."

"I want you home now..."

"Bye... Love you." He hangs up. He sits back on the couch. Feels the teeth of withdrawal pains, a need at his stomach. A vitamin for the baby, feed the baby now. Back it up. He reaches down in his jacket pocket on his sleeping couch of pillows in a sheet and blanket of summer calm warmth. Myrthe was his explanation of every woman. A wife, sister-friend that serenaded the man she was with and the people around her, her upbringing as a hostess on Embassy Row. He walks out of the house into the tapered blue star night. He stands on the screened porch. Late night snoozes, his friend asleep in his wife's arms. A family dreams above his head into the stars. He rolls up a joint, lights, puffs the smoke down. Blows it out his nose into the coolness of the difference of night. And after the beginnings of a day, moist, chocolate hands of his sons. Pete sucks the weed down his lungs. He gently dreams up in the stars. A symphony of violins sing in his ears.

Pete finishes, toddles off back in the quiet house to the couch. He takes off his shirt, shoes, pants. All he wants is his wife and his happy daughter clapping her hands in his lap. Instead, he hides under the sheets and dreams.

He is back on the train going down a digit dark track. No people around. Except one man. Him and Haile Selassie, on the Freedom Train. They shake, rattle, rock on the tracks. He is a short, frigate man. They're the same size. Pete hasn't seen him in years. He's glad to shake the emperor's hands again. The concept of a man and king on the same train, rolling down the track. Medals on his chest, down to his stomach. His beard a mass of soft cotton. His eyes blaze with the fires from the burning bush. His uniform of white, green and gold is stained. He has a hold on Pete. He has him feeling empty, at an adjacent destination.

"Young man, why do you follow me?"

"Huh?" Pete points at his chest. "You are following me, aren't you?"

"Yes, I guess I am." He laughs like a weird tropical bird, full of feathers, waiting for someone to talk to from his cage. "Somebody tore up the page."

"Excuse me, Your Highness?"

"Somebody tore up the page."

"Sir. What page?"

"This page." He shows him a book bound in green and gold. "This page is missing." His fat fingers of gold rings direct him to the missing page.

Pete looks at the pages. "Page twenty-three." He spits out. "Your Highness, what is this book about?" He gazes in the face of an old man watching the world from his throne of gold lions' heads. All the skeletons of a man, who once took inventory of his life during World War II.

"Minutes." He pushes his gold leaf cap back off his head. "This book is about people running to catch a train. All they have are minutes… It's like a little child looking at a book of dinosaurs." His voice rises. "A foundation of the past."

"I don't see the pages." Pete searches around the empty section.

"Look for it… Ask around." He looks at him as if he's a rolling satellite. "This is my stop. See you around, Petey-Pete." He vanishes as the train slows… at track twenty-three.

At some point Pete looks out the window. He sees his mother, his father waving at him from some corn fields. He sees his grandmother Emma, granddad Poppie, aunts, uncles, cousins waving at him from the barn. He waves back. The train keeps going by. "Let me off! Let me off!" He sees Sam, Duck, Kenny, Posie, Ralph, Sam's wife. He sees clowns doing back flips. All acting like tourists, none of them worried about missing the train. He runs to the door and starts banging at the window. "Let me off! I said let me off!" The train doesn't slow down.

• • •

Easter Sunday morning. Myrthe slips behinds her husband dressing in the mirror in the bedroom. "You ready?" She plays with the pearls around her neck. "You look nice."

"For a man who don't wear suits every day like my brother, huh?"

"You don't have to." She slaps his butt. "You Sam the man."

He gives her a stupid grin. "That's right... and don't forget it." He points back at himself in the mirror. "Was Pete up?"

"He's been up," she says. "Drinking coffee and reading the paper."

"I have to get a cup too."

"Go on downstairs and fix you a cup." She taps some hair back to its original place in the bun set around her head. "Or you need me to get it for you?"

"No, I'll get it." He lifts his chin, slips a knot in his red tie.

"Good. That gives me time to get Zara ready."

"What time are we leaving?" He looks at his wrist-watch; almost seven-thirty.

"Mabel and Ray will be over here at eight-thirty." She puts tiny gold earrings in. "We'll follow them... Pete can ride with us."

"Okay." He feels funny. Acting like a little woman getting dolled up for a tea and biscuit set at the Wimbledon. "Honey, where are my gold cufflinks?"

"Top middle drawer."

He pulls them out.

"I see you getting all pretty on this day." Myrthe looks at them in the mirror. A complete couple actually ready to hear a sermon on being good everyday, not just this day.

"Going to a Baptist church. No hummin' in that house."

"Oh, you saying us Catholics don't know how to celebrate the Lord?" She twists the clasps in the shirt hole. Locks it down.

"Just sayin' yaw put the dead to sleep."

"And why did you become one?"

"To eat at the table with Peter and Paul." He turns away from the mirror to see a funny-girl stare from her eyes of brown gold and neck of pearls.

"*Kisa*!" She sticks her hands on her hips; asks him again in English, "What?"

Sam loves to tease her about religion and the way different little Christian rituals seem to slap themselves across your face. Make you sit up and take a stand for this religion or that religion. It's a game to him. He grins as he thinks about the fun him and the saints would have on a Saturday evening or Sunday afternoon, if they were alive to see what was happening in Rome today. "Men stuff. Talk sports... Take bets on the Dallas and Redskins games in the fall." He turns back to his image in the mirror to see a man sharp as the wind. "Call me Mr. Hollywood."

"Make fun." Rolls her eyes over him. "You look fine enough." Myrthe turns around to the mirror, adjusts her beige silk dress. "Button me." She turns her back around to him.

"Come here, let me show you."

"Don't touch me... button me."

He buttons her dress up. "There." Her perfume is about to make him fall over her.

She sticks her hands up to keep him from her lips. "Now go make your coffee," she says. "And I get Zara up."

"Bye." He walks down the stairs whistling with his blue blazer draped over his right shoulder. Pete's on the couch. Sunday paper, coffee cup in front. In white shirt, black tie, a gray pin-stripe on with black wingtips on his feet. The neo-conservative look of an urban jungle-brother with class. "Mornin', Pete."

Pete unlocks his eyes from the sports page. "Morning, Sam." He lifts his cup up to greet him from the couch.

"I see you way ahead of me... Let me get a cup."

"Water's ready."

Sam puts his blazer around the back of the chair. He goes to the kitchen of blue and white walls. Bronze pans over the dish rack, table with straw placemats. A calendar of a bowl of fruit stuck to the refrigerator, detailing the dates of his wife's periods, dentist appointments, mortgage payments. Onion smells and trash bags in the corner from the party last night. He reaches in the cupboard, takes down the jar of instant coffee, cream. Sugar in stone-white canisters. Cup, saucer from the rack. Scoops coffee, pours his water, sticks in two spoons of sugar and stirs to get the addictive roasted bean boost for the rest of the day. Tastes, searches for the perfect cup of coffee throughout his whole life. This was close. He closes his eyes. Sniffs up the steam-beans in his nose. This is his morning. He's getting ready for church with his family and friends. Peace throughout the day. Quiet morning, just the birds talking to him. Just the sun from the blue curtains telling him how lovely the day is going to be.

41

All pews full at Mt. Eastern Shore Baptist Church. Reverend Hodge shouts out the words of the Lord from his pulpit. His robes of red and gold have the distinction of flapping like a giant crane. He flies off the stage with mike in his hand, for them to fly behind him.

The preacher man shouts. "Help me, Lord! Help me, Lord!" His hot, greased head of waves is a mess of sweat down his face. His handkerchief shakes with thunder at the three hundred guests in his great house this Sunday. His voice is mean, soft. A finishing act for a Broadway play stuck in its final week. A rousing applause from the people in the seats has him look to the tall ceiling of wooden beams. Tiffany stained windows that cost plenty from their pockets. Babies cry in the back of the aisles, listening to his voice go down the road of hoarseness.

Glass stained windows display the angels of the Eastern Shores. They help children out of the darkness of the woods. Daniel in the lion's den prays to one for safety. A mother over her dying baby. An angel stands with a sword in his hand by the bed. "Oh no! They are with us! They walk with us! They talk to us! They hear us!" He sticks his hand to his ear towards his audience.

A choir of twenty-five strong gather this day, all with delicious smiling faces. Silver-African tongues. Men, women clap in unison; twist their shoulders to the beat of the big man at the piano. Shouting to the call and response of the reverend directing them in song:

> We cherish thee, O' Lord
> We want to pray with thee, O' Lord
> For the first time I called
> You came to me, O' Lord
> How much you care
> How much we climb the mountain
> To overcome our sins, O' Lord
> How much we pray! Stop! Listen!
> To thee, O' Lord
> Give love a try
> In the bosom of Abraham
> O' my Lord
> Until the day we lay
> The day we lay
> In your arms!

Sam, Pete, Mabel, Ray his family and his partner Llosa he invited to their church and Myrthe holding the two children in her arms. Sit in the fourth row, left side of the church. They all clap. Bow their heads in the folly and quest of happiness as objects of bitterness melt away from the voices of the song. Time and time and time and time again the sermon of this man sparks the existence of a good and evil. Nurses pluck down beside some of the women in the seats, who threaten to keel over in the light of the Lord. Sun comes through the red, blue windows of angels. The stage is a conversation of bounty as more smelling salts come out of the nurses' pockets. Palms, the Crucifixion; his mother and a giant sun statue behind the choir stream out over the stage.

Reverend Hodge says, "We will all return to him someday! Alllll aboard! Alllll aboard!" He jumps. Hops. "Pack it up! Leave your sinning behind! Because it's time to answer to the man! I know good men do bad! I do bad! Mothers do bad! Children do bad! I know good men do bad! My good friends..." He leans on the podium. "But we all going to see him one day. We will see him... Our children are seeing him now! Every day! Every day!" Shakes his mop wet head in sadness. Tears fall from his eyes. Spit dribbles from his lips. He dabs his head with his handkerchief. "Our chuldren! Our chuldren are dying in the streets! From the deeds of good men... We are going to destroy the very fabric of this house... this neighborhood... I object to what we are doing around here! Now some of us even selling the dope ourselves from our own homes!" He points at the rainbow people. "I have failed thee, O' Lord! I have failed thee, O' Lord! I have failed thee, O' Lord! Two... three of our chuldren died just last week. Round the corner... in that very playground where I bring my own! Nobody cares! Nobody cares!" He warns, "I say to you! Know your past! We are in bondage! Know O' Pharaoh who has put us all in chains! Know that we must find

Moses! We must find a man to lead us out of Egypt!" He crashes his fist on the podium. "Dere ain't none! Dere ain't no Moses dis time! We killed them alllll!" He drops to his knees. "O' Lord, I love thee!"

He directs them to their Bibles, "Second Timothy, Verse one… This know also, that the last days, perilous times shall come!" He moves back to the stage, arms out. "One… two, three of our chuldren gunned down in the street. Just around the corner… the other day. The Lord tells us! We aren't listening!" He puts his hand back to his ear. "We aren't listening, we cannot stop this prophecy… It is upon us. Pray for your chuldrens, our mothers, our husbands are not next… but if they do go, justify why you are on this earth today! Justify why we smell the flowers, buy presents, help old people across the streets. Justify why we say good morning! Justify that we are kind and courteous to each other… each and every day! Justify why the wheat grows, the cows give milk, the tigers roar. Justify why we are here on this earth today! Justify your love for him… before you go see him later on!"

He slides the handkerchief over his jaws. "On this Easter Sunday I would like to thank the many guests for coming, and our regulars too! Before we leave the house of the Lord this day, I want you all to stand. Hug, kiss each other. People of every hue on this earth. Black! White! Yellow! Purple! I want you… husbands, wives, children, enemies and friends… arise!"

Sam stands with the others. He hugs his wife, Pete, his daughter, the baby and Mabel. He looks up, taps his brother on the shoulder. They grab each other. Ray kisses Myrthe and his wife. Tears stream like a broken pipe from his eyes as he hugs up Petey-Pete. Pete holds Myrthe, clutches her around the neck. Wheelchair-bound old men and women dying of some form of cancer reach out to their children's arms like newborns coming out of their mothers for the first time. The church is a volcano of organ music. Lights filter the puffy, wet faces as the choir breaks into a song. A solo starts up by Sister Louise Rodgers:

> He is with us on this day!
> Our daily bread… must come to
> His table and eat up the flesh!
> Rejoice in the lamb!
> Rejoice in the son
> On his day of sacrifice!
> He is there! He is there!
> He is there!
> Waiting for us!

The Choir:

> Oh! Jesus! Oh! Jesus! Oh! Jesus!
> We come to you this day!
> March on the road
> March in your footsteps!
> To Calvary!
> Oh! Jesus!
> Oh! Jesus!
> He is with us every day!
> He is with us all the way!
> He is with us!
> Oh! Happy day!
> Uh! Uhhhh! Good God!
> Uh! Uh! Good God!

Passageways of a tired, singing crowd leave out of the church after a rousing sermon by Reverend

Hodge. Outside at the top of the stairs, a long line of people hug him around the neck for the spirited dictates of what Easter is all about. They can see with their hearts the light through the darkness of the clouds coming overhead. Rain stops. The sun comes through just after noon. Bible in his left hand, a face to find the lost and lonely sleeping in doorways. A man who cares so much that he cries when he thinks how hard it is for all of them to make it in this world today.

Ray and Mabel come to him, embrace him around the waist. He kisses the baby, takes Little Ray up in his arms. "This boy is getting big."

"It's that soy milk, Reverend Hodge."

"Mabel, I knew you would be a most cherished mother to think of your child and giving him the utmost nutritional value… The Lord be with you." He gives the baby back to her. "Ray, let me talk to you for a second." He then takes Ray away from her a few feet. Whispers in his ear. "You bring your gun to the house of the Lord?"

Ray is shocked that he says something about this. "I'm sorry, sir. But the devil is here too." He pats under his arm. "Next time I'll leave it in the car."

"Next time,"Reverend Hodge is concerned."Next time leave it in the car…"

"I will, sir." Ray walks back to his wife and son. He takes them down the steps to the car. Opens the door for Mabel and the baby.

Sam, Myrthe walk up to him. Zara beside them. Petey-Pete strolls leisurely behind them. He makes some wolf grins at some of the nice, green-grass women in the congregation.

"I see you, Sam... Glad you and your wife could come."

"I got tired of the Peter and Paul show," Sam laughs. Myrthe pinches him. "Ouch!" He shakes the reverend's hand. "Just kidding."

"Sam, don't forget we are all in the band... Just some of us play a little Chopin and some of us play a little Rhythm and Blues... But it's all telling us the same message... God is alive!" He bends down, hugs the pretty child in pink dress and pink bows in her hair. "You and your mommie look lovely today in your pink Easter bonnets with all the frills upon it."

"I enjoyed your sermon, Reverend Hodge... It bought tears to my eyes." She wipes a gloved hand across her cheeks. He hugs her around the shoulder.

Pete says, "Just a home-made charge!"

"I just did my job, son... carrying the Lord's message."

"Amen," Pete says, praising him with a handshake.

"Amen!" Sam says, "You enjoy your Easter, sir."

"You too."

Other people come up in the line. He watches the couple go down the steps. He thinks he's met this man with thick braids and a fine suit before. A group of Baptist converts mingle. Say their last goodbyes and arrange church functions for the future. It's a good day under blue skies. Clouds part overhead as children run. Play hide and seek behind the reverend.

Just before Ray gets in his car, a woman calls out on the blueberry spring day: "Ahhhhh! He's got a gun! He's got a gun!"

"Petey-Pete pulls his gun.

People scramble before bullets start flying. Children run-spill. Mothers lose their minds in the streets, hide behind cars and trees. All parties to a killing on a day of servitude in front of the cross.

Sam pulls Myrthe down to the ground. Peeks up, wife, child safe. But six feet up the steps, Pete has a gun.

"Put it down, Mr. Sturdivant! Put it down now!" Ray hollers, aims.

Llosa Perez circles slowly to the other side. She completes the triad of staring down the man they want.

"Not today!" Pete screams. "Bring on the wedding cake!" Flinches.

Ray gets off two rounds. Llosa gets off one; right to the head. Silver gun muzzles flash. Police sirens come in the twisted distance.

Sam gets his wife and child off the ground. Myrthe keeps her hands over Zara's face and head. She gets hysterical. "What happened? What happened, Sam?"

"I don't know..." He holds her tight. "I don't know."

Ray cries out, "Goddamn! Goddamn!"

Llosa walks up slow. She kicks the gun from his outstretched hand.

"Sam, it's Pete! Go to him," Myrthe said. "Go! We'll be okay."

He touches his little girl's face. He walks back, petrified at the sun and the pool of blood under his friend.

Llosa is disgusted. "Shit!" She didn't want it like this... not today. Not ever.

"Is he…?" Sam asks, stares down at an easy face with his long hair flowing under him.

"He's dead, Sam." Ray stands up. "I'm sorry, man." He frowns down at the hurricane-twisted man. "Damn!" He looks up at a valueless God in the sky.

Cops arrive, push the crowd back.

"He had this in his pocket." He hands him a blood soaked yellow pamphlet.

Mabel runs up the steps with the baby. "Honey!" She asks him, "You awright?"

"I'm fine, Mabel," Ray says. "I'm cold… but I'm okay."

Sam notices the pamphlet is called "El, Zorro."

"What is it about?"

"Just some stupid poems," Sam says.

Ray scratches his ear. "Go ahead, Sam. I'll take care of your friend."

He walks back to Myrthe… his bridge, and a little girl to take care of for the rest of his life. He drives back to his home, past streets he once drove in his dented-up truck. Drank his gin. Rubbed the pretty ladies' asses. Felt up the world and sang its songs. Let the smoke come out his nose whenever he wanted to dance between the purple valley city and white corner moon. He left Petey-Pete back on those steps.

He touches his wife's pretty-flower knee as they go over a pothole. He looks over at his daughter's head resting back on her mother, quietly going to sleep.

"You okay, Sam?" Myrthe just watches the lights blink, change to stop or go. She looks at the man who makes her feel like she's on a road to safe passage in the greatest and latest romance novel.

It's true, she's in love with him all over again. He's a good man, father to both of them. She picks a tear out of her eye, blows her nose with a Kleenex.

"You okay, baby?"

"I'm feeling better," Myrthe says to him without pause in her voice. She has to be strong for him to carry on, for him to love her, for him to love their little girl... that's what it's about with him anyway... just give him room to love... room to show he can love.

"Petey-Pete, my man, damn!" Sam shakes his head down at the steering wheel; slaps tears from his face, blood on his hands. He leans over, touches his daughter's rosebud cheeks. "Baby you okay?"

He hugs them both...

"I'm okay," she smiles up, "daddy."

"Sam, I love you," Myrthe kisses him, "home."

"Okay," he touches her shoulder, "home." He wipes his bloody hands on his white shirt, Sam hugs his little girl. Green light pops on as he drives his family between the purple valley and white corner moon.

ABOUT THE
AUTHOR

G.Franklin Prue was born in Washington, D.C. in 1952 and worked in the defense industry, public health, and education, after receiving his Masters Degree in Education Administration and Supervision. He attended George Washington University Writers Workshop and the University of Georgia Writers Conference. He has two other novels published, *A Year of Madness* and *Mammie Doll*. He is a Vietnam era veteran. He is well-traveled in Central and South America, and now resides in Seattle, Washington.

Made in the USA
Charleston, SC
11 June 2013